TARGETS
OF
OPPORTUNITY

JEFFREY S. STEPHENS

POCKET **STAR** BOOKS

New York   London   Toronto   Sydney   New Delhi

The sale of this book without its cover is unauthorized. If you purchased this book without a cover, you should be aware that it was reported to the publisher as "unsold and destroyed." Neither the author nor the publisher has received payment for the sale of this "stripped book."

Pocket Star Books
A Division of Simon & Schuster, Inc.
1230 Avenue of the Americas
New York, NY 10020

This book is a work of fiction. Names, characters, places, and incidents either are products of the author's imagination or are used fictitiously. Any resemblance to actual events or locales or persons, living or dead, is entirely coincidental.

Copyright © 2011 by Jeffrey S. Stephens

All rights reserved, including the right to reproduce this book or portions thereof in any form whatsoever. For information, address Gallery Books Subsidiary Rights Department, 1230 Avenue of the Americas, New York, NY 10020.

First Pocket Star Books paperback edition May 2012

POCKET STAR BOOKS and colophon are registered trademarks of Simon & Schuster, Inc.

For information about special discounts for bulk purchases, please contact Simon & Schuster Special Sales at 1-866-506-1949 or business@simonandschuster.com.

The Simon & Schuster Speakers Bureau can bring authors to your live event. For more information or to book an event, contact the Simon & Schuster Speakers Bureau at 1-866-248-3049 or visit our website at www.simonspeakers.com.

Manufactured in the United States of America

10 9 8 7 6 5 4 3 2 1

ISBN 978-1-5011-0769-6

Rave reviews for the first Jordan Sandor novel by

JEFFREY S. STEPHENS

TARGETS OF DECEPTION

"A very solid, fast-paced thriller that carries the reader on a globe-trotting adventure into the world of counterterrorism."
—Robert K. Tanenbaum, *New York Times*
bestselling author of *Betrayed*

"A fast-paced tale of international intrigue and suspense . . . with a terrific lead character in Jordan Sandor, and many plot twists. . . ."
—Steve Alten, *New York Times* bestselling author of the MEG series

"Move over, Jason Bourne. I want Jordan Sandor."
—*Romantic Times*

"Grabs your attention from the first page . . . as ex–CIA agent Jordan Sandor races against time to prevent a worldwide terrorist plot."
—Howard Kaminsky, bestselling author of *The Glow*

"An intricate, suspense-filled plot that propels the reader to the final page."
—Jean Stone, author of *Trust Fund Babies*

"A must-read tale of worldwide peril and intriguing double cross."
—William F. Brown, Tony Award–winning author of *The Wiz*

"Will keep you on the edge of your seat to the very end."
—*Joint Forces Journal*

for Hoccos, who never left a man behind

TARGETS
OF
OPPORTUNITY

PYONGYANG, NORTH KOREA

O N THE EIGHTH floor of a nondescript office building overlooking the harbor in Pyongyang, two men faced off across a small table. Hwang Hyun-Su, host of the meeting, was one of Kim Jong-Il's most trusted advisors. His guest from South America was only identified to him as Adina.

The Great Leader maintained a strict need-to-know policy, even among his closest and most prominent associates. All that was required was for Kim's deputy to attend this meeting, hear what the man had to say, and report back.

The view from the austere conference room offered a revealing portrait of North Korea's industrial dilemma: the warehousing and docks, with their antiquated equipment and vessels, appeared largely deserted—the port was far too quiet to comport with Kim's claim of national prosperity. In sum, the harbor evinced all the activity of a New Hampshire lake in January.

Nevertheless, Hwang pointed to the port with pride, claiming it was proof of Kim's true genius.

Responding without irony or sarcasm, the Latin man said, "We very much respect the spectacular growth of your economy," then waited for his host's interpreter to explain his statement. "If we are to make progress in these discussions, however, we must be candid about your dependence on foreign sources of oil."

Hwang stared at his guest. "The Democratic People's Republic of Korea is an independent nation. We are not reliant on any other government."

The man called Adina could not resist a thin smile. "I am well versed in your Great Leader's Juche ideology, his commitment to total autonomy, and the impressive strides he has made to ensure the success and the security of your beloved nation."

Hwang nodded his approval as the statement was translated.

"But sir, the DPRK consumes more than thirty-five thousand barrels of oil every day, an extremely conservative estimate based on a damaged economy. Even at those numbers, your country produces less than two percent of its requirements. If that is not dependence, what is?" The Asian winced slightly. "If you are uncomfortable with the word *dependence,* then perhaps we should speak of cooperation."

"Cooperation with whom? We already have friends who help us to meet our needs."

"Ah, yes. But your so-called friends engage in wars with the imperialists of the West, then withhold production of oil and intentionally cause the price of crude to skyrocket. What sort of friends will they be when the cost has doubled again? Who will offer you protection?"

Hwang sat silent.

"The Korean People's Army you have assembled cannot rely on the promises of those who are consumed with their own difficulties. You cannot run your tanks and ships on those questionable assurances. And what of your financial infrastructure? Your people have suffered great deprivation in the name of industrial progress, but how will that end if you cannot afford the oil you need to grow?"

"The people are devoted to following our Dear Leader."

For the first time, Adina did nothing to disguise his impatience. "It is difficult for people to remain in lockstep when they are starving to death. Let's be frank, shall we? Your country has suffered food shortages for over a decade with no end in sight. You have chosen to cut off foreign aid, even from nongovernmental agencies such as the World Food Program. This has only worsened the situation. Your stranglehold on the people is enforced not through devotion, but through martial law. Your policies have resulted in famine, chronic poverty, and a decline in productivity. As the price of oil climbs, your troubles will only increase. Your military remains strong, but to what purpose? You have two million men in uniform doing nothing more than guarding a border that separates you from your own brothers in the south. How will that end for you?" Hwang stood up as the translation was completed, but before he could speak, Adina said, "Sit down, I'm not finished."

The Korean stared at him in disbelief. "Do you understand that I am here on behalf of the Great Leader? Do you realize, that if I so choose, you will never leave this room alive?"

Adina remained utterly composed as he replied, "And to whom do you think you are speaking, some fool toady you can intimidate with your threats? Kim would not have sent you to meet with me unless he believed I had something important to say."

"Insulting my glorious country, is that what I should find important?"

"No, my friend," the Latin replied, speaking slowly so that nothing would be missed by the translator. "What I have come to say is that I have a solution to these problems. A strategy, if you will, that will benefit your country and mine."

Hwang hesitated for a moment, then sat back down. "Well?"

"What if we could arrange a means of using your military intelligence and capability to deal a mortal wound to our common enemy? What if we could do it in such a way that the blame was not laid at your doorstep or mine? What if we work together to ensure that you will have access to oil at a fair price for decades to come, while crippling the United States in the process?"

"You want us to go to war against the United States?"

"Quite the contrary. I want to help you *avoid* a war with the United States, a war that is inevitable if your economic issues worsen and your flaunting of their demands increases. Let's be frank in our assessments for a moment. Try to put aside the patriotic claptrap you're forced to recite for the masses and look at the realities here." The Korean translator visibly flinched as he delivered this sentence, but Adina went on. "Where will all the hunger and oppression in your country inevitably lead? Eventually you will be left with a disenchanted people and a huge army with war as the only rationale for its use. Just as the United States needed the Second World War to lift itself from the Great Depression, the DPRK will be left with no alternative but bloody conflict. Then who will you fight? The Chinese? The Japanese? The Americans? With their resources, it will spell disaster for you." Hwang began to protest, but Adina held up his hand. "Right now our enemies in the West face an ongoing battle with the extremists in the Middle East. Instead of becoming entangled in those hostilities, let us embark on a mission that will use the fanaticism of the Islamic lunatics for our benefit. Let them escalate their conflicts with the United States, let them deflect all attention away from us while we actually deal the Americans a crushing blow. Let our two nations become the core of a great new alliance for this young century."

"Who are you?" Hwang said, regretting the question as soon as it was uttered.

Adina waved the question away as if swatting at a noisome insect. "Who I am is of no consequence for now. What *is* important is that we are already moving ahead, swiftly and secretly and effectively. We already have men in place to begin the first part of this mission."

"Already moving?"

"Yes, with the approval of your Great Leader."

Hwang appeared stung. "Where?"

"In the Caribbean."

Hwang would have laughed, if humor were any part of his limited emotional arsenal. "The Caribbean? What sense does that make?"

"All the sense in the world," Adina said with a smile. "As you will come to see, once you are prepared to listen, it makes all the sense in the world."

CHAPTER ONE

TEHRAN

SEYED ASGHARI WAS a true believer. He had dedicated much of his adolescence and all of his adult life to the glory of Allah, pursuing what he perceived to be God's purpose—the destruction of all Western infidels. He was devoted to this calling and therefore honored to have been recruited for his latest assignment, serving Iran in a multinational assault upon the United States.

And yet, almost from the start, he was troubled.

He first became anxious when he learned his cell would be led by an Asian. Throughout his years of loyal service to the Islamic Revolutionary Guard Corps, Seyed had always taken orders from fellow countrymen, or from Syrians or Palestinians with whom he shared a cultural and religious bond. This stranger from the Far East was different in style and approach from any of the other men he had followed, and the unconditional authority he wielded disturbed Seyed more and more as the days wore on.

He was also bothered by the inclusion of three Spanish-speaking men in his unit. Not only was it unusual for Hispanics to be involved in an operation originating in this part of the world, but these three seemed to share a private bond with the Asian that alienated Seyed.

And there was one further issue. Seyed presumed he had been selected for this mission because of his expertise in clandestine methods, skills that involved far greater subtlety and technical proficiency than those possessed by most of his compatriots. As the planning proceeded he was not entrusted with details of the impending assignment, but what little he was told left him wondering how his particular talents would be useful in what appeared to be a paramilitary strike.

Something did not feel right about any of this.

For the past few years Seyed's handler in the IRGC had been Ahmad Jaber, a man well respected within the organization for engineering terrorist assaults and who, as a consequence of his service to the cause, was being actively hunted by the governments of the United States, Argentina, and Israel, among others. Jaber had become a mentor to Seyed, the only person to whom the young man would dare confide his apprehension. And so it was to Jaber that he brought his concerns.

Seyed was seated on the edge of the sofa in the comfortable living area of Jaber's home, a place he had visited only once before. He spoke slowly and deliberately, wanting to be certain he was giving a fair account of everything he had seen and heard.

After listening intently until his protégé was finished, Ahmad Jaber slowly shook his head and admitted, "I have been told nothing of this operation."

Seyed was dark skinned and bearded, short and powerfully built, clothed in a traditional, free-flowing Arabic aba and sandals. His eyes, ebony dark and normally filled with defiance, now betrayed his growing fear. "How can that be, emir? How can such a thing be arranged without your knowledge?"

Jaber calmly held an upraised hand in response to the question, then stood and paced thoughtfully back and forth across the room as his young charge waited. Jaber was tall, clean-shaven, and well groomed, his thinning hair combed straight back, his nails buffed and trimmed. He was finely dressed in an Italian suit and French shirt, worn open at the neck. His Western bearing was what one might expect from a corporate executive in Europe, not a murderer in the service of a distorted faith. Jaber finally stopped and looked down. "I honestly do not know how this can be," he conceded. "What else have they revealed to you of their plans?"

"I told you all I know. They have not yet discussed plans for the attack with me. They act as if I cannot be trusted, as if I should not really know everything until the last moment."

"And how many of our own countrymen are involved?"

"Only two others," Seyed told him, then recited the names of the other Iranians in the cell. "I had never heard of them before."

Jaber shook his head again. "Nor have I."

"How can that be?" the young man asked again.

While Seyed was anxious about his individual role in this mission, Jaber had a broader concern. In the past year he had repeatedly clashed with other IRGC leaders over their use of foreign agents, fearing that the purity of their jihad was being compromised. Jaber warned them that they were beginning to look more like some international conglomerate run by the Americans than an Islamic crusade.

Now he was being informed of a major assault being prepared without his participation, an operation led by an Asian and run with South Americans. The implications for his own future were obvious.

Jaber returned to his seat opposite Seyed, still trying to make sense of this.

"Emir?" Seyed interrupted his reverie.

Jaber stared at the young man without speaking. Then he said, "It is clear that you must continue your role, learn everything you can and then report back to me. First, recite for me again everything you have been told. Everything."

Seyed restated the major points he had already shared, then Jaber pressed him for details, seeking to piece together as much information as he could about the others who were involved, particularly the Asian. Seyed believed he was either Chinese or Korean, his nationality having not been disclosed. He had not been told which country the South Americans were from, but believed they were from Venezuela. He vowed to find out. "I am sorry I do not know more," he said.

Jaber smiled warmly and assured him it was only a beginning. "But you must not come here again. There may be danger in that for both of us."

"I understand. But please know that I was most careful in my journey to your home."

Jaber smiled again. "Good, good. I am certain you were. And you must be just as careful when you leave." Then he gave instructions for contacting him.

Seyed pledged his loyalty, then went on his way.

———

As Jaber suspected, Seyed had been less cautious than he believed in traveling to this prosperous suburb of Tehran.

The men who organized Seyed's mission had assigned watchdogs for everyone involved and, even as the young man followed a circuitous route back to his own home, his meeting with Ahmad Jaber had been tracked and reported.

"A shame," the Asian man told his three Spanish-speaking lieutenants, speaking in their native tongue. "Seyed might have been valuable to us at some point." He thought for a moment. "That leaves only two Iranians in our unit. We may need to recruit another. What a waste of time."

The others said nothing.

"He must be removed at once."

One of the men asked, "Can we be sure that he revealed anything to Jaber? After all, they have had a long relationship. Is the visit so unusual?"

"It is when you consider the pains he took to conceal his destination."

The others could not disagree.

"And it is the nature of their relationship that persuades me he would certainly have discussed our plans. There is no question, Seyed must be interrogated and then eliminated. And quickly. There is no telling who else he might speak with."

One of the other men hesitated, then asked, "What of Jaber?"

"Yes, I know, a troubling complication."

"He is a high-ranking operative in the IRGC."

"I am aware of that." The Asian paused, then said, "It must be made to look as if someone else removed him. The Americans, the Israelis. Do what needs to be done, but clean this up now."

Later that evening Seyed received a text message summoning him to a meeting. There was nothing remarkable in either the short notice or the late hour. His cell had been gathering frequently, often at odd times. In each their Asian leader assured them that the time for action was drawing ever closer, even if specifics were scarce.

Seyed deleted the message, completed his prayers, then headed out.

Unlike the IRGC briefings he attended in the past, which were conducted by Jaber in an impressive high-rise at the center of the modern Elahiyeh district, tonight Seyed traveled on the Kordestan Highway, taking an exit that led to an old neighborhood of broken-down buildings and industrial yards.

During the ride he thought a great deal about Jaber. Until today Seyed had always known the man to be beyond fear. His mentor thrived on power and control. Now he was obviously distressed at the prospect of a major offensive being planned, right here in Tehran, without his knowledge. Seyed had repeatedly asked him, "How can it be so?" It worried them both that neither had an answer.

It was also apparent that Jaber, although he voiced no criticism, was upset Seyed had visited his home to deliver this information. Seyed was certain that he had taken the necessary precautions, that he had arrived and departed from their meeting undetected, but he recognized that Jaber was not convinced. It was up to Seyed, then, to prove himself. He was determined to learn what he could and report back.

Seyed turned off the service road and drove to the end of

a long, dark street, guiding his car around a squat structure. He parked in the rear lot and took the stairs to the second floor.

Hurrying up the two flights, he reached the warren of offices they used for their meetings, strode through the unfurnished vestibule, and entered the inner room. As soon as he walked in he saw that Jaber had been right, his betrayal had been discovered. There was nothing tangible, just a feeling, an intuition about danger he had developed over the years, an instinct that up to now had kept him alive. Tonight he saw that his fate had been written. He saw it in the face of the Asian, and in the fact that only this stranger from the East and the three South Americans were present.

"Where are the others?" Seyed asked.

The Asian was standing beside a large drafting table they used for their meetings. He stepped forward as two of the others moved behind Seyed and barred the door.

"We need to talk," the Asian said simply. His Arabic was rough, but understandable.

"Of course."

"I trust you will be professional, so this does not have to become unpleasant."

Seyed blinked.

"You have gone outside our circle, contrary to all instructions. We need to know how much you have revealed, how much damage has been done."

Seyed held on to the fleeting hope that this was only a bluff, a test. Perhaps they were not sure. He said, "I have no idea what you are talking about."

As he uttered the final word of that denial he felt the

crushing blow of a metal pipe across the backs of his knees, dropping him to the floor. Before he could catch his breath he was struck a second time, the heavy iron rod now brought crashing down on his right shoulder, the sickening sound of breaking bone followed by his cry of pain.

The Asian stared down at him. Then, without speaking, he gave a slight nod, and another blow was inflicted from behind, this time just below the left side of Seyed's neck. The young Iranian crumpled face-first onto the cracked tiles.

"I asked you to tell us the truth, and was hoping to conduct this inquiry in a civil manner," the Asian said. "The offer will not be made again."

Seyed twisted his head slightly, excruciating pain searing through his neck and shoulders as he struggled to look up. The Asian waited, but all Seyed Asghari muttered was *"Allahu Akbar."* He already knew he was a dead man.

Ahmad Jaber had not survived these many years in his violent profession by taking chances or relying on the competence of others. When Seyed came to his home and revealed what he knew about this mission, Jaber realized that his own life had taken an inexorable turn.

There was no way that a major assault was being planned by the IRGC without Jaber taking part, not unless his own people had turned against him. This left only two possibilities.

The less probable scenario was that the IRGC was indeed involved and that Jaber had been betrayed for reasons he did not know. The more likely alternative was that outside forces had initiated this scheme and decided to exclude him. In either event, Seyed Asghari would not have been permitted to roam the streets of Tehran without surveillance, or perhaps an escort—Jaber had to weigh the possibility that Seyed was being used to set him up.

Whichever of these was true, Jaber was certain that his enemies, whoever they were, already knew of the meeting. Whether Seyed put him in harm's way by mischance or was a willing instrument of his demise, Ahmad Jaber understood that he had become expendable.

Whoever was running the operation had no choice but to liquidate him. If the situation were reversed, Jaber grudgingly acknowledged, he would do the same thing.

Living one's life as a terrorist requires this sort of cold pragmatism. It also involves constant vigilance and the need to maintain any number of escape strategies. Whatever the facts proved themselves to be at some later date, he had to move swiftly to save himself and so, shortly after Seyed had departed that afternoon, Jaber initiated his plan.

Only his wife, Rasa, and their servant, Mahmud, shared the house. Their sons had died years ago, in faithful service to the forces of Iran in its struggles against Iraq.

He called his wife into the study, shut the door, and calmly explained that she must immediately take her car and leave for Tabriz to visit her sister. He offered neither an explanation nor a final good-bye. "If anything should happen, if you should hear anything that gives you cause for worry, you must then depart from Tabriz and follow the path to safety we have spoken of in the past."

After years of marriage, Rasa Jaber had come to terms with the constant danger that was a part of their lives. The tragic loss of both children had hardened her, and so when Ahmad explained what she must do, she asked no questions. Only when her husband completed his instructions and handed her a case containing a large amount of cash did her dark, trusting eyes well with tears. They had been through difficult moments before, but this time she felt an eerie sense of finality.

"We will always meet on the bridge to Paradise," he told her, invoking the name Al Sirat. Then he added, "Allah be praised." He spent the next hour with her, seeing to it that she packed and was on the road before nightfall.

Once his wife was gone, he told their servant that he would also be leaving for several days. He knew that in their absence Mahmud would avail himself of the luxury of his master's bedroom, a far more comfortable situation than his own. Since he and Mahmud were approximately the same age, height, and weight, this would serve Jaber well.

After dismissing Mahmud, Jaber locked himself in his den, where he opened the wall safe and removed its contents. Then, using a keypad secreted on the wall inside the safe, he entered a series of codes. He had long ago planted explosives throughout his home, which remained benign until the day arrived when it became necessary to bring them to life. He was convinced that day had arrived. Once activated, they could be set off with the remote detonator he now held in his hand.

——————

As soon as darkness fell, Jaber bid Mahmud good night, wished him well, and left the house. He took the various papers, weapons, and cash he had removed from the safe and placed them in his car. He then drove off, as if he were leaving town, but eventually circled back to his own neighborhood, arriving on the bluff high above his home. He parked, got out of the car, and took a position on the hill, where he prepared to wait.

Jaber had no doubt they would be coming for him, and he suspected it would happen soon. Given what little Seyed had described of his mission, it was obvious that the planned attack was a major offensive. Loose ends would not be tolerated. Assuming that everything Seyed had told him was the truth, the young man was already dead, or at least in custody, and anything they did not already know about his visit with Jaber would soon be revealed. Seyed might try to protect him by lying, but they would know the two had met and would not take any chances.

Even if they did not make their move against him tonight, Jaber understood that his time was limited. He was willing to spend a few hours here to see if he could discover anything, at least about the identity of these people. Either way, he was prepared to take the action he knew he must and make his escape. His plan was simple. If the assassins arrived tonight he would wait until they entered the house, then set off the explosion. It would kill his servant—who was standing in for Jaber in this tableau—as well as the men who would have come for him. If they did not arrive, he would initiate the explosion anyway and, by all accounts, Ahmad Jaber would be reported as the victim of some Western reprisal, a martyr in the cause of Allah, an Iranian hero.

Either way, it would take time for the authorities to properly identify the mutilated corpse in his bedroom, which would give him the opportunity he needed to follow his route to safety, through the back roads of his native land, moving west and into the border area near the Iraqi city of Erbil, where several Iranian diplomats were seized a couple of years before by American Special Ops personnel. The last leg of his journey would take him into the Sulaymaniyah province of Iraq, a Kurdish territory controlled by the United States. There he would turn himself over to the Americans, who would gladly accept the surrender of a senior IRGC official.

He allowed himself a grim smile as he sat on the stony ground, staring at his home below. This was a well-to-do area by Iranian standards, the houses set comfortably apart, offering that illusion of privacy enjoyed in residential areas everywhere. It left Jaber to wonder who among his neighbors might have guessed at the secret life he had led all these years. What a convoluted world he inhabited. What an ironic end to his illustrious career.

As the night wore on, he could not help but consider another option. The notion of his own redemption was nearly irresistible. What if they came for him and he managed to capture one of these assailants, to have the chance to question him, perhaps to learn what all of this was about? What if he could then prove that he was still loyal to the cause, that he had not betrayed his country? A tempting prospect, of course, but he admitted to himself that he was not suited to such a confrontation. He was a terrorist, not, as the Americans would call it, a gunslinger. His job was to plan destructive actions to be carried out by others, not to put himself in the line of fire.

For the present, escape was the most viable path.

As the moments dragged slowly by, Jaber had no problem remaining alert—the fear of death is a dependable adrenal trigger. He spent the time staring at his home, a squarish structure of classic architecture. He looked around this affluent neighborhood, set just to the north of the Pasdaran district. Unlike the modern towers that reached to the sky near the Niavaran Highway, this was a quiet area, set among hills, with a view of the Alborz mountain range in the background. He allowed himself a melancholy thought, realizing how much he would miss this home and this life, while knowing that things had developed too quickly for him to allow emotion to influence his judgment. He had made his decision and would yet have to make other difficult choices in the moments and days ahead.

And then, as he rued this situation, he saw three men approaching his house from three different directions.

Very professional, he observed approvingly.

Even in the darkness he could make them out through his small field binoculars. They appeared to be Hispanic, just as Seyed had told him, and each was carrying an automatic weapon slung over his shoulder, each wearing a backpack. They stopped and removed their packages, then laid out the materials before them.

Interesting, Jaber thought as he watched them prepare incendiary devices. It had not occurred to him that they might arrange his death by planting explosives instead of a straightforward assassination, such as a gunshot to the head or a knife to the throat. Whoever they were, they wanted it to appear that he was a victim of terrorists, not thieves. From the look of things, they also wanted to leave no trace of him behind.

He wondered who these people might be, these foreigners who were so well organized and equipped, operating with such impunity in his own country. They could not be IRGC, he decided, and for a fleeting moment he reflected again on a reversal of course. Perhaps he should let them believe they had successfully played out their murderous plot, then he could arrive this very morning in IRGC headquarters to report everything he knew.

But what if he was wrong? What if the IRGC had condoned their plans? He would be walking into a firing squad, and suicide was certainly not a path Ahmad Jaber was prepared to travel, not even for the glory of Allah. That sacrifice, he had long ago decided, was best left to others.

He shook his head as if to wish away all of this double thinking, then quietly rose to his knees. Leaning on a pile of rocks that protected him from view, he had a better look at the proceedings below. As the three men continued to prepare their materials Jaber became convinced they were not going inside the house before setting off the explosives. That meant they would be able to make their escape before Jaber could detonate his own blast.

What a pity, the Iranian reflected bitterly.

He could ignite his charges first, when these three assassins approached the perimeter of the house. Perhaps the explosion would kill them, and there was certainly gratification in the idea. But what if one or more survived and came after him then and there? No, he decided, these were enemies he would have to fight another day.

He would set off his charges immediately after theirs, and they would be allowed to flee. They would be unlikely to notice the additional conflagration as they ran from the scene, but Jaber's bedroom would certainly be vaporized and any chance of positive identification of the body inside would then be impossible, unless the government spent the time and effort to recover body fragments and do DNA testing. Even if they were so inclined, he would be far gone by then.

Jaber watched with a sense of morbid detachment as the three men went about the business of placing explosives around the base of the walls to his home. When they had completed their work they met at the bottom of the hill, where one of them suddenly pointed upward. Jaber crouched down, his pulse quickening. He waited a moment, then peered out into the darkness from behind the rocks. He felt his heart pounding even harder as they began climbing in his direction. He drew back, weighing his options. He realized his handgun and limited physical resources were no match for these three younger men. He had no time to run; the rocky hillside would give him away as soon as he moved.

Then he thought about setting off his own charges. The distraction might give him enough time to get away. It might even trigger their explosives, which would surely create enough mayhem to provide him an opportunity to get to his car.

Before he acted he risked one more quick look and was amazed to see that they had stopped halfway up the steep incline. As one of them pointed off to his right, Jaber understood. He had not been spotted. Apparently they had only been looking for a better position.

Jaber drew a deep breath as they clambered to a spot a hundred or so yards off to his right. He slumped down with his back against a large rock as he tried to control his heavy breathing. He stared at the detonator in his hand and prepared to wait.

He did not have to wait long. As soon as the three men settled in at a safe distance from the house a booming noise rocked the night. Seconds later Jaber hit the red button on his remote, and a combination of fire and noise lit the sky and filled it with a deafening thunder and a spray of stone and dust.

People in the homes all around them were jolted from their sleep, rushing to their windows to see what had happened. The damage was confined to Jaber's home, but the explosions propelled debris into the dark sky.

Jaber held his ground, not moving until the three men had stolen away over the hill. He allowed himself a final look at the flaming remnants of the place he had called home for so many years, feeling a sadness he had not expected. Then he turned and began his journey to safety.

CHAPTER TWO

ONE WEEK LATER, AN ESTATE OUTSIDE LANGLEY, VIRGINIA

AN IMPOSING STONE house sits amid a rolling lawn on a large tract situated some forty miles southwest of Langley in suburban Virginia. Once jokingly referred to by an agent as the House of the Seven Gables, the estate had since become affectionately known to insiders simply as the "Gables." The property rolls on for more than a hundred acres, the perimeter marked by a wood fence inconspicuously braided with enough high-intensity electrical wire to stop a charging bull moose in its tracks. The fortifications at the gatehouse and outbuildings are also well disguised, giving the place the look of a stately manor while concealing tracking devices, day and night surveillance, a full complement of armed guards, and enough weaponry and communications paraphernalia to stand off an assault by a well-equipped battalion.

The Central Intelligence Agency's most elaborate safe house, it is used only for the most distinguished and valued guests, such as Ahmad Jaber, until recently a senior officer in Iran's state-supported terrorist network, the Islamic Revolutionary Guard Corps.

Jaber's defection from the IRGC was greeted by considerable skepticism within the CIA unit devoted to countering Islamic terrorism. In the long history of counterintelligence gambits, practices of disinformation, false flag deceptions and other similar ploys had created a healthy level of paranoia whenever an enemy agent appeared on the scene claiming to bear unexpected gifts. Jaber was known to have been involved in the attack on the Israeli embassy in Buenos Aires and the training of operatives for the IRGC in Lebanon. He was also presumed to have been instrumental in planning the 1983 bombing of the Marine barracks in Beirut that left 241 American servicemen dead. Deputy Director Mark Byrnes endorsed the suspicion that Jaber's sudden departure from a career orchestrating murder and havoc might be a ruse of some sort. That view was shared by senior officials up and down the line, including the Director of Central Intelligence, the Director of National Intelligence, and the President's National Security Advisor. Byrnes, for his part, was intimately familiar with the carnage caused by Jaber and his minions, and he was charged with the responsibility of rooting out whatever scheme was being hatched by the Iranians.

When Jaber made his way out of Iran and into Iraq he promptly surrendered to the Allied Forces—which essentially meant American soldiers backed by the encouragement, and little else, of United States allies—and sought asylum through a back-channel connection he claimed to have in Washington. Jaber's contact turned out to be someone in the State Department he had met only once, at a peace conference in Paris ten years before, and the

American quickly disavowed having had any communication with the terrorist since then. Learning this, Byrnes insisted that Jaber be transported stateside and turned over to Central Intelligence for vetting, which was quickly agreed to by the President's National Security Advisor as well as the Agency's Director. The CIA medical team began by subjecting the Iranian to a complete physical. One of Byrnes's theories was that Jaber, now almost sixty, might have contracted some fatal illness, and was intending to play out his final days doing as much additional damage as possible by feeding the Agency a giant helping of disinformation.

The DD was mildly surprised when the tests revealed Jaber to be in excellent health.

When the Iranian was placed under a mild anesthesia for his exam, he was also treated to a cocktail of so-called truth serum. Once he had regained consciousness he was still under the influence of a pharmacological mix far more sophisticated than sodium pentothal. The ensuing discussion, which is admittedly never as fruitful as an unfettered interview, was at least intended to determine if his defection was genuine or part of an IRGC mission.

While a regimen of intense psychological programming might have prepared Jaber to withstand this sort of drug-fueled colloquy, he said nothing to suggest that his presence was any sort of hoax. Moreover, Jaber seemed to have information about a planned attack that was coming from someplace other than Iran, a compelling bit of information if any part of it turned out to be true. The specifics were muddled, which is often the case when confessions are chemically induced, and Byrnes looked forward to a further inquiry, once his prisoner was fully alert.

And so, notwithstanding the DD's continued misgivings, he had Jaber transferred from the CIA infirmary to the Gables for a formal interrogation. Then he called Jordan Sandor.

CHAPTER THREE

NEW YORK CITY

IT WAS JUST after dawn, and Jordan Sandor was in his Manhattan apartment, grinding through the last sequence of his daily exercise routine. Not yet forty, he worked hard to keep in shape, his current regimen including some rehab moves intended to bring him back to top form after the injuries suffered during his recent mission in Europe.

He was in the middle of a series of sit-ups, working each elbow to the opposite knee in turn, twisting hard in alternating directions, when he heard the ring on his BlackBerry that told him he had a text message. He finished the cycle of crunches, stood, wiped his face with a towel, and grabbed the PDA from the table. The coded message instructed him to call on a secure line.

He went to his bedroom closet, reached inside and unlocked the overhead panel, took down the metal box he kept there, and brought it to his desk. He removed the satellite phone reserved for these communications, turned it on, and, as he waited for it to power up, entered a series of numbers on his computer keyboard that emitted a frequency that blocked any eavesdropping in the room. Then he picked up the phone, which was now at full signal, punched in the familiar number, and said, "Sandor encrypted."

Sandor had not spoken with Deputy Director Byrnes since the debriefing at Langley that followed the mission he completed in Italy. He worked several weeks at rehabbing his leg, first at Bethesda Naval Hospital in Maryland and then back home. He also spent time in the New York office, monitoring the work being undertaken by the Counter-Terrorism Task Force to undo the residual damage caused by the rogue agent Vincent Traiman, whom Sandor had successfully dispatched in Portofino. Now Sandor felt he was nearly back to full strength, regardless of what the Agency doctors had to say. He wanted clearance to return to action and so was not unhappy to receive a message from the Deputy Director. After a few moments he heard the familiar voice.

"Good morning, Sandor."

"You're up early, sir."

"We have a situation I'd like you to have a look at. I need you here, pronto."

"I can get to LaGuardia, be down to you in a few hours," Sandor said.

"No, I've already arranged transport. There's a car waiting for you downstairs."

Sandor nodded at the phone, knowing that meant a few things. Urgency, of course. Also that Byrnes might want him armed, not wasting time with the security issues he would face on a commercial flight. And, most important, this was not going to be a meeting at Langley, it was likely going to be a private audience at the Gables, hopefully with Ahmad Jaber. "Am I going for a drive in the country?"

"You are."

"I'm on my way," Sandor said.

Sandor had heard the rumors of Jaber's defection while spending time in the Company's Manhattan office a few days before. He was surprised he had not already been contacted by Byrnes but hoped that was the reason he was being summoned to Washington.

He quickly showered and dressed, choosing gray slacks, black loafers with rubber soles, and a crisply pressed white shirt. He had a look in the mirror, his uneven nose a reminder of too many close-action battles, his complexion tanned and a bit weathered. His dark hair was cut just long enough to allow him to run his fingers through the thick waves, front to back—which he habitually did when he took time to reflect on something important. He was doing that now as he continued to stare ahead, his intense eyes no longer seeing his reflection, instead visualizing Ahmad Jaber. It was a confrontation he had looked forward to for a very long time.

Back in the bedroom he pulled out his black leather "go" bag, already packed with two changes of clothes, toiletries, and other sundries. Then he returned to the metal container. He removed his bulky Smith & Wesson .45 semiautomatic with two magazines, his passport—and a spare passport with a NOC, or non-official cover, in the name of Scott Kerr, one of his favored aliases—and tossed all of them in the bag with the secure cell phone. After he replaced the box in the overhead safe, he checked the magazine of the smaller, Walther PPK .380 he always carried with him, placed it in its leather holster, and shoved that inside his belt at the small of his back. Then he pulled on a navy blazer, headed downstairs, and climbed into the Town Car that was waiting to take him crosstown to the East River heliport.

————

Sandor figured Byrnes would eventually call him in for these debriefings. Ahmad Jaber was a major force in an area where Sandor had been involved in several operations. More than that, Sandor guessed that the DD would share his doubts about the authenticity of the defection. Byrnes might also want him to participate in the interrogation since there was some personal history there.

Sandor suspected that Michael Walsh, Director of Central Intelligence, might be the reason he had not been contacted earlier. Walsh was not Sandor's biggest fan, and he particularly disliked anything that reeked of vendetta. Sandor took no offense. He had long ago concluded that Walsh was just a typical executive at the top of a large corporate structure. The higher up the food chain, the more conservative the approach. The Director's job was not only to run the Central Intelligence Agency, it was also to cover the President's ass. It was the President, after all, who had given Walsh the job and who was, in the final analysis, Walsh's boss.

It was therefore inevitable that Walsh would worry about field agents who were constantly on the brink of skirmishes that could create international tensions, embarrassing incidents, or outright disasters. The DCI did not want those risks multiplied by anything personal that might pollute the decisions or actions of his men. On top of those concerns, Walsh felt that the more proactive and insubordinate the agent, the worse the risk.

Sandor smiled to himself. He knew that, on some days, he was the Director's worst nightmare.

Fortunately, Deputy Director Byrnes had the ability and integrity to balance the risks and rewards of having men like Sandor out in the world, handling the necessary dangers inherent in covert operations. Byrnes was a career intelligence officer, not a political appointee or someone running for office, and even if he shared an Ivy League background and club membership with Walsh, he was willing to stand up to the Director for what he knew was right. He and Sandor sometimes disagreed about missions, and frequently about tactics, but they always had the same goal—to keep America safe by fighting her unseen enemies.

———————

As Sandor boarded the Sikorsky chopper that would take him across the Hudson to the private airport in Teterboro, he reviewed what he knew about Ahmad Jaber, an enemy who had dwelled in darkness for the past decade. They knew that Jaber had been involved in the planning of several devastating attacks throughout the Mideast, South America, and Europe. He had engineered these murders in the name of an extreme Islamic vision that the governments of Iran, Syria, and even Saudi Arabia refused to publicly acknowledge, even as each of them provided undisclosed support.

These clandestine battles were still being waged along with the fierce struggles on the ground in Afghanistan and Iraq, but somehow they did not touch the rhythm of life at home, not in the way past battles had gripped the nation.

Americans did not actually feel they were at war, not

really. There were no rallies to sell savings bonds as there were during the Second World War, or marches in protest such as the ones we saw against the debacle in Vietnam. As the horrors of 9/11 faded in the rearview mirror of the national consciousness, America simply parked its worries in an opinion poll and went back to the mall.

Unfortunately, as Sandor knew with painful intimacy, these dangers remained real and present, and he was one of those sworn to repel the ongoing assaults on our security and our freedom. A secret war against the United States was being waged every day, and Sandor knew that someone had to stand and fight.

Sandor also knew that Jaber had worked with Vincent Traiman, who was directly responsible for the murder of Sandor's local operatives during a mission in Bahrain. When his team was exposed in Manama, Sandor was the only one to make it out alive, and he looked forward to the opportunity to confront the IRGC terrorist who may have been behind that massacre.

So, even if Jaber's defection made no sense, Sandor was willing to hear what he had to say.

Then, if it was up to him, he would be pleased to rip the man's throat out with his bare hands.

CHAPTER FOUR

ST. BARTHÉLEMY, FRENCH WEST INDIES

T HE FLIGHT FROM St. Maarten to St. Barths lasts just ten minutes, but the final moments seem like an eternity. The airport is small and the only runway is so short it cannot accommodate a plane larger than a sixteen-seat twin prop. The final sixty seconds of the approach require the pilot to navigate through an ever-present wind shear as the small aircraft passes from the calm air above the open Caribbean across the rocky hills that form the port of Gustavia below. At the entrance to the airstrip the plane must squeeze the tips of its wingspan through a narrow V formed by mountains on either side, forcing the captain to execute a drop of a hundred feet until the wheels bounce onto the runway, then struggle to bring the aircraft to a stop before it slides onto the beach of St. Jean and into the sea.

This morning, two men sat in the last of the three passenger rows, watching as they passed through that mountain cut, the wheels of the small plane nearly touching the tops of the cars traveling on the road below before the precipitous drop to the sun-bleached tarmac and then the rush toward the runway's end. When they were finally brought to a halt at the edge of the tarmac, the plane made an about-face, then taxied safely back to the small terminal. Almost immediately the rear hatch was pulled down, and a welcoming breath of tropical air greeted them as they disembarked down the short stairway.

Hicham was a French-speaking Moroccan, a tall man in his thirties, with an olive complexion and handsome features, his head shaved clean, his amber eyes sleepy, his manner deferential. He led the way to the immigration booth, where he presented his passport, then exchanged pleasantries in the local language with the officer behind the glass-fronted counter.

The man beside him, known as Cardona, said nothing as he handed over his Venezuelan passport, waiting for it to be stamped and returned. Unlike his more elegant companion, Cardona was short, dark, and brutish looking, his deep-set eyes distrustful, his gaze constantly in motion as if endlessly surveying the landscape from side to side.

They picked up their luggage from the small carousel, one large suitcase each, and Hicham led them to a small row of courtesy booths where a local car rental service had a chalkboard with his name on it. He had reserved a small Japanese SUV for three weeks and, after presenting a credit card, he signed some papers and was handed the keys. They found the car in the parking lot and were on their way.

Hicham was at the wheel, guiding them along the island's main road toward the area known as Pointe Milou. "Nothing to it," he said in English as he took a hairpin turn that spun them up a steep rise.

Cardona grunted in response.

They followed the hilly path through St. Jean, around Lorient, and ultimately toward a small circle at the road's end that sat above a large cliff overlooking the sea. There they found the entrance to a steep driveway, which led to a compound of small, attached buildings that sat on a promontory jutting out over the water.

Hicham stopped the car and had a look at the spectacular views. "Nice, eh?"

Cardona said nothing.

Many of the beautiful villas in St. Barths were available for lease when not in use by their owners. The place they had chosen, known as Villa du Vent, was one of the finest on the island, its remote location well suited to their needs.

Hicham put the car in gear and wound his way down a steep, curved driveway that ended in a narrow turn. As they pulled to a stop, the housekeeper emerged from her *maisonette* to greet them. She was an attractive young Frenchwoman dressed in a short cotton skirt and an undersized halter top that displayed all of her significant assets to the best possible advantage.

Hicham introduced himself in French. She said her name was Stefanie. He politely declined her offer to help with the bags.

"We are here for rest and quiet," he told her with a diffident smile. "I know of the services provided with the villa, but we will require very little from you."

Stefanie appeared slightly displeased at the news, responding with that signature pout Frenchwomen use when expressing anything from unhappiness to flirtation.

"All we require," he went on, "is that you come every morning at ten, make the beds, clean the kitchen, and take care of the towels and so forth. Otherwise, we would prefer to be left to ourselves."

"You do not want your beds turned down in the evening?" she asked in her heavily accented English. "No assistance with cooking?"

"No," he replied pleasantly. "We are quite self-sufficient."

Stefanie responded with a curious look, obviously reaching a conclusion about the intimate preferences of these two guests. She told him that she understood.

Hicham read her thoughts, but ignored them. "Other than your morning chores, we prefer not to be disturbed," he told her again.

Stefanie nodded. "Would you like me to show you around before you settle in?"

"Of course," he agreed.

She led them down the cobbled path to the main entrance and into the entry foyer, where they dropped their bags. She took them outside again, to a concrete deck that surrounded the entire property. There were wraparound paths, stairs, and short walls all running to the edge of the property, which stood more than eighty feet above the sea and provided a panoramic vista three-quarters of the way around. The sea cliffs allowed for no entrance to the villa from any of these sheer sides. A large swimming pool on the far side of the deck was lined with a dark-blue tile that reflected the color of the sky, creating the illusion that the water disappeared into the horizon.

After Stefanie concluded her brief tour of these spectacular views she walked them through the open-air dining room, then the kitchen and living room.

"I can show you to your rooms now," she said.

There were four bedrooms, each a separate structure with its own bath. Cardona grabbed his suitcase from the entry foyer and tossed it on a bench in the master suite. Hicham was left a comfortable room that faced the pool.

"Please let me know if I can help with anything else."

Hicham said, "*Merci bien*," then handed her five one-hundred-euro notes, which finally earned them a slight smile.

"Let me know if you need anything else," she said again, a bit more sincerely this time, then the two men were left to admire her rhythmic walk as she exited through the main entryway, closing the door behind her.

Cardona nodded his approval.

"Forget it," Hicham told him. "There's more of that on the island, just not here, eh?"

Cardona frowned. "Come," he said.

They returned to the master suite, where Cardona opened his valise, lifted out his clothing and toiletries, placed them on the bed, then went to work on the false linings within the four sides of the rectangular bag. He extracted four packages of C-4 explosive, all of which had been coated and then molded into the corner frame of the suitcase. They had passed through security without arousing the slightest suspicion.

"I told you there was nothing to worry about," Hicham said.

Cardona dismissed him with a wave of his beefy hand. "Why was this necessary? They're coming by sea anyway."

"I told you, they had a point to prove."

"Bullshit," the burly man growled.

Hicham shrugged. "Perhaps you're right. Meantime, we have a couple of days to organize ourselves," he said. Then with a smile he added, "And to relax."

"Too much planning, not enough action," Cardona grumbled.

"You may be right again," Hicham agreed. Then he turned for the door. "As for action, I'm going for a swim."

CHAPTER FIVE

AN ESTATE OUTSIDE LANGLEY, VIRGINIA

On his arrival at the Gables, having been cleared through the outside security checkpoints, Jordan Sandor was admitted to the large stone house. Mullioned windows framed bulletproof glass, metal detectors and X-ray machines were discreetly set behind the wainscoted panels of oiled walnut, and multiple layers of crown molding disguised the ubiquitous surveillance cameras. All in all, the subtlety of these precautions left the Gables with the appearance of a proper men's club in London.

Sandor was ushered downstairs and shown into a sound-proof room in the basement. The Deputy Director was waiting.

Byrnes was a handsome man of about sixty with narrow, well-defined features, short, graying hair, and shrewd blue eyes that his subordinates, other than Sandor, often found unsettling. He was attired in his customary gray suit and white shirt. When Sandor entered the room Byrnes looked up from the armchair in which he was seated, but he did not stand.

"Sir."

Byrnes nodded to a large screen on the wall to their right. "There's our boy."

Sandor had never met Ahmad Jaber, but as he viewed him on the closed-circuit monitor, he recognized him from surveillance photos. Although he looked older than Sandor had expected, the agent knew him at once. "What have we got so far?"

Byrnes motioned for Sandor to have a seat opposite him, then quickly brought his top counterterrorism agent up to speed. Jaber's physical was clean. He still had family in Iran, including his wife, which put them at risk, unless, of course, the entire defection was part of a larger subterfuge. Thus far he had been candid about his past, admitting his complicity in the Israeli embassy bombing in Buenos Aires, the attack on the Marine barracks in Lebanon, the training of insurgents in Iraq, and several other terrorist missions.

"I assume he agreed to a chemically enhanced interview."

Byrnes nodded. "What I've told you are the highlights of everything we've gotten from him."

Sandor shrugged. "Those drugged-up interrogations are only as good as the questions asked."

The DD raised an eyebrow.

"No offense meant," Sandor said, "but we know all about Jaber and the IRGC. All he's bringing us is last month's newspaper. What does he expect for that, a house in Malibu and a book deal for his memoirs?"

Byrnes responded with a thin-lipped frown that Sandor had often seen from his superior officers. He figured it was something they taught in the first year at the State Department. "Actually," the DD explained, "he does have some requests, and that's one of the reasons I brought you down here. He asked to speak with you."

The statement took Sandor by surprise but all he did was nod. "Did he mention the topic?"

"No. He just said he wanted you here."

"Uh huh. Well, I'm here," Sandor said as he stood up. "Let's go see what he has to say."

Byrnes also stood, placing a hand on Sandor's shoulder. "Remember, this whole thing is being recorded. No antics, no violence, no gun in his ear."

Sandor offered up his best impression of an innocent look. It was not convincing. "I get to say whatever I want though, right?"

Byrnes responded with a resigned shake of his head. "Where's your weapon?"

"They checked it at the door."

"Sandor. Your weapon. Now."

Sandor reluctantly reached his hand under his blazer and removed the Walther and holster from the small of his back.

"Just put it on the table," the DD ordered. "You can have it back when we're done."

———————

The room in which Jaber waited was furnished as a small, comfortable den. The walls were painted a dark green with walnut wainscoting. There were several easy chairs set in a circle and an oval cocktail table in the middle that held a tray with coffee and tea carafes, cups and saucers, cream, sugar, and pastries. This was obviously the soft sell, Sandor noted as he followed Byrnes inside. He would have chosen something a little less comfortable.

Jaber stood when they entered. He ignored Byrnes, with whom he had already spent considerable time, and said in thickly accented English, "Mr. Sandor, I am glad to see you are here."

Sandor stared at him for a moment, then said, "If I wasn't already standing I wouldn't have gotten up for you." Then he sat in the chair directly opposite the Iranian.

Jaber nodded, then retook his seat. "All the same, thank you for joining us."

Sandor stuck out his lower lip as he looked his man up and down. Then he said, "Let's be clear where we stand, you and I. I don't believe your defection is real and, even if it is, I wouldn't care if you could tell me where to find the Holy Grail; if it were up to me I'd take you out right here and now—"

"Sandor!" Byrnes barked.

Jaber waved off the DD with a sweep of his hand. "As you Americans say," he observed in a polite tone as he continued to look squarely at Sandor, "at least we know where we stand."

"Not quite. It's bad enough that you're responsible for the deaths of hundreds of my countrymen and allies, but I believe you and my old friend Vincent Traiman also had my men killed in Bahrain. Then you tried to have me murdered, which makes this personal." Sandor leaned forward as he added, "Just so you really know where we stand."

"This is war, Mr. Sandor."

"War? Is that what you claim this is? Tell me, Ahmad, where are your soldiers? What uniform do they wear? What country do they represent?"

Jaber responded with a blank stare.

"This isn't war, and you're not in any army. You're just a

gang of murderers from countries without the guts to admit their involvement, and that's only because we'd kick your Arab asses up and down the Gobi Desert if you did. So instead you send suicide bombers into crowded plazas and claim they're on a holy mission for Allah. I've got news for you, pal: if Allah stops by anytime soon he'll tell you that you're not even close to what he had in mind."

"Are you done, Mr. Sandor?"

Sandor sat back, but said nothing.

"Good, because it may have occurred to you that I, as your enemy, must have had some compelling reason to request that you join this discussion. You must have realized I am aware of your hatred for me. It is obvious. Is it not?"

"It is to me."

"Excellent. In that case, what I have to tell you will be all the more effective, since you and I have what you might want to call a history."

Sandor nodded slowly as he studied the Iranian. The sonuvabitch was a cool customer, he would give him that much. "History, is that what we have? All right, I'm listening. But I have to warn you, I tend to have a short attention span."

Now Jaber leaned forward slightly. "It is no secret that the governments of our nations are enemies. I make the distinction between government and people because, as you are well aware, under prior regimes the people and governments of Iran and the United States were closely allied. In fact, Iranians are more Western than any other country in the Middle East."

"Except Israel."

"You will forgive me if I postpone a discussion of Israel to another time. As far as I am concerned, the Israelis are nothing more than a filthy herd of desert-dwelling, land-grabbing goatherders. My countrymen are far more civilized and far more European in their ways than your Israeli friends can ever hope to be."

"Glad you don't want to discuss that right now."

"My point is that the governments of Iran and the United States are very much at odds, even if our people are not."

"Your man Ahmadinejad would call that statement treason."

"He might, which may be part of the reason I am here. There are many within my country who fear the consequences of the ongoing nuclear program, the incursion of the Islamic Revolutionary Guard Corps into Iraq, and the general hostilities between your nation and ours. Iran has problems within the region that it must address, some of which originated centuries ago. As you have suggested, it may not choose to face annihilation by the United States for actions in which it actually has no real part."

"Are you trying to sell me the idea that your defection is part of some unofficial peace initiative?"

"No, not at all. My defection is quite a personal matter. What I have to offer, however, is information about coming attacks that will neither serve my country nor yours."

"From the IRGC?"

"No."

"Al Qaeda?"

"No. In this instance, I believe your enemy will only appear to be from among these groups. No, this threat is actually from the East."

Sandor looked to Byrnes. The Deputy Director said nothing.

Jaber continued. "I will have to admit that I am lacking certain details, but I think it will become clear that an offensive is being launched by North Korea." For the time being, he had decided not to mention what Seyed had told him about the involvement of the South Americans. There was an old saying in the desert about never displaying all your wares until the very end of the trade.

Sandor shook his head in disgust. "You want us to believe that we're going to be attacked by North Korea, but it's going to be made to look as if it came from Iran?"

"Not Iran, necessarily. From what your media calls Islamic extremists."

"And how would you have come into possession of this information?"

"An excellent question. In order for their plan to succeed they would obviously need to involve certain personnel, to have it appear the source of the attack was Islamic and not Asian. They have been extremely careful in their planning, but nothing is beyond detection or betrayal in the modern world, as you gentlemen know only too well. Thus far I only have fragments of information, but it is enough for me to piece together a large part of this puzzle."

Byrnes said, "If you've already discovered this, presumably others would also have access to the information inside Iran. The plot could be easily exposed, if and when the time comes."

Jaber showed his white teeth in a grim smile. "That may be a false presumption. I am fairly certain that the man who provided this information, Seyed Asghari, has been removed, and I was the only one to whom he reported."

Byrnes and Sandor shared another quick glance. "Removed by you?" Sandor asked.

"Of course not. I would have been happy to learn more from him as things moved forward but, unfortunately, time became extremely limited. Given the events that followed our meeting, I am certain Seyed is gone."

Byrnes gave one of his thin-lipped looks of disapproval. "Before he was liquidated, what makes you think they didn't force him to reveal the name of the person to whom he was passing information?"

Jaber grinned again. "Naturally, Mr. Byrnes, I have proceeded on the supposition that he was coerced into divulging precisely that. Which is why an attempt on my life was made and which is why, as a result of the ensuing explosion at my home, I am presumed dead by one and all. At least for the time being."

"Which is also why," Sandor continued the thought, "you are here."

"As I said earlier, I have a personal reason for this defection. The motive, simply put, is that as long as I am believed dead and given a new identity, I can live out my years without fear of reprisal. If, however, it is learned that I am still alive, well, as you can imagine, that would be remarkably inconvenient for at least two governments."

"Not to mention the IRGC."

"Precisely."

"And the members of your family still in Iran."

Jaber conceded that point with a slow nod of his head.

"Their safety is only secured at the moment by the belief that I am dead."

"All of which means you are not really a defector."

"Alas, in the technical sense, I must confess this is true. I concede that I have not suffered a change of heart or a shift in my allegiances." Jaber smiled pleasantly. "Think of me instead as someone with information he is willing to trade in exchange for safe harbor."

CHAPTER SIX

AN ESTATE OUTSIDE LANGLEY, VIRGINIA

SANDOR AND BYRNES returned to the sanctuary of the smaller room for a private discussion. Although the entire mansion was regularly swept for audio bugs and surveillance devices, these soundproof spaces provided an additional measure of security.

"He's a liar," Sandor said as soon as the Deputy Director shut the door behind them.

Byrnes turned. They were standing face-to-face. "To what end?"

"I haven't figured that out yet."

"You don't really believe he surrendered to us, put himself in our hands, merely to send us on some wild-goose chase."

"I'm not sure."

"Intelligence reports and satellite photos have confirmed the explosion in his neighborhood in Tehran. It was his house."

"What about his story about the informant, this Seyed who reported to him?"

"Nothing on him yet. We have only the sketchiest intel on Seyed Asghari. A bit player. Nothing to indicate that he's dead or that he's involved in plans for an attack."

Sandor shook his head. "Something about this just doesn't feel right. He's lying. Or at the very least he's holding out on us."

"I completely agree, at least with the latter view," the DD replied calmly, "but if what he says is even half true, we need to track this lead as far as it takes us."

"I know," Sandor grudgingly admitted.

"If Iran is working with North Korea, it takes things to an entirely different level. The worst-kept secret in the Middle East has been Kim's attempt to clone their Yongbyon nuclear reactor in the Syrian desert. If they're getting in bed with Iran, we're no longer discussing the militant subcultures of Al Qaeda or the IRGC."

"Come on," Sandor said. "You want to discuss poorly kept secrets, how about the fact that the IRGC is really state sponsored."

"Of course. But in the past few years we've avoided a worldwide catastrophe by battling terrorist groups, even when we knew they were being covertly funded by unfriendly regimes. Now we're confronting the possibility that paramilitary actions are being officially sanctioned by foreign governments."

Sandor could not suppress a grin. "In other words, if you'll allow me some of your Washington lingo, we're talking about acts of war by sovereign nations."

"Yes," the DD conceded in what was little more than a whisper. "That is exactly what I'm saying."

"So, whether it turns out to be bullshit or not . . ."

"We need to find out." Byrnes finished the thought.

"I take it there's more."

Byrnes motioned to the armchairs and the two men sat. "We have independent sources confirming that there has been significant intelligence traffic between Iran and North Korea." He went on to explain that SIGINT, or Signals Intelligence, had developed the information at the National Security Agency. Formerly working out of Fort Meade, and now located in new high-tech headquarters in Laurel, Maryland, the NSA had processed recent data convincing them, in Byrnes's words, "that something is going on." The stakes were raised when one of South Korea's KCIA agents disappeared after reporting this activity.

"We have a highly placed source in North Korea," Byrnes went on. "He's deeply imbedded, but this is important enough that we'll have to use him."

"You mean risk his exposure."

Byrnes nodded.

"So where do I start?"

"We need you to go there. Communications are difficult, but we have reason to believe our man on the inside can get you to the people in Kim's administration most likely to be leading this sort of initiative."

Sandor smiled again at the choice of words, then ran his hand through his hair. "Initiative," he repeated.

"We're going to set up a team of four agents. We've already chosen the others; you'll lead."

"A team? In North Korea? What happened to the old maxim about traveling swiftest who travels alone?"

"Not this time, Jordan. It's too complicated and it's too risky."

"In other words, you want to quadruple your chances

of someone actually making it through and making it out?"

"In a word, yes."

"It's good to feel loved." Sandor sat back in the comfortable club chair. "North Korea? How the hell do we get inside? Better than that, how do we get home?"

"Getting in should not be a problem. The DPRK is allowing trade missions into the country to see the Arirang Festival." When Sandor responded with a puzzled look, Byrnes said, "I'll explain that later. The point is, you'll go through China, on Canadian passports. You'll be briefed, then you can meet with your team at the Farm."

"But the idea of four of us entering the country at the same time?"

"I know, bad form. We just don't have time to arrange it any better than this."

"And if their immigration forces smell a rat and detain us when we enter Pyongyang?"

"Then we're screwed."

"Is that the royal 'we'?"

Byrnes gave him a look that was all the response he was going to get.

"You haven't answered my question about coming home."

"We expect it to get a bit messy once you get inside and reach our source."

"Which means we're not getting out the way we go in, is that the bottom line?"

"Frankly, yes. We don't anticipate you being able to acquire the information we need without some, uh . . ."

"Persuasion?"

The DD nodded. "Our man in Pyongyang has an escape

route and some contingency plans. And you'll likely need to improvise."

"I'll bet," Sandor said, although he could not disguise the fact that he would be pleased to be back in action. "I take it Director Walsh has signed off on this."

"I've spoken with the Director as well as the President's National Security Advisor. With our findings on movements between North Korea and Tehran, the consensus is that the operation is worth the risk."

"The risk for whom?" Sandor asked with a wry smile.

"You in particular," Byrnes replied with no humor in his tone or manner. "You were the number one choice for the mission."

"And that comes from . . ."

"The top."

For the moment, Sandor was silent.

"Timing here is crucial," the DD said. "We have no idea how quickly this terrorist assault is moving, and we have limiting parameters on the movements of Kim's man."

"In plain English, please."

"We have to get to Kim's delegation as soon as possible, and in the most vulnerable setting."

"So we aren't going to march into the palace and ask for an appointment."

Byrnes replied with another of his classic frowns. "No, you are not."

"So how quickly are we going to move?"

"Immediately," Byrnes said as he rose to his feet. "There's a car waiting for you. You'll meet with your men this afternoon."

"And what about Jaber? Why do you think he asked to see me?"

Byrnes had already given that some thought. "He wanted to goad you, I think."

"For sport?"

"No, probably because he believes you're the best man for the job, and he actually wants you to succeed here."

"Well, that certainly is a bit of sad irony." Sandor stood. "Jaber has been involved in killing a lot of our people. Marines, diplomats, civilians, my team in Bahrain. When he talks about retiring into the sunset on our dime, I want to gag."

"Don't worry, Jordan. I won't forget who we're dealing with."

Sandor picked up the Walther and its holster from the table and tucked it into his belt. "That's good, because if everyone really does think he's already dead, that means no one is looking for him. And that can cut both ways."

CHAPTER SEVEN

ST. BARTHÉLEMY, F.W.I.

Hicham and Cardona were enjoying a pleasant lunch in an outdoor café along the quay that fronts the southwesterly side of the main harbor of St. Barths. Gustavia is the capital of the small island, named by Swedish settlers who were but one of the various nationalities that have controlled this rocky outcropping in the Caribbean between its discovery by Columbus and its ownership by the French. As a modern haven for the rich and beautiful, St. Barths has asserted a measure of independence from its mother country, but remains decidedly Gallic, from its cuisine to its attitude.

Hicham was describing what he knew of the history of Fort Oscar, which sits on the highest promontory at the mouth of the U-shaped port. It remains a military installation, originally built centuries before as the first line of defense against intrusion by sea.

"Now it houses the local *gendarmes* and the few remaining French military staff still assigned here," he explained. "But the true purpose of the site has become the electronic monitoring conducted from three stories below, buried deep inside the mountain." He pointed, and Cardona reached out and knocked his hand down.

"Be careful," he grumbled. "And keep your voice down."

Hicham laughed. "We're just two tourists admiring the sites. No one is looking at us anyway, brother; they're checking out the babes."

Beautiful women, young and old, clothed in diaphanous cotton covers or barely clad at all in their string bikinis, had been parading by them as if in a procession. "This is St. Barths. Let's take in the view." This was a far cry from the somber atmosphere of his briefings in Tehran, and Hicham intended to enjoy himself.

Cardona frowned. He was about to admonish his companion, to tell him that he was not serious enough about his responsibilities, to ask him how a Muslim could be so cavalier about women and alcohol and the sybaritic pleasures of this island. But he held his tongue.

At that moment, the cell phone in Cardona's shirt pocket began to vibrate. He connected the call without speaking.

"Are you in place?" the voice on the other end inquired in Spanish.

"Yes."

"Good. I am en route to my rendezvous in Tortola. From there we will travel directly to you. Did you have any difficulties?"

"None," Cardona told him. "Not so much as a glance."

"Excellent." The voice uttered a brief laugh. "Are you enjoying the local pleasures?"

Cardona looked across the table at Hicham. "We are preparing for your arrival," he said.

CHAPTER EIGHT

THE CIA "FARM," OUTSIDE LANGLEY, VIRGINIA

SANDOR WAS LESS than delighted that his incursion into North Korea would require the involvement of a team. His last group mission had ended disastrously in Manama, and as Byrnes well knew, Jordan felt responsible for every one of those casualties. Byrnes also knew that Sandor preferred to work alone whenever possible.

However, this was the DPRK, a country dedicated to the most ruthless and oppressive qualities of tyranny. Successfully engaging in espionage within its borders, not to mention escaping the country with the information sought, was going to require both skill and luck.

It was simply not a one-man operation.

The briefing was arranged at the Farm, the CIA's main training facility, located more than an hour from Langley. When Sandor arrived he was pleased to learn that the DD had chosen three men he knew well.

Craig Raabe was a former Navy SEAL, an expert in explosives with a subspecialty in arranging diversions that could provoke absolute mayhem when required. He was tall and fit with a shaved head, an easy laugh, and a gaze that could bore through lead. He also had a reputation of indestructibility.

Jim Bergenn was an expert marksman who had worked with Sandor in Afghanistan. Like Sandor and Raabe, he was in his late thirties, a handsome man with dark blue eyes, light brown hair, a charming manner, and a well-deserved reputation as a ladies' man in his off hours—and sometimes while on duty as well. Attractive female recruits were cautioned about Bergenn shortly after arriving at Langley. Some of the women at headquarters thought the warning should be included in the CIA handbook.

Kurt Zimmermann was in his late forties, a career Company man recently relegated to duties as an instructor on the Farm, legendary for his facility as a linguist. He spoke several languages without detectable accent. He was not as tall or athletic looking as the others, but he was broader and more muscular, with a renowned scowl of disapproval that intimidated some and amused others. His regular features gave him an everyman look that allowed him to pass as Scandinavian, Slavic, or numerous other nationalities in between. As far as his new assignment was concerned, he was certainly not going to convince anyone he was Korean, but he spoke the language fluently and that could prove valuable.

The three of them were waiting in a conference room in the main administration building. When Sandor strode in they greeted him warmly, or at least Raabe and Bergenn did. Then Zimmermann came forward and shook his hand, not letting go.

"Not your style, is it?"

"Sorry?"

Zimmermann treated him to the famous glare. "You don't much like moving in a pack."

Jordan grinned. "Depends on the pack, Kurt."

With that, Zimmermann gave Sandor his hand back and offered up his lousy impression of a smile.

"How much have they told you so far?" Sandor asked.

"Only that we're going on safari with you," Jim Bergenn said. "The DD was short on time, said you'd give us the skinny."

Sandor motioned to the chairs and they all took seats around the conference table. "Here's what I know," he began, then shared what he had learned in the past couple of hours.

When he finished, Craig Raabe said, "Ahmad Jaber? Why would we believe a single thing that asshole has to say?"

"Good question," Sandor admitted, "and I don't have a good answer, except to tell you that he's left his country and family and surrendered to us. His house has been blown to bits and the intel network has him as a probable casualty in the explosion. That means, as far as everyone else is concerned, it appears he's dead. If he's lying to us, that appearance could become reality very quickly."

Zimmermann grunted.

"As I've explained, we had a report from a guy in the KCIA who since has gone missing, and we've had one brief communication from our man in Pyongyang. Both confirm the basis of Jaber's story, that a deal is in the works between the DPRK and the IRGC."

"Well," Raabe said with a grin, "I guess that's some kind of answer anyway."

Zimmermann was obviously less satisfied. "Why send us into North Korea, then? Why not just bring our man out?"

"I asked Byrnes that very question," Sandor told them.

"Seems our source is highly placed. Too valuable an asset to waste if this whole thing turns out to be bullshit."

"We're not as valuable, is that the bottom line?"

Sandor allowed himself a brief chuckle. He had known Zimmermann a long time. "No, that's not it at all. Look, gentlemen, our Korean mole is an informant, not a field agent, and whatever this plan is, it is being handled on a high level within the Kim regime. Our man's access to the information is limited."

"Meaning what?" Bergenn asked.

"Meaning that we're not going in to simply retrieve a package," Craig Raabe said.

"That's right," Sandor admitted.

"We're going in there to develop the intel ourselves," Zimmermann said, finishing the thought.

Sandor nodded. "Our man inside doesn't have the dope, he just knows where to point us so we can get it."

"Perfect," Zimmermann said.

"How the hell do we do that in Pyongyang?" Bergenn asked. "That place is sewed up tighter than a frog's ass."

"Charming image," Raabe said.

"We're going to visit the famous Arirang Festival," Sandor told them, making it sound like some sort of afternoon at the county fair. When Zimmermann and Bergenn responded with blank looks, he said, "I never heard of it either, just got the lowdown in my briefing. It's their version of a Super Bowl halftime show, without the football game. Our boy will be there with some key players from Kim's inner circle. All we need to do is find them, get some answers, then come on home."

The three of them stared at Sandor in silence. Then Raabe burst out laughing. "That easy, huh? Just breeze in, slap around a couple of Kim's henchmen, then catch the next stagecoach out of Dodge."

"Something like that," Sandor replied, then described the plan to get them into the country posing as Canadian businessmen. "It gets a little worse," he told them, then explained that their identities would be non-official covers. The risk in using a NOC is that in the event of capture the government will deny involvement.

"In plain English, we'll be hung out to dry. Perfect," Zimmermann said again.

"That's not even my concern," Sandor told them. "It's the exfiltration that could get hairy."

"You think so?" Raabe said. "Not to mention the part about getting the information. Unlike you philistines I've heard of the Arirang Festival and, as I understand it, the stadium holds over a hundred thousand people. And nearly as many performers."

"Top marks for cultural knowledge."

"Thanks."

"And you're worried about being caught in the middle of that many people."

"We're not exactly being asked to grab some guy in a deserted alley, right?"

"Look on the bright side," Sandor replied. "With so many people around, it shouldn't be tough to get lost in the crowd."

"Yeah," Zimmermann said, "four Americans and two hundred thousand Koreans."

"Four Canadians," Sandor corrected him. "Look, anybody who doesn't want in, speak now or forever hold your peace. There'll be no hard feelings, because this is going to be a dangerous mission, make no mistake about it. It's strictly a voluntary deal."

They were quiet for a moment, then Raabe said, "I'm not about to miss this barbecue."

Bergenn said, "All for one and one for all, right?"

Sandor said, "I sure hope so," as he turned to Zimmermann.

Kurt finally responded with a quick nod. "Why not? I've got to get the hell off the Farm, that's for sure. I'm starting to feel like a schoolteacher."

"Good," Sandor said. Then he laid out the contingency plans the Agency had devised for their escape.

CHAPTER NINE

ABOARD THE YACHT *MISTY II*, IN THE CARIBBEAN

Rafael Cabello, the man known as Adina, had departed from Pyongyang immediately after concluding his business there, then flew through Beijing to Sydney and on to Mexico City. He traveled by car to a private airfield, where a charter flight took him south to meet the large and luxurious yacht *Misty II* in Tortola. He had remained aboard as other preparations were being made, and now the crew prepared for the journey to St. Barths.

Adina was in his sixties, trimly built with fine features, straight gray hair, and dark, unsmiling eyes. He was expensively tailored and carefully groomed, a man who had come to appreciate personal comfort and elegant living, even as he continued to extol the virtues of socialism for the masses.

He began his professional life as an instructor at Simon Bolivar University, an institution named for the Venezuelan revolutionary who preached pan-Americanism in the nineteenth century. At the college, Professor Cabello taught Marxism and espoused his worship of Lenin and Castro. Ultimately, however, he decided their approach to the worldwide spread of the new order was too passive for his taste. Eschewing his scholarly pursuits in the name of action he took to ground, adopted the code name Adina, and organized a paramilitary political group focused on support for his country's great new hope, a former pupil by the name of Hugo Chavez.

Chavez admired his former teacher, but Adina's philosophic lessons paled in importance when compared with the strategic advice he provided the future leader of Venezuela after the failed coup attempt of 1992. A brilliant tactician, Adina was known by insiders to have been invaluable in the subsequent resurrection of the Chavez machine and the ascendancy of his protégé to the presidency. After that success, Adina helped Chavez consolidate his power. Adina was instrumental in the growth of Venezuela's position on the world stage, using his country's natural reserves of crude oil and enormous refining capabilities as leverage for international influence. He engineered plans that won the allegiance of neighboring South American leaders in oil-for-support programs. He advocated an aggressive posture toward the United States, which Chavez zealously adopted, repeatedly vowing to wipe America off the map. Adina was even behind the renaming of many Venezuelan-owned gas stations in the United States, after Citgo became the target of conservative activists who were less than pleased to support a leftist regime. He essentially conceived the overall restructuring of Venezuela's modern petro-economy and—a personal favorite of Adina's—he scored a public relations coup when he persuaded the naïve scion of a famous American political family to become a shill for the Venezuelan government in exchange for a few paltry barrels of heating oil donated to the poor within the United States.

As the years passed, however, Rafael Cabello was present less and less among Chavez's inner circle, until he had become what he was today—a legend who was rarely seen but for those closest to the Venezuelan dictator. He had long ago cast off any idealization of the socialist state. Remaining an avowed enemy of democracy, he became a staunch supporter of rule by force. In the end, he had evolved into the most dangerous of adversaries, a socialist zealot who was neither ideologue nor true believer, but a brilliant and ruthless pragmatist.

———

"Sir." A steward interrupted him as he sat on the sundeck of the large yacht, admiring the blue of the sea and sky.

"Yes."

"The captain asked me to inform you that we will arrive after dawn tomorrow, as you requested."

"Excellent," Adina replied, then sent the young man on his way.

He sat back and reached for the beverage on the table beside him, taking a sip of the cold, fruity drink. He reflected on his meeting with Hwang, Kim Jong-Il's plenipotentiary for subversive activities. He was surprised the man knew so little of the plans that were already under way, but he allowed himself a silent nod of respect for Kim's obvious caution, if not paranoia. At least the North Koreans were now fully on board and would fulfill their end of the bargain. That was the important thing.

A few moments later, one of the other passengers on this voyage came on deck.

"Renaldo. Sit," Adina said in Spanish. "Have a look at this beautiful day."

Renaldo, some thirty years Adina's junior, took the chair beside him.

"Would you like a rum punch? Quite delicious."

Also speaking in their native tongue, Renaldo declined the offer. Then he said, "We have had further confirmation from Tehran."

"Indeed?"

"The authorities have completed their search through the rubble at Jaber's home. They recovered the remains of one body in the bedroom."

Adina considered that for a moment. "Remains? Have they verified that the deceased was Ahmad Jaber?"

"Not yet."

"The death of such an important man and still no positive identification?" Adina shook his head, as if disappointed in the Iranians for such inefficiency. "Has DNA testing begun?"

"I am not sure, we're attempting to find out."

"Do that," Adina told him, then took another drink of the punch. "Was there no one else found in the house?"

"Not that I know of."

"No sign of his wife?"

"Not that we have been told."

"Isn't that interesting?" He turned from the glorious scenery, having been nearly mesmerized by the steady wake of the large ship. Now he cast an inquiring look at his companion. "As I recall the dossier, Jaber was married, was he not?"

Renaldo nodded.

"Odd, then, don't you think, that after a morning visit

from Seyed Asghari, he meets his end that very same night amid the total destruction of his home and yet his wife is nowhere to be found?"

Adina did not await a reply, sending Renaldo on his way to make further inquiries. Then he returned to his ruminations about Hwang, regretting that these developments might require him to have further dealings within Iran.

CHAPTER TEN

NEW YORK CITY

Sandor and his team were told to put their affairs in order before they left for Toronto the following morning. The true risk of this sort of mission went unspoken, but it was understood that certain matters must be attended to before they became four Canadians en route to Beijing.

Each went his separate way, dealing with their families and personal issues. Sandor was flown back to Teterboro, then driven into Manhattan. He made a few phone calls from the road, then headed for his first stop, dinner with his best friend, Bill Sternlich.

Sternlich was an articles editor for the *New York Times*. He and Sandor had been close for many years, dating back to Bill's assignment in the Washington bureau when Sandor was working out of Langley. They had both since returned to New York, their friendship intact despite the huge political divide that separated them. Sternlich was a confirmed liberal, his perspective having become even more skewed, as Sandor taunted him, by his long-running association with America's most shamelessly slanted newspaper. Sandor, according to Bill Sternlich, was just slightly to the right of Attila the Hun.

In fact, neither assessment was true. Sternlich was possessed of a far more moderate perspective than one would usually find in the daily screeds on the *Times'* op-ed page. Sandor, although an archconservative in matters of national security and the sort of advocate for individualism that would make Ayn Rand proud, could be something of a social liberal, for which he was frequently teased by his friend.

Political differences aside, there were indeed professional considerations that weighed heavily on the friendship. Sandor was limited in what he could discuss about his work for the government and, what little he might share, Bill generally could not print. Nevertheless, Sandor provided leads when he could, and Sternlich had been helpful in acquiring background information on more than one occasion, even managing to publish a piece that Sandor had penned when he was posing as a retired State Department attaché working as a freelance political writer. The friendship had survived, even in the face of recent events that had shaken them both.

By the time Sandor arrived back in the city it was after seven in the evening. They agreed to meet at one of their regular haunts, Esca, on Forty-third Street and Ninth Avenue. Sternlich had reserved a table in the corner of the back room, where he was waiting when Sandor arrived.

Bill stood and greeted his friend with a warm hug. "Been a while, pal."

"Yes, it has."

Sternlich was a few years older than Sandor, nearly forty-one, with the unmistakable look of a man devoted to a lifelong desk job. He sported a soft middle, pale complexion, and receding hairline, and his bespectacled gaze always bore that slightly weary look of someone who simply did not get out in the world enough. "So," Sternlich said as they took their seats, "it's time to catch up."

Sandor began by inquiring about Bill's wife, of whom he was very fond, then about Bill's children, a young boy and girl Jordan found endlessly amusing. After that he hesitated before asking about Beth Sharrow.

"She's coming along," Sternlich said. "Time for you to see her again, I think."

Beth was an Agency analyst in the New York office. She and Sandor had been an item a few years back, and she became close with Sternlich and his wife. Beth remained friendly with the Sternlichs after her romance with Sandor ended, as all of his romances ended, without resolution or reason. During Sandor's most recent assignment, Beth had unfortunately become embroiled in the action when she was identified as someone with access to him. She suffered a vicious beating that would certainly have killed her if Sandor's backup team had not arrived in time to take out the assassin and save her life. Sandor felt completely responsible.

Beth was hospitalized for several days, then spent time in rehab, where they worked on her broken jaw as well as her shattered psyche. Sandor visited her in the hospital as soon as he returned from Europe, but the doctors thought it might be best for him to stay away for a while.

Sternlich had agreed at the time.

"It might actually help for her to see you at this point," Sternlich admitted.

Sandor nodded. "As soon as I get back."

His friend responded with an uneasy smile. "Are we going on the road again?"

"Tomorrow."

"I thought you were still on some sort of medical leave."

"Some sort, but I'm ready to go."

"Right back into the deep end of the swimming pool, eh?"

"Something like that."

Sternlich gave him a curious look. "So our get-together is more than just a social catching-up session."

Sandor scanned the room quickly for what must have been the fourth time. "You've heard about the Jaber incident in Tehran?"

"We heard Ahmad Jaber was blown to pieces in his home," Bill replied in that straightforward manner Sandor so admired. Not only was his friend informed, but he never played games when it came to these discussions. Sandor wished he could be as candid, but Jaber's survival and defection were still classified. "No group has taken responsibility, at least not yet."

"Right," was all Sandor could say for now.

"From what I understand, we're well rid of him."

Sandor nodded. "Bad guy."

"Word in the media says a heightened security alert is coming down the pike. Any connection to the late Mr. Jaber?"

Sandor nodded. "It turns out he may have had information that led to his early exit. I'm assigned to find out."

"You're going back to the Middle East?" Sternlich knew the last time Sandor was there he was involved in the aborted mission in Manama, Bahrain. He also knew it was less than a happy memory.

"Not exactly."

"Not exactly?"

"No. I'm heading a little farther east than that."

"That so?"

The waiter came by and each man ordered a *quartino* of red wine, Sternlich a Sangiovese, Sandor a Montepulciano. As the server walked away, Sternlich asked, "That all you're able to say?"

Sandor hesitated. "No. Actually, this time I've got to tell you some things. I'm going to a place where getting in is going to be a helluva lot easier than getting out, especially after I take care of what I have to do there."

"Meaning what?"

Sandor stared across the table at his friend. "Meaning, I may not make it back."

Bill shook his head. "Jordan . . ."

"Hold on, please." He leaned forward and lowered his voice. "I'm only telling you this because if something happens, something unexpected, I may need someone to contact, someone outside the normal channels. I have a feeling about this for reasons I can't explain, and I want you to know that I may need to get you information I wouldn't trust with anyone else. I need you to have a way to verify that the information is coming from me." He reached into his sport coat pocket, removed a small piece of paper, and slid it across the table. Then he leaned even closer and whispered in a voice so low he was practically mouthing the words. "Take a look at this and don't say anything."

As Sandor removed his hand, Sternlich looked down at the paper, a code in numbers and letters. "These are . . ."

Sandor held up his hand, then smiled. In another barely audible whisper, he said, "Damnit, Billy, didn't I just tell you not to say anything?"

"Right."

Sandor then turned the paper over, revealing the words that read, "Memorize right now, then destroy."

"Those are the numbers, so you'll know the communication is coming from me. Just in case," Sandor said. "Just in case."

CHAPTER ELEVEN

ST. BARTHÉLEMY, F.W.I.

EARLY THE FOLLOWING morning, the yacht carrying Adina and his retinue arrived in Gustavia. The premier berths along the main dock were situated between the old St. Barths and the new, just down the street from Le Select—the Rastafarian hamburger joint that remains one of the few affordable places to eat on the island—and only a short stroll from a dazzling assortment of glamorous boutiques. Hermès. Cartier. Cavalli. Bulgari. Chanel. Dior. Vuitton.

Cardona had driven into town early, grabbed a café au lait from the patisserie on the Rue du Roi Oscar II, then waited on the quay. Hicham had been instructed to remain at the villa, a one-man welcoming party constituting quite enough attention at this hour.

Cardona watched patiently as the crew of the *Misty II* went through the slow and careful process of docking the large yacht, then he boarded and was escorted into the main stateroom, where he was soon joined by Adina.

Cardona was clothed in wrinkled linen slacks, a button-front short-sleeved shirt, and sandals. Adina was dressed in well-tailored beige slacks, a pressed white linen shirt, and tan loafers of soft woven leather. He was holding a wide-brimmed Panama hat.

"You had a good trip?" Cardona asked.

Adina shrugged. "We shall see. I believe our Asian comrades are finally in lockstep with us. All that remains is to execute our plans with the required precision. That, my friend, will make it a good trip."

Cardona responded with a nod, saying nothing. Adina reflected on how he had taken a particular liking to this man—affection would be too strong a word—appreciating his no-nonsense style and the unquestioning way in which he followed orders.

"We need to begin our work here."

"As you say."

"We've revised our thinking," Adina told him. "We think it will be best to have the Americans begin their chase sooner rather than later. The weather forecasts seem to favor an earlier timeline."

"Good."

Adina smiled. "It is therefore time for us to send Hicham on his mission."

———

Cardona drove Adina and his lieutenant Renaldo along the mountainous road that led back to the compound on the cliff. When they reached the house, they strode quickly from the parking area to the main building.

Hicham was in his bathing trunks, soaking up the early morning sun on a chaise beside the pool. When he saw the three Venezuelans enter he jumped to attention. Cardona made the introductions.

Adina gave a nod of the head without shaking hands. Then he turned and stepped to the railing to have a look out at the sea. "Beautiful view," he said simply.

When Hicham assured him that he would enjoy the villa, Adina explained that he and his aide would remain with the others on the yacht. Then he asked to see the layout anyway. Hicham grabbed a T-shirt and pulled it on, then led them from room to room. As they finished their walk along the concrete path overhanging the cliff, Adina said, "So, we are completely undisturbed here."

"Yes, except the housekeeper living in the *maisonette* at the foot of the driveway there. She comes in once a day for about an hour." Hicham had a quick look at his watch. "Just about twenty minutes from now. Quite attractive," he added.

Adina glanced at Cardona. "I do not want to meet her." Turning back to Hicham, he said, "Go and tell her she is not needed today."

When Hicham was gone, Cardona led the other two men back into the master bedroom suite. He took his suitcase from the closet and displayed the explosives he had successfully smuggled into the country.

Adina nodded approvingly. "Time to get started, my friend."

"What do you want me to do?"

"Our sun-loving North African friend will begin the operation for us."

Cardona nodded.

Adina placed a hand on Cardona's powerful shoulder. "I have already arranged his passage, from here to St. Maarten, then connecting on the afternoon flight to New York."

Speaking to Renaldo, he said, "While we have lunch on the yacht you can arrange for his boarding pass."

Renaldo said that he understood, but Cardona seemed to be mulling it over.

"Is something wrong, my friend?"

"No, I'm sorry, no, I was just thinking, that was all."

The older man smiled indulgently. "Thought is the assassin of action. Do you know who said that?"

Cardona gave a confused look, then shook his head.

"I did," Adina announced, followed by a hearty laugh that he prolonged until the two younger men joined in. When he resumed his serious demeanor, he said, "Tell me your concern."

"Well, once he arrives in St. Maarten, won't he have to claim the bag and run it through customs?"

"Ah, a good question. You see, Renaldo, why I tell you I am so pleased with this man? He leaves nothing to chance." Turning back to Cardona, he explained: "There is a service here that allows a check-through, as well as a connecting boarding pass, both of which Renaldo will arrange for a small fee. We'll take care of everything."

Cardona responded with a satisfied look.

"Good," Adina said in a way that made it clear the subject was closed to any further discussion.

Cardona closed the suitcase and followed Adina and Renaldo from the bedroom back to the deck, where Hicham had just returned.

"Well," Adina said, "this is quite a glorious setting, is it not?" He did not await a response. "And you will also enjoy our yacht. Your comrade here has already had the pleasure," he said, giving Cardona a fraternal clap on the arm. "Your turn will be for a fine luncheon on board."

"Thank you so much," the Moroccan replied with obvious satisfaction.

"It's settled," Adina said as he held out his hand and led them to four chairs arranged in a circle around the small table on the deck. "First it is time for you to tell us what you two have learned about the technology inside the depths of Fort Oscar."

CHAPTER TWELVE

EN ROUTE TO PYONGYANG

Sandor rejoined his team early the next morning. They met in a conference room adjacent to a private hangar at Reagan International Airport in Washington, where they were presented passports, visas, credit cards, and dossiers containing background information on their identities as Canadian businessmen. Then they were flown by charter to Toronto, where they would connect with the Air Canada flight that would take them nonstop to Beijing.

"Canadian," Craig Raabe mused on the ride from D.C. "I don't have to fake some silly accent, do I, Zimmermann? Sound like a Canuck or something?"

Kurt Zimmermann grunted.

"Hey, you're the language expert." He turned to Sandor. "What if they start grilling us about hockey? I hate hockey, don't know diddly about it. They'll see right through me."

Sandor responded with a sage nod. "Yes, I'd say it's your lack of hockey knowledge that's putting us at risk here, Craig. Tell you what, we have twenty hours or so on the flight to Beijing. I'll spend the entire time regaling you with the history of the NHL."

Bergenn laughed. "Just make sure you're sitting at least three rows away from me."

At Pearson International Airport in Toronto their first-class check-in went without a hitch. Their bags held no weaponry and no electronics. Only Raabe's suitcase was fitted with plastic explosives and they were undetectable, or so Craig was assured at Langley. He knew the real test of that would come at airport security in Beijing and then Pyongyang. Meanwhile, the other three carried no contraband, not wanting to risk an arrest before they even made their way inside the DPRK. As Sandor reminded them, they would be unarmed and very much on their own.

Sandor also told them that it was important, right from the start, that they assume the identities they'd been given. "Four businessmen on a trip like this don't move like a Special Forces advance unit." Once they received their boarding passes, he said, "Do your own thing, we'll meet back at the bar in the First Class Club in an hour or so."

Sandor spent the time seated in a comfortable armchair in the lounge, going over the information that Byrnes had furnished, for his eyes only, to be destroyed before he boarded the flight to Beijing. There were several aspects of the mission he had been told that his men had not. The DD had left it up to him to decide when and how much of the data to share.

Sandor put the file on his lap and stared out the window. Given the level of danger he and his men were facing, he wanted to be sure his mission would not be complicated by any information leaks.

As he knew only too well, when people in government start talking, the discussions are quickly picked up by the media. That meant the secret of Jaber's defection was not likely to stay secret very long, which would have a wide range of consequences.

One aspect of those consequences was particularly troubling.

If Jaber was telling the truth—that he had defected for fear of his own safety—those who believed they had already murdered him would not take kindly to the news that Jaber was still alive, especially since he was now cooperating with the Americans. It would be no leap of faith for his enemies to assume Jaber was sharing any intelligence he had about the scheme being hatched with the North Koreans.

Carrying the thought forward, Sandor knew that the only edge he had in his incursion into Pyongyang was surprise. If the North Koreans learned that the CIA had information about these plans, the danger of their mission would increase by an exponential factor.

He reached into his pocket, pulled out his cell phone, and called Sternlich. "Bill, it's me."

"How do I know it's you? Recite the code."

"Not funny. This is likely the last time I'll be able to call you in the next few days. I need you to check something for me."

"I'm listening."

Sandor believed the best place to gauge whether a breach had already occurred was among the denizens of the fourth estate. If the channels of confidential communications had been penetrated, the media would be the first to know. Sandor trusted Sternlich as much as he could trust anyone, and time was short, so he elected a frontal approach. "Bill, I have to ask you something, but the entire discussion, even the topic we discuss, ends with this conversation."

"I understand," Sternlich said.

Sandor hesitated. "You remember our discussion about Ahmad Jaber yesterday?"

"Of course."

"I never asked if you'd heard anything about him."

"I haven't, but I can check around if you want."

"I do want you to. But tread lightly, Bill."

"I will."

"I need to know what the rumor mill is churning out about him. Anything at all you can dig up in the next twenty-four hours. Then I need you to text me 'yes' or 'no' on my international cell number at this time tomorrow. If it's yes, I'll know I need to get back to you."

"All right."

"And Bill, there's one more thing."

"Go ahead."

"It's extremely serious."

"I'm listening," Sternlich assured him in a grave voice.

"I forgot to cancel my newspaper delivery," Sandor said, then started laughing.

Sternlich took a moment to name the anatomical part of a horse his friend most closely resembled, then hung up.

Sandor went to the men's room. In one of the toilet stalls he tore up the contents of the file Byrnes had given him and flushed them away. Then he broke his cell phone in two, removed the battery, and gouged the internal transistor board with his pen. When he left, he deposited each piece in a different trash bin, then made his way to the bar and ordered a Jack Daniel's on the rocks.

CHAPTER THIRTEEN

TABRIZ, IRAN

THE WIFE OF Ahmad Jaber did not learn of the destruction of her home until several days after it happened, when the Iranian minister of communications finally gave Al Jazeera permission to release the story. She was sitting in the living room of her sister's home in Tabriz, watching the evening news, when the report was aired.

An overwhelming sense of disbelief quickly turned to shock as the sketchy details were recounted. She stared at the screen as video footage displayed the wreckage of her demolished house from several angles. The reporter on the scene offered the government-sanctioned view—that the blast was caused by a faulty gas line. She sat motionless, gazing at the television, realizing that she had been waiting for something like this, expecting something like this, ever since her husband sent her away a week ago.

And then the fearful moment came when the reporter said, "Only one body was recovered at the scene." Then he said, "It is believed to be the body of a longtime civil servant in the administration."

Rasa Jaber waited, but they gave no name. She managed to draw a deep breath, then let it out slowly, unevenly, but she did not weep. She had been the wife of an international terrorist for three decades, so she watched the entire segment in stoic silence, then stood and trudged slowly into the kitchen, where her sister was preparing dinner.

"Something has happened," Rasa said, fighting back tears. Then, as calmly as she could manage, she recounted what she had just heard.

Her sister nearly fainted.

"Please," Rasa implored her as she helped her sit down, "we must be strong. This situation remains dangerous." What she did not say was that the danger now extended to her sister, her brother-in-law, and her two nieces. "Does anyone know I have come to visit with you?"

"Only my neighbors."

Rasa shook her head. "All right. I will finish preparing the dinner. You need to go out and buy every available newspaper from Tehran. They are available nearby?"

Her sister nodded.

"See if you can find *Hamshahri* and *Shargh*. And your local paper, what is it called?"

"*Durna*."

"Yes. And also try to find them from yesterday, even the day before. I need to look for every possible report."

"What about the English paper?"

"The *Tehran Times*? Yes, that too, if you can get it."

The younger woman hesitated before speaking. "You know that they will all carry the same story, the one the government has approved."

"Yes, but every detail is important if I am going to find Ahmad." Her sister still appeared unconvinced. "What is it?"

"I am sorry to have to ask this, Rasa, but if Ahmad survived, would he not have contacted you by now?"

Rasa shook her head slowly and managed a grim smile. "No, that is exactly what he would not have done. Now go, quickly."

Once her sister left, Rasa went to the closet, removed her suitcase, and began to pack. She forced herself to methodically fold each article of clothing, placing them neatly until she suddenly stopped, gripped by a painful spasm of fear, a palpable sense that froze her in place. She dropped the sweater she was holding and wrapped her arms around her shoulders, as if that might alleviate the awful chill. In a moment the sensation passed, but she still did not allow herself tears. There was too much to do.

She knew her sister would protest her leaving, but Rasa realized she must depart immediately. It was for her safety as well as the protection of her sister's family. At some point the people responsible would come for her, and this would be one of the first places they would look.

Only one body had been recovered at the scene, Rasa reminded herself, and the reporter said the remains were yet to be conclusively identified. Rasa believed her husband was still alive. He had sent her away abruptly, so he must have known there was serious trouble ahead. Now her home was in ruins and a man was dead.

She believed that man was their servant, Mahmud, and she suspected Ahmad had arranged things to make it appear that he was the one who perished in the explosion. She also believed her husband's ruse would soon be discovered and, assuming Ahmad was beyond their reach, they would search for her.

All of this was more than mere speculation, Rasa told herself as she finished packing. She actually felt certain of these things. She had no idea how her husband knew their house would be destroyed, or why he would have anticipated events so as to leave Mahmud behind, but she knew the cleverness of Ahmad Jaber. Whatever he had done had bought them time, and now she must use that time wisely. Over the years he had tutored her in the means of escape, preparing for the possibility that flight would become necessary. He had mentioned it again last week, as they parted. Now that day had arrived, and she must act with both dispatch and caution.

She took a moment to organize the cash that Ahmad had given her that night. Some was in rials, some in euros, some in American dollars. It was quite enough to fund her way to safety. She also removed from the inner compartment of her valise the handgun he had left her. She was no marksman, that was sure, but she knew how to load, to disengage the safety, to point, and to fire. If it ever became necessary, and now it well might, she would be prepared to act.

Rasa replaced the gun and the cash, closed the suitcase, and returned to the kitchen. This would be a sad dinner, likely the last time she would ever see her sister and her nieces. She only hoped no trouble would befall them from all of this.

She also hoped Allah would permit her to survive.

CHAPTER FOURTEEN

EN ROUTE TO PYONGYANG

THE FLIGHT TO the People's Republic of China was un-eventful, and the four men got as much sleep as they could, knowing rest would be at a premium once they reached their destination. In Beijing they collected their luggage, passed through the "In Transit" procedures, then were directed to the North Korean airline desk.

Sandor powered up his international cell. There were various voice mails and e-mails, but only one he was looking for. Just an hour before, Bill Sternlich had sent him a text that said, "No."

Sandor took a quick stop in the men's room and subjected this cell to the same fate as his other phone in Toronto, then moved on.

———

At Air Koryo each of them was questioned, their visas and passports scrutinized, their bags subjected to a double round of scanning. The four men engaged in ongoing banter, four chums on holiday without a care in the world, none of them so much as glancing at Raabe's suitcase. Even if the weapons experts at Langley were right, and the C-4 was essentially invisible to a normal scan, the four agents also realized it would likely be discovered if the suitcase were opened and the lining torn away. Sandor could not help but think of his conversation with Sternlich, could not help but worry over the possibility that word of Jaber's defection had already leaked and that he and his team were at a much greater level of risk than anyone had foreseen. So far, at least, Sternlich had said, "No."

As they continued their banal chatter, Raabe's valise was passed through with the rest of their luggage and they were permitted to head to the boarding gate. Once aboard the plane, Sandor realized the dangers they faced may have more to do with aeronautics than espionage. The aircraft was an ancient Russian model, something Moscow had probably given away twenty years ago in lieu of turning it into scrap metal.

The Air Koryo staff was efficient, but when the steward offered them beverages and Raabe made a joke about Coca-Cola being the world's dominant power, his attempt at humor was met with an icy silence.

Sandor knew there would also be nothing friendly once they entered the ironically named Democratic People's Republic of Korea. Known in diplomatic circles as the DPRK, and to the world at large as North Korea, it makes other dictatorships look positively tame by comparison. The lack of basic rights and freedom, not to mention communications, is nearly absolute, and these restrictions apply to nationals and foreigners alike. Unlike other countries, which welcome tourists, there is no unfettered movement within the DPRK. Sightseeing tours are precisely choreographed. The few restaurants which visitors may patronize are strictly identified and regulated by the state. The hotels are likewise designated, thereby simplifying the task of military surveillance, which is maintained even with regard to the most innocent guest. The only Internet use must be accessed via satellites controlled at state facilities, meaning that all messages are subject to monitoring and censorship. No cell phones are allowed. Television and radio programming are limited to news and entertainment approved by the Great Leader and his administration.

Sandor watched as Raabe made another failed attempt to charm the stewardess, then sat back and stared out the window.

After a couple of hours, and a surprisingly smooth ride, they landed at Pyongyang International Airport. They were led down a metal staircase onto the tarmac and into the main terminal. The building was small and squat and utilitarian, the roof adorned with an enormous billboard containing the watchful visage of Kim Jong-Il. They were herded along with the other passengers and required to fill out yet another series of forms, including the usual acknowledgments that they were not carrying any prohibited goods. Then they were subjected to a new round of interrogation and inspection.

None of the four Americans cast so much as a glance at Raabe's suitcase as it passed through a final scanner without incident.

At the conclusion of the formalities, a Korean gentleman of about fifty, with closely cropped hair and unexpressive mien, stepped forward and introduced himself as Choi Ki.

In heavily accented English, he said, "I will be your guide during your visit to the Democratic People's Republic of Korea. You may call me Mr. Choi."

Sandor and the other three men introduced themselves, then grabbed their luggage and followed Mr. Choi outside to the small bus that he explained would be their transportation for the next three days. The driver gave his name, which was Sang Chung Ho. Mr. Choi then apologetically explained that Mr. Sang spoke almost no English.

"Gentlemen, I must ask for your passports. I will hold them for safekeeping during your stay with us."

Sandor and his team were prepared for the request, but feigned some appropriate reluctance before handing over the forged documents.

"Now please sit back and enjoy the ride into Pyongyang."

Sandor nodded to himself. He had no weapons, no means of outside communications, no one to count on when the action started except for these three men. The small bus might as well have bars on the windows, he thought. For all practical purposes, they had just been taken prisoner.

CHAPTER FIFTEEN

ST. BARTHÉLEMY, F.W.I.

HICHAM DISLIKED CARDONA. He disliked him the first time they met.

They were certainly different, he and this brutish Venezuelan, but the differences were not merely stylistic. Hicham would be the first to acknowledge that his relaxed approach to religion was troublesome to his stricter Muslim brothers, but Cardona was not a son of Allah. He was nothing more than an ignorant mercenary who viewed everything in life with a cynicism that precluded any commitment to a greater cause. Hicham was not a secular opportunist, he was loyal to his faith and committed to doing Allah's work. So, although they were both engaged in this treacherous business, their reasons were worlds apart.

Why should he have to suffer the disapproval of this infidel?

Adina was another matter entirely. The man was refined. He was a gracious host at the sumptuous lunch they were served on the yacht. Their discussions revealed that he was a Christian who nevertheless understood the teachings of the Koran.

Hicham realized, however, that this was a serious man, a man to be feared.

When Hicham was recruited for this mission he was contacted outside normal channels, to the extent normal channels exist for such things. He was assured his services were required in the name of Allah, and that he was going to be an important part of a massive strike against the Americans, a plan being organized by a consortium of various nations. Since then, however, his involvement had been marginalized and, although he could not complain about a few days of relaxation on this island paradise, he was becoming increasingly unsure of his true role.

So, when Adina told him that his responsibilities had changed and he was ordered to board a flight that day to New York, Hicham was disappointed. His assignment in the Caribbean had never been detailed. All he knew was that his mission had something to do with the electronic installation at Fort Oscar. Hicham assumed he would be asked to either take control of the communications systems there or, at worst, help to destroy it.

And now he was to fly to New York to meet a man he had never heard of, for reasons he would only be provided once he arrived.

He was committed to playing a useful role in the upcoming attack, but he had been given these instructions by Adina and there was nothing to be done about it.

After their lunch on the *Misty II*, Cardona was ready to drive Hicham to the airport.

"What about my things?" Hicham asked.

"Renaldo picked them up for you," Adina told him, then called to Renaldo, who had just returned. He produced Hicham's carry-on bag and his boarding pass. "Everything has been arranged."

"My suitcase . . ."

"You'll be returning day after tomorrow, my boy, no need for a suitcase." Adina tilted his head slightly and offered him a wry grin. "Unless you don't trust us with your things while you're away," he added, evoking laughter from the others, and a forced smile from Hicham.

"I thought I would be here when the action started."

"You'll be back in time. You are a key part of this team," Adina assured him.

————

When Hicham and Cardona arrived at the airport, the Moroccan said, "No need to wait. It's a beautiful day. Bad enough I have to leave the island, go enjoy yourself."

"You're the one who enjoys these things," the burly Venezuelan responded. As punctuation, he offered a disdainful look at the tropical scene that surrounded them as they stood in the parking lot outside the small terminal. "I'll wait."

Hicham shrugged. "Then let's go upstairs and have a beer."

There was a bar on the second level that served Stella Artois on draft. Hicham ordered one for each of them. They sat at a table by the window where they had a view of the airstrip and the St. Jean beach just beyond. The barman served them, and Hicham said, "Good beer, eh? I love Stella."

"I thought Muslims don't drink."

Hicham smiled. "How long have you been waiting to mention that?"

"Since we arrived."

Hicham nodded. "Some men are more religious than

others," he said. "And some of us celebrate our faith in different ways."

They spent the next ten minutes in silence. Then the announcement came for Hicham's flight. Downstairs they parted without any gratuitous show of affability, merely nodding good-bye. Hicham passed through security and strode out the glass door to the tarmac, where he climbed the few steps into the single-engine plane.

When the flight took off, Cardona pulled out his cell phone and reported to Adina, then returned to the villa at Pointe Milou.

PYONGYANG

THE GRANTING OF a tourist visa into the Democratic People's Republic of Korea carries with it obligations that transcend the temporary abandonment of privacy and freedom. For one thing, guests are required to suffer through a mind-numbing sightseeing tour, every feature of which pays homage to the Great Leader.

Sandor and his men had no sooner boarded the van being piloted by the taciturn Mr. Sang when their bilingual guide Mr. Choi stood up and described the mandatory itinerary they would enjoy on the way to the hotel. Sandor responded with a bemused smile. He had been fully informed of this ritual and the fact that it was compulsory. There was no artifice here, no inquiry by Mr. Choi if these visitors would like to drop off their luggage first, take a shower, or perhaps relax for an hour before they began their predetermined journey through Kim-land. They were simply informed of what was to come next, then instructed to remain in their seats as the van whisked them along their way.

The vehicle was large enough for a contingent more than twice their size, so each of the four men occupied a two-seat bench, with Raabe across the aisle from Sandor, Zimmermann and Bergenn behind them. As they entered the high-way to Pyongyang, the most striking feature of the multilane road was the absence of traffic. In a country where the leadership extols the illusions of its extraordinary economic success and the triumph of the "Juche Idea"—Kim's ideology of national independence—the general population had somehow been left out of the equation. Not only are they lacking cars, televisions, and other amenities the Western world takes for granted, they are also lacking food. The people of North Korea had been facing a deadly famine for more than a decade, with no end in sight.

As if no such problems existed, Mr. Choi stood facing his guests, droning on about the magnificence of his great country until they reached Mansu Hill, where the bus came to a stop at a large plaza, in the center of which stood an enormous statue of Kim Il-Sung, father of Kim Jong-Il.

Towering over Pyongyang below, the image of the country's former leader stands with arm upraised, apparently exhorting his minions to worship him as they would a deity. When Mr. Choi informed them it was time to leave the vehicle and admire the monument, Craig Raabe turned to Sandor and muttered, "You've got to be kidding."

"Easy, big guy," Sandor said as he stood. They had all been briefed on what was to come, but Sandor knew more about it than any of the others.

Mr. Choi led them outside with Sang remaining in the driver's seat as they filed past him. He looked as if he were bolted in place. Choi carried a small bouquet that had been sitting beside him on the front seat.

Out on the street he said, "It is our custom that visitors

honor the Great Leader by placing flowers at the base of our Glorious General's statue." Then he held them out straight-armed, as if part of some formal ceremony.

Knowing this moment would come, the four agents had drawn straws on the flight to Beijing. Zimmermann had lost. Now he stared at the bouquet as if it might be contaminated.

"Kurt, why not do the honors," Sandor urged him with a grin.

Zimmermann glared at Sandor, then reached for the flow-ers, resisting the urge to snatch them from Choi's tiny hands and throw them on the pavement. He walked toward the monument and set the bouquet on the ground at the base of the gigantic shrine, then backed away.

Mr. Choi hurried forward and stopped him. "Please, you must bow," he said in a tense voice that told Sandor and the others that they were being watched and, by definition, that Mr. Choi was being judged. Sandor had a look around, but the plaza was almost completely empty. Then he glanced at Mr. Sang, still in the bus, who was silently observing the proceedings. Sandor nodded, but Sang did nothing to ac-knowledge him.

Kurt Zimmermann shot the other three a dirty look, then turned back to the gigantic image of the Supreme Com-mander, gave a brief nod of his head, then stepped back.

"Very nice," Raabe said with a grin.

"Screw you very much," Zimmermann replied.

Choi told them they must now observe a moment of si-lence, after which he herded them back onto the bus.

The other stops on their route involved similar protocols, minus the floral offering. As they approached each one of these highlights, Choi would tell them how fortunate they were to have the opportunity to visit whatever they were about to visit. Then they would leave the bus, admire something that Mr. Choi ordered them to admire, reboard the bus, and move on to the next attraction. These included the Tower of the Juche Idea; communist carvings honoring Marx, Lenin, the proletariat and, of course, Kim Il-Sung; and their final stop, the Arch of Triumph.

Unknown to the rest of his team, this was Sandor's first contact point.

The DPRK's Arch of Triumph, situated within the city limits of Pyongyang, is larger than the Arc de Triomphe in Paris, which is the only way Kim Il-Sung would have it.

"You've got to be kidding me," Bergenn said as they climbed off the small bus for the fifth time and stood on the sidewalk, staring up at the monument. "What, exactly, was the great triumph that this arch is supposed to commemorate?"

Mr. Choi, hearing the comment, explained how the North Koreans had driven the Japanese from Korea in 1945 and, in the process, ended World War II.

"Uh, call me crazy, but according to what I've heard, Korea wasn't split in two until after the war," Bergenn said. "And speaking of revisionist history," he went on, but Sandor stopped him when he saw Mr. Choi's sallow complexion growing paler by the moment.

"We understand that we are guests here," Sandor said. "We will enjoy this opportunity to see your Arch of Triumph."

Mr. Choi responded with a quick nod, then led them toward the monument.

It was notable, again, how quiet things were within the

capital city. As they walked together along the spotless sidewalk of this wide boulevard there was almost no vehicular traffic and very few pedestrians. Sandor felt the eeriness of this utterly antiseptic scene, remaining alert to the fact that—despite all appearances—everything they did was being carefully monitored.

As they reached the plaza at the base of the arch they spotted the first tourist stand they had encountered since arriving in the capital city. A country purporting to encourage foreign visitors to come and honor the Great Leader offered very little in the way of souvenirs of the event. The group had not come across so much as a postcard up to now. Even at this small booth, unlike Western tourist stands, the selection was limited. They had a few packaged snacks, some soft drinks, and a vast array of photographs, mostly of Kim Jong-Il. The rest of the counter and walls were covered with pins of various colors, sizes, and designs. Koreans are fond of pins, and it is not unusual for citizens of the DPRK to wear several at one time. As the other three men followed Choi toward the arch, Sandor fell back, wandering back toward the stand.

An older woman stood inside the kiosk, while a younger, attractive woman was waiting alongside the counter.

"Do you speak English?" Sandor asked them.

The older woman did not reply. The younger girl said, "Yes, a little."

Sandor nodded. "This arch is taller than the one in Paris," he said.

"But not wider," she told him.

Sandor looked around, then returned his attention to the

young woman. "I would like to buy some pins. I think four should do it," he said.

"Yes, here are four very nice pins." She reached behind the display and held out four enamel-covered pins. Two had a colorful design surrounding the flag of the DPRK. The other two featured the same design around the image of Kim Il-Sung.

Sandor began to hand her some *won,* the North Korean currency he exchanged for at the airport.

"Take these," she said softly, placing them in his hand. "The design is what you will seek in others. You understand?"

He nodded, putting the pins in his jacket pocket.

She turned to the other woman and handed her the bills. When she made change, the young woman turned back to Sandor and handed him some coins. "You are Sandor?" she asked in a hushed tone.

"Yes."

"I am Hea," she said with a shy smile.

A voice behind Sandor said, "A name that means grace. And quite fitting, I must say, young lady." It was Zimmermann. "Making friends, Jordan?"

"A wise man once told me that whenever traveling abroad, we are diplomats for our nation."

"Our beloved Canada, you mean," Zimmermann said with a sarcastic smile.

"Of course."

The others were approaching, led by Mr. Choi, and so the pretty young woman named Hea displayed the wares of her kiosk with a graceful wave of her hand. "Your friends, they would like a pin? A soda?"

Mr. Choi was eyeing Sandor with more than his usual level of anxiety. Sandor smiled at the girl and shook his head. "No, I believe it's time for us to go."

As their small group began to walk away, Sandor stayed back long enough to hear the girl whisper, "Look for this design at Arirang." When he turned to her she mouthed the words, "I will see you there."

CHAPTER SEVENTEEN

ABOVE THE CARIBBEAN, NORTH OF ST. MAARTEN

Hicham WAS SEATED comfortably in his first-class seat on the large jet that would carry him from St. Maarten to New York. He had made the connection from St. Barths without incident, and was now working on his cocktail and gazing out the oval window at the blue sky, wondering for a moment if perhaps Cardona was right. Hicham mused over the sins he had committed against his religion, both in the name of pleasure and in the service of his people, and wanted to believe that Allah would forgive him these transgressions. After all, he assured himself, he was a soldier in the war against the Western infidels, and that should be enough.

As he took another drink he didn't feel the first explosion, coming as it did from deep within the cargo hold, a small charge that an instant later ignited the larger blast. Everyone felt that one, as the device detonated several pounds of augmented C-4 plastique, blowing a hole in the side of the plane, rocking it off course as the entire belly of the aircraft suddenly caught fire below them.

Passengers began to scream as their oxygen masks were released, hanging before them from their clear plastic tubes, impotent symbols of the horror they were about to endure.

Inside the cockpit the crew struggled to level out the airliner as their emergency panels lit up with an array of emergency warnings. The navigator was already on his radio, calling for help, as the captain initiated rescue sequences, turned on the manual sprinkler systems, and ordered the first officer to assemble the staff, telling them to gather every fire extinguisher on board and take them below.

But it was too late. When Adina's men wired the C-4 into Hicham's luggage, they also rigged lines that appeared on the scanning machine as the spine of the suitcase, but were actually tied to a second round of devastation—a highly combustible plastique that now exploded upward in another blast, tearing through the floor and followed by a flash of fire that began to engulf the passenger cabin.

The screams were deafening as Hicham looked around him, feeling a mix of both terror and rage. He damned Adina and cursed his own stupidity. Then he realized in a final moment of awareness that this would be his last memory, the earsplitting screams of all these people with whom he was about to die.

CHAPTER EIGHTEEN

NEW YORK CITY

Bɪʟʟ Sᴛᴇʀɴʟɪᴄʜ ᴡᴀs in his small, postmodern office in the new headquarters of the *Times*, standing high above Eighth Avenue. He was editing a magazine piece about celebrities in Southern California who were promoting solar energy, hybrid cars, and other environmentally fashionable options. He stopped, removed his glasses, and took a moment to consider how these pampered children of Hollywood could possibly reconcile their endorsement of a green lifestyle with their private jets, fur coats, and cocaine snorting. Then he leaned back and stared up at the ceiling, replaying for the hundredth time his last conversation with Sandor.

He did the checking Sandor requested and, as instructed, sent him a text twenty-four hours later, letting him know that he had not turned up anything new on the death of Ahmad Jaber. But since then he had heard a rumor that Jaber was not dead, that he was in the hands of United States intelligence.

Sternlich was considering the consequences of that information, how he might get word of it to Sandor, and whether Sandor already knew.

Just then Frank Donaldson barged into the room.

Donaldson was in his late twenties, a graduate of Avon and

Yale. Square-jawed and blond-haired, he was a go-getter from a wealthy family that subsidized his nascent career as a political reporter, not only because they could, but because they assumed it was the start of an ascending path that would ultimately lead him to the anchor desk of some network's evening news program. Sternlich was alternately amused and bewildered by the fact that, given the young man's privileged background, Donaldson's views were even further to the left than his own.

"Heard about the plane in St. Maarten?"

Sternlich responded with a blank stare.

"Get this," Donaldson said, then shared the sketchy information that had just come through about the crash.

"Any survivors?"

"Doesn't look good. Navy, Coast Guard and Air Force are on their way."

"Was it mechanical?"

"Planes don't just blow up in midair, Bill."

Sternlich nodded but said nothing.

"What about that friend of yours?" Donaldson asked.

Sternlich blinked.

"Come on, you know who I mean, that guy from Washington. He seems pretty wired into what's happening, right?"

"And?"

"And how about we give him a call? See if he can clue us in, get us a little advance info."

Sternlich shook his head slowly. "He's unavailable right now."

"That so?" Donaldson planted himself in the chair opposite his editor. "He wouldn't already be on his way there, would he?"

"You have an overactive imagination, Frank."

"Hey, you're the one who told me to follow my nose, right?"

Sternlich leaned back and had a look at the young reporter. "If you follow it too closely you'll get cross-eyed."

"Come on," Donaldson said, "for the team."

Sternlich had never much liked that ex-jock chatter. "My friend is out of town," he said.

"So was this airline crash."

"He's nowhere near the Caribbean, Frank."

"Okay, but there are some stories flying around; he might help us piece things together."

Sternlich waited.

Donaldson pulled his chair closer to the desk and leaned forward. "You remember that story about the explosion in Tehran a week or so ago?"

Sternlich nodded.

"A source I have in D.C. says there may be more to it than Al Jazeera is letting on."

"That would certainly be a shocker."

"Right. Well get this—there's a rumor that Ahmad Jaber isn't dead, that it wasn't his body they recovered."

"I heard that rumor too."

"Did you also hear that Mr. Jaber might actually be a guest of our government at the moment? Right now, here in the States. At the Langley Hilton."

Sternlich did well to hide his surprise. "I'm listening."

"What if this plane crash is somehow connected to Jaber? What if it's retaliation for his capture?"

"That's quite a stretch, Frank. What have you got, other than a wild guess?"

"Nothing," the young man admitted, sitting back as if deflated by the notion. Then he perked up again and said, "Unless maybe your pal can give us something to run with."

"My friend is in the Far East at the moment," Sternlich told him, regretting the statement as soon as he uttered the words. "At least he was, as far as I know."

"The Far East?"

"As far as I know."

"Can you check? I mean, this could be huge, Bill."

"I don't know what you expect him to be able to tell me."

Donaldson responded with one of those knowing smiles that belong to the privileged few who are graced with the realization that, in the end, they are better than you because of breeding, education, heritage, and, above all else, money. "Look, it's not as if we all don't know your pal is a spook. Least you can do is see if he's got anything he can tell us, then we can huddle up again. Right?"

Sternlich frowned. Huddle up? "I'll see what I can do," he lied.

CHAPTER NINETEEN

AN ESTATE OUTSIDE LANGLEY, VIRGINIA

WHEN MARK BYRNES received word of the airplane explosion outside St. Maarten, he immediately called for his car and headed directly for the safe house where Ahmad Jaber was still in residence. Unlike some of his subordinates, notably Jordan Sandor, the Deputy Director was a man with an even temperament not given to easy fits of anger. Today, however, was another matter. By the time he reached the estate he was not disposed to a diplomatic approach.

Byrnes stormed into the room and demanded, "What the hell kind of scam are you running here, Jaber?"

The Iranian responded with a blank stare.

"Answer me, damnit."

"Mr. Byrnes, I, uh, I am at a loss here."

"You're going to be at a loss. Now tell me what you know about the destruction of a commercial jet in the Caribbean."

As Sandor had observed just a few days before, either Jaber was a great actor or a great traitor to his people. He said, "I have absolutely no idea what you are talking about."

Jaber was in an isolated environment with no access to television or newspapers or radio or the Internet. Even if he was part of the plot to destroy the airliner, Byrnes realized that he had no way of knowing the sabotage had succeeded.

"Sit down," the DD said gruffly, then took a chair opposite Jaber, drew a deep breath, and gave the man a summary of what he had learned so far.

Jaber's look of surprise turned to a pensive expression. "Could that have been their plan?"

"I beg your pardon."

"When Seyed came to me, as I have described to you, he knew little of their intentions. For my purposes, the identity of the men involved was more important than their mission. Seyed Asghari knew practically nothing of their plans, so I felt it would be more valuable to find out who was involved."

"The men who were involved, according to your information, were Asian, probably Korean. That was as much information as this Seyed Asghari gave you?"

Jaber nodded, then stared down at the floor, holding his forehead in his left hand, his left elbow resting on the arm of the chair, apparently lost in his own thoughts. He was not ready to divulge what Seyed had also told him about the Spanish-speaking men who were involved, undoubtedly the same men who had engineered the destruction of Jaber's home as he sat on the hillside and watched. There were only a few things he had managed to keep to himself, knowing that in the end his fate would become a negotiation and he had very little else to trade.

"And you believe this was their scheme?" Byrnes demanded. "To destroy a commercial aircraft in the Caribbean?"

Jaber paused, then finally looked up. "Frankly, I do not."

"So," Byrnes said, less angrily this time, "I return to my original question. What scam are you running here?"

"I am not the one running the scam, as you put it, Mr. Byrnes. I have come here, as I told you, to share whatever information I have. If you are asking me for an opinion, then I must say I do not believe this was their ultimate goal. No. It makes absolutely no sense. Why travel to Iran? Why involve so many different people? I say again, no. In my opinion, this was merely a diversion."

"A diversion? Over two hundred people are presumed dead. What the hell kind of diversion is that?"

"In my estimation," the Iranian responded calmly, "an extremely effective one."

CHAPTER TWENTY

ST. BARTHÉLEMY, F.W.I.

THERE ARE THREE types of people who inhabit St. Barths. The first are the true natives, that group of hardy islanders descended from French, Swedish, and assorted other ancestries. The second are the visitors who fall in love with the natural attributes of the island, who rise at dawn, jog on the beaches, soak up the sun, eat salads for lunch, and are at home in their rented villas or expensive little hotels by ten. The third are those who come to St. Barths, not for its innate splendor, but for its reputation as the place to see and be seen. They are the late-night revelers who eschew gorgeous sunrises, opting instead for drunken sunsets. They are the denizens of the hilltop palazzos, the suites in the finest of hotels like the Isle de France or Guanahani, or the occupants of the megayachts that choke the small harbor of Gustavia.

Yachts like the *Misty II*.

Adina was well aware of these three disparate worlds, interested not for sociological reasons, but for how the movements of these people would affect his plans to infiltrate the telecommunications center at Fort Oscar.

He was seated on the uppermost deck of the *Misty II*, puffing calmly on a Partagas D4, staring across the clear blue water at the cliff where the walls of the old fort were visible. Ironically, it was the portion of this fortress that was not visible that presently held his interest.

Adina had just received word that the airliner had gone down. He chuckled aloud at Hicham's concern that he might not be part of the operation here in Gustavia. Their departed Arab friend had indeed been an integral part of that plan.

The destruction of the airliner was critical to his scheme. Adina had instructed Renaldo to line Hicham's suitcase with plastic explosives, then check the bag through to New York. Once Renaldo obtained the boarding passes for the flights from St. Barths and St. Maarten, he destroyed the luggage receipt.

Making Hicham the unwitting carrier of the bomb was easy. The Moroccan never even knew a suitcase had been checked in his name.

The difficult part was finding a way to detonate the explosives. Adina's men realized there was no effective way to implant a timing mechanism. Such gadgets could be too uncertain and even the most casual security check would detect the equipment. They opted instead for an altitude-sensitive device. It was constructed of clear glass that contained mercury, sulfuric acid, and an explosive cocktail containing liquid oxygen. When combined in the proper sequence the concoction would have enough firepower to set off both the C-4 and the secondary inflammables.

Unlike the interior of the passenger and crew areas, the luggage compartment of the airplane was not fully pressurized, so the device would work as the plane rose. The crucial feature was to have the glass container strong enough to withstand the large bag being tossed about by luggage handlers in the transfer from one airplane to the next—they obviously did not want the suitcase to explode on the ground—but delicate enough to shatter when the mercury and acid expanded as the flight rose somewhere above twenty thousand feet. Once the glass membrane separating the components cracked, the mixture would ignite.

The appearance of the tube and the liquid, seen through the airport scanning machine, approximated a large bottle of cologne, nothing that would raise undue suspicion inside checked luggage. The top compartment contained the mercury, and it was full and airtight, designed to appear on the X-ray machine like the cap of the bottle.

As anticipated, no one in security gave it a second look, not in St. Barths, nor in the check-through baggage area at Princess Juliana International Airport in St. Maarten. As the aircraft rose high above the sea and approached the critical level, pressure built until the lethal container detonated.

Now, as the authorities occupied themselves with a downed aircraft, Adina could proceed with the next phase of his operation.

CHAPTER TWENTY-ONE

PYONGYANG

THEIR COMPULSORY SIGHTSEEING tour con-
cluded, Sandor and his men were taken to the Yanggakdo
International Hotel, a huge rectangular building of no ar-
chitectural distinction which was set on a small island in the
middle of the Taedong River.

On their arrival, Craig Raabe made a comment about
the likeness between the setting of this large, monolithic
structure and New York's Rikers Island prison facility. Not
only were they similar in style, but each was only accessible
by a bridge. "Tourists here are like inmates in a detention
center, right? Easily monitored and not able to enter or leave
without permission."

Mr. Choi was not amused. He was quick to point out
that the Yanggakdo had a nightclub, assorted dining rooms,
a revolving cocktail lounge on the top floor, conference
rooms of various sizes, and spectacular views across Pyongyang and beyond. All of this was available to be enjoyed and
explored by Sandor's group under the watchful eyes of their
ever-present guide and others who remained unseen but were
obviously in attendance.

Choi shepherded them through the check-in process,

explaining that they would be sharing two rooms, and that once the room assignments were given there would be no switching. Sandor glanced at Raabe. They understood that limiting them to two rooms made surveillance that much easier than four.

"Is there any way to pay for a single-room upgrade?" Raabe asked. "These jokers all snore."

When Choi shook his head, Sandor said he would bunk in with Raabe, Bergenn with Zimmermann.

"You may rest now," Mr. Choi advised them, "or have a look around our wonderful hotel. Almost two hours before dinner, in Dining Room Three. Six o'clock."

"Dining Room Three?" Raabe asked. "Is that the steakhouse, or do I have it confused with Dining Room Two?"

Mr. Choi ignored him. "After dinner, you will be honored to attend the Arirang Festival."

"That's what we're here for," Sandor said. Then the four of them followed Choi, their suitcases in hand, to the elevator bank.

They realized the rooms were probably wired for audio, and perhaps even video. Their discussions would therefore be limited, as would their ability to organize the explosives Raabe had secreted in his luggage.

Before entering the lift, Sandor said, "I'm not tired. After I clean up I'll be heading for the revolving bar."

The others nodded.

"Thirty minutes," Sandor told them.

————

They were all staying on the tenth floor at the Yanggakdo, undoubtedly to further ease the surveillance of their movements. They were shown to their rooms by Choi, where they found the accommodations spacious but cold, in keeping with the character of the building. The rooms were identical, each containing two double beds, a square nightstand between them, and two rectangular dressers against the wall. There didn't seem to be a curved line anywhere. A television was secured to the top of one of the bureaus. It offered exactly two channels, each broadcasting state-created news.

One side of the room consisted of floor-to-ceiling windows overlooking the harbor. Two others had large mirrors built into them, a perfect arrangement for covert placement of the audio and video equipment that was undoubtedly rigged behind the glass. Sandor and Raabe bid the others good-bye, then shut the door. They looked over the setup and then at each other. Neither man spoke, neither voiced the obvious need to find a way to remove the small charges of plastique and magnesium fuses from Craig's bag without being observed.

Sandor headed for the bathroom, where he turned on the shower, all hot water, at full blast. With the door closed and the shower curtain pulled back, the mirror in there steamed up in just a couple of minutes.

He came back and said, "You want to shower first?"

Raabe nodded, grabbed his suitcase, and disappeared into what had developed into a humid cloud.

Sandor turned one of the small armchairs toward the large window and sat, treating himself to the panoramic view of North Korean countryside as it stretched out toward the horizon, wondering what the evening would bring.

Their plan was actually quite simple, but Sandor knew the execution was going to be complicated.

Inside the Rungrado May Day Stadium, where the Arirang Festival was held, they would wait for the conclusion of the first act. When the second act began, Sandor would leave his seat. Their guide would not want him wandering off on his own, so the other three would agree to accompany him, just to make it more convenient. Once they were out of view they would dispatch Mr. Choi in any manner they deemed best, then head up two levels to the private boxes. There they would need to locate the suite where their mole would be meeting with key players from Kim's inner circle. It was Sandor's assignment to find these men, extract whatever information he could without compromising their North Korean collaborator, then make an escape.

They had no weapons and no clear plan for extraction from the stadium, relying as they must on agents within the country to provide them help along the way. They would not be able to return to the van, since the driver, Sang, was certainly not going anywhere without Mr. Choi. This meant that timing, stealth, and luck would be imperative.

Not to mention the assistance of the young woman who had given Sandor those four pins at the Arch of Triumph.

CHAPTER TWENTY-TWO

NORTHWEST IRAN

Rasa Jaber steered her late-model Mercedes along the Marand Road beltway, heading northwest from Tabriz, bypassing the town of Marand en route to the Turkish border. She realized that time was critical, but was careful of her speed, repeatedly forcing herself to slow the car. She knew that if she were stopped in Iran and her identity discovered, she would be taken into custody to face repercussions she could not even allow herself to contemplate. Ahmad had schooled her well, so she proceeded with caution, once again bringing herself back into line with the flow of traffic.

In the silence of her car, left to think about her husband and the predicament she faced, she became increasingly distraught. How had things gone so wrong? She had already suffered enough for the perils of Ahmad's chosen life—they had lost both of their sons in the war with Iraq and had a tragic familiarity with how suddenly things could change. Over the years she was forced to admit to herself, infrequently and with the greatest reluctance, that death was a specter under which they constantly lived. But this was something else, a fate she had never imagined. This was a threat coming from her own country.

Her husband obviously knew of the coming danger. He had moved her out of harm's way to protect her and, she told herself, had somehow managed to escape himself. But now so many days had gone by and there had not been a word or a message. He knew where she was, where she could be found. He could have sent her some sort of signal, could he not?

So where was he? What did he expect her to do? Had he abandoned her forever?

The visit to Tabriz had placed her sister's family in jeopardy. Ahmad had been thoughtless in arranging that as her safe haven. Rasa left her sister's home as soon as she learned of the explosion—remaining there would have been worse for all of them, and she hoped she had acted quickly enough so that her sister would not suffer. But now she was alone, on a journey into oblivion, to give herself up to the despised Americans, to seek quarter from those Ahmad had spent his life battling. She was traveling a route her husband had outlined for her long ago, in anticipation of the day when he was gone and she would be expendable in the eyes of his enemies. What lunacy, she told herself. Could her own people have become the enemy? If Ahmad was alive, as she was sure he must be, why had he left her to this fate?

Rasa became so upset that she failed to notice her speed increasing again, but it no longer mattered. They had already spotted her vehicle, and their sirens suddenly pierced the haze of her tortured thoughts with the harsh chill of reality. Two official cars swiftly pulled alongside her, one remaining even with her sedan, the other moving out in front. Together they forced her to the side of the road.

CHAPTER TWENTY-THREE

ST. BARTHÉLEMY, F.W.I.

THE REAL FUN in St. Barths begins long after nightfall. People are done with frolicking on the beach, shopping in overpriced shops, and enjoying their late-afternoon rendezvous and siestas. After a late dinner session the bars fill up, the discos swing into action, and the party gets under way. Fortunately, Adina told his men, by then almost everyone on the street will be drunk or stoned, or both. His two teams would be able to move around the harbor undisturbed and virtually unnoticed. Their only issue would be the increased level of security at Fort Oscar.

Adina had favored this timing, carrying out the disruption of the telecommunications at the fort after the plane was downed. In reverse order, word of an assault on the fort might have caused the airport in St. Maarten to cancel flights or, at the least, wake up and pay attention to the luggage passing in transit through its porous checkpoints. An attack on Fort Oscar, coming after the crash, would be seen as part of a larger conspiracy focused on this sleepy corner of the Caribbean—exactly as he intended.

In addition to the team leaders, Renaldo and Cardona, there were six men assigned to this mission. They were now all on board the *Misty II*, and tonight, just after midnight, they convened in the main salon. All eight men were dressed in large tropical shirts of various patterns and shapes, the loose-fitting fabric serving to hide their body armor, automatic weapons, radios, and assorted other gear. They were assembled for final instructions.

Adina reveled in these enterprises. The former college professor turned militarist had come to prefer action over analysis, regretting only that he would not accompany them on this operation tonight.

"Men," he said, addressing them in their native Spanish, "I remind you again to take nothing for granted. Do not let these tropical surroundings fool you. There are French soldiers and local *gendarmes* on duty inside and outside the fort. These men are professionals, and the crash of flight six sixty-one will only serve to intensify their vigilance."

The eight men nodded without speaking.

"Cardona will command your team," he said, pointing to the three men on his left, "Renaldo is in charge of the rest. You will move separately, advancing on the hill from two directions." He pointed to a map on the table, depicting the U-shaped harbor. "Cardona's team will arrive first and circle here, to the west. Once Renaldo is in place on the south hill, on his signal, you will both move toward the two entrances. As we have discussed, there should be little resistance at ground level. The real assets within this fortress lie beneath, and that is where the fighting will come," he told them with a grim smile. "Any questions?"

No one spoke.

"Good. I will be in radio contact at all times." He gestured to the wireless setup on the table. "You have already been briefed on your extraction. Two powerboats will be awaiting you here," he said, pointing again to the map, "at the northern end of the Rue des Quais." He looked around the room. "You know your assignments. Now go."

CHAPTER TWENTY-FOUR

MARAND, IRAN

THE THREE IRGC agents who had taken Rasa Jaber into custody commandeered the interrogation room of a local police station. Once their identities as members of the Revolutionary Guard had been established, the Marand police had no problem relinquishing the room and staying clear of whatever this was about.

Mrs. Jaber sat at a small table, two of the men seated opposite her, the leader of the group pacing behind them.

"You are not providing the help we had hoped for, madame. This will not go well for you if you refuse to cooperate."

Rasa Jaber was a proud woman. She sat upright in the uncomfortable metal chair, fighting back tears as she stared at this stranger. "As I have already said, there is nothing for me to tell you."

He stepped forward and slammed his fist on the table. "You have nothing to tell us or you are unwilling to speak? Which is it?"

She drew a deep, uneven breath. "My husband is a loyal Iranian. He has fought for the IRGC and for the glory of this country."

"He is a traitor," the man bellowed. "And," he added in a modulated tone, "may I remind you that he has also abandoned you to this fate."

Rasa had been struggling with the possibility that this was true, that she had been forsaken by her beloved husband. It did not seem plausible, nor was she prepared to believe that he had betrayed his country. She shook her head. "Ahmad was murdered, our home destroyed. Why are you not chasing the villains who are responsible for this atrocity? Why are you persecuting me?"

"Is that what you really think, madame? That your husband is dead?"

She stared at him without blinking.

"Odd, then, that we discovered you driving across the country rather than returning to Tehran to mourn your great loss."

Rasa stared down at her hands.

"Dead indeed," the man said disdainfully, then reached for a leather portfolio on the table, shuffled through some papers, and removed a group of photographs. "Perhaps this will change your mind," he said as he placed a series of eight-by-tens in front of her. The first was a photograph of Ahmad Jaber. Two men were standing on either side of him.

"What is this supposed to mean to me?"

"Please, have a more careful look," he said. "We have gone to the trouble of having it enlarged, so that all of the details are evident. Have another look."

And so she did, not trusting her own eyes as she studied the picture more carefully. It was obviously a recent photo of Ahmad, that much was clear. But now she realized the two men were American soldiers. As she looked through the other prints she realized that he was being escorted into an American military vehicle. He did not appear to be under arrest or in handcuffs or otherwise coerced. He seemed to be acting voluntarily, apparently cooperating with these men. She looked up, her expression a mixture of outrage and confusion. "This is a lie," she insisted. "This is some trick."

"No, Madame Jaber," the man said in a voice that now bordered on sadness. "I am afraid it is the truth," he said as he pointed at the image of her husband. "You will see that these photos were taken over the border, in Iraq."

She stared at the photographs once again, then returned her bewildered gaze to this tall stranger.

"Now," the man said more calmly, "perhaps you are prepared to share with us everything your husband said to you in the days before his defection."

CHAPTER TWENTY-FIVE

PYONGYANG

THE FOUR MEN were seated at a round, black lacquer table in the lounge on the top floor of the Yanggakdo Hotel. The entire room revolved slowly atop the tall building, treating each of them in turn to the full spectrum of the view below.

Craig Raabe made a show of craning his neck around, then said, "This would be great, if there was something to see."

Sandor smiled. "Easy, big guy. We Canadians are polite guests, remember?"

"Sure," Craig said, then took a gulp of his club soda and lime. He was taking no chances with alcohol, not with an explosive pack strapped to the small of his back. "It is one helluva view, though."

Sandor nodded, then had a look around the almost empty bar. "Not exactly doing land office business, are they?"

"Maybe it's too early for most tourists," Jim Bergenn suggested. "They're probably still out there oohing and aahing over the Arch of Triumph."

"Quite an authentic history tour," Raabe said. "Sort of like visiting Epcot Center in an alternate universe."

Bergenn and Sandor laughed.

"We've got company," Kurt Zimmermann told them as he spotted Mr. Choi making his way across the room to their window table.

"Gentlemen," the slightly built Korean greeted them. "You are enjoying our beautiful views?"

"Oh yeah," Craig Raabe told him. "Breathtaking."

Sandor took a sip of his scotch—no American bourbon was in evidence—and looked up at their guide. "I thought we were going to be allowed some time on our own."

Choi gave a theatrical look at his watch, then said, "Just wanted to remind you, dinner in forty-five minutes."

Raabe nodded thoughtfully. "Thanks for the update. You'll be coming by every fifteen minutes, I expect, like a town crier?"

Choi began to say something, then stopped, turned, and headed off to whatever vantage point they had assigned him to keep an eye on this foursome of travelers.

Bergenn was about to speak, but Sandor held up his hand. "How about those Toronto Blue Jays," he said. Then he laid three pins on the table. He was already wearing his. "Put these on," Sandor said. "You'll feel like a local."

Dining Room Three was as cavernous as the penthouse bar upstairs and as antiseptic in décor as their rooms. The four men suffered no surprise to discover the cuisine was consistent with the surroundings. What the food lacked in visual and culinary flair it made up for in the variety of hot sauces offered, each intended to mask the inferior quality of the ingredients. Mr. Choi joined them for dinner, which

Sandor did not see as any particular hindrance, since open conversation was out of the question anyway.

Shortly after their plates were cleared and tea was served, Choi announced that it was time to go. They followed him downstairs, out through the lobby, and into the van, where the reliable Mr. Sang awaited their arrival.

Each of the four men was carrying a small bag, knowing they would never see the Yanggakdo Hotel again. As they took their seats, Choi frowned, then told them, "You will not be able to bring anything into the stadium."

Sandor did his best to look surprised, then said, "Well, that's okay. We'll just leave them. We all trust Mr. Sang."

Choi appeared to be thinking that over, then with a short nod gave permission to Mr. Sang to set off. As the van pulled away from the curb, Choi said, "You should be prepared for one of the world's greatest spectacles."

He was not wrong, but he had no idea the spectacle would not be provided on the field.

The arena, Rungrado May Day Stadium, is a colossal structure housing one of the largest arenas in the world, seating more than 150,000 spectators and accommodating more than 100,000 performers. The Arirang Festival is part circus and part gymnastics performance, famous for the human mosaics that are so intricate and so precisely executed they dazzle even the most jaded observer.

As they approached the stadium Mr. Sang circumvented the throngs of native attendees who were coming on foot toward the eight main entrance gates. Sandor had not discerned any special markings on their van, but somehow they were allowed to bypass these pedestrians, as well as several remote parking areas and the ubiquitous security check-points, eventually finding a special access area reserved for foreigners and dignitaries.

Sandor tapped Mr. Choi on the shoulder as they came to a stop. "This is rather an elitist entrance for a socialist country, don't you think?"

Choi fixed him with a cold stare. "I understand that you and your associates enjoy your Western sarcasm. It would be best, however, to refrain from such comments while you enjoy the festival."

Sandor returned the hard look. "Best for whom, Mr. Choi?"

The Korean gave no answer. He stood and faced the four of them. "You will leave your bags on your seats and follow me. I have your tickets. It is most important that you remain close to me at all times for the rest of the evening, gentlemen. Do you understand?"

Craig Raabe said, "It's good to feel loved, Mr. Choi." When their guide did not react, Raabe said, "I don't suppose this show opens with a stand-up comedian from Pyongyang?"

At least that earned him a frown. Then, without giving any instructions to Mr. Sang, Choi led them off the bus and into the crowd.

———————

The DPRK often hosts large excursions of honored guests at the Arirang Festival, particularly from the People's Republic of China. Those contingents are typically accompanied by several thousand Chinese security personnel, making the arena virtually impenetrable. Byrnes and his team checked timing with the KCIA to be sure that Sandor's team would not be encumbered by that additional problem.

The four men followed Mr. Choi, wading into the crowd around the perimeter of the stadium. The walls were buttressed by massive support arches that covered the entrances. Inside there were several stands featuring posters, soft drinks, tiny mementos, T-shirts, and the ubiquitous Korean pins. "So this is where we can stock up on souvenirs," Sandor said, but Choi hustled them past, clearly not wanting any of his charges to become lost in the crush of people on either side of the exclusive, narrow entryway. "Come," he said, and hurried them inside.

They obediently remained in lockstep, following Choi through the gateway and along a series of concrete ramps to an upper level. There they were handed programs and led to the front row of a mezzanine section. Sandor noticed the military presence everywhere—on the field, in the stands, and, to his dismay, on guard within the interior corridors behind them. He and Bergenn exchanged concerned looks, but said nothing. The only good news was the continuing mystery about the health of the Great Leader. As Sandor and his team knew, Kim Jong-Il had not been seen in public for months and was certainly not going to be at tonight's performance. That meant the security, although in evidence, was at a much lower level than it would have been if Kim were on-site.

They found their seats, Jordan taking the aisle and Choi placing himself in the middle of them.

The field below, which was the size of several football fields, was already populated by more than seventy thousand people, all of whom were working with a series of colorful cards, readying themselves for the upcoming display of coordinated colors that would depict everything from vivid sunsets to martial arts to pictures of Kim Jong-Il. In between, acrobats of all ages would perform.

Choi chattered away about the spectacular colors and precision movements and how it all served to exemplify the Juche ideal.

Sandor tried not to yawn.

Following a preliminary array of automatonic card flipping that was a sort of visual overture, Act 1 began. The programs they had been provided contained several languages, thankfully including English. A quick review informed them that they were about to sit through a pictorial history of the North Korean motherland in all her resplendent glory. Amazing, Sandor thought, that they can mount a production like this while their people are starving to death in the countryside nearby. He waited impatiently as the show slowly made its way through displays of carefully chosen historical events, a few of them real, but most of them imagined. The finale was an enormous replica of the North Korean flag presented by two hundred thousand perfectly aligned hands wielding small cards. As this first act concluded, the performers began rearranging themselves for the next series of choreographed moves. After a long break, when they were almost ready to begin Act 2, Sandor stood up.

"Very impressive," he said to Choi, "but I've got to use the facilities."

Mr. Choi became instantly flustered. "No, no, I am sorry. Act Two to start."

"That may be, but I've got to take care of Act One, if you know what I mean."

Choi was also standing now. "Please, sit down. You are blocking the view of these people," he said, then bowed slightly in apology to those behind them.

"Okay, I'll find my way, no problem," Sandor replied, starting up the aisle.

Choi protested again. "You must not go."

At this point Zimmermann stood. "Hey, if it makes it easier, I could use a pit stop myself. I'll go with him."

"Sure," Raabe said as he and Bergenn got up from their seats. "We'll all make it easy on you. Come on, Choi."

Choi suddenly found himself surrounded by them, a short Korean bracketed by four tall Americans as they headed up the stairs toward the passageway that led to the men's room. They reached the concrete hallway behind the stands, passing a few other spectators who were returning to their seats.

"Which way?" Sandor asked.

Choi pointed to the left, and they followed him, past a soldier who was standing guard with an AK-47 slung across his chest, and into a large, tile-lined bathroom.

Two other men were inside, and the foursome took their time at the urinals, waiting as the strangers quickly washed up and left, apparently in a hurry not to miss the next series of card flips. Sandor had been told that the Koreans consider it disrespectful to leave your seat during the performance. He had counted on the bathroom being empty, and was pleased to see the two stragglers go on their way.

Choi, who had been pacing back and forth, moved impatiently toward the door. "Come, come," he said. "Let's go."

Sandor was the first to finish and he walked to the row

of sinks. After rinsing his hands, he turned to Choi. "Paper towels?"

The Korean could not believe the man was so dense. "Right there," he said huffily as he pointed to the dispenser on the wall. That brief move was all Sandor needed.

He stepped forward and grabbed Choi's outstretched arm with his left hand. Then, with a quick, powerful thrust, he hit him under the chin with the heel of his right hand. As the Korean staggered backward against the wall Sandor moved swiftly to the side, taking him around the neck, then grabbing Choi's wrist, forming a tight hold that choked off both sound and air as the smaller man struggled to wrench free until he finally succumbed to the sinewy garrote that rendered him unconscious.

Raabe reached under his shirt and removed two strips of duct tape from the small of his back. The first he pressed against Choi's mouth. The second, longer piece, he used to bind the unconscious man's hands behind him.

Sandor pointed to Zimmermann, then to the door. The team's linguistics expert stepped into the corridor and called to the sentry, who was standing at a portal, viewing the extravaganza below. In Korean, Zimmermann said calmly, "We need some help here. Our guide has fainted."

Zimmermann's relaxed tone, and the fact that he spoke flawless Korean, gave the guard no reason for alarm. The soldier stepped forward, and Kurt politely held the door for him as he entered the bathroom. Before the man had a chance to assess the situation, Zimmermann hit him from behind, using the side of his hand to land a crushing blow across his neck. Bergenn was waiting, unleashing an open-handed uppercut that shattered the guard's nose, sending blood flowing down his face as he crumpled to the floor. Kurt was immediately on him, driving his knee into the Korean's back before grabbing his head with both hands and smashing his face into the tile. Then he took the tape Raabe was holding out and trussed the inert figure the same way they had Choi.

"Bind their legs too," Sandor said. "Take the AK-47, his radio, and whatever else he's carrying, then stuff the two of them into those toilet stalls and lock them in."

As they quickly went about their work, Zimmermann said, "Why not take them out right now?"

Sandor shook his head. "No need."

Zimmermann responded with a scowl. "The guard is going to be out cold for a while, but how long you think your polite little choke hold is going to keep Mr. Choi asleep?"

Sandor stared at him.

"Not long enough," Zimmermann warned. Then, before stuffing Choi into the stall, he took the guard's automatic pistol from its holster and drove the butt of it into the side of Choi's head three times. As he drew his hand back for a fourth blow, Sandor grabbed his wrist.

"That's enough, Kurt," Sandor said angrily.

Zimmermann lowered his arm and Sandor took the gun.

"Grab some paper towels, wipe up the blood as best you can," Sandor told Raabe and Bergenn. "We need as much time as we can get before we set any alarms off." He pointed at the unconscious soldier as Craig sat him on a toilet and shut the door. "What'd we get from him?"

"An extra magazine for the AK-47," Bergenn reported. "And that Tokarev, with two eight-round magazines in the pouch." The Tokarev Type 68 is a Russian-style handgun, eight-shot, 7.62 mm. "Two-way radio. That's it."

Sandor nodded. "Better than what we came with. Jim, you hold the rifle, I'll hang on to the gun. Kurt, you take the radio, should come in handy later and you speak the lingo."

Bergenn finished wiping up the blood on the floor and against the wall. Raabe locked each toilet stall from inside, then climbed over the top of the divider.

"Okay," Sandor said, tapping himself on the lapel of his jacket. "Time to find someone with a friendly face who's wearing this pin."

CHAPTER TWENTY-SIX

ST. BARTHÉLEMY, F.W.I.

THE FIRST OF Adina's teams made its way around Gustavia harbor on foot. Led by Cardona, they strolled past the various dockside restaurants and *tavernes* like a curious crew from one of the yachts in residence, attracting no attention from the well-oiled patrons who were sitting at outside tables or milling about in the bars. The four men turned left at the end of the Rue des Quais, passing the Wall House, a popular eatery that was winding down its service for the night. They continued on the Rue Pitea, then circled off to the right, approaching the base of the hill that formed the westerly embankment just below Fort Oscar. As they began their climb there was nothing behind them but the peaceful expanse of the Caribbean.

The evening sky was clear, but the crescent moon did little to illuminate their ascent. The fortress loomed above them, constructed of imposing brown stones that had withstood centuries of baking sun, vicious hurricanes, and foreign attacks. Their raid would not require them to breach these walls, however. They knew, from the surveillance done by Hicham and Cardona, that the exterior of Fort Oscar was no longer treated as a high-security installation, its massive profile more of a landmark than an active military stronghold.

They also knew that the nighttime guard on this side of the fort was actually stationed just inside the main wall and, even following the airliner explosion in nearby St. Maarten, Fort Oscar maintained its usual laid-back appearance as they scrambled quietly upward.

When Cardona determined they had come close enough to the entrance, he held up his hand, halting their progress, then motioned for them to stay low on the ground. They could see the entry now, but were hidden from sight amid the scruffy vegetation along the hillside. Cardona checked his watch, then held up five fingers.

————————

Renaldo and his three compatriots had traveled across the harbor in a small tender, then tied it off at the far end of the concrete dock alongside a large sailboat. They had chosen this route since they were carrying most of the equipment, two of the men wearing backpacks. A late-night saunter through town lugging explosives and electronic gear might have provoked some inquiries even among the drunken denizens of St. Barths.

Once on land they hurried along the paved path that led to the southerly wall of the fortress, Renaldo timing their arrival to coordinate with the four men on the other side. As they neared the main gate, he engaged the electronic transmitter that would jam all cellular and radio phone signals in and out of Fort Oscar.

At the appointed moment, exactly 1:45 A.M., the two teams approached their respective entrances to the fort.

Fort Oscar has two entry points, one on the west, the main gate on the south. The fortress is a large rectangle. Inside the imposing walls is an open corridor that rings the interior structure, a smaller rectangle housing the main building with its offices, barracks, armory, and the communications center below ground level.

Cardona's men stayed in place on the hill as he stood and strode toward the small guardhouse within the opening on the western wall. The man on duty was seated at a desk. When he looked up he first saw the stocky Venezuelan, then the silenced barrel of an automatic 9 mm pistol leveled directly at his eyes.

"Do not move, do not even speak," Cardona said in Spanish, making no effort at French. If the man did not understand him, it would be his loss. "Slowly, very slowly, let me see your hands."

The guard had been reading a book, which now fell to the ground as he lifted his arms above his head.

"Good. Now stand, very slowly, and turn around." When he did not immediately respond, Cardona used his left hand to make a motion directing him to get up from his seat. The man's eyes widened with terror as he stood. Cardona said, "If I wanted to kill you, my friend, you would be dead already. Now, turn around." The guard hesitated, then slowly showed his back to Cardona and, as he did, the Venezuelan struck him across the head with the butt of his gun, a violent blow that dropped the man to the floor.

Cardona raised his left arm and the other three men stood and hurried forward. Two of them quickly bound and gagged the guard, then all four made their way into the wide corridor.

––––––––––

At the same moment, Renaldo's team came through the main gate, where they knew there would be two guards on duty. His men moved together, guns drawn, taking the two *gendarmes* before they had time to react. The sentries were disarmed and then subjected to the same fate as their comrade on the west wall. They were left trussed and unconscious against a stone wall.

Renaldo checked the time. They were on schedule so far, but they understood that breaching the interior would be far more difficult than their initial incursion. The two outer entrances were manned by local police. The lower levels, however, were protected by French military.

All eight men had memorized the schematics obtained by Adina. They knew that once inside the corridor, they would likely be detected on the security system being operated from below. Each team had one man assigned to disable the surveillance cameras, and that was accomplished without finesse, the devices being taken out with silenced gunshots. There was simply no way to hide their assault from this point forward. The best they could manage was to cut off the video feed, then move quickly to their next point of attack.

––––––––––

Cardona and one of his men were already racing along the wide passage, heading for the rear entry leading downstairs. The other two on his team hurried left toward the ground-level garrison. The off-duty soldiers on-site would have been asleep, but alarms would now be triggered. The two men took their positions on either side of the door to the barracks, prepared to take out anyone who might wander into the corridor.

Meanwhile, down the passageway at the steel door that provided access to the lower levels, Cardona's man took two small charges, set them in place, and wired the fuse to a small digital timing device. He motioned Cardona back, and the two took cover around a turn. In thirty seconds the blast rocked the door from its hinges, the sound loud enough to be heard by Renaldo's team around the other side of the wide, square hallway that ringed the facility.

That was the signal. Renaldo had his lead man set charges of his own at the southern door.

Cardona and his accomplice were already running along the corridor, again to the right, stopping just before the turn. When they heard the second blast go off they came around the corner and joined Renaldo's group.

Cardona and his man were handed Uzis from the packs Renaldo's team had carried. Now all six terrorists were armed with rapid-firing weapons. They also pulled on gas masks. Cardona, his man, and one of Renaldo's team then hurried back to the door they had blown open on the west wall. Renaldo stood ready at the southern entrance. When Cardona fired a signal shot, each team leader led his men past the twisted metal of the shattered doors, through the smoky entryway and into a common vestibule with stairways on the left and right.

By now the French soldiers stationed below were girding for the attack, taking their posts at the base of the stairways, their FAMAS F-1 multifunction assault weapons raised and at the ready. But the teams led by Renaldo and Cardona had stopped at that first landing, not advancing until they pulled the pins on four grenades and tossed two down each of the stairwells. They made a chilling, clattering sound as they rattled their way down the metal steps.

The soldiers scattered but it was too late, the series of explosions coming quickly, shrapnel cutting into them from all angles while creating chaos throughout the large room. The intruders followed this by tossing tear gas cans that exploded into a cloud of choking fog. Now the six men, proceeding from two directions, made their way carefully into the smoky bedlam below.

———————

The explosions were not loud enough to carry into the night beyond the thick stone walls of Fort Oscar, but the *gendarmes* and soldiers who had been asleep inside the barracks had already been awakened by the alarm sent from the communications center in the basement. They had quickly dressed and started for the door, where they were greeted by an announcement from the other side, the voice loud and speaking in clear French.

"You come out here, you die." One of Cardona's two rear guards had given the warning as he stood off to the side of the barracks entryway. He had heard the alarm and was listening to the activity within, prepared for an onslaught from the off-duty soldiers. "There is no need for anyone to be a hero," he told them, then punctuated his threat by reaching out and, without standing in front of the entrance, firing two silenced gunshots, splintering the wood of the door. He followed that demonstration by saying, "Your friends out here have not been hurt, just disarmed. I tell you again that no one needs to be harmed. Just stay inside and we will be gone in ten minutes."

The barracks were presently occupied by three policemen and four soldiers. The seven had been moving toward the small foyer at the entry to their quarters until the shots were fired. Now they quickly retreated to the rear of the large room. The senior policeman looked to the ranking military officer. "What do we do?" he asked in a quiet voice.

The lieutenant shook his head. "We have no idea how many there are, or what weapons they have." He was still shaking his head. "But in ten minutes, who knows? They might kill us all if we don't take action."

"What could they want here? What is it that you people are doing down there?" The *gendarme* was looking at the floor, as if it might hold an answer.

"I'm afraid that is still classified, regardless of the circumstances."

"Classified. *Merde*," the French cop spit angrily. "They want to kill us for something and we don't even have the right to know what?"

As they argued their inequitable fate, the voice from the outside corridor said, "I advise you gentlemen to stand down. And maintain silence."

The policeman shrugged his shoulders and looked at his two fellow officers. "We should do what he says," he told the others in a whisper. "I will take my chances in here. Why should I be killed for an answer no one is willing to give me?"

As he led the other two policemen farther away from the door, the lieutenant ignored them and said to his soldiers,

"Collect your weapons, see how many men here will fight with us, then we'll sort this out. We can't sit here hoping they won't rush in and kill us all."

"Have you tried your cell phone again?" one of his men asked.

The lieutenant, name of Henri Vauchon, nodded. "They must be jamming the signals. I get nothing."

"Neither do I."

"Well," Vauchon said, "we've got to do something. The question is, what?"

_____

The action on the level below had accelerated as the terrorists entered from their opposite sides in a pincer move designed to gain immediate control of the facility downstairs. Each of them stayed in a crouch as they reached the floor level, taking cover behind desks and cabinets while they assessed the situation.

In addition to four French soldiers, three of whom were bleeding from injuries sustained in the grenade attack, there were men and women who had apparently been working in front of computer screens and other electronic equipment and were now seeking refuge under tables and wherever else they could hide. All of them, military and civilians alike, were coughing and gagging in the haze of the putrid gas.

Two of the soldiers, off to the right and partially hidden by a half wall, immediately began shooting as Renaldo's team entered. Renaldo called out to them, "Cease your firing, there does not need to be more injury," but they persisted, so the six intruders unleashed a barrage that came from both sides, slaughtering the two soldiers in a rapid fusillade. Witnessing the brutal conclusion to that exchange, the other two French soldiers surrendered. They were swiftly disarmed by Cardona's men. Cardona then picked out an older man from among the huddled workers, grabbed him by the arm, and pulled him to his feet.

"Who is in charge here?" Cardona demanded.

"I am the supervisor of these people," the tall Frenchman replied nervously as he struggled with the effects of the tear gas.

"Well you listen to me, supervisor," Cardona said, jabbing the barrel of the Uzi into the man's side, "you do what I say or I'll kill you."

"I can't breathe," the man gasped, spittle and vomit running down the side of his mouth.

Cardona ignored him, shouting through his mask. "First, you tell these people to get together in a corner." He looked around the large room. "Over there," he motioned with his head. "They will be safe from the explosions over there."

"Explosions?" the man asked in a quavering voice.

Cardona ignored the question, nodding at Renaldo, whose team went about attaching explosive charges to various components that appeared to be the most vulnerable and important pieces of equipment in the room. Cardona returned his attention to the supervisor. "If you don't want me to kill you right here, you will do as I say." When the man hesitated, followed by a nauseating cough, Cardona again prodded him with the gun barrel. "Tell them," he growled.

The man managed to call out the instructions. The venting system was finally alleviating some of the effects of the acrid smoke, and he watched as his coworkers left their hiding places and fearfully huddled together at the far end of the room, not sure if they were being given sanctuary or herded together for ease of execution.

Cardona watched them, ever fascinated at the cowardice of people when faced with life-and-death choices. He turned back to the man in his grasp. "Now, tell me how we get below, and make sure we do not have any problems getting there. You are understanding this?"

The man nodded, his eyes wide with fear.

"I know there are more soldiers down there. We do not want to have to kill anyone else, do you understand?"

"Yes," the man moaned.

"Good. Now lead us downstairs."

CHAPTER TWENTY-SEVEN

RUNGRADO MAY DAY STADIUM, PYONGYANG

ONCE SANDOR LED his team out of the tiled restroom into the deserted concrete corridor, he knew moving around the arena would become increasingly dangerous. There were military guards posted throughout the facility, and access from one level to the next was well protected.

Sandor pointed to the right and Bergenn moved first, Zimmermann following him. They reached a portal that opened to the ramp leading above, and Bergenn gave the all clear. Sandor checked behind him, then he and Craig Raabe ran down the corridor, past the other two men, pausing at the opening, bracketing the entryway.

Sandor nodded to Raabe, who immediately sauntered out into the open and up the incline. He was met by an armed soldier before he could reach the next landing.

The sentry showed Raabe his palm, the international signal for "Halt!" His other hand was now on the grip of his North Korean–made AK-47. "Where are you going?" he demanded gruffly in his native tongue.

Raabe, displaying no comprehension of Korean, responded with a blank stare and a shrug, then held up his ticket and offered a friendly smile.

The soldier took his eyes from Raabe just long enough to have a look at his seat assignment, but that moment was enough. The much taller American rammed his closed fist into the man's neck, then, as the Korean reeled backward, Raabe followed him down, his thumbs pressing hard against the man's larynx as he took him to the ground, keeping him quiet as he choked the air out of him, the soldier instinctively letting go of his weapon as he reached for his assailant's wrists.

The instant the others heard the first sound of the struggle they came charging up the ramp. Bergenn rendered the guard senseless with a hard blow to his left temple from the butt of his automatic rifle.

"Kill him," Zimmermann hissed.

Sandor shook his head. "He's out, now let's go."

But Zimmermann was not taking any chances. He bent over and picked up the man's assault rifle, then made a move to step away from the inert figure sprawled on the concrete. Before Sandor could react, Zimmermann spun around and kicked the man, very hard, three times in the side of his head. "Now he's out."

Sandor gritted his teeth but said nothing. He ordered Raabe and Bergenn to grab the man and carry him with them, not willing to risk leaving the body in plain sight. Then, with a wave of his hand, he led them on a run up the ramp to the opening at the next level. He made a quick check to see if anyone was coming in response to the sound of the quick scuffle, but all seemed quiet. They made the turn and moved cautiously up another ramp to the elite level, where they knew the private boxes were located.

Sandor stopped a few paces before they entered the corridor. "There are going to be more men up here," he reminded them in a hoarse whisper. "Probably teams of two."

The other three nodded.

"Craig and I go first, you two hang back until the fun starts."

Bergenn and Raabe dropped the dead soldier on the cement floor, then pushed him against the wall. Sandor was holding the pistol he had taken from the guard downstairs. He shoved it into his waistband and covered it with his jacket. Then, without another word, he and Raabe finished the short walk up the cement rise, holding out their tickets like two lost tourists.

As they came to the portal they were prepared to see armed soldiers. They moved to their right, where, suddenly, someone stepped out of the shadows.

It was Hea, the girl Sandor had met at the kiosk near the Arch of Triumph that afternoon.

"Where have you been?" she asked. "You're late."

Sandor nodded. "Where are the guards?"

"They patrol back and forth on this level," she said as she guided them back onto the ramp. "They'll be here in a few seconds."

"How many?"

"Two."

"How did you get here?"

"I'm part of the international hospitality crew," she answered with a nervous smile.

Sandor nodded. "How far is Hwang's box?"

"Three to the right," she told them, then said, "Shhh."

They could hear the guards coming.

With no silencer on his weapon Sandor knew he could not fire the gun, not unless it became absolutely necessary. A single gunshot would bring scores of Korean soldiers on the run and the mission would be over, not to mention the lives of his entire team. He watched the attractive young girl, her face taut with both fear and resolve as she said in a hushed tone, "Just follow me."

Sandor and Raabe exchanged a quick look but she was already stepping into the corridor, so they moved right behind her into the open, where they were promptly met by two approaching soldiers. Bergenn and Zimmermann remained around the corner, on the ramp, their AK-47s in hand.

Hea began speaking quickly, in Korean, and Sandor assumed she was telling them that she had found these tourists wandering around looking for their seats. Sandor responded with a smile and held up his ticket. The problem was that Hea was standing between them, making it difficult for him to initiate the first move. The girl must have sensed this, because she stepped to her left as if allowing the two uniformed guards to have a better look at the tickets. But these two were not looking at the tickets, they were staring directly into the eyes of the two Americans.

When they barked something, Hea turned to Sandor and said, "They want you to step back, against that wall."

Sandor nodded, still smiling, then turned slightly, as if about to move toward the wall. As he did, he shot a quick glance at Craig. Raabe responded, leveling a rapid kick aimed at the neck of the shorter soldier on the left, while Sandor spun back and lunged at the man to their right.

This time the Koreans seemed ready for the assault. The first made a deft move, Raabe's karate kick glancing off the top of his head, the other man averting a direct hit by Sandor, then reacting with a sweeping maneuver that just missed knocking Sandor off his feet.

Sandor knew that time was against them. These men had weapons they would not be afraid to use and radios that, once engaged, would be equally fatal. He regained his balance and drove forward with the crown of his head, crashing into the Korean's chin, knocking him backward as Sandor hit him again, this time with the heel of his hand. He followed with three short chops into the man's throat, snapping his windpipe, leaving him to clutch desperately at his neck as he gasped his last breath.

Raabe, after missing with his kick, was left in a more vulnerable position than Sandor, and the soldier had time to level his automatic weapon at Craig's chest. But Hea had come from behind and dug two fingers deep into the man's right eye, jerking his head to the side as he reached up and let out a shriek, giving Craig time to hit him several times in the solar plexus, knocking the air out of him, the weapon falling back on its sling and slapping across his chest as he stumbled backward on top of the girl.

By now Bergenn and Zimmermann had reached the scene. The first soldier was dead and Sandor was holding down the second man's arms as Raabe put his knee into the man's chest and then, using both hands and a forceful twist, broke his neck.

No one spoke as Hea, Raabe, and Sandor got to their feet and retrieved the weapons and radios from the two dead Koreans. Sandor looked to the girl.

"Any of these other suites vacant?"

She nodded and pointed to a door down the hallway.

"Let's get rid of these two," he told his men. "And the other guy on the ramp. Fast."

Hea let them into the unoccupied luxury box, where they deposited the three corpses, then shut the door and headed for their destination, two doors away.

CHAPTER TWENTY-EIGHT

ST. BARTHÉLEMY, F.W.I.

CARDONA WAS STILL holding Fort Oscar's graveyard shift supervisor tight in his grasp. Together they moved toward the door that led to the basement level. Adina's men were not about to risk a ride on the elevator, too many things could go wrong there. When the elderly Frenchman hesitated at the head of the stairwell, Cardona shoved him forward. The muscular Venezuelan was not as tall as his hostage, but he was much younger and much stronger. And he was carrying a gun.

"Move," he ordered.

Adina's men had removed their gas masks, the ventilation system having already cleared the air of most of the nauseating smell. This gave them better visibility, which would be crucial as they descended to the main nerve center downstairs.

They realized that the staff stationed on the lower level was already aware of this invasion. Even before the grenades went off, security cameras and silent alarms would have alerted them to the incursion. As soon as Cardona, Renaldo, and their four men entered the inner sanctum on the main floor, everyone would have been on alert. The ensuing explosions and gunfire, even through these thick, reinforced walls, would have been heard throughout this part of the compound. With a welcoming committee gathering for them below, Adina's men were not going to take any chances.

They also assumed that calls for help had been transmitted. They were successful in temporarily jamming cell phone signals from the fortress, but this was an international communications center, and there was no way to block their satellite capabilities. They only hoped that the help the fort staff sought would not arrive in time.

As Cardona made his way down the stairs, he kept the French supervisor in front of him. Renaldo and two of his men were right behind them. The remaining pair from the assault team was still wiring explosives to the computer banks against the wall, all the while keeping an eye on the men and women huddled in the far corner of the room.

"Now," Cardona said slowly to the Frenchman, "when we walk through the door down there, you will be our human shield. Do you understand?"

The terrified man nodded.

"You call to them, tell them to put aside all of their weapons or everyone upstairs will be executed. *Comprende?*"

The Frenchman nodded again.

"Good. Now move slowly."

With the computer supervisor in the lead, the group had nearly reached the bottom of the staircase. Cardona roughly pulled him to a halt. "Now. Tell them now."

The frightened man steadied himself, then called out in French, "Please, these men are dangerous. You must lay down your weapons or more people will be killed."

There was a tense silence, then a voice from below asked, "How many are there?"

Cardona understood enough French to understand the question. He swiftly clamped his hand across the man's mouth, then pressed the barrel of the submachine gun into the side of his neck. "You tell them there are too many of us for them to fight," he whispered directly in his ear. "Tell them they have ten seconds to lay down their weapons or we will begin killing hostages on the main level."

When Cardona pulled his hand away, the tall Frenchman did as he was told.

There followed another eerie silence, broken by the clatter of guns being dropped to the hard, tiled floor below.

Renaldo shouted out in French, "Move your weapons to the landing, where we can see them, then back away."

They watched as two pistols and two automatic weapons slid into view.

Cardona leaned toward his man again. "How many guards down there?"

"Only two at this hour."

Cardona yanked on the man's hair, pulling his head back at an awkward angle. "Don't lie to me, I'll kill you right here."

"No, I'm telling the truth," the man wheezed, his throat tight from the tear gas, fear, and the pressure his tormentor was applying. "Two men."

Cardona nodded to Renaldo, who shouted out, "Now all of you step back, and stand together. Anyone we find not standing with the group will be immediately shot."

They listened as the people shuffled about. When it became quiet again, they resumed their descent.

Lieutenant Vauchon, the ranking army officer present in the Fort Oscar barracks, decided it was time for action. There were four French military and three local policemen on hand. They could not simply stand by while people were being murdered on their watch. "We need to move," he told the others.

They were all standing in the rear corner of the barracks. Whatever they decided to do, each man had grabbed his sidearm. As they spoke, they kept their voices low and an eye on the door, mindful of the possibility there could be a sudden attack.

"They said they would be gone in ten minutes," the ranking *gendarme* replied. "Let's give it a little time."

"A little time?" Vauchon asked him. "There could be a slaughter under way." He was glaring at the captain of the *gendarmes* now. "You want us to sit here and wait it out? Is that your plan?"

"We can't be rash," the policeman protested.

"We are seven. How many of them can be out there?" Vauchon spoke in a hushed but firm tone.

The police captain looked to the door, then back at the younger man. "Even if we outnumber them, how do you propose we get out of here without being cut to ribbons? We don't know how many are stationed out there, and they're certainly prepared for an attack."

Vauchon acknowledged the problem with a nod. "If only we had grenades, or something to make some noise, to cover a rush down the steps." He looked around their drab quarters, the barest of sleeping accommodations with no windows and the latrine outside and down the hall.

"Well we don't," the captain said, feeling a momentary sense of relief. "I say that we remain here, in a defensive posture. If they come, we'll be ready. If they leave . . ."

"If they leave after they've murdered the people below, you mean? The people we are here to protect, you mean?"

The others were silent as these two faced off, their fates and the fates of those inside the fort riding on the decision they would make.

"No," Vauchon said firmly. "We'll rush them. We can draw straws to determine the order of the charge, then we go."

The police captain shook his head. "No. No. My men and I are with the local force. You are with the army. Our duties and responsibilities are different."

Vauchon sneered at him. "We are not discussing duties here, captain, we are talking about saving the lives of innocent people who are apparently being executed while we stand here engaged in this debate."

"I am sorry, lieutenant, but our suicides will not solve the problem."

Vauchon turned away in disgust and faced his men. "We go as four, then." He paused, looking each of them square in the eyes. "I'll take the lead," he said.

———

Cardona and Renaldo entered the telecommunications center in the basement of Fort Oscar, the tall Frenchman ahead of them. One of their men trailed behind, covering the rear flank. The other remained in the stairwell, as backup.

They found themselves facing an array of modern technological paraphernalia that was incongruously secreted in the bowels of this old fortress. The room was rigged with large screens on three walls and banks of computer systems that were connected to international satellites and fiber-optic lines and wireless hookups, making this one of the most sensitive monitoring facilities in the Western Hemisphere. Everything from air traffic to naval movements were tracked here, both civilian and military, as were climatic and seismographic changes. The entire operation was classified as top secret and existed on a strict need-to-know basis within a multinational intelligence initiative begun by the United States and France.

Cardona and Renaldo had a quick look around. The staff, perhaps a dozen men and women in all, were dressed in casual island attire. They were standing, as ordered, against the wall to the left. Two men in uniform stood in front of them. There did not seem to be anyone lurking behind the desks or the large mainframes, but Renaldo said sternly to the gathered group, "If there is anyone else here, you will all be shot."

"No one else is here," one of the soldiers said, taking a step toward him. "What do you want?"

Renaldo ignored the question. "If you take another step forward, I'll kill you and then the woman behind you."

The soldier slowly moved back.

"All right," Cardona called over his shoulder to the man from Renaldo's team who had been covering their backs, "get this done quickly."

The man moved swiftly, removing his backpack, and, as his team members had done upstairs, he began to wire explosives to the mainframes.

Lieutenant Vauchon made sure that he and his three men had full magazines in their handguns, a chambered round and two extra magazines apiece. The three policemen watched as the soldiers prepared to make their move.

"The least you men can do," the lieutenant said without looking at the police captain, "is man this area at the top of the stairs. And try not to hit any of us in the crossfire."

The four soldiers then moved silently across the barracks to the top of the stairs, two on each side. It was only a half flight, just six steps to the door below, just outside which the invaders stood watch over them. The lieutenant gave the signal that he was ready to go. When all three of his men nodded, he drew a deep breath and took off down the short staircase, staying in a crouch, hitting the door with his shoulder and rolling into the corridor.

Adina's sentries were alert, but Vauchon had moved too quickly and too quietly. Bursting into the hallway, he knew exactly what he meant to do when he got there. Seeing only two men, he opened fire, hitting the man on his left several times before he was able to return a shot. By then his three men had emerged, taking out the second terrorist with a furious close-range barrage that tore through his neck and head and dropped him, dead before he struck the concrete.

The first man had slumped against the wall and slid to the floor but he was still breathing. Once they disarmed him the lieutenant kneeled down and asked, "Who are you? What do you want here?"

The dying man gave no answer.

Vauchon asked, "How many men are with you?"

Drawing a painful breath, the man said in a weak voice, "Closer." When Vauchon leaned toward him, the man spit in his face, then slumped to his side, dead.

The lieutenant stood up and wiped his cheek with his sleeve as his men watched. "Let's go," he said.

Before they headed off to the communications center, the three policemen joined them with guns in hand, the captain in the lead, offering up a diffident smile. "What the hell," he said. "You took on the tough part."

Lieutenant Vauchon nodded without comment. He and one of his men picked up the Uzis from the dead sentries, then raced off down the hall, pausing at the turn to have a look, then rounding the corner and sprinting to the entrance that led downstairs to the first level.

"You heard the shooting earlier," Vauchon reminded them in a quiet but stern tone. "These men are not here to take prisoners or to negotiate. Remember that. Shoot to kill." Without another word they split up, just as Adina's men had done earlier, and raced along the corridor and charged down the two staircases.

The two terrorists who remained on that first level had heard the gunfire from above and attempted to contact the men who had been left to guard the barracks. When they received no response they radioed Cardona and Renaldo to warn them of the problem. They were ordered to hold their positions.

The two men shared a conspiratorial look. Their explosives were already rigged and they were closer to the main level than the men downstairs. That meant they were closer to a means of escape. They had no way of assessing how the fight up above had gone, but whatever had happened in the barracks, all they had to do was fend off a counterattack and then get the hell out of there.

When that assault came, just moments later, they were stunned to see seven uniformed men rush into the room.

———————

The group of French soldiers and policemen burst into the first-level room at almost the same moment, arriving through the portals on both sides. They quickly assessed the situation, diving for cover as the two terrorists opened fire. The civilian personnel were left exposed in the corner of the room and, as his men took aim, it was obvious to Lieutenant Vauchon that there would be serious casualties if he did not act swiftly.

"Hold your fire," he told his men. Then to the two intruders, he hollered, "Throw down your weapons. Do it now."

One of Adina's men, crouched behind a desk to the left, said, "We'll kill these people first if you make another move against us."

Vauchon did not hesitate. He leapt to his feet and made a mad rush toward the sound of the man's voice. Seeing this, his men stormed across the room behind him.

The sound of gunfire became deafening in the confines of this tiled facility, the acrid stench of gunplay replacing what remained of the tear gas. As he charged ahead Vauchon was hit with a bullet that ripped into his left shoulder even before he got off his first round, but he continued forward, emptying the first magazine from his Uzi in mere seconds, three of the shots finding their target. The others surrounded and disarmed the second of Adina's men after a furious barrage that hit the police captain and one of the soldiers, while ricochets and misplaced shots struck three of the staff as they attempted to scatter for safety.

It seemed blood and smoke were everywhere, backed by the dissonant screams of fear and pain.

The first of Adina's men was dead, the one Vauchon had shot. The second was dragged up, onto his knees, his arms raised above his head. "Listen to me," the terrorist warned them, "this room is armed to explode in just a few minutes. We must leave or we'll all be killed."

Two of the workers called out, saying that they had seen the intruders wiring devices all around the room.

Vauchon stepped forward, holding his bloody shoulder with his right hand. The others kept their guns trained on the kneeling man as the lieutenant approached him. "Disarm the bombs," he ordered. "Disarm all of them."

The terrorist shook his head. "They're on timers. They cannot be changed, they cannot be touched."

"I don't believe you."

"Why would I lie at this point? What would I have to gain?"

Vauchon stared into the man's cold, dark eyes. "How many more of you are here?"

Before he could respond, one of the other staff members stood up, a woman in her thirties. She had a red-brown stain on her blouse from tending to one of her injured coworkers. "There are four more," she told them. "They've taken Alain and gone downstairs."

Vauchon asked her, "How many more of you are down there tonight?"

"Twelve, I think, including Alain."

The lieutenant looked back at his prisoner, who remained on the ground with his hands raised. "What are they doing down there?"

"The same thing," the man told him. "Setting explosives."

"How many men you have posted outside?"

"Only the two at the barracks. We were eight in all."

"No backup?"

"No, I'm telling you, just eight of us. Now please, let's get the hell out of here."

Vauchon ignored him and turned to the police captain. "You and your men lead the staff outside. No telling if he's lying about backup, so be careful."

"You've been hit," he said.

Vauchon noticed for the first time that the captain was also bleeding. "You all right?"

The policeman forced a weak smile. "I'm too old for this shit. What about you?"

"I'm fine," Vauchon told him. "Just go. And take François too," he added, referring to his corporal, who had also been wounded. "The rest of us will hold on to our friend here and see about the group below."

CHAPTER TWENTY-NINE

RUNGRADO MAY DAY STADIUM, PYONGYANG

JORDAN SANDOR AND his team knew their window of opportunity would be slammed shut very soon. If Mr. Choi and the soldier they left in the men's room on the lower level were not soon discovered, the three guards they had just eliminated would certainly be reported missing when they failed to check in as part of any standard patrol detail. Time was tight as the four Americans moved quickly behind Hea toward the luxury suite just down the corridor.

Given the security throughout the stadium, Sandor was not surprised to find the door unlocked. He was surprised, however, that no guards were posted inside. There were only four middle-aged Korean men in business suits seated around a square table, obviously in the midst of a discussion, with no particular interest in the colorful proceedings on the field below. Each of them appeared shocked at the intrusion. Sandor knew that each of them truly was, but for one.

As instructed, Hea did her best to appear terrified, which was not all that difficult since Sandor was holding the barrel of his automatic against her right temple as the five of them filed in.

"Good evening, gentlemen," Sandor said. "We have borrowed this young woman to act as our interpreter." He gave her a nudge, so she might begin to fulfill her role, but the Korean seated to his left held up a hand.

"We all speak English, sir," the man told him. "You may release this woman and state the reason for your outrageous behavior."

Sandor gave the girl a rough shove and Hea fell into a chair against the wall. "We won't be releasing anybody, not just yet."

Zimmermann was the last man in. He took a final look in the passageway, then shut the door and leaned against it, covering Sandor's back. Bergenn and Raabe had already positioned themselves in opposite corners of the room, out of view from anyone who might have a sight line through the glass panels that looked out onto the field below.

"Our outrageous behavior results from the fact that your government is presently involved in illegal activities against the United States." Sandor spoke slowly to be sure he would be clearly understood. "If you answer my questions to our satisfaction, we'll go away. If you don't, we'll kill you."

The same man responded. "You are mistaken, sir. Now lay down your arms before someone gets hurt."

Sandor understood the culture well enough to know that the first of them to speak would not be the senior man present. Sandor stepped forward and, as he did, he casually eyed the lapels of each man's jacket. As was the fashion in North Korea, even highly placed dignitaries sported lacquered pins, including at least one featuring the visage of the Great Leader. Only one of these men, however, had the pin with the border design Sandor was seeking. He was seated to the right and Sandor was careful to evince no recognition. Instead he raised his left hand and struck the official to his left who had been doing the talking.

The blow sent the man reeling backward, his chair toppling over as he fell to the floor. Another of the foursome, the man just in front of Sandor, who had been seated with his back to the door, began to rise, but Sandor grabbed him by the shoulder and forcefully shoved him back into his seat.

"You see, gentlemen," Sandor said calmly, "someone's already been hurt." He eyed each of them in turn. "I agree that violence should be unnecessary, but our time together is short and we need answers."

The man on the floor stared up, his eyes alive with fury. "Your time is short, that is certain."

Zimmermann, Raabe, and Bergenn waited in silence as Sandor glared at the man, then turned to the three Koreans who remained seated at the table. The man wearing the designated pin responded with a quick glance to his right that told Sandor what he needed to know. Sandor bent down and placed the muzzle of the automatic against the head of the man on the floor. "I don't have time for this bullshit, so someone had better start talking," he said.

The man who sat facing the door finally said, "We had nothing to do with the airplane explosion." His voice was eerily calm, and Sandor knew he was hearing from the man in charge. "You have made a tragic mistake in coming here."

Sandor stood, righted the toppled chair, and took a seat at the table. "The airplane explosion?"

"Is that not why you are here?" The senior official looked

to the other men at the table, then returned his attention to Sandor. "Ah, of course. You have probably been guests of our great country for at least the past day or two. You might not have heard of the airliner that went down in the Caribbean. It was on its way from St. Maarten to New York." He then offered up a cruel smile. "I understand the flight carried many of your countrymen. What a pity." Shaking his head he added, "What is the expression? Ah yes, foul play is suspected."

The four Americans were obviously rocked by the news. Since their arrival in the Beijing airport they had been cut off from any of the usual news sources. They had certainly not heard of an airplane crash. Sandor did his best to retain his composure, insisting, "I haven't come about the sabotage of a plane." The problem was that he had no way of knowing if this was the truth. With a sickening ache in his gut he realized he might have arrived too late to avert the disaster they had been assigned to prevent.

Shaking his head the Korean asked, "If you are here not about that, then why have you come?"

Sandor stared at the Korean, realizing that all he could do was press ahead. "You know why I'm here."

The man maintained his thin smile. "You are bluffing. As you Americans like to say, you are on a fishing expedition. Your government has sent you here on a mission for which you will surely die, and now you are not even sure of the reason."

The man was right, based on what little the Agency had learned from Ahmad Jaber, but Sandor was left to make a guess that any liaison between North Korea and Iran would include petro-politics. He said, "You're wrong if you believe we don't know what your government is up to, just as you and your friends are wrong about trading oil for terror."

It wasn't much, but the flicker of recognition in the man's eyes was unmistakable. "You are speaking nonsense," the man replied.

"Am I?" Sandor spun around and faced the man to his right, leveling the gun at his face. "Why don't you tell me, pal? Am I wrong?"

The terror in the man's eyes was plain, but Sandor gave him high marks for keeping his cool. He said, "You are wasting your time if you expect me to reveal anything to you. I am a patriot, loyal to our Great Leader, and I do not fear death."

So Sandor turned his attention to the man across from him, the man wearing the pin. "What about you?" he demanded.

With another, almost imperceptible eye movement, the mole again told Sandor what he wanted to know.

"What's your name?"

"Kyung."

"Well, Mr. Kyung, are you prepared to die like your friends here?"

"I am prepared to do whatever I must," he responded. "Mr. Hwang and I will tell you nothing," he said, with a nod of his head to the senior man in the group.

Hwang. That was the name Sandor wanted, the name of one of the most influential ministers in Kim's cabinet. Byrnes had not been wrong in wanting the opportunity to interrogate him, but what could Sandor get him to divulge here? They had little time for coercion and few options, so Sandor turned back to the man on his right and lashed out, smacking him on the side of his head with the butt of his pistol. As the Korean rocked back, Sandor drove a stiff arm into his sternum, knocking him off his chair. Then he said to Zimmermann, "Toss him over there next to the girl. If I don't get the answers I want in the next sixty seconds, kill him and the other sonuvabitch on the floor." Then he turned back to Mr. Hwang, still seated to his left, still wearing an implacable look of superiority. "You and Mr. Kyung here are not martyrs. You're not the type. That's for your robots down on the field. So please spare me the patriotic song and dance and tell me what I want to know." Before Hwang could answer, he added, "And if you say anything stupid, like 'I don't know what you're talking about,' I'm not only going to have your friends shot, I'm also going to start taking you apart, one bullet at a time. And trust me, I'll make it really hurt a lot, and I'll make it last for a really long time. So," he said, leaning back comfortably in the chair, "connect the dots for me from here to Iran to the United States."

Mr. Hwang offered nothing but a blank stare.

"Uh huh," Sandor said, turning his attention to the man across from him, the man wearing the pin that identified him as the CIA mole. "What about you, Mr. Kyung? Can you tell me what I want to know?"

Kyung looked from Sandor to Hwang, but did not speak.

"Come, come, gentlemen. I'm not exactly renowned for my patience."

"I do not know as much as Mr. Hwang does," Kyung said in broken English.

For the first time, Hwang could not control his temper. He turned to Kyung and began scolding him in Korean. Sandor turned to the girl. "What are they saying?"

Hea hesitated, but Bergenn put a gun to her head, making sure her cooperation still appeared to be under duress. "Mr. Hwang is calling him a traitor," she explained. "He is telling him to be silent, that it is only a matter of a few minutes before the soldiers discover there is a problem and come to take you Americans away."

Hwang now leveled an angry tirade at the girl, but Sandor simply nodded. "Okay, Kurt, shoot the guy on the floor."

"Enough violence," Kyung called out before Zimmermann could follow the order. He looked at his senior officer. "Tell them what they want to know. They will not live to use the information anyway, is that not correct, sir?"

Hwang thought it over. The notion seemed to amuse him. "Yes. You are correct." He turned back to Sandor. "You are here to uncover some plot, is that it? Like the typical American cowboy, you ride into danger with no sense of perspective or honor or intelligence. Just guns blazing, as the saying goes, all violence and no forethought, an apt summary of your country's foreign policy. And that is how you have come here, because your people are convinced that my great nation has become a partner in some dark conspiracy." Hwang shook his head. "What incredible arrogance. Does it not occur to you Americans that free nations might form an alliance without initiating a plot against the United States?"

"North Korea is entering into an alliance, is that what you're telling us?"

"Our great nation is expanding its global influence. That is all you need to know."

Sandor stood abruptly. "I don't have time for a civics lesson from a government that controls its people with martial law and then starves them to death. I want answers and I want them now."

When Hwang stared at him without speaking, Sandor nodded at Zimmermann. Kurt grabbed a pillow to stifle the sound, then kneeled over the man on the floor and prepared to fire a shot into his head.

Kyung leapt to his feet. "Enough of this!" he shouted at Hwang. "Tell them about the man from Venezuela. What harm will it do? They are dead men anyway. What purpose will our deaths serve?"

The two Koreans locked eyes, and suddenly Hwang understood. "You," he said coldly. "You are the traitor in our midst. I could not believe it when they told me it was so."

"What are you saying?" Kyung demanded.

"You are the traitor," the older man repeated. Then he turned to Sandor and fixed him with a cold look. "If he is the man you have come for, his help will be of no use." He managed a grim smile. "You may think this is some sort of victory, but you are wrong. I will not tell you a thing, and he does not know enough to matter."

Sandor turned to Kyung, the time for pretense having passed. "I hope he's wrong about you not knowing anything."

Kyung shook his head, stealing a quick glance at Hwang. "I know he had a meeting with a man from Venezuela, and I know that Kim Jong-Il approved their plans."

"Who did he meet with?"

"A man called Adina. He had another name, but I do not know it."

"Cabello," Sandor said with a nod of his head. "Rafael Cabello."

"They are planning something in the West, but I am certain the airliner explosion was not their purpose."

"How do you know?"

"Because their arrangement had something to do with an alliance that would provide us a supply of oil into the future."

"So what was the plan, damnit?"

"I am sorry, I do not know. I think they began suspecting me. I was excluded from key strategy meetings. I believe that is why I was brought here tonight, to be questioned."

Raabe was standing at the door, listening to the sound of shuffling boots on the concrete floor down the hallway. "They're coming," he told them.

Hwang was still staring defiantly at Sandor. "You see? The only truth this traitor has spoken is that you and your men are dead already."

From the moment Sandor entered the room he realized he might have to kill the other three Koreans to protect Kyung. If his cover was blown there was no way Sandor could leave the CIA mole behind with witnesses to his betrayal. Now they understood that Kyung did not have the critical information they had come for and they needed time to work on Hwang. He stared at the senior minister. "Well, if we're dead then so are you," Sandor said, pointing the barrel of his pistol at the man's face. "Get up."

Zimmermann was now standing beside Raabe. He said,

"If you two can finish up your chat later, we've got some action down the lane here."

Sandor looked from Hwang back to Kyung. "I hope your escape plan is better than your intelligence gathering," he said.

"Yes, we have two possible routes, once we get out of the stadium."

"Once we get out of the stadium? I hope you have a plan for that too." Sandor turned to Bergenn. "Knock those two out; they've heard enough for now."

Bergenn, using the butt of the automatic, rendered the man on the couch unconscious with a couple of violent blows to his head, then leaned over the man on the floor and did the same.

"You're leaving these bastards?" Zimmermann asked. Before the others could react he grabbed the large pillow from the sofa and, using it to muffle the sound, shot each of the two Koreans in the head.

As Hea turned away, Sandor stared at Zimmermann for a moment but said nothing. Turning back to Kyung, he asked, "How the hell do we do this? Drag you and Hwang down the hall past twenty soldiers?"

"No, there's a tunnel under the stands, for government officials and honored guests." He pointed at the smoked glass wall that separated them from the private area outside. The suite included twenty exterior seats facing the field below, but he was pointing to a door outside to the left. "There," he said.

Sandor looked to Craig Raabe. "First we'll wire up a warm reception in here."

Raabe nodded and went to work, placing a charge at the entry door.

"All right," Sandor said, jabbing his pistol into Hwang's ribs. "Anything else you want to tell me before we say good-bye to the Arirang Festival?"

Hwang stared at him sullenly.

"Have it your way," Sandor said as he shoved him forward. "We're moving out."

CHAPTER THIRTY

INSIDE FORT OSCAR, ST. BARTHÉLEMY, F.W.I.

LIEUTENANT VAUCHON WATCHED as the police captain led his two *gendarmes*, the injured soldier François, and the staff of Fort Oscar's main workroom up the stairs to safety. Vauchon was left with his two men and their prisoner. He looked down at the Venezuelan, who remained on his knees with his hands clasped behind his head.

"What is your name?"

"Fredrico."

"Well, Fredrico, you are able to contact your compatriots on this radio, yes?"

The man nodded anxiously.

"Good," the lieutenant said. "Then it's time for you to tell them exactly what I want you to say. You understand?"

"Our time is short," was the nervous reply, but Vauchon shook him off.

"I'm sure we have more time than you say. After all, your men below have not even returned here, have they?" His pleasant demeanor was abruptly replaced with a brusque tone. "Now get these bastards on the radio."

Fredrico took the radio from Vauchon, prompting the lieutenant to shove the barrel of his rifle at the man's eyes.

"Easy," he said. "And remember, I speak perfect Spanish."

The prisoner acknowledged this with a brief nod, then moved more slowly as he pressed the send button and made contact with Renaldo.

Vauchon said, "Tell them all their other men up here are dead and you're our prisoner. Tell them they have no way out except through this room. They are in a dungeon, and we are now their gatekeepers, tell them that."

Fredrico did as he was told. There was no reply.

"Now tell them we have five men positioned in this room, and the remaining members of my unit are waiting at the two doorways on the main level." When this was greeted with a skeptical look, Vauchon jabbed the barrel of his FAMAS into the center of the man's forehead. "Tell them," he ordered through clenched teeth.

Again the man complied.

"Now, tell them that if they want to save their lives they must immediately release the staff and send them up here. And tell them I mean immediately."

Fredrico again spoke into the radio and then waited, until the response finally came crackling over the handheld device. It was Renaldo's voice.

"Tell our French heroes that unless they give up their weapons and retreat, we will begin murdering these people, one every thirty seconds. There is no time to negotiate, this is a final order."

Vauchon did not much care for the idea of having orders dictated to him by a murderer. Concluding he had no further need of Fredrico, he took the radio from his prisoner's hand and passed it to one of his men. Then he calmly raised the

French-made rifle and brought the metal butt crashing down across the back of Fredrico's head. As the man stumbled to the side Vauchon struck him again, this time imparting an underhanded blow with the stock of the FAMAS that caught the Venezuelan under the chin and sent him reeling backward until he hit a desk and fell to the floor, unconscious.

Taking the radio back from his corporal, Vauchon pushed the transmit button. "You see, it is you who have no time. You are quite correct. This is not a negotiation since we do not negotiate with terrorists. Your man has already informed us that these rooms have been wired with explosives, so according to him we are all dead anyway, are we not?" He gave the man a chance to answer. When he did not, Vauchon added, "We are prepared to wait you out. We can even seal off these rooms and leave you to the fate you have created for yourselves. Our proposal is a simple one. Release the hostages and we will allow you to surrender into our custody. If you stand and fight, you will all die."

While they awaited a reply, Vauchon instructed one of his men to try one of the landline phones again to make another attempt to contact their superiors in Guadeloupe. As expected, the phones were still dead.

"Try your cell again."

André shook his head. "I have tried. Nothing."

The other soldier said, "At least the automatic warning systems must have been triggered."

The lieutenant nodded, his expression grave. "No matter. If this Fredrico told us the truth, help will never arrive in time."

"We should go above, sir," André said. "Respectfully,

there is nothing more we can do from here that can't be done upstairs."

Vauchon thought that over as his other officer examined the explosives that had been rigged at strategic points around the room.

"I'm no expert," the young soldier said nervously, "but there appears to be some serious firepower wired into this place, sir. I agree with André."

"What about those innocent people below?"

André spoke up. "There are four armed men down there and three of us. If we attack, we'll be ducks in a shooting gallery the moment we come through the door. Here we had surprise on our side, sir, not to mention we had seven men against two."

Vauchon could not argue his logic. And yet, what of all those people downstairs?

At that moment the three Frenchmen were startled by the unmistakable echo of gunfire from the level below, followed by the sound of the radio in the lieutenant's hand crackling to life. "We have killed the first hostage," the voice announced, backed by a chorus of wailing and screaming in the background. "One of your soldiers has given his life for no reason, and his blood is on your hands. Now, are you prepared to give up your weapons and permit us safe passage?"

CHAPTER THIRTY-ONE

RUNGRADO MAY DAY STADIUM, PYONGYANG

CRAIG RAABE WAS working on the door of the suite that led to the main corridor. He fastened a simple trip wire to the door handle and connected it to one of the packages of C-4 plastique he had removed from the small of his back. It was a crude mechanism, but it would buy them some time. When he completed his work he looked to Sandor. "Ready," he announced.

Kyung nodded. "Follow me," he said.

Before they moved out, Sandor borrowed a strip of duct tape from Raabe and slapped it roughly across Hwang's mouth. "You touch this tape, you die. Now let's go."

In a single file headed by Kyung, the six men and Hea left the suite through the smoked-glass door that led to the outer seating area of the private box, then passed through the doorway to the left that led into a tunnel that circled its way beneath the infrastructure of the arena. Each of the four Americans was now armed with a North Korean–manufactured AK-47 and extra magazines. Bergenn and Sandor also had the Type 68 pistols.

Raabe was last through the door and he again rigged a special greeting for those who would be following them.

Once he completed the task, he rushed to catch up with the others.

"Only one charge left," he called out to Sandor.

"Okay," Sandor said. "Hopefully one is enough."

The passageway was a dimly lit concrete channel, narrow with a low ceiling and no stairs, a winding ramp down to ground level. Kyung led them in a trot, no one speaking until they heard the distant sound of an explosion from above. All seven of them stopped for a moment.

"Our first greeting card," Raabe said.

Sandor ordered them to get moving again and they did.

Kyung said, "Almost there," just before they heard the second blast, this one much louder, the noise reverberating throughout the long tunnel. Seconds later it was followed by the sound of automatic gunfire, the prelude to soldiers entering their passageway.

"Let's go," Sandor urged them.

The group ran ahead until they reached the final turn. Kyung brought them all to an abrupt stop. He looked at Sandor. "The soldiers on the ground level will already be on alert," he said, then pointed ahead. "The tunnel branches off in two directions from here. There are exits to the outside, left and the right."

Sandor nodded. "The longer we wait, the worse it'll get." He turned to Hwang and ripped the tape from his mouth. "Since you don't care about dying for your country, I figure you'll lead the way. That plan work for you?"

The Korean stared at him coldly. "You are all dead men."

"So you keep telling me, but I think you should go first anyway." Sandor grabbed Hwang by the collar and looked to Kyung. "Which way?" he asked.

Their mole in Pyongyang ignored the angry glare of his superior officer in the DPRK as they stood in a tight circle under the murky lights of the narrow corridor. "I had planned our escape to the right," Kyung said, his admission of complicity in this American incursion now complete. "But I never expected this much resistance. I am not sure what we will face."

Sandor was tempted to laugh. "What we will face, my friend, is a vigorous counteroffensive." They heard the first echo of dozens of footfalls on the concrete ramp behind them, which now grew louder by the second. "Let's stay with your plan."

Kyung said, "We have one thing in our favor—they will not want to kill Hwang."

"Great," Sandor said with a wry grin, "at least we've got that going for us. Now lead the way."

Kyung took off toward the right and they all fell in behind him.

Strange, Sandor thought as they raced toward the door. The group chasing them from above would have had the chance to radio to the ground patrol. Why had they not entered the tunnel ahead of them, positioning themselves at this junction where they would have had the superior position to attack Sandor's team? It might just be that Kyung was right. As they reached the exit door, he said, "Our friend Hwang really is valuable property, eh?"

Kyung responded with a nod that appeared more like a lowering of his eyes in deference to the other Korean.

Sandor turned to Bergenn, who had come up just behind him. "This could work," he said, then without hesitation he stepped forward and kicked the door open, one hand holding his submachine gun, the other swinging Hwang in front as a human shield. To his amazement, there was not a single Korean soldier in sight. In fact there was no one at all on the small plaza. "Snipers," Sandor said to Bergenn. "They're not going to risk hitting this sonuvabitch in a firefight, they're going to try and pick us off."

As Bergenn passed that information back to the others, the sound of the onrushing soldiers from above grew louder.

"Time to get going, chief," Bergenn said.

Sandor nodded. "Where to?" he asked Kyung.

"Your van, you see it there?" He pointed across the courtyard to the familiar bus.

"Not bad," he told Kyung. "What about the driver, Mr. Sang?"

Kyung nodded. "He is one of us."

Sandor smiled. "Nice. So then, all we have to do is get across the plaza, board the van, and not stop for red lights." With the soldiers above fast approaching, Sandor knew they were out of time. "All right everybody, stay low, move fast, and let's try to get there in one piece." He looked at Hea. "You know how to use this?"

She nodded, so he handed her the automatic rifle and removed the Tokarev from his waistband.

"There are probably snipers all around," he told them, "three-hundred-sixty-degree coverage from above. Allow everyone a few paces before you move outside. Don't give them any cluster targets. Let's go."

Sandor moved first, shoving Hwang forward and breaking into a run toward the small bus. The shooting began immediately and any ideas Hwang might have had about resisting Sandor's push forward vanished in an instinctual drive for self-preservation. Sandor knew his handgun was all but useless against the fusillade of automatic fire, so he concentrated on running as fast as he could to the vehicle.

His men, armed with the automatic rifles taken from the Koreans, managed to give him some cover, and he made it to the relative safety of the van without being hit. Hwang was not as fortunate, taking a round in his right shoulder. As Sandor and his wounded prisoner dove into the bus, they found Mr. Sang crouching on the floor beside the driver's seat.

Bergenn quickly followed them on board, Hea close behind.

"Damn," Sandor growled as he scrambled to his knees and had a look at the fighting on the plaza. He saw that Kyung had been struck in the crossfire and was lying on the ground. When Raabe made a move to reach him he was also hit. Zimmermann, trying to take aim at the sniper above the parapet who was doing the most damage, was caught in a fusillade and spun to the stone floor in a bloody heap.

Sandor snatched the rifle Hea was holding and yelled at Sang, "Get this damn thing going." Then he turned to the girl. "I have a better idea, you drive. Jump that curb there and circle back so we can get those men on board."

Hea stared at him, panic in her eyes. "Kyung is dead. So is your friend. They will kill the other one next."

Through clenched teeth Sandor hollered, "Do what I tell you, and do it now!" Then he turned to Bergenn. "They're coming through the door," he said, pointing at the soldiers who had followed their route into the courtyard.

Even as Sandor spoke, a hail of gunfire rained down on the van from above. Bergenn aimed high at the snipers as Sandor fired at the onrushing soldiers on the ground, giving Hea time to swing the bus up onto the curb and head for Craig Raabe.

Raabe was in a crouch, blood visible on his shirt and pant leg as he returned fire at the men who were coming at him.

Hea may have been a reluctant driver, but once she sent Sang back to the floor and took the wheel, she steered the van dead ahead, directly into the dozen or so men who poured through the door onto the plaza. She then swerved hard to the right, giving cover to Craig and the fallen Zimmermann and Kyung, bringing the bus to a sudden stop. Bergenn and Sandor struggled to pull everyone aboard.

Raabe managed to crawl into the vehicle on his own. Zimmermann was still breathing, but only barely, and he was apparently not long for it as Bergenn dragged him inside. Kyung was dead, but they also lifted him into the van. Then Sandor hollered, "Go, go, go," and the girl took off again, this time spinning the bus around and flying away from the gunfire, leaping off the curb and careening wildly to the left as shots continued to shatter the van's windows and pierce its sides.

Bergenn did his best to tend to Raabe's wounds as Sandor kneeled over Zimmermann. The big man was covered in blood, his breath shallow and arrhythmic, his face contorted in pain.

"Kurt, where's the worst hit?" Jordan asked.

Zimmermann looked up at him through the vacant eyes of death, somehow managing one more cynical grin. "Not sure," he managed in a raspy whisper. "It was either the fifth or the sixth shot." Then the smile vanished as he grabbed at Sandor's arm, squeezing it with all of his remaining strength until the grip went slack, his head fell to the side, and, with a final gasp, he was gone.

"Damn," Sandor groaned. He turned to Bergenn. "How's Craig?"

"He'll make it if we get him help, but he's done playing commando for today."

Sandor nodded, then had a look at his friend's anguished face. "Hang in there, Craig, we'll get you home."

Hea had the van racing forward and they were beyond the range of gunfire for the moment. Whatever elite units of the DPRK army might be dispatched to pursue them, at least they had a lead.

Sandor stood up, holding on to a seat back to keep his balance as Hea floored the accelerator. "I don't think they're going to hit us with anything large, they probably still want to try and get their pal Hwang back in one piece." He gestured toward the Korean, who was lying on the floorboard to the rear of the bus, moaning from the pain in his damaged shoulder. Sandor, in a voice loud enough for the man to hear, said, "If he moves, Jim, shoot out both of his kneecaps."

Bergenn nodded. "Consider it done."

Sandor went to the front of the van and kneeled behind Hea. "Nice driving."

She responded with a slight nod.

"Do we have a plan here or are we driving all the way to Seoul?"

"Sang has two cars waiting for us," she told him as she

maneuvered her way past the outlying parking areas onto an auxiliary road, keeping her foot to the floor as she hurtled through the night.

"We're switching vehicles?"

She nodded again, and so Sandor turned to Mr. Sang, who was still seated on the floor, his back against the front firewall, facing the rear. "You're on our side, eh? You actually speak English?"

When the man looked up, his eyes were moist with grief. "A little, yes."

"You worked with Kyung?"

The man was finding it difficult to speak. "My cousin," he finally said. "Like a brother."

"I'm sorry."

"Yes. Like a brother."

"I understand," Sandor said. "These men are my brothers."

Sang responded with a look that said he also understood.

"So, how do we get out of here?"

Sang explained that there were two cars parked at the end of a deserted road. The idea was for them to split into two groups. One would make their way south, for the Yellow Sea. From there they would travel by boat to South Korea. The others would head north for the Russian border.

Those were the two options Sandor discussed with Byrnes when they considered the most logical exfiltration routes.

"We have information I need to get to my government. You understand that, right?"

Sang nodded.

"We don't have much time, and we need to get the message out of the country even if we don't make it."

"Yes," the man said thoughtfully, "very difficult."

Sandor paused, then broke into a loud laugh, causing everyone in the van, except Hea, to look up at him.

"Are you kidding me, Sang? We just broke into the private boxes at the Arirang Festival, took out half a dozen guards, kidnapped one of Kim's top men, and outran the North Korean army. Now you're telling me it's going to be difficult to get an e-mail or phone call out of here?"

Sang nodded sadly. "Yes," he said. "All transmissions, wireless telephone, Internet connections, all go through satellite. State controlled. Very difficult."

The humor drained from Sandor's face. "Look, at this point I don't care if it's traced, I just want to be sure the communication goes through."

Sang nodded, but offered nothing more.

"Okay," Sandor replied, then got up and marched to the back of the bus, where he stood over Hwang. "Listen to me," he said, his voice devoid of any emotion. "I'm only going to explain this to you once. You need to tell me everything else you know about the deal your country has made with Iran and Venezuela. Then I need to know the fastest way to transmit this information. I have two men dead, another man down, and an entire unit of your beloved army on my tail, so I have no time for negotiations. Am I clear?"

Hwang stared up at him, his arrogance gone, his face betraying both pain and fear.

"Am I clear?" Sandor shouted at him.

When Hwang gave no answer, Sandor pulled out the Tokarev sidearm and pressed the barrel against the man's knee and cocked the hammer.

"Yes, yes," Hwang groaned, "I understand."

"Then answer me."

When he did not reply, Sandor moved the gun from the man's knee and jammed it into his wounded shoulder. Hwang writhed in agony. Sandor pressed harder.

"Answer me."

"I do not know all the details." Hwang spoke haltingly. "I only know we have made an alliance with the man in Caracas."

Sandor pressed harder.

"Oil for military aid," the Korean gasped.

"What sort of military aid? What is the aid going to be used for?" When the man's eyes widened, Sandor knew they had arrived at the critical moment reached in any effective interrogation. Hwang had the choice to save himself or to die an unsung hero. "Come on, Hwang, you said it yourself, we'll never live to tell the tale." When the man hesitated, Sandor increased the pressure on his bloody shoulder.

"Attack on your oil reserves," the Korean blurted out. Then, as Sandor continued to prod him with the barrel of the automatic pistol, Hwang passed out.

CHAPTER THIRTY-TWO

INSIDE FORT OSCAR, ST. BARTHÉLEMY, F.W.I.

LIEUTENANT VAUCHON REALIZED that he had run out of time and that his options were woefully limited. The terrorists below were still transmitting the screams of the hostages, which sounded like human static being broadcast on the handheld radio. Their cries could also be heard through the open stairwell, creating an eerie, stereo effect.

Vauchon could retreat, sealing off the rooms and leaving those people to die along with their captors. Or they could attack, risking their own lives in what might be a futile effort, since the explosives would likely kill them all in the end.

Vauchon turned to the younger soldier who was still examining the detonators. "You know something about these things. Is there any chance they can be disarmed?"

The junior officer shook his head gravely. "No, sir, not without risk of setting them off."

"Are they on timers, can you tell that? Or are they set to be remotely detonated?"

Again the man responded with a solemn frown. "I can't tell, sir, I'm sorry. The main devices are inside plastic housings. I can't see if it's on a digital timer or not."

The chaotic sounds from below were suddenly overridden by Renaldo's voice as it crackled over the radio. "What's it going to be? In ten seconds we're going to shoot another one of your friends down here."

The lieutenant pushed the transmit button. "All right," he said. "But you have to tell us how to disarm these explosives."

"I told you this was not a negotiation," came the reply. "I can delay the mechanisms down here, but in a few minutes you will all be dead if you don't clear out." There was a pause, then, "You simply cannot win this standoff, do you understand? You have the choice to either control the damage or cause everyone to die."

Vauchon looked at his men. "Whatever happens, we've got to try to save those people," he told them.

Both of his men nodded their understanding.

Vauchon spoke into the two-way again. "All right, we're leaving. Bring the hostages out and we will allow you safe passage."

Renaldo laughed into the radio. "I will dictate the terms here. First, you and your men will toss all of your weapons down the staircase. And I mean all of them, including whatever you took from my men. Then you and your men will stand at the top of the stairs, where I can see you, with your hands raised. You say there are five of you?"

"We are only three," Vauchon admitted.

"Where are the others?"

"They have escorted the others to safety."

"If you are lying, more of these hostages will die unnecessarily."

"I am telling you the truth. There are only three of us remaining."

"And my men?"

Vauchon paused. "One is dead," he said, "and so are your two guards at the barracks. The man called Fredrico is unconscious."

There was silence for a few moments, then, "All right, throw the weapons down now."

The two young soldiers stared at Lieutenant Vauchon. "They'll murder us all," André said.

Vauchon nodded. "You men go." When they hesitated, he said, "That's an order. Go. Now."

They looked to each other, then at their superior officer. "We will not leave you here," André protested.

"I gave you an order. There has been enough sacrifice, you're right about that. We do not need two additional martyrs. You'll do more good stationing yourselves outside with the others." Vauchon turned back to the radio. "My men have fled. I am alone." His men reluctantly turned and made their way upstairs as Vauchon stepped forward to the landing and tossed his FAMAS automatic rifle down the steps, the loud clatter on the metal stairs echoing above and below. "I have given up my weapon," he said.

"Ah, my French hero," Renaldo replied. "If only I could believe you."

Vauchon felt for the handle of the pistol tucked inside his belt at the small of his back, then eyed the FAMAS automatic he had leaned behind the desk to his right. "I have done what you said," he told them. "I am waiting."

The door below swung open and Vauchon could see several staff members being prodded forward, one of his own soldiers at the front of the group. All of the hostages moved slowly, with their hands on their heads. He had an obstructed sight line on one of the terrorists, who was crouched in their midst, automatic rifle in hand, using the captives for cover.

As they moved up the staircase, the man called out, "Keep your hands high and do not move."

"Let these people go and you will be allowed safe passage," Vauchon replied.

Another of the men stepped into view in the doorway at the base of the stairs. "Of course we will," he said. It was Renaldo, the voice on the two-way radio. "We will be safe until we are ambushed outside. Now get on your knees."

Vauchon did as he was told as he watched the entourage move ever closer, the group reaching the landing in front of him.

"Stop there!" Renaldo hollered. Then he directed his lead man to see if there were others waiting.

The man moved cautiously, one hand on his rifle, the other clutching the arm of one of the hostages, shoving him ahead as he moved out from the protection of the small group of prisoners. He stood near the doorway and surveyed the room. "Looks all clear," he called out in Spanish.

"Good," Renaldo responded. "Now shoot the Frenchman."

As soon as the order was given the hostages began shrieking again. Vauchon used the momentary distraction to roll quickly to his side and clamber behind the desk, grabbing for the FAMAS.

Before Renaldo's man could react, Vauchon was shocked to see André step out from the far stairwell on the left and open fire at the terrorist. The man fell to the ground dead, but the hostage he had been hanging on to was also hit and dropped beside him.

When Vauchon ordered him to leave, André had actually run up the near staircase and doubled back down the other, while his young comrade had remained hidden in the first landing. Now he too stepped out, looking for a target.

The din of yelling and gunfire was deafening in the small, metal-encased room. Vauchon hollered at the top of his lungs, telling the hostages to get down. "On the floor!" he shouted repeatedly.

The French soldier from the lower level, who had now reached the top of the staircase, lunged forward and tackled two of the workers, shielding them as the exchange of shots intensified. Others fell on the stairs, their hands covering their heads. Lieutenant Vauchon was up now, taking a position off to the side of the doorway with the FAMAS in hand, sending a spray of gunfire below, shots caroming off the metal walls, hitting hostages and terrorists alike. Vauchon's men came forward, each of them understanding that there was no turning back. Hostages were being hit, maybe even killed. He signaled to the soldier on the ground, who took the cue to shove the two hostages beneath him, forcing them to crawl forward until they all made a run for it to the staircase and safety above.

In the midst of the uproar, Vauchon heard a man downstairs shout out a cease-fire. Suddenly an eerie silence fell over the scene until the man below hollered again. "These explosives are set and cannot be disarmed. The charges will be detonated in a matter of minutes now. Either you let us through, or we will begin firing directly at the remaining hostages."

Vauchon did not hesitate. "Let them go and drop your weapons, then you can all leave."

"You are not listening," Renaldo said, then leveled his weapon at one of the prone bodies on the stairs. "You have five seconds to back away or my men and I will commence firing."

What Renaldo did not remember in the commotion, and what Lieutenant Vauchon could not possibly know, was that Adina was remotely monitoring these proceedings as he sat alone on the upper deck of the *Misty II*. He was receiving all of Renaldo's radio communications, and so he heard the exchanges with Vauchon and, of course, the repeated volleys of gunfire.

What neither Renaldo nor Vauchon knew was that Adina had arranged to have the explosives rigged with a remote-detonation option.

At the moment of the cease-fire, Adina stared at the triggering device in his lap, listening through his headphones to the latest threat made by his men in the hopes of extricating themselves from what had become a disastrous turn of events.

He heard Renaldo say, "You are not listening. You have five seconds to back away or my men and I will commence firing."

Adina shook his head sadly. Renaldo was one of his best men. He did not care about any of the others, but Renaldo's death would be a loss. He would even feel something of a personal sorrow.

Nevertheless, this mission had been bungled. The escape of the French soldiers from the barracks and the murder of his guards were unforgivable. Adina was not concerned about the loss of his men, but he was furious about the possible compromise of his plan. He listened intently as the French soldier replied. He decided to give Renaldo one final opportunity to remedy his blunders.

———————

Vauchon held firm. There would be no negotiation. He figured there were only a few more hostages still in harm's way. Some had already been shot in the gun battle, some of those might already be dead.

He nodded to his two men, then all three opened fire, aiming high as he shouted to the remaining Fort Oscar staff who were huddled on the staircase, "Run for it, run!"

What ensued was utter pandemonium. The three remaining terrorists at the bottom of the stairwell returned fire, aiming at their attackers and the fleeing hostages.

The surviving workers made their way up the stairs as best they could, screams of fear and cries of pain intermixed with the clamor of gunshots. One after the other took hits in their shoulders, legs, and backs. Still, they struggled ahead as the three French soldiers gave them cover.

When the last of the hostages had clambered onto the landing, Vauchon reached for the man who had come through earlier, the one who had been wounded when André took out the terrorist who had been sent up first to scout out the room. Vauchon helped the worker to his feet, then, with the injured staff member in tow, he and his men herded the others to the near stairwell that led above.

Suddenly, as the gunshots continued to fly while Renaldo and his remaining accomplices scrambled up the stairs from the lower level, a brief rumbling sound was followed quickly by the sound of a loud blast, a thunderous crash chased by a fireball that followed the three Venezuelans up the stairs and engulfed them in flames.

Only Renaldo made it all the way to the top, where he lurched forward onto the floor of the main level. Just he and Vauchon remained there, the terrorists below having been incinerated in the blast and the surviving workers having already reached safety above. Renaldo had dropped his weapon and was covered in blood. Vauchon, who was himself injured in the explosion, leaned over him, gun in hand. The two men stared at each other and then Renaldo began to speak.

"Listen to me," the terrorist gasped as the lieutenant dragged him toward the staircase.

Renaldo spoke quickly, gasping for air, barely able to complete what he wanted to say before a second series of explosions were ignited, coming from the charges on this main level, sending another roiling plume of fire and smoke upward. The sound was deafening as the series of concussive blasts knocked Vauchon backward, smashing his wounded left shoulder into the corner of a metal desk as he went sprawling onto the floor. He struggled to his knees and crawled toward the doorway.

Renaldo was dead.

Vauchon staggered up the stairs into the open corridor on the main level of the fort, where he stumbled to the safety of the stone floor.

———

Adina put down the remote detonator on the table beside him and removed the earphones. He could no longer hear his men, their communications having been destroyed.

The sounds of gunfire, the explosions he had triggered and the wretched screaming of his innocent victims instantly vanished. He picked up his drink and took a long swallow.

It was his intention to create chaos in the balmy and peaceful Caribbean, and that had been accomplished. The loss of so many key men was an unfortunate consequence. His purpose was to send his enemies scurrying about these islands, searching for a connection between the downing of the airliner and the destruction of the communications center at Fort Oscar, all the while distracting them from any sense of his true intentions, his catastrophic plans for the southeastern United States.

He took another drink, uttered a sigh, then lifted the receiver that connected him to the wheelhouse.

"Weigh anchor," he told them, and hung up.

CHAPTER THIRTY-THREE

IN THE COUNTRYSIDE, OUTSIDE PYONGYANG

Hea DROVE THE bus to the end of a quiet, secondary road. She had long since switched off the headlights and, as far as Sandor could tell, had been guiding them forward by some innate radar. She now turned into a wooded area, making her bumpy way through trees and shrubs where there was barely enough room on either side for the small bus to pass, eventually coming to a stop beneath a canopy of large poplars.

They had successfully outdistanced the soldiers who made the first attempt to chase them. Given the element of surprise and the fact that Hea and Sang had already mapped out a circuitous escape route, they took and held an early lead. In the past few minutes they heard the sound of helicopters, but now their van was hidden from an aerial view in the darkness of this thickly forested glen. Sandor stepped into the cool night and saw, just a few yards away, two parked cars hidden under a spread of well-placed boughs.

"So," he said to the girl as she followed him out onto the soft ground, "when you get to the States you can race Danica Patrick at the Indy 500."

Hea responded with a blank stare. "You have a very American sense of humor, I think."

"Is that good?"

She forced a smile. "Let me just say, it is confusing."

Bergenn joined them now. "Don't worry," he said in response to Sandor's look of surprise. "I tied our friend Hwang to the seat in the back."

"We're just about to get the lowdown from Hea." He pointed to his right. "There are the two cars. Which way is home?"

The girl resumed her serious demeanor as she laid out their plans. "Most people escaping my country travel east to the Sea of Japan or west to Korea Bay. The only possible way to safety is by water; the border with the South is too heavily guarded." Both men nodded their understanding. The border between North and South Korea is the most heavily fortified crossing in the world. "Since this is well known, the shores are constantly under observation by the military. This makes the shorter routes to water also very dangerous."

Sandor frowned. "So what do you suggest?"

"I suggest surprise," she said proudly.

Sandor stifled a smile. "We're all ears."

"Sorry?"

"I mean, we're listening."

"I see. Well, it is less than seven hundred kilometers from here to the Russian border at Khasan."

"Four hundred miles," Sandor said thoughtfully.

Bergenn responded with a concerned look. "Four hundred miles by land? In North Korea?"

"This was our fallback route according to the DD," Sandor explained.

"There are also troops along that border," Hea went on, "but it is much more open because there are many railroad lines passing back and forth between my country and the Khasansky district."

"And because it's not a border with South Korea."

She responded with a respectful nod. "There is a rail bridge across the Tumen River. We can get through on the railroad cars or beneath the bridge."

"Sounds like fun. What's the other option, tie that little sedan to a hot air balloon and float into China?"

"No, the other plan is to drive south, right through Pyongyang. They will not expect this. Then go west to the Yellow Sea, where it is a short boat trip to the South."

"It certainly is bold, I'll give you that." Sandor turned to Bergenn. "Name your poison."

"Your mission, chief, you give the orders."

Sandor looked behind him, as if someone might be coming. "Whatever we do, our lead is going to evaporate quickly." He nodded to himself, as if confirming his decision. "You go south. Take Sang, let him do the driving, he'll know the way." He turned to Hea. "Sang can be trusted, yes?"

"Yes," she told him.

"It's a much shorter trip," Sandor said.

"Which means a much better chance for Craig," Bergenn agreed.

"Exactly." Sandor paused. "He'd never survive the trip north."

They were quiet for a moment, reflecting on the impossibility of their circumstances, not to mention Craig Raabe's chances of making it through.

"You're taking Hwang?"

"Yes," Sandor said. "For whatever good it might do as a bargaining chip."

"Remember, if he gets in your way, don't let him get in your way."

Sandor smiled. "Roger that."

"So you'll take Hea?"

"She's been one helluva driver so far."

"She certainly has," Bergenn agreed.

Sandor glanced at the young woman, who was waiting patiently for these arrangements to be sorted out. She said, "You are right that time is short, Sandor. We really must go."

"Okay," Sandor agreed, then turned back to Bergenn. "You know, Jim, this is going to ruin your reputation."

"How's that?"

"Rumor has it that you always get the girl."

"I've heard a thing or two about you too, chief." He had a look at Hea. "Careful with him," he warned.

Hea responded with a frown.

———

Sandor, Bergenn, Sang, and Hea went about loading the weapons into the cars and preparing to leave. Sandor took Hwang, trussed his hands and legs with tape, and shoved him in the backseat.

Then Sandor and Bergenn faced their toughest decision.

The bodies of Zimmermann and Kyung were still in the van. There was no way they were going to leave them behind to their possible desecration by the North Korean army. Taking the bodies was out of the question.

Bergenn stood there, facing the small bus, trying to read Sandor's mind. "Even if we set a long fuse to torch the van, once it goes off they'll be all over it, then they'll have our tire tracks and we'll lose most of our advantage here."

Sandor nodded. "But they're going to find this van sometime."

Hea was standing behind them. "You are right," she said in a whisper. "But there is a paved road not far from here. We will go north and they will go south. All they will know is that there are two cars."

Sandor grinned. "I'm getting those last pieces of C-4 from Craig," he told Bergenn.

Craig Raabe was already laying across the backseat of the second small sedan. He parted with the explosive material and fuses as Sandor explained his plan.

Raabe responded with a weak nod. "I'll see you back in D.C.," he said.

"You bet you will," Sandor told him, then hurried back to the van.

A couple of minutes later Sandor and Bergenn had rigged explosive charges to both entrances into the van. "This way," Sandor said, "we save the fire until they find the van. And when they do . . ." He paused. "Kurt would have liked that kind of send-off, don't you think? Sort of a Viking funeral."

"He would," Bergenn agreed. "Group cremation, where you take your enemies along for the ride."

"Right," Sandor said. Then they shook hands. "Good luck."

"You too."

"Whatever happens, let's get as much of this information to Washington as we can."

CHAPTER THIRTY-FOUR

CIA HEADQUARTERS, LANGLEY, VIRGINIA

DIRECTOR WALSH HAD an office full of people with staff shuttling in and out bringing him current updates. Deputy Director Byrnes was at his side as they faced the videoconference monitor on the far wall. Peter Forelli, the President's National Security Advisor, was demanding a full explanation of everything that happened at Fort Oscar. Urgent communications were flooding in to the White House from all over the world, including Great Britain, Germany, Canada, and, of course, France. The early reports were grim and, in addition to information, President Henry Forest wanted to know just how in hell this mess had become his problem.

CIA Director Walsh told the President's advisor that he had no answer yet.

"Well, damnit, get one. The President gets blamed for everything from floods to famine. Now he's getting tagged because the French can't protect their own fort, which, by the way, hasn't seen a battle in over two hundred years."

"You're well aware of the operation that was in place inside that fort," Walsh replied calmly.

"Yes, Michael, I know what was going on there. And incidentally, it was supposed to be a top-secret communications installation, which begs another level of inquiry, once the smoke on this clears."

The DCI said nothing.

"We've got an airliner down off of St. Maarten and now a fort invaded in St. Barths. What in the name of all get-out is going on down there?"

"We're working on it," Walsh said.

"Perfect," Forelli said, then took a deep breath. "And what's the hubbub in Pyongyang?"

"You saw the satellite feed?"

"Yes, yes, yes, of course we did. Is that one of your black ops?"

Walsh turned to Byrnes. He responded with a short nod. "It was likely one of our operations," the Deputy Director told them.

"Likely, huh? Do I want to know what's going on in North Korea?" the advisor asked.

"No, sir," Byrnes replied without hesitation, "you do not."

"Uh huh. Well, based on what we've learned from the satellite surveillance, it appears there was one helluva gunfight outside that ridiculous stadium over there."

"We have the same information," Byrnes said.

"Anything more than that?"

"Not yet."

"Don't bullshit me, Mark," Forelli warned.

"We have nothing else from there yet."

"Great. I suppose our wacko friend Kim will be issuing a statement soon, some clever ditty about Western imperialism."

"I'm not so sure about that," Byrnes said.

The National Security Advisor hesitated, then decided to let it go. Sometimes, in dealing with the Agency, plausible deniability was more important than information. "All right, you have any other good news for me today?" When neither Walsh nor Byrnes replied, he said, "Keep us posted. And I mean up to the minute." Then he reached for the panel in front of him and Forelli's image on the screen went black.

The Director turned to Byrnes. "Do we need to talk?"

"Yes, sir, we do."

Walsh cleared the room, leaving the two of them facing each other across the Director's conference table. "I'm listening."

"We assume the firefight in Pyongyang was Sandor's team," Byrnes reported. "So far we have no intel on the result."

"In other words, we don't know if he made it out or not."

"Exactly."

"Anything more from Ahmad Jaber?"

"We received word his wife was taken, apparently on her way out of Iran."

"Jaber knows this?"

"Not yet." He paused. "But she apparently knows that he's here."

Walsh pressed his lips together, thinking that one over. "Any sense of what sort of relationship they have?"

"As in, does Jaber give a damn about his wife?"

"For example."

"I'll find out."

"You do that. And you find out what else he's holding

back. If he doesn't give us everything he has, and I mean right now, then all deals are off."

"Understood."

"You tell him from me, if he screws with us I'll feed him to Jordan Sandor, one piece at a time."

"Yes, sir," Byrnes said, resisting the impulse to smile for the first time in days.

CHAPTER THIRTY-FIVE

IN THE COUNTRYSIDE, NORTH OF PYONGYANG

HEA DROVE THROUGH the night along poorly paved back roads. The absence of traffic was a problem, especially at this hour, and she was not going to make it easier for them to be spotted by driving on the main highway north. They stayed close to the Taedong River, she and Sandor agreeing that the inland route, although longer, was safest. As Hea had explained, their pursuers would expect them to make a run for one of the coastlines, either the Sea of Japan to the east or Korea Bay and the Yellow Sea to the west. Instead they would circle around the mountainous area near Hyesan and continue north to their destination, just across the Russian border.

There was little moonlight, but the sky was clear and the girl continued to find her way forward without the benefit of headlights. Sandor admired the way she navigated these byways in virtual darkness, keeping a steady speed as they motored ahead. He studied her finely chiseled features, realizing for the first time that she was an exceedingly attractive young woman. He wondered how she had been recruited, who had contacted her, even how old she might be.

And then his mind wandered back to the news of the

airliner that had exploded after taking off from St. Maarten. At first he tried to imagine how that incident could be tied to the information he had uncovered thus far from Jaber, Kyung, and Hwang. It made no sense, and he struggled to piece together some connection between the random terrorist destruction of a commercial airliner and an alliance among North Korea, Iran, and Venezuela.

But soon his thoughts turned to the jetliner explosion itself. He had no idea what altitude they had reached before the blast, but he imagined the stunned passengers as the aircraft was torn apart and began its accelerating dive into the Caribbean. How long had people remained conscious? How many were thrown from their seats? Was any part of the main cabin ripped away, causing some to be drawn into the vortex of depressurization and flung helplessly into the sky?

He began to do the math on how quickly the horrific end would come for these unsuspecting vacationers, travelers with spouses and with friends, parents with sons and daughters, clutching their children for those final seconds of life as they confronted the inevitability of their violent ends. Would they pray to God? Would they cry out? Would some try desperately to comfort their doomed children?

Sandor felt his stomach tighten as he considered the deranged bastards who would wreak this devastation on innocent people, on people who had done nothing wrong except to have unknowingly boarded a condemned flight.

Those poor souls, he thought. He was not able to shake the image of their last chaotic moments. He drew a deep breath and blew it out hard, as if exorcising the sense of abject evil that gripped him. Then he swore to himself that if he ever made it back from this mission, whatever it took, he would track down the sonuvabitch responsible and kill the man himself.

———————

The army of the DPRK is a well-trained and rigorously disciplined group. Their elite units were assigned to posts along the border with South Korea and throughout Kaesong and Panmunjom, maintaining an uneasy peace and keeping their two countries separated. The troops assigned to the Rungrado May Day Stadium were more policemen than combat soldiers, assigned to preserve order, not prepared for the invasion Sandor and his men had engineered.

Now, as the squadron assigned to the Arirang Festival mobilized half of its remaining men to chase down the intruders, the word went out for assistance to the various battalions in the neighboring provinces. Before they were in place, however, the advance unit had managed to track Mr. Sang's van to the clearing twenty miles north of the stadium.

The officer in charge ordered his vehicle to halt more than a hundred yards short of their target as two armor-plated personnel carriers behind his did the same. He deployed his men in a semicircle around the small bus, careful that no soldier was in the line of friendly fire. They moved quickly in the darkness, each man taking cover behind a tree or bush, no one moving any closer until given the order.

When the assault team was in place, the night became deadly quiet. No one spoke, no one moved. It was apparent, even from this distance, that the bus had been abandoned. The officer in charge ordered four of his men forward. They kept low, crawling slowly ahead as he watched and waited.

His orders were to recover Hwang alive. If there was any chance he was still aboard he could not simply riddle the bus with gunfire or launch a shoulder-mounted grenade attack. He worked cautiously, instructing his men to take special care that this esteemed member of their government not be harmed.

Once the four advancing soldiers fanned out and were just yards from their destination, they stopped. There was no sign of life inside the van. He sent another six soldiers ahead, waiting anxiously until they were in place. Then, in a firm but quiet voice, he issued the one-word order. "Attack!"

The ten soldiers reacted as one, lunging ahead in a crouch as they rushed the van, front door and back, the lead four separating, two men bursting through each of the doors. Then, for an instant, it seemed as if everything came to a halt as a flash of fire was followed by a massive explosion as the C-4 Sandor had wired to the gas tank ignited. The entire vehicle became a huge, burning pyre as it leapt off the ground, seeming to hang in the air until it came crashing back to earth, engulfing everyone inside and all those around it in a sea of flames.

———————

Hea saw a small flash of light in her rearview mirror. She told Sandor, who spun around to catch a glimpse of the explosive greeting they had left behind. It had been less than ten minutes since they had separated from Bergenn and Raabe, and Sandor had anticipated a longer head start. He could only hope that the destructive blast would create a delay as the military regrouped for its search. Then he thought of Kurt Zimmermann and felt his stomach go cold and empty, but he shook it off. If they were lucky there would be time for mourning later. If not, they would have all died for nothing.

Hwang was in the backseat, bound hand and foot and gagged tight for the ride. They had treated his injured left shoulder with a primitive bandage that did little more than stanch the bleeding.

"Hope you're comfortable," Sandor said. "Anytime you have something important to say, you let us know." When the man responded with a defiant stare, Sandor turned to Hea. "If you need a break, I'll drive," he offered.

"I am fine," the girl told him. "I know these roads."

They were determined to make as much time as possible under the cover of night as they sped in the direction of their ultimate destination, the Russian border. They intended to make their way across at Khasan, a city just south of Vladivostok.

And then Sandor heard it, that faraway noise of the fast-paced *thwup-thwup-thwup*. "Helicopters," he warned as the sound grew louder, intruding into the quiet night.

Hea turned off the road and stopped amid the inky shadows of a wooded glade.

"Just a few hours till daylight," Sandor said after a quick check of his watch. "We're not going to get far if we have to play hide-and-seek with an air reconnaissance mission."

She nodded, not sure what an air reconnaissance mission was, but getting the idea nonetheless.

"And they'll be sending a road unit this way soon enough, moving at top speed, headlights on, what we call hot pursuit."

"They will," she agreed quietly.

"So we're not going to do ourselves any good just sitting here." He had a look out the open window. "They seem to be veering off, probably checking those routes to the coasts."

"Yes," Hea agreed again.

"But other choppers will be coming back this way too. I think we need to take our chances and move out."

Without another word she put the car into gear and made her way back onto the road.

Sandor turned back to their hostage and undid his gag. "So, our friends Kim and Chavez have put themselves in play together. Isn't that a pretty picture?"

The Korean stared back at him without speaking.

"Nice doubles pair, those two lunatics. And Ahmadinejad too? But why the hell would they blow up a flight in the Caribbean? What does that get them if their deal is an oil-for-arms exchange? If they want to hit our oil reserves, why blow up a commercial airliner?"

Hwang allowed himself a thin smile, one of those looks that said, "We're so much smarter than you stupid Americans." It made Sandor want to reach out and pummel his face with a brick, but he offered up a grin instead.

"Come on, Hwang, I'm never making it out of your country alive, you keep telling me that. Indulge me with your brilliance."

Hwang looked at the back of Hea's head, then turned to Sandor. "You and this treasonous bitch will pay for this."

"Okay, we'll pay, but let's just say we'll pay later. Meanwhile, what gives? Why an airplane? What the hell does that have to do with an attack on our oil reserves?"

"It is not for me to understand these things," Hwang replied in his dull affect.

"I know, I know, you're just a faithful follower of the Great Leader. All the same, you've got to wonder why he'd want to piss off the United States with a move like that, killing all those innocent people just when he's about to cash in on some badly needed oil at a bargain price from Venezuela and Iran. If you're planning to go after our oil why not hit a tanker instead?" Hwang looked away, and so Sandor asked, "Is that it, you're going after tankers in the Caribbean?"

When Hwang did not respond, the girl motioned to Sandor. He leaned toward her, their cheeks brushing together as she kept her eyes on the road ahead. The wind whipping through the open windows created enough noise to render her inaudible to Hwang in the back. "There's a safe house," she whispered, "about two hours from here. If we can make it there we should be fine."

"Good."

"You need to blindfold him."

Sandor nodded, then reached back, tore off a piece of Hwang's shirt, and tied it roughly around his head. When he was done, he moved next to Hea again. "Do they have access to an overseas telephone?"

"They should."

Sandor smiled as he moved away from her and sat back in his seat. "I guess I'm still on a need-to-know basis, eh?"

Hea reacted with a puzzled look. Then, as if suddenly comprehending, she nodded solemnly. "This is all very dangerous," she said.

"So I've noticed."

"I mean to others as well."

"I see. So these are friends of yours we're going to see?"

She turned to him, removing her gaze from the highway for a nervous moment. "Family," she whispered.

Sandor frowned. "Two hours, will we make it before sunrise?"

"I hope so," the girl said. "If we don't have to stop, I hope so."

CHAPTER THIRTY-SIX

AN ESTATE OUTSIDE LANGLEY, VIRGINIA

IT WAS BEFORE dawn and Deputy Director Mark Byrnes had been up all night. He spent the previous evening with Director Walsh, speaking with the President's National Security Advisor and various officials at the National Transportation Safety Board and interspersing those political duties with reviews of the preliminary intelligence reports that came pouring in. He then worked furiously through the dark hours to organize current data being collected about the catastrophic crash of the airliner in the Caribbean. In the midst of this squall of technical information, false leads, and general confusion, just before sunrise he received a communiqué from an imbedded source in Tehran. He read it through, then hurried from the office at Langley into his chauffeured Town Car and made his way back to the safe house for another interview with Ahmad Jaber.

"I have already told you," the former IRGC operative said, "I knew nothing of an airline explosion, nothing. And it makes no sense to me, based on what little Seyed knew. Whoever these men were, they did not need to travel to Tehran to sabotage a plane in St. Maarten."

Byrnes was seated across from Jaber in the comfortable,

soundproof interview room where they had met with Jordan Sandor just a few days before. "What could they have been planning in Iran, then?"

"I've told you, I do not know."

Byrnes shook his head in disgust. "You've come here, an avowed enemy of my country, seeking asylum, and all you have to sell is some rumor about a planned attack without any detail and without a target. Before that plane went down, we were willing to work with you, we were willing to try to develop the intelligence and see where your lead would take us. But now your value has plummeted to the point where it is hard to justify any sort of accommodation at all. Do you understand what I'm telling you?"

Jaber returned his unblinking gaze. "I understand fully, just as I understood the risk I took when I surrendered to your troops in Halabjah."

"I hope you do."

The Iranian permitted himself a slight smile. "You and I know that my position in Iran became untenable. The attempt to assassinate me could not have been undertaken without the approval of the IRGC."

"What if it had been an outside group, on a rogue mission?"

"Possible, but not likely, not in Tehran. Violence is not tolerated there, not without receiving prior sanctions. It is not New York City, Mr. Byrnes."

The Deputy Director ignored the remark. "So you became expendable. Simply because this Seyed spoke with you."

"It appears so."

"And life here, even in custody, was preferable to death in Iran."

"So it would seem." The grin returned. "Despite the recent devaluation of my value to your government, you Americans are not butchers."

"Whereas your people are."

"Let us say that my people have a different cultural and religious perspective."

"Including a complete lack of respect for the sanctity of human life, just to mention one notable distinction."

"Come, come, Mr. Byrnes. A moral debate in the face of what we have to confront here? What am I to say in response? Vietnam? The invasion of Iraq? Lynching of African-Americans? The annihilation of what your media so charmingly calls Native Americans?"

Byrnes responded with a world-weary sigh. "You must be kidding me, Jaber. You consider the war in Southeast Asia a fair comparison to the random killing and mutilation of schoolchildren? Suicide bombers on commuter buses? Rockets launched into the middle of open-air markets?"

"Casualties of war."

"Victims of terrorism, you mean. When you call Ahmadinejad and the IRGC butchers, you're insulting butchers everywhere."

Jaber offered no reply.

"And what of our American family values your media is so quick to mock?"

"Excuse me?"

"The way you described your hasty departure from Mother Iran, it seems you left behind the graves of your two sons. And what of your wife of thirty years? You also left her behind to fend for herself."

Jaber was silent again.

"How long did you think she would be safe, hiding at her sister's home?"

The Iranian shifted in his seat, eyeing the CIA Deputy Director warily now as he shuffled through the papers in his lap.

"Yes," Byrnes continued, "we have sources too, as you may recall." He removed his reading glasses from inside his suit jacket pocket and made a show of perusing one of the documents he was holding. "After you sent Mrs. Jaber to her sister's home she took flight. By the time the authorities tracked her there she had already gone, apparently making her way west on a path not unlike the one you took toward northern Iraq." He looked up. "She was not as successful as you were."

As the color drained from Jaber's face, Byrnes was fascinated to see that there was actually something or someone in the world about whom this cold-blooded killer cared, other than himself. "They have Rasa in custody?" he barely whispered.

"Yes," Byrnes told him, "they picked her up on the beltway northwest of Marand." Then, with no attempt to conceal his satisfaction, he added, "What is worse, we believe they confirmed that you're here, in the United States."

Jaber's formal posture sagged, his arrogant mien dissolving into a careworn expression of sudden and utter despair. The implications were inevitable. He would be branded a traitor, not only to his country but now to his wife as well. Whatever she would have refused to divulge in loyalty to her husband she might now reveal in consequence of his abandonment. Or worse, as a result of torture. Whatever cooperation she might offer, the IRGC would not forgive his betrayal and his wife would be made to suffer for his treason.

"You are certain?" was all Jaber could manage.

"As certain as we can be in these matters. We know that your sister-in-law and her husband were questioned, but your wife had already gone. The latest report has her in a detention center in Marand."

Ahmad Jaber drew a deep breath and let it out slowly as he stared at his hands, clasped tightly in his lap.

"So," Byrnes said. "If there's any chance we can help you with this, it's time for you to share whatever you've been holding back."

When he was first taken into CIA custody and Byrnes arranged a chemically engineered interrogation, the results made it clear that the man had information, although the particulars elicited in his drug-induced haze were typically vague and confused, as they generally are in that process. He had since volunteered enough to confirm the initial reports—that something appeared to be in the works between the regimes of Kim and Ahmadinejad. Byrnes had been willing to give Jaber some time to bargain his way through the hoary process typical of most defections, since the Agency believed it would be helpful to have Jaber's cooperation as they developed more data on their own. Now, however, the downing of the airliner had foreshortened the timeline, and Byrnes cursed himself for his indulgence.

"I've had no sleep," the Deputy Director said. "I'm being

pressured for answers and my tolerance level is extremely low. I am only going to ask you once more. We know that you are holding back on us. You apparently think this is some sort of a negotiation but I am here to tell you that you are mistaken in that belief. This is not some rug sale in the bazaar. You have no leverage here. I can snap my fingers and they'll put you on a plane back to Tehran within the hour. So it's your choice. What is it going to be?"

Jaber looked up slowly, then began to speak. "My wife," he said, but Byrnes cut him off.

"No trading. You give me everything you have, then we'll talk about what we can do for you."

The Iranian nodded slowly. "The North Koreans," he said. "They have been in discussion with highly placed people in South America. They want to trade arms for oil, according to what Seyed understood."

"And you're just telling me now?"

Jaber said nothing.

"South America is a continent. I need better than that."

"I don't know more than that, but I would guess Venezuela."

"Venezuela?"

"That's my guess."

Byrnes shook his head. "Why does that involve terrorist action? They can make an economic trade like that anytime they like. What does that have to do with destroying a commercial aircraft?"

"I don't know," Jaber admitted. "Since you told me about the airplane explosion, I have been trying to put it together. It makes no sense." He paused. "Seyed came to me because he was confused about several aspects of this operation."

"I'm listening."

"Neither of us understood why I was not involved or informed. Why was this being done outside normal government and IRGC channels? If North Korea wanted to trade for oil with Venezuela, why would Iran be involved if the oil was not to come from us?"

"Who were the North Koreans talking with? I need names."

He shook his head. "Seyed never had names. As I told you, his involvement was peripheral; it almost made no sense."

Byrnes shook his head. "You're still holding out on me," he said, but before Jaber could reply they were interrupted by a knock on the door. The DD rose slowly from his chair and said, "Come in."

The duty officer entered and held out a folded piece of paper, then left the room. Byrnes read it, then looked at Jaber.

"This is the latest report on an attack made yesterday on Fort Oscar."

"Fort Oscar?" Jaber appeared genuinely perplexed.

"Yes, in Gustavia. St. Barths," Byrnes said, but none of this seemed to be registering with the Iranian. "You're going to tell me you know nothing of this either?"

"Nothing."

Byrnes uttered a long, frustrated sigh. He suspected that Jaber had likely given him all he had. The unfortunate truth was that the Iranian had come here with little to trade other than some vague rumors of an arms-for-oil deal between

North Korea and someone in South America, most likely the Venezuelans. Anything else he had given them was old news—names of Al Qaeda assassins the CIA already had in their databank, details of Iranian-led terrorist attacks that had long ago been vetted by others and solutions to bygone mysteries that had already been solved. As Jaber conceded in the meeting with Jordan Sandor and again this morning, he had not chosen to defect based on an ideological change of heart, or some epiphany about the monstrous nature of the work he had done over the years, or even the obvious lunacy of his dictator Mahmoud Ahmadinejad. No, the fact was that Ahmad Jaber believed he had been betrayed by those he served for reasons he could not fathom, and so he was simply in search of shelter from that storm.

"This just isn't enough," Byrnes said.

Jaber nodded slowly. "I understand. I wish I knew more. For so many reasons."

"We have a downed airliner, an attack on a vital communications center, and all you can tell me is that Kim made a deal for oil, probably but not positively with Chavez. What do I tell my superiors?"

Jaber thought that over, then responded with a grim smile. "Perhaps you can convince them that it is better to have me here than operating from Tehran."

Byrnes was far too tired and much too depressed to find any humor in that notion. "What about Ahmadinejad's nuclear installations?"

"I've told you already, that was not within my area of expertise or authority."

Byrnes winced at Jaber's euphemistic description of his

career. "All right," he said, getting slowly to his feet, "I'll report our conversation. It's all I can do."

Jaber also stood. "My wife," he said.

"Nothing to be done about that. Not right now," Byrnes replied, leaving that last thought hanging between them as he left the room.

CHAPTER THIRTY-SEVEN

SOUTHWEST OF PYONGYANG, NORTH KOREA

As Hea drove Sandor and Hwang north toward the mountains near Hyesan, Mr. Sang guided the small Fiat sedan carrying Jim Bergenn and Craig Raabe in a circuitous route around the main roads of Songnim. He was heading west, toward the coastal town of Namp'o, which was situated at the mouth of a large inlet to the Korea Bay. Sang was not as cautious as Hea, using his headlights and opting for wider, well-paved roads, racing toward what he believed was their best chance of escape as quickly as possible. Their journey to safety was much shorter than Hea's, and he regarded speed as more important now than stealth.

Once they arrived outside Namp'o, Sang knew there would be numerous small fishing boats docked at the piers, any one of which could easily be commandeered if they could elude the military patrols along the shoreline. Once at sea, surrounded by the darkness, he would navigate their passage south, to one of the villages just north of Inchon, in South Korea.

As they barreled ahead into the night, he explained his plan to Bergenn. Bergenn leaned over and described the situation to Raabe, who was laid out across the backseat.

"You hear that, cowboy? Just a little boat ride to freedom."

Raabe barely managed a grunt in response.

"You holding up okay?"

Raabe uttered something that Bergenn took for a yes. Craig had taken shots in the side of his chest and his leg, although the hemorrhaging had stopped under the pressure Bergenn had applied with strips of torn cloth. Now the initial shock had been replaced by severe pain and a dizzy weakness from the loss of blood.

As Bergenn turned back to face the road ahead he heard the unwelcome sound of approaching helicopters. The route they had taken was too exposed for Sang to take cover now, their headlights a homing beacon for the pursuing choppers.

"Step on it," Bergenn barked instinctively, but Sang had already accelerated into a sweeping curve that for a moment took them out of view of their pursuers. They sped over a slight incline, then banked off to the left.

But the helicopters were quickly gaining and bracketed them on the left and right. In the darkness, Bergenn could make out a pair of Hughes MD 500s, probably bought by the North Koreans back in the seventies, before Reagan slammed the door on any more deliveries. The choppers were antiquated by modern American standards but they were agile, and most of the eighty or so that the DPRK purchased had since been retrofitted as gunships.

Bergenn had no weapon capable of taking the helicopters down, so the best they could do was outrun them until they found some sort of shelter along this open stretch of road. "Kill the lights," he ordered Sang, and the husky Korean complied. The small Fiat Palio he was driving surged ahead at eighty miles an hour, but the chopper to their right circled around and suddenly shined its high-powered halogen spotlight, sweeping the highway until it found them.

Sang did the best he could, but racing forward at this speed without headlights left them too vulnerable. When the beam of light from the chopper found them, Sang was momentarily blinded. He instinctively hit the brake, causing the sedan to swerve wildly, glancing off a high curb on the right that sent them careening across the road and onto the dirt-covered median. Sang struggled to bring the Fiat back under control, but the second helicopter rose into view on the left, using its light beam to further disorient him as the car caromed back onto the pavement.

Then, arising from the darkness ahead of them, they saw the headlights of several vehicles coming at them. The helicopters had obviously radioed their position to the shore patrol at Namp'o.

Sang slammed hard on the brake again, this time bringing the car to a screeching halt. He turned to Bergenn with a look of desperate fear.

"It's all right," Bergenn said. Then he held his automatic pistol to Sang's head. "We'll tell them you were our prisoner. You understand? You tell them you were a hostage. A prisoner. Okay?"

Sang responded with a nervous nod of his head.

By now several North Korean soldiers had rushed from their transports and were surrounding the car. A voice over a loudspeaker ordered the occupants to get out.

When Sang began to say something, Bergenn shook his head. "No translation required. Let's go."

As they got out of the car, Bergenn was still holding the Tokarev in one hand and the AK-47 in the other. Sang climbed out of the driver's seat and stood beside the door, motionless.

The amplified voice, this time in English, ordered Bergenn to drop his weapons.

He looked around, seeing the situation was hopeless. There were already soldiers in position to the left and right, and other vehicles had arrived, coming to a halt on the road behind them. He bent down and placed the pistol and automatic rifle on the ground. "I have a wounded man in the back of the car!" he shouted.

"Get him out," the voice demanded.

"He cannot be moved. He needs medical attention."

There was silence for a few moments. Then, out of the glare of the numerous lights, an officer came walking toward them. "Where is the other man?" he demanded in English.

"In the backseat," Bergenn told him, turning toward Raabe.

"Do not move. Put your hands in back of your head."

Bergenn did as he was told, facing the officer again and waiting. Sang began to speak quickly in Korean, apparently protesting his innocence.

The officer continued toward them, a gun in his hand. Bergenn could now see there were several other soldiers advancing on his flanks. The officer stopped a couple of yards from the front of the Fiat. Sang was still talking when the officer barked something at him, and Sang became quiet. The officer looked Bergenn up and down. Then he pointed to Sang and said in English, "This man is a traitor to his country and to our Great Leader." He then raised his pistol and fired three quick shots. Sang crumpled to the ground.

The officer walked around the car, looking down at Sang as if admiring his work. Then he kicked Sang's inert body a couple of times, just to be sure. He peered into the backseat, where Raabe lay, barely conscious. When he returned his attention to Bergenn, he said, "We have other plans for you, my American friends." Then he shouted some orders and his men came forward, handcuffing Bergenn and dragging Raabe onto the road.

CHAPTER THIRTY-EIGHT

IN THE NORTH KOREAN COUNTRYSIDE, SOUTH OF HYESAN

BY THE TIME Bergenn and Raabe were captured, Hea had reached a small village outside Samsu, just south of Hyesan. Dawn was not long to arrive, but they still had the cover of darkness as she brought the sedan to a stop behind an ancient wooden structure. Sandor and Hea got out and stood facing each other.

"We will have to walk from here," she said. "We cannot let the other villagers see the car arriving at my parents' home."

"What about him?" Sandor asked, pointing a thumb over his shoulder.

"We cannot take him and risk being seen. We will have to come back for him."

Sandor yanked Hwang from the backseat and dropped him on the ground. He double-checked the tape around Hwang's ankles and wrists, then said, "Anything you want to tell us before you take a nap?" The Korean glared at him, so Sandor replaced the tape over Hwang's mouth, then struck him across the temple with the butt of his gun. "Okay," he said, and he and the girl lifted the unconscious man into the trunk and slammed it shut.

———

At the small farmhouse just down the road, Sandor asked for no introduction to the members of Hea's family and he received none. He assumed the elderly man and woman were her parents. The young man with whom she did most of her talking appeared to be her brother.

After a quick conversation in Korean, Hea took Sandor aside and explained their escape route. They would be hidden in the back of a truck with Hwang. Then, as soon as people began setting out for work just after sunrise, her brother would drive them northeast, near the edge of the Yalu River valley and then along the towering range of mountains to their west, until they neared the border with Russia. At that point they would be on their own.

Sandor knew they were close to China, but that route would certainly be more dangerous than the two-hour drive north. Diplomatic relations among these neighboring countries made it all but impossible to smuggle Hwang out of the country through China. Moscow was likely to be far more cooperative than Beijing and, as Sandor well knew, the post-Soviet Russians were also easier to bribe.

"What about an overseas communication in the meantime? Phone, e-mail, anything?"

Hea shook her head. "Kwan tells me it is too dangerous to try that now, not with so much driving ahead of us. Too much time to intercept the communication and then locate us. Then we would be, uh, how do you say . . ."

"Screwed."

She managed a smile.

"Any chance we can put a call through as we get closer to Khasan?"

"Yes, Kwan thinks we can."

"Good. So explain to me why all three of us need to go. Why can't you remain behind?"

A sadness filled her pretty eyes. "I cannot. After what has happened I have no future here."

Sandor nodded but said nothing.

"I am worried about my family. We must leave no trace of our being here."

"Will they get rid of the car?"

"Yes, after we are gone."

Sandor reached out and took her hand. "Everything will be all right," he told her. "Everything."

She looked into his eyes, her unflinching gaze saying that she only wished she could believe him.

————

Just before first light, Hea and Jordan hurried out the door of the small house and climbed in the rear of a Korean lorry. There was a shallow compartment beneath the floorboards where Hwang had already been placed, still bound and gagged and quite unconscious.

"I didn't hit him that hard," Sandor said.

"No," the girl explained, "he was drugged when my brother retrieved him from the car."

Kwan, who had climbed into the back of the truck behind them, simply nodded, then said something in Korean to which his sister could not manage a reply. All she could do was wipe her eyes. Then Sandor lay down beside Hwang, and Hea got in beside him as her brother laid the AK-47 at their feet and placed a wooden lid atop them, casting the three of them into total darkness. Above them they could hear Kwan rearranging boxes overhead, then slamming and securing the tailgate. A few minutes later the engine of the truck sputtered to life, and they began to move.

Of the many fears Jordan Sandor had conquered in his years of military and covert espionage service, a slight case of claustrophobia was not among them. Now he was trapped in a virtual coffin, his fate belonging to a man to whom he had not even been introduced and a Korean girl he had met less than forty-eight hours before. He remained still in the blackness as they rumbled ahead, feeling there was barely enough room to take a deep breath, struggling against the anxiety of this total helplessness, eased only by the fact that his right hand was clutching the Tokarev he had taken from the soldier back at Rungrado May Day Stadium, and the pleasant sensation of being pressed up against this attractive young woman.

"I just want you to know," he whispered to her, "I never kiss on the first date."

He hoped she was smiling as she said, "Shhh, we must be totally silent."

He waited a few seconds, then said, "Who could possibly hear us with all the noise this truck makes?"

When she offered no response he thought about his teammates, hoping they had made it to safety. If Bergenn and Raabe had been captured he knew there was no way they would be broken, no way they would divulge Sandor's route north. Raabe was so badly wounded he had no idea which way Sandor's car was heading. Bergenn was never going to cave in, certainly not through torture, not even with chemical inducement. By the time they managed to extract anything at all from him it would be too vague to be of use, and by then Sandor and Hea should be safely out of the country. Or so Sandor told himself as he managed his nerves, just as he had been trained, one slow, deep breath after another.

———

As the truck rolled on, Sandor tried to keep track of the passing time, but it was nearly impossible in this deprivation chamber. His legs and back began to ache, and he felt there was barely enough room to breathe, let alone stretch. When he felt the truck slow to a halt his sense of relief was overwhelming but he said nothing. He listened as the engine was turned off, and wondered if they had reached their destination. Then he heard loud voices and the sound of the tailgate being opened. His sense of elation was immediately replaced with apprehension as his instincts told him they had reached some sort of roadblock. His fear was confirmed when he heard the sound of boots boarding the rear compartment, moving boxes around as they stomped about overhead.

He recognized Kwan's voice, calm and deferential in tone, and the angry voices of other men, obviously soldiers, demanding answers that Kwan was doing his best to provide. Hea's body tensed up as she lay beside him, and he only hoped that whatever narcotics they had administered to Hwang earlier that morning would keep him out for a few more minutes.

There was no way for him to understand what was being said and for an instant he thought of Zimmermann, with all his linguistic skills, now a casualty of war in the North Korean countryside. By the sound of it, there were at least three other men up there besides Kwan. If they found the lid to their hiding place, Sandor knew he would be momentarily blinded when it was lifted and the light from above hit them. His chances of raising his hand and getting off three accurate shots was almost nil, but he opened his eyes as wide as he could, preparing to squint when he heard the floorboard being moved, giving him the best chance to adjust. He also placed his finger on the trigger of the Tokarev, preparing for the moment when surprise would be his only ally.

After another interminable minute or so the tone of the voices above him told Sandor that the conversation was winding down. The noise of boxes being shuffled around came to a stop. That was followed by the sound of men leaving the truck and the tailgate slamming shut.

In a few moments the engine shuddered to life and they were back on their way.

CHAPTER THIRTY-NINE

GUADELOUPE

Lieutenant Vauchon had been removed from the carnage outside Fort Oscar and was taken by air with the other victims to the hospital at Guadeloupe. All things considered, he had fared better than most.

The casualty list included several of the workers on the lower level. The entire team of terrorists had been killed, including the two guards Vauchon and his men had disposed of outside their barracks. All of the survivors from downstairs had been injured to one extent or another by the explosions and gunfire. The workers from the upper level had made it to safety, but several of them, as well as Vauchon's men and the French police, had sustained gunshot wounds and various levels of lacerations, broken bones, and assorted other injuries in the aftermath of the blast. They had all been shot at, were covered in debris, pelted with flying metal fragments, and subjected to the fire that resulted from the explosions.

In the midst of this devastation, the entire communications center in the basement of Fort Oscar had been demolished.

Officials from the French Ministry of Defense were dispatched from Paris to Guadeloupe, along with an assortment of representatives from other countries. No one as yet had any idea what to make of these attacks in the Caribbean. The downing of a commercial jetliner, followed by the destruction of Fort Oscar, simply made no sense and, more surprising perhaps, no terrorist group had yet taken credit for the assaults.

Since all of the perpetrators were dead, and the surviving police, soldiers, and staff workers all credited Vauchon with the rescue of those who made it out alive, he appeared to be the only man left to question. After treatment for some cuts and bruises, the gunshot wound to his left shoulder, and a fracture of his left forearm, Vauchon was released from the infirmary and whisked by car to the French military headquarters at Pointe-à-Pitre. No one with sufficient authority or information to undertake a meaningful debriefing had yet arrived in Guadeloupe from Europe, and so the thankless task befell the colonel on duty. An officer accustomed to dealing with issues no more complex or intriguing than chasing down drug smugglers and enforcing immigration procedures, he was the wrong man for the job.

Lieutenant Vauchon and Colonel Picard sat across a conference table from each other. The colonel began the interview by heaping praise on the French soldier for his bravery under fire, perhaps hoping to string enough superlatives together to allow time for someone with the proper credentials to arrive and take him off the hook. Eventually, however, the congratulatory monologue came to an end.

Although Vauchon had endured an extremely traumatic night and morning, he still managed some sympathy for a superior officer who he knew, even before he arrived, was way out of his depth. "Colonel, I know this is a difficult situation for all of us," he said. "Do you think it would be helpful if I simply provide a narrative of what occurred? It would spare you the need to ask questions until I have offered my full report."

Colonel Picard's enthusiasm for the suggestion was worthy of news that he had just won the national lottery. "Yes, yes, by all means. Excellent," he said.

Vauchon waited a few moments, then said, "Sir, perhaps we might want to call in a stenographer. This would save you the trouble of taking notes." Not to mention the trouble of finding a pen and pad, which were clearly absent from the table.

"Excellent." The colonel picked up the phone and ordered his aide to join them with a recording machine.

While they waited, Vauchon said, "There is something I should mention before we begin." Picard leaned forward. "At the end, after the first explosion was ignited, there was pandemonium, of course, with people rushing from below, trying to escape. The second series of blasts came soon after, but in those few moments I came face-to-face with the man I believe led this attack."

The colonel waited.

"He was mortally wounded, and he knew it, sir. He spoke to me and told me three things that may have great bearing on this matter."

"This man spoke to you, knowing he was dying?"

"Yes, sir."

"Credible statements, they say, these so-called deathbed confessions."

"Yes, sir."

The colonel leaned back in his chair, not encouraging Vauchon to continue, but rather signaling that the lieutenant should wait a moment as he thought this through. When a knock came at the door, Picard ordered them to hold off, then leaned forward again. "I take it that you view this information as being, shall I say, of a sensitive nature."

"I do. And critical to this investigation."

Colonel Picard shifted nervously in his seat.

"I want to impart this information to you in case, well, in case of anything happening, I think someone else should know before we go on the record."

Picard replied with a reluctant nod.

Vauchon lowered his voice as he said, "The man told me that he had been betrayed. I don't believe he ignited either of the explosions. His team wired them, certainly, but he was not there to commit suicide."

"You mean they were set off by someone else in his cell?"

"No, sir. I believe from what this man said that they were set off remotely, although I cannot be sure. But I believe that is what he was saying. Something about betrayal and a remote detonation. Second, he gave me a name, and I believe it may be the name of the man responsible for the plan. He said 'Adina.'"

"Adina," Picard repeated dully.

"Yes. And then he said one more thing before he died, just as the next explosion occurred."

"Yes, lieutenant?"

"He said something about a bay, or a town by a bay."

The colonel was intrigued in spite of himself. "Gustavia perhaps?"

"No, sir."

"Well, what exactly did he say?"

"Well, as you can imagine, the circumstances were difficult at best, but I believe he was saying the words 'bay town.' I believe that was it."

"'Bay town.' Those were the words?"

"Yes, sir."

"And what did you make of it, lieutenant?"

"I'm not sure, sir, but they were his dying words."

The colonel leaned back again and had a look at his watch. "All right, you'll make your full statement, but we'll deal with this last part when they arrive from Paris later today."

CHAPTER FORTY

SOUTH OF THE BORDER BETWEEN
NORTH KOREA AND RUSSIA

BY THE TIME the truck ground to a halt again, Sandor felt as if he had been buried alive beneath the floorboards for days rather than hours. If this stop turned out to be another military checkpoint he preferred to shoot it out rather than spend one more moment stuffed in this dark hole. He hadn't slept in more than twenty-four hours, his muscles ached, and the air within the cramped space was hot and fetid and thin. Still, he fought against his emotions as he waited and listened.

Hea was lying motionless, her soft breathing telling him she had willed herself to sleep.

Smart girl, he thought.

On the other side Hwang remained thankfully unconscious, which was one less problem to deal with, at least for now.

When the noisy truck engine was silenced, Sandor tightened his grip on the Tokarev once again and waited.

He heard the tailgate opening, then someone boarding the rear of the lorry. One man, or so it seemed. Then the sound of the boxes above them being shoved aside was followed by the board being lifted and the sudden rush of fresh air felt like an ocean wave passing over him.

He blinked repeatedly, trying to make a quick adjustment to the dim light inside the truck as he scrambled from the compartment. He found himself staring up at Kwan.

The young man was not smiling. He stood there, holding his finger to his lips.

Sandor nodded his understanding, got to his feet, then helped Hea to stand as she roused herself into full consciousness.

As Kwan whispered something into his sister's ear, Sandor stretched out, first his legs, then his back and neck and arms. Hea turned to him and said quietly, "We must get out of here right away so Kwan can leave. There is a path that will take us to the Khasan railroad yard. We must go on foot."

"What about him?" Sandor pointed to the inert form of Hwang.

Hea asked her brother something, then said to Jordan, "We cannot leave him here, it is too dangerous for my brother."

"And the rest of your family," Sandor reminded her.

"Yes. He might somehow be able to identify our village, or . . ."

"You," Sandor interrupted. "Believe me, I understand, and I need him anyway. Just didn't count on having to carry him." He had another look at their hostage. "Ask Kwan how long he expects Hwang to be out."

The question raised a smile from the young Korean before he answered.

Hea said, "He thinks he will be out for quite some time."

Sandor shrugged. "So that means I'll be lugging him around for quite some time. How in hell are we going to get past the guards like that?"

"Kwan has a planned route for us," the girl told him.

"What about that overseas communication?"

Kwan understood. Reaching into his pocket he pulled out a cell phone. He said something to Hea, who explained that it was a disposable phone, a valuable commodity in North Korea, but traceable once powered up. It should only be used when they were near the end of their journey.

Sandor nodded. "But this will definitely get me an overseas connection?"

"Kwan says it will, but you must be careful. They will track the signal as soon as you make the call."

"Got it. Okay, let's move out."

Kwan helped Sandor drag Hwang to the edge of the truck bed. Hea then had a look outside. They were parked off the highway, beside a large rock outcropping that hid them from view.

"Quickly," Hea urged him.

Sandor jumped to the ground and, despite the stiffness in his back and neck, hoisted the inert man over his right shoulder. He wanted to say something to Kwan, to thank him, but Hea's brother was busy replacing the floorboards, rearranging the boxes, and closing the tailgate. When he was done, he and his sister paused, but only for an instant, looking at each other as if for the last time. Then the young man nodded and, with a sad smile, climbed into the cab of the truck and drove away.

After a momentary pause, Hea said, "Hurry," then led Sandor to a path amid the trees, away from the road.

Fortunately, Hwang was not a large man and Sandor had little difficulty carrying him over his shoulder as they trudged north through the woods. Their direction was easy enough to discern with the hot sun on their right filtering through the dense foliage above them. Neither Sandor nor Hea spoke for ten minutes or so, they just moved ahead until Sandor asked, "So what, exactly, is our plan? We just going to walk across the border with Hwang on my back?"

Hea did not break stride as she said, "There is a railroad siding. A couple of miles more and we will see it. We can board a Russian freight train as it slows through the yard. That will take us into Khasan."

"And if we're seen running for the train?"

"We can pay off the attendant if we have to. Or use these," she reminded him, hoisting up the pistol she still held, then pointing to the gun in his hand. She had the AK-47 slung over her shoulder.

"Uh huh. And what about the fact that the DPRK military is going to be on the alert for a border crossing?"

"What choice do we have?" she asked, still marching ahead of him.

Sandor nodded approvingly. There were several things he liked about her style, especially the ability to keep her focus while knowing, just a few minutes earlier, she had likely cut off all contact with her family. Forever. "So," he said, "we're just like a couple of Depression-era hobos, jumping a boxcar, that's the plan?"

"Excuse me?"

"Sorry," he said, "I'll explain that later. Let's keep going."

And so they did, the trail becoming narrower and more overgrown with vegetation the farther north they went, which suited Sandor just fine. The less trampled their path, the less likely they would be intercepted before reaching the yard.

In half an hour the tracks came into view and soon they could hear the sound of trains rumbling along, somewhere off to their left. Hea slowed, then stopped and moved behind a large tree. Sandor fell in behind her and dumped Hwang on the ground. He took the opportunity to stretch his neck back and forth, trying to loosen up the tightness in his shoulders.

"Time to find the road less traveled," he said, smiling at the blank look she offered in response. "Another story for the flight back to the States, okay?" Then he lifted Hwang again and began to move through the trees with Hea trailing behind.

It was not long before they could see the train yard that Hea had described. It was a large, open area, with tracks accommodating traffic north and south. The tracks leading up to Khasan were closest to them, but there was a large expanse of open ground they would need to traverse if they were to reach the train as it came through.

"This isn't going to work," he told her as they stopped behind a large rock to survey the area. Sandor pointed to a couple of structures, two stories high, across the way. "Probably railroad offices and switching stations, but today I guarantee you they're full of local military, all equipped with high-power binoculars, not to mention rifles." They were too far away to determine if anyone was positioned on the roofs, but Sandor guessed they were. "We try and make a run for it in the open there and they'll cut us to ribbons."

"Can we wait until dark? Would that be better?"

"Better, yes, but they'll have infrared and night-vision goggles. Or they can easily throw floodlights on, and then what? And who knows what patrols they already have in the area? We can't just sit here for ten hours and hope that we're not discovered. Our friend Hwang is going to wake up eventually, which will create another issue." He thought it over as he watched an old locomotive pull a line of freight trains slowly past, traveling south. There was no sign of a military presence, no one boarding the cars as they moved along. "No, I believe our best move is to act now. But not here," he told her. "Come on."

Sandor hoisted Hwang one more time, then led Hea back through the woods, staying as close as he could to the rail line without coming out from the cover of the trees, not stopping until they were more than a mile south of the yard.

Now they were much closer to the tracks, although Sandor knew the train would be moving faster here, making it tougher to board. He did not have to wait long before the sound of an approaching locomotive announced it was on its way.

"Not yet," he said as he watched, gauging the speed, judging how he would make his move. When the entire line of cars had passed, he said, "Okay, we can do this. First thing, it has to be a Russian train. No sense complicating our lives by getting aboard a North Korean line."

Hea nodded. "Both Russian and North Korean trains run back and forth."

"Right. Second, and this is the tough part, I don't think it'll work for us to board one of the cars in the back. There's likely to be a customs check, and we'll be dead if they find us there. I need to get into the locomotive, to make sure they don't stop when they come to the border. You understand?"

"Yes."

"Which means I have to try and board first. The question is, what the hell do we do with Hwang? You're not going to be able to carry him onto a moving train, and I can't risk lugging him on my back if I'm going to reach the engineer."

As they talked it over, Hwang finally started to stir. "All right," Sandor said, "here's what we'll do."

After he explained his plan, Hea asked, "What if the next train is North Korean?"

"The one that just passed was North Korean, which should improve our odds the next one will be Russian. If it's not, well, then Mr. Hwang turns out to be unluckier than we thought. Right, Hwang?"

Hwang was emerging from his narcotic haze. He heard the plan and began to struggle against his bindings. Sandor reached out and gave him a slap on the cheek. "You just stay nice and quiet, pal. I'd hate to think I hauled you all this way just to shoot you."

Hwang gave him a venomous look, but stopped writhing around.

Sandor turned back to Hea. "If this stretch of rail is being watched they'll see me as soon as I move into the clearing with our friend here." He took the cell phone Kwan had given him and handed it to her. "If anything should happen to me, you get the hell out of here, try and jump the next train going north." He stood and led her beyond the earshot of his prisoner, behind a large tree. There he recited a set of numbers. "Once you're on the train you turn on the phone and enter those numbers, then ask for a man named Byrnes, tell him you were with me, tell him everything that happened. He'll get you out of here. All right?"

She stared at him, not moving, not speaking.

"Hey," he said, "just a precaution. Now, repeat the numbers," he insisted, and she did. Then he returned to Hwang and, without warning, leaned over and hit him with the side of his clenched hand, striking him just between the man's neck and shoulder, a vicious chop that would quiet the Korean down for a little while longer.

Sandor lifted Hwang over his shoulder and, moving as fast as he could, entered the clearing. As he raced for the tracks he expected something, sniper fire or a shout from a sentry, but nothing came. They were far enough from the main yard with no sign of anyone in sight.

Sandor laid the insensate man across the northbound rails at the end of a long straightaway and turned back for the woods. There was no reaction from anywhere, all was quiet, and Sandor made his way back to safety.

When he reached Hea, she smiled slightly, then held out the phone.

Sandor nodded as he took it. "All we can do now," he said, "is wait." Then, as he caught his breath, he grinned. "One way or the other, at least I won't have to carry that sonuvabitch around anymore."

CHAPTER FORTY-ONE

CIA HEADQUARTERS, LANGLEY, VIRGINIA

Deputy Director Mark Byrnes was again seated in the office of CIA chief Michael Walsh, and again they were facing the large screen, which this time displayed the image of the President himself, as well as National Security Advisor Peter Forelli, members of the National Security Council, and other administration officials. The group assembled at the White House was in a somber mood. All of them, that is, except for President Forest. He was downright angry.

"How in hell is this possible?" he demanded. "Where was the breakdown?"

At the moment, he was addressing the problem of the downed airliner. They had not even reached the next agenda item, the destruction of the communications center in Fort Oscar.

"So far," DCI Walsh replied, "we believe it occurred in the pass-through of luggage from one of the smaller islands. A lot of these commuter flights check baggage through when they come into St. Maarten. We're checking into all of them. We're also trying to determine the means of detonation."

"Excuse me?"

"Well, sir, preliminary tests indicate that the explosive device was placed somewhere within the cargo hold. We have not determined if it was ignited remotely, on a timing device, or by an altitude-activated triggering mechanism."

"No," the President said, "that's not what I'm asking, Mike. What's this about the luggage passing through?"

Walsh turned to Byrnes, the classic Potomac handoff.

"There are local airlines that operate between the smaller islands and St. Maarten," the Deputy Director explained. "To save time, sir, some of them have arrangements with the international carriers that allow passengers to check their bags through. Without reclaiming them in the Princess Juliana Airport," he added.

The President turned to Forelli, fixing him with a look that could have bored a hole through a lead shield. "Are you guys telling me that they allow luggage to be checked through from these puddle-jumper flights onto a jumbo jet heading for the States?"

"Yes, sir," the NSA replied unhappily, "it appears some of them do. The bags are scanned by the security personnel in St. Maarten."

President Forest shook his head. "That's comforting. What do they do, have a glance at the screen in between sips of their piña coladas?" He turned his wrath on the head of the NTSB. "Is this procedure sanctioned by your department?"

Saul Adler nodded glumly. "The airlines are permitted certain latitude on how they handle connecting flights. In the Caribbean . . ."

"Don't give me any bullshit about the Caribbean," the President barked. "I got over two hundred people dead in the Caribbean, not to mention this disaster in Fort Oscar. What I don't need, Saul, is a damned travelogue. What I need is for someone to tell me what the hell is going on here." He turned back to the screen and said, "Byrnes, you have anything for me so far that means something?"

"Given the attack on Fort Oscar, I think we should focus on flights that came into St. Maarten from St. Barths."

"Don't overwhelm me with the obvious. What else have you got?"

"You've been briefed on the Jaber defection, sir?"

Forest nodded impatiently.

"It appears he knew nothing about the jetliner, Mr. President. His information and the leads we've been developing indicate that all of this may have something to do with energy resources."

"Energy resources? Like what, a play against one of our nuclear power plants?"

"No, sir, but this is all highly classified . . ."

"Everyone in this room is cleared," the President announced impatiently. "Just lay it out for us. Why would they blow up an airplane and then Fort Oscar if this is a play against a reactor or something?"

"No, sir, we believe it's some sort of oil-for-arms play."

"What in hell does that have to do with downing a commercial airliner?"

Byrnes drew a deep breath. "We believe the attack on the airliner might have been a diversion, sir."

"A diversion?" the President roared. "These bastards killed two hundred people as a diversion?"

"Yes, sir, that's how we see it. They may want us to link the airline explosion with the attack on Fort Oscar, send us spinning in the wrong direction, but we believe their real plans have something to do with our oil supplies. This appears to be an offensive coordinated between Pyongyang and someplace in the West. Most likely Caracas. We are still unsure if Iran is actually involved."

Now the President was listening. "Go on."

"We have one of our best men leading a covert operation in North Korea. We're waiting to exfiltrate him as we speak."

"What sort of operation?"

"Fact-finding, sir. We believe, if we can get him out, he may have information that will help us connect the dots on this."

President Forest turned to Forelli again. "This have to do with the mess you told me about at that ridiculous festival they hold with all the cheerleaders in Pyongyang?"

The NSA confirmed it was.

The President turned back to the screen. "When you say 'one of our best men,' who do you have leading the ops over there?"

"Jordan Sandor, sir."

"Sandor, eh?" For the first time, the President allowed himself one of his well-known smirks. "Way I hear it from Peter, satellite photos show they had quite a firefight at that stadium yesterday. That was Sandor?"

"We believe so, sir."

"You really think he got anything out of that?"

"I hope so, Mr. President."

"Me too," he agreed, with a quick nod of his head. "All right, then, you fellas do whatever it takes to pull him the hell out of North Korea, then let's start to get us some answers."

CHAPTER FORTY-TWO

SOUTH OF THE BORDER BETWEEN
NORTH KOREA AND RUSSIA

WHAT SANDOR'S PLAN lacked in finesse it made up for with surprise. Hwang lay across the northbound tracks, bound at the wrists and ankles with his mouth taped shut. Sandor had also done his best to strap Hwang in place with his belt, so escape would be nearly impossible.

Hea was hiding in the bushes directly across from where the Korean lay. Sandor was a hundred yards south, so he would have the first look at whether the train was Russian or DPRK. They remained that way for nearly an hour, watching as Hwang tried unsuccessfully to wriggle out of danger. Then they heard the sound coming from the south.

As soon as Sandor spotted the Russian logo he signaled Hea, who ran from cover and knelt beside Hwang. Sandor was racing north through the trees as the freighter barreled ahead to where the girl now stood waving her arms, the incongruent scene causing the engineer to reflexively blow his horn and order his assistant to hit the brakes.

What could possibly be going on, they must have wondered.

But before they could make sense of a man tied to the

tracks and a woman calling for help, they slowed their long line of cars just enough for Sandor to charge on the full run from beyond the siding and leap onto the running board of the locomotive with the Tokarev in hand and the AK-47 strapped across his chest.

The engineer was a burly man in his mid-fifties, his brakeman younger and thinner. "Stop this thing!" Sandor hollered at them in their native language, and the operators were too stunned to do anything but comply. As they did, Sandor relieved them of their sidearms.

There was not enough time to bring this huge linkage of rolling steel to a halt before hitting Hwang, but Hea had already managed to free him from the tracks and drag him to safety as the train continued slowly past them.

With the train still creeping ahead, Sandor instructed the brakeman to get down and help bring the girl and Hwang into the cab. "And no heroics, right? No one here is going to get hurt if you cooperate," he said, still speaking in Russian. "We just need a quick lift into Khasan." Then he tossed one of the Russian pistols down to Hea, keeping the engineer covered with the AK-47.

The brakeman got down and helped Hea lift Hwang, all three of them clambering aboard. Sandor said, "If you touch the radio, if you try and trip an alarm, I'll kill you both. You understand?"

"Perfectly," the engineer replied. "Your Russian is quite good."

"I've had plenty of practice. Now, get this crate going again and tell me the procedure you have to follow when you enter the rail yard up ahead."

The engineer described the protocol. When they came south into the country, filled with Russian products, they would be stopped and examined. On the way back they were basically empty, since North Korea did not have much to export. There was little to look for except possible defectors. Normally they would be asked to slow the northbound train, but nothing more. Occasionally they would be subjected to an inspection. This morning, however, the engineer said that he had noticed an increased military presence along his route.

"Now I understand why," the man said.

"Well, I appreciate the warning," Sandor replied with a nod. "Now you and your friend have a choice. You can die here for no good reason that I can think of, or you can get us safely into Khasan, where I promise you, the financial reward will justify the risk. You understand?"

"You are American," the man replied, now speaking in English. "I am happy to help you. The North Koreans," he said with a disgusted look, then spat on the deck of his engine house to make the point.

Sandor frowned. "Even if you're telling me the truth, I have no time for political agendas, simple greed works fine for me. I just need to get across the border."

"Don't worry," the burly engineer assured him. Then he turned and spoke to the brakeman in Russian, telling him they would not slow as much as they normally did. They would not want to raise unnecessary suspicion, but they wanted to maintain enough speed to be sure they would be able to get through to Khasan if there were trouble. "The North Koreans are crazy," he said to Sandor, "but not crazy enough to do anything once we cross into Russia."

"That's how I figure it," Sandor agreed. "I just hope this old crate has some sort of turbo drive if we need it."

The switching house in the rail yard north of Najin was antiquated but it did have certain modern equipment, including a tracking device covering all of the rails near this border with their neighbor to the north. One of the switchmen on duty noticed that the next northbound train, due just after noon on its way to Khasan and then on to Vladivostok, had slowed to a near stop just a few miles south of the yard. Under normal circumstances this could mean one of several things, including the pickup of defectors, the off-loading of contraband, or a mechanical issue. Most days he would not even mention the incident, since the train had not actually come to a halt and reporting this sort of occurrence would inevitably cause him additional work and the need to complete various forms he would rather avoid. Today, however, there was a nationwide alert from the military, and there might be more risk ignoring the situation than not.

So, when the young switchman saw that the freight train had slowed and then resumed its prior speed, he brought it to the attention of his superior.

"Very interesting," the older man replied. "Is this something you have observed before on this run?"

"From time to time there is a changing of speed, sir."

"But you found this unusual enough to report it today?"

"Yes, sir."

The older man responded with a knowing look, then

went to his phone and called the *sangjwa*, or colonel, in charge of the local military unit.

The DPRK army already had a squadron positioned in the area, although no one in the hierarchy believed that Sandor could have eluded the dragnet they had set for him in Pyongyang and safely made it all the way to Najin. They assumed he was still in the southwest, hiding somewhere, and that his capture was imminent, particularly once his two comrades, now in custody, were forced to divulge whatever they knew of his whereabouts.

Nevertheless, the order was given for the dispatch of additional men to the site with instructions to conduct a thorough inspection of every car. As the Russian freight train entered the southern entrance to the yard, the engineer received a radio communication telling him to stop along the siding just across from the main terminal building.

———

The stocky Russian engineer was leaning out the window of the locomotive, his assistant beside him. Sandor was seated behind them, keeping just below window level. Hea was crouched on the metal floor, armed with one of the Makarov pistols they had just taken from the Russians. She was keeping an eye on Hwang.

"Don't reply," Sandor said to the engineer when he heard the order come over the radio.

"Won't that make things worse?"

Sandor shook his head. "Keep moving slowly. In another minute ask them to repeat what they said. Go back and forth on the radio with them. Say you don't understand them. We've got to get past the main building without stopping."

This time the engineer exchanged a nervous look with his second in command. "You don't know these Koreans, they are crazy," he said to Sandor. "They'll open fire without warning."

"On a Russian freight train? No way. But I can tell you who definitely will open fire if you don't do what I say, then I'll run this old jalopy myself. *Pon'yal?*"

The man reluctantly complied, receiving an instant and irate reply over the air. "Stop now," he was instructed.

Sandor nodded. "Slow it down a bit, just make it appear you're going to stop. We had a look at this yard earlier today. We've got to get past that last switch where they can send you off to the siding. After that they can't divert us. Tell them you're stopping. Ask them what's going on."

The Russian nodded and said in English, "Buy time, you Americans say."

"Exactly."

Speaking into the microphone in his friendliest tone, the engineer inquired as to why he was being delayed. The reaction over the radio remained angry, telling him he was in the Democratic People's Republic of Korea, that he was under their jurisdiction and had no right to question their authority. The arrogant speech was just long enough to get them to the last of the switching tracks.

"How far to the border now?" Sandor asked.

"A few kilometers."

"Good. Ask them if you can stop up ahead. Then, while they're answering, let's get this bucket of bolts rolling." Sandor, moving in a crouch, had a look out of the port window. He could see soldiers lined up in front of the main terminal building. Several were already making their way on foot across the far tracks toward the train. "You better get it going now, Boris, or you're not going to make it home for dinner tonight."

As soon as the Russian moved the throttle forward, the old locomotive belched out a dark cloud of smoke. The line of cars accelerated slowly, and Sandor grabbed the brakeman by his shirt collar. "The emergency release," he hollered in the man's face, his Russian crystal clear. "Cut the line of cars loose right now."

The brakeman led him to the rear of the locomotive cabin, pointing to a series of switches and a huge lever. "It will take both of us," the man said in Russian.

Sandor eyed him warily, then shoved the gun inside his waistband. "You screw with me and I'll kill you where you stand."

The man had a look into Sandor's steely dark gaze and responded with a nod. "I understand," he said. Then, after hitting several switches, the two men bent to the task of unhooking the line of boxcars by raising the long steel lever.

As if a great weight had been lifted from its back, the entire trail of cars was set loose and the old engine surged forward. The unit of North Korean soldiers broke into a run, but it was too late. Sandor watched as a few turned back, hustling toward vehicles that would pursue them by road as they steamed toward Russia.

Not a shot had been fired, at least not yet.

Sandor took Kwan's cell phone from Hea and turned on the power. If North Korean intelligence was going to intercept the signal, it wouldn't matter now.

Sandor entered the series of numbers he had recited earlier for Hea and was soon connected to a secure line. He used one of his code names, then demanded an immediate connection to Byrnes. Within moments he heard the DD's voice assuring him, "We're clean on this end, go ahead."

"I'm doing a Casey Jones to the Bolshoi."

"Copy that," Byrnes replied. The route through Khasan was one of their contingency exfiltration plans. Byrnes knew exactly where Sandor was headed.

"I'm on my own," Sandor reported, "but we have company for dinner, one for each side of the table. We also have unfriendly locals on our tail."

"I copy. How far are you?"

"Couple of miles, but the stretch run is going to be hot."

"We'll work on the border stop for your trailers."

"Good. But I need a taxicab home, and pronto."

"We'll get that done too."

"I hope so, because we're very close to curtain time."

"I read that," Byrnes told him. "Any reviews for me on the out-of-town performance?"

"Yes, we have reason to think the bird was a diversion."

"We have the same indications here."

"I believe this is being orchestrated by Adina," Sandor told him. "You copy that?"

"I do. Is that confirmed?"

"Best I can for now. We may have some help getting more specifics."

"We'll talk once you're secure on your end." Byrnes paused. "Any word on the other ticket holders?"

Sandor dreaded the question. It meant that Bergenn and

Raabe had not been heard from. "That's a negative. Z is definitely going to miss the show. Not sure about the other two."

"All right," Byrnes replied, the concern audible over the garbled wireless connection. "Let me get your ride set up."

"If the others have been taken, I have something they may want to exchange."

"Thank you for that," Byrnes said. "See you back here."

CHAPTER FORTY-THREE

KHASAN, RUSSIA

R**ELATIONS BETWEEN** R**USSIA** and the United States had turned chilly under Putin's leadership, which had morphed without convincing artifice into the Putin shadow regime. Putin was no Gorbachev and there was no Ronald Reagan to confront him. President Forest had his hands full with the struggles in the Middle East, the collapse of the global economy, and re-election. Prospects were far less rosy than they had once appeared for a lasting friendship between these two great powers.

Nevertheless, Byrnes had mobilized his skeleton crew of operatives in Vladivostok, and they had traveled to Khasan long before Sandor phoned in from the freight train. This border between the northeast corner of North Korea and the eastern edge of Russia was one of the potential escape points for Sandor and his team. Well aware of the logistical difficulties in exfiltration, the Deputy Director left nothing to chance that was within his power to control, especially after hearing of the skirmish outside the Arirang Festival. Diplomatic lines had been humming for the past ten hours and Moscow realized this was no time to quarrel with the Department of State in Washington. A commercial jetliner had been downed in the Caribbean and the communications center at Fort Oscar had been demolished. President Forest and his intelligence team were in no mood for a negotiation. If Sandor made his way into Russia, cooperation was expected.

Now that Byrnes received Sandor's call, his American operatives and Russian liaison were waiting at the offices of the Khasan stationmaster. Even so, Sandor was far from being out of danger. As the engineer did his best to outrun the North Koreans, the front line of DPRK soldiers opened fire. A fusillade of shots were striking the old locomotive and ricocheting treacherously around the cabin. The thick steel that lined the compartment made it a sort of lethal pinball machine.

Sandor ordered Hea, Hwang, and the brakeman to lie flat on the metal floor, and he told the engineer to keep as low as he could.

"There's nothing to see out there," he reminded him, "it's a damned train and it's running on tracks, so all you have to do is keep it moving forward."

The AK-47 Sandor still held did not have the range or power to answer the assault from their rear. He also knew his ammunition was limited, so he held his fire in case any of their pursuers got close enough for him to take a meaningful shot. He crouched behind the metal-plated cab of the locomotive, watching as the foot soldiers behind the accelerating train fell back. But trucks suddenly appeared off their left flank, charging up the road that ran parallel to the tracks.

Sandor had not warned the engineer that his kidnapping of Hwang might embolden the Koreans to ignore the usual border restraints and remain on their tail all the way across the Tumen River into Khasan. Sandor was counting on Byrnes to lean on the Russians to have their military stop the convoy, at least long enough for him to escape. He was also counting on plain old Russian arrogance, expecting their border guards to bring the Koreans to a quick halt.

They were only a minute or so from the crossing when the soldiers in the troop transports opened fire. The road rose above the level of the train tracks along this section of the route, and the trucks were moving faster now, giving the North Koreans an excellent vantage point. Several shots crashed through the windows of the cab and caromed off the steel, one of them striking the engineer, who fell to the floor. Sandor raced forward, finding the man clutching his arm, his face a dark scowl.

"Bastards," he grumbled in Russian.

"You all right?"

The man nodded. "Let's get home," he said as he struggled to his feet and retook the controls.

As the train surged ahead, the firing diminished. Sandor saw that the road had veered off farther to the west, now separating them from the tracks by a dense stand of trees as they emerged from the woods into the opening above the Tumen River. The only concern was that the Koreans, figuring all had been lost, might forsake the rescue of Hwang and launch a rocket attack at the locomotive.

"Ah!" the engineer cried out, and Sandor turned quickly, thinking the man might have been hit again. Instead he saw him pointing in front of them, to the border just ahead, where Russian guards had gathered outside to see what was going on.

Without reducing speed, they swept past the checkpoint and the Russian soldiers who were lining the tracks. Whatever Byrnes had done, he had obviously done it well. They proceeded on for the last kilometer with no shots being fired and no sign of the DPRK military. They only slowed when they entered the Khasan rail yard.

Sandor freed up Hwang's ankles but kept his hands secured behind his back and his mouth taped. "Come on," he said to Hea, "time to go."

The train rolled to a stop and the five of them were met on the ground by several armed soldiers, an elegant Russian man in a well-tailored suit, and two Americans. It was the Russian who spoke, his English impeccable.

"We have interceded on behalf of our countrymen, who reported coming under improper attack from the North Korean military. The three of you," he continued, eyeing Sandor, Hea, and Hwang, "were never here. Is that understood?"

When Hwang tried to speak through the tape over his mouth, the Russian reached out and unceremoniously ripped it from his face. The Korean uttered a loud yelp.

"You wish to say something?"

But when Hwang began an angry diatribe, three soldiers leveled their rifles at his head.

"Does anyone else have anything to say?"

Sandor grinned, gesturing toward the engineer and brakeman. "Only that these two men are heroes, and should be well provided for." He directed himself to the two Americans. "Is that understood?" The two agents nodded their assent as Sandor eyed the attaché cases they were carrying. "I assume one of you has something to give these gentlemen."

The older of the two agents nodded as he held out his case.

"Nice work," Sandor said as he took the briefcase. "I thought you'd show up with the money in a paper bag."

The man from State said nothing in reply.

Sandor passed the attaché to the engineer. "This is a thank-you from me and my Uncle Sam. And get that arm fixed."

The burly man nodded.

"It was nice never having met you," Sandor said.

The younger man responded with a confused look, but the engineer uttered a chuckle. "Go ahead," the engineer said in English, "before I think that maybe you were really here."

Sandor took his hand and said, *"Do svidaniya,"* then followed the two Americans to a waiting car where he, the girl, and Hwang were whisked away for the flight home.

CHAPTER FORTY-FOUR

BAYTOWN, TEXAS

Peter Amendola WAS never going to win any popularity contests at the Baytown oil refinery, not among his superiors and certainly not among his coworkers. He was arrogant, irritable, and generally unpleasant, even if his most vocal detractors would concede he was one of the most effective supervisors on the line. He was a pain in the ass to work with, but they couldn't deny he got the job done.

Amendola was also an intensely private man. He did not spend his after-work hours carousing at the local pubs, would not attend company picnics, and could not be persuaded to play in the corporate softball league. He generally kept to himself.

In short, his behavior presented the classic profile of a man who might engage in just the sort of treachery the security forces at the plant were charged to root out. Yet somehow, perhaps due to his talents on the job, his peculiarities were overlooked. It just never seemed to occur to anyone that Amendola posed a risk for information leaks.

Sometimes what is most obvious is not seen.

———————

The facility at Baytown is a massive complex but, contrary to what some might assume, the largest oil refinery in the

Western Hemisphere is not in the United States. Venezuela owns that distinction for its combined enterprises at Cardon, with a capacity that is nearly double that of the refineries in either Baytown or Baton Rouge, America's two largest plants. Nevertheless, these refineries in Texas and Louisiana, just miles from one another along the Gulf of Mexico, are enormous, satisfying a large portion of the nation's oil needs.

Security is obviously a major issue since oil, being a highly volatile and flammable substance depending on the form of its refinement, poses numerous safety and health hazards. Leaving aside the geopolitical implications of how the need, supply, and use of oil has reshaped the world in the past hundred years, there is a simple truth that transcends these imperatives—oil is dangerous. It is disastrous if a single tanker disgorges its cargo into the ocean. It creates horrendous environmental implications if an oil rig is damaged and its bounty is allowed to leak onto the land or into the sea, as the nation witnessed with the BP disaster. And it would be cataclysmic if the holding tanks in a large refinery were somehow compromised, if overall safety precautions were breached, or, worst of all, if the facility were attacked.

Precautions are taken and defensive measures put in place, anticipation of problems being of the utmost importance in an uncertain world. In simpler times, tours of large oil refineries were routinely open to the public. No such access is provided anymore. Employees are vetted before hiring, periodically subjected to screening and subjected to spot checks. This sort of scrutiny intensifies for those workers occupying higher and more sensitive positions. Anyone dealing with classified data is carefully watched.

An insider who determines to pass on such information must therefore be incredibly furtive in his actions. Those seeking it have to be more careful still.

The first approaches made to Peter Amendola came slowly. The fishing line was let out a little at a time until the hook could be set. Originally, the information requested seemed utterly benign and the cash rewards welcome. His benefactors were corporate spies, or so he was assured. This was nothing more than keeping up with new processes, maintaining a competitive edge. It was like Nike and Adidas, they told him, or, for those with longer memories, Macy's and Gimbels.

As the money increased and the demand for records grew, so did Amendola's doubts, and he was not shy about expressing those feelings. His handler was empathetic, claiming that he was going out on a limb by revealing the second layer of the tale. In the end, he said, Amendola's doubts were well placed—his benefactors were not corporate competitors after all. The truth, his contact ruefully admitted, was that the principals were well-financed environmental activists interested in having an inside look at the workings of a refinery, wanting to ensure that proper safeguards were in place and that no shortcuts were being taken at the expense of a green planet.

Sounds like bullshit to me, Amendola told himself, but he took the money again, even as his misgivings grew. He had a demanding wife, a spoiled daughter, and a young son with serious health issues, all of which helped him rationalize his deceit.

And yet he was no one's fool, at least he thought not, and he realized that the data he was now being asked for could not possibly square with the story he was being fed. When he voiced his latest doubts, his contact assured him everything would be all right, that from here on they would just ask for periodic reports.

And then he was summoned to a meeting at a local Starbucks for a little chat after work. That had been their modus operandi, brief meetings in public places such as bars, coffee shops, malls, which were followed by exchanges of cash for information at various drop-off locations. The meetings were typically brief and reasonably cordial, but this evening the tone of the discussion was different. When his handler completed an explanation of what was being requested, Amendola leaned forward in his chair, his blunt features expressionless while his eyes flashed anger across the small table.

"Why the hell would a bunch of tree huggers need information about perimeter defenses?"

The man facing him was dressed in tan slacks and a white polo shirt, his sandy-colored hair slightly tousled, his appearance altogether forgettable, just as intended. He was the sort of man you might walk past four times in a single day and never notice once. "It's all about the safety of the refinery, I suppose. I don't try to figure these things out, Peter," he said with a friendly smile, his manner relaxed as he sat back in his seat. "Just doing a job, like you."

Amendola shook his head without realizing it. "This is not my job, buddy. This may be your job, this is not my job," he repeated.

"Have it your way," the man replied affably. "All the same, we need the information."

"You told me there wasn't going to be anything more than some periodic reports on operations," he protested.

"Hey, things change."

Amendola looked away, making a quick scan of the room. "Well I can't get that sort of information anyway. It's way beyond my pay grade. Outside the scope of my duties."

The smile did not leave the man's face as he said, "You're lying, Peter. It may be beyond the scope of your duties, but we know you can get it."

Amendola finally sat back, taking a moment to study the man. Then he said, "But I won't." He picked up his coffee and took a sip.

"I have to disagree," the man said as he slowly shook his head. "I think you will."

"Really?"

"Oh yes. You see, we need this data, we know you can get it, and that's the basis of our little, uh, arrangement. Right?"

Amendola leaned forward again, straining to keep his voice low. "You never said anything about defense systems. You wanted to know about safety measures, cross-checks, fail-safes. This goes way too far."

"Too far for whom?"

"For me, that's *whom*."

The man raised up from his seat slightly and reached into his hip pocket, pulled out an envelope, and placed it on the table. "Our affiliation is almost done, Peter, I promise you that, but I also assure you that we need what we've asked for." He slid the brown envelope across and stared at Amendola, his grin having momentarily vanished. "I think you'll cooperate."

Amendola hesitated, finally picking up the wrapper and pulling out several photographs and a printed card. The pictures included his wife, his children, and an array of candid photos of him retrieving envelopes containing cash from various drop-off points. He looked at the card, which was a list of all his wife's immediate relatives, as well as his own.

"You see, Peter, I didn't want to be heavy-handed about this, but we have no time to negotiate here and, to be blunt about it, you simply have no bargaining leverage. I hope you understand our position. We never meant this to become unpleasant." The smile returned, as if he were about to pass on some good news. "So then," he continued as he lifted his cup of coffee, "shall we say day after tomorrow?"

CHAPTER FORTY-FIVE

OVER THE PACIFIC, EN ROUTE TO WASHINGTON

AFTER HIS CLAUSTROPHOBIC ride beneath the floorboards of a Korean truck and a bumpy ride on an old Russian prop jet, Sandor appreciated the luxury of the Gulfstream that carried them from Osan Air Base in South Korea, then on to Elmendorf Air Force Base in Alaska for refueling, and finally, to Washington. After nearly two days of continuous action without time to rest, exhaustion swept over him like a series of crashing waves.

He was seated next to Hea, who, as an undocumented foreign national, posed some interesting issues for the officials he had spoken with in Osan. As far as Sandor was concerned, there was no doubt that she would be coming along for the ride. As he patiently explained, she had been the reason he had gotten through and he was not leaving her behind. The word from Langley ultimately came, endorsing that position.

Hea was already more than a little nervous, less from the aftershock of all they had been through than the realization of what might lie ahead. She was traveling to the United States for the first time, leaving her entire family behind to God only knew what fate, and she had no idea what the future held. Sandor stayed close to her, making sure she had something to eat and drink, encouraging her to rest, and trying his best to assure her things would all work out.

After they boarded for the Alaska–Washington leg Hea turned to Sandor and said, "I had never been on an airplane before today."

"Nothing to it. Takeoff was the tough part. You did just fine."

"I was a little frightened," she admitted. "I did not want to tell you."

Sandor smiled at her. "You've certainly been through tougher moments these past two days."

She looked into his eyes. "All those men, all the dying, it was very difficult for me."

"I understand. It was for me too."

"It did not appear so." She hesitated, then said, "You have killed before."

It was not a question so he offered no reply.

"Can I ask you how many men you have personally killed?"

Sandor pressed his lips together, then said, "The number is not important but believe me, if I killed them it was always personal to me."

Hea turned to look out the window and, before long, she fell into a deep sleep. Sandor watched her for a while. He knew her life was about to become an unpredictable jumble of bureaucratic decisions largely beyond her control. He promised himself he would do everything he could to help her through that transition.

He fought to stay awake long enough to make some final

notes on his report for Byrnes, then had a look to the back of the plane, where Hwang was handcuffed hand and foot and watched over by two armed escorts. Somewhere over Vancouver he finally gave in to sleep.

————————

It was morning in Washington, more than twenty hours after they began their journey from Khasan, when the plane landed at Dulles. Two waiting Suburbans took the three travelers and their military escort to the safe house in Virginia.

Hwang remained in custody, shuttled off to the infirmary, where his shoulder was treated again. He was then placed under lock and key and twenty-four-hour surveillance.

Hea was treated far more cordially. She was shown to a suite where she could bathe. Fresh clothing was provided, as was a sumptuous meal. Still, there was no mistaking the fact that she too was being detained, at least for now.

Sandor was led to one of the secure offices in the basement, where Deputy Director Byrnes awaited him.

"Good to have you back," the DD said as he extended a welcoming hand.

Without so much as a hello, Sandor asked, "Any word from Bergenn yet?"

Byrnes shook his head. "Nothing. And no indication from any of our sources that Kim's people are claiming their capture. Whatever went down with Bergenn and Raabe, the North Koreans are playing this one very carefully."

Sandor sat in one of the comfortable armchairs. "That'll change. At this point they know I got Hwang out of the country. They've had the best part of a day to figure out how to approach us on that."

"Agreed."

"But they're involved in a larger plan, and they're not going to screw it up over one man."

"Unless that one man can screw it up for them."

"Exactly," Sandor said.

"Do you think he knows enough to throw a monkey wrench into the works?"

"I'm not sure," Sandor conceded. "He's certainly impressed with his own importance, I'll give him that much. I got what I could, but the circumstances were limited, if you know what I mean."

"I understand. But now we've got him here. Let's find out what else he knows."

Sandor frowned. "He's a tough old bird. And time is not on our side."

"I know. So let's see what you have."

Sandor reached in his pocket and took out the four handwritten pages of notes he had made during the flight. "Here's my report," he said as he handed the papers to Byrnes. "What have you got so far on the airliner?"

"You're up to speed on the mess at Fort Oscar?"

Sandor nodded. "I downloaded the intel from the satcom link during our flight. Have we been able to tie the two events together?"

Byrnes frowned. "Not yet. They obviously seem to be of a piece, as they say. So far it appears the bomb that took down the plane was passed through luggage coming from St. Barths into St. Maarten. Other than that, we're at a dead end."

"And I take it from what I read that our pal Jaber thinks the downed flight was a diversion?"

"I believe he really does. He thinks the operation has to do with some sort of attack on our oil reserves."

"That's consistent with what Kyung and Hwang had to say. If it's true, why take out a commercial flight and the communications hub at Fort Oscar? What sense does that make?"

Byrnes looked up from Sandor's notes. "None, as far as I'm concerned. Which is why you've got to head down there and make sense of it for us." He stood. "You want to get yourself a shower and something to eat before we go through everything?"

Sandor waved him off as he also got to his feet. "Later. First I want to know what we're going to do about Bergenn and Raabe."

Byrnes nodded. "We're working on it already, believe me."

Sandor stared at him with that look that the DD had come to recognize only too well. "I realize they may be willing to make a trade for Hwang," Sandor said. "If not, you and the Director know I'm going back to get them out myself."

CHAPTER FORTY-SIX

NEW YORK CITY

Byrnes allowed Sandor a few hours at home before he sent him off to the Caribbean. The DD arranged to have Sandor flown back to Westchester Airport and driven to his apartment on the west side of Manhattan. There Sandor packed some clothes for the trip and picked up the past week's mail from Florence, his downstairs neighbor. As with most of his assignments, Sandor could never be sure when he would return, and he couldn't have weeks of mail spilling out of the box in the small vestibule of their brownstone. Florence, an attractive African-American woman who alternated careers between waiting tables and attending casting calls, collected the assortment of catalogues and bills and watered his plants whenever he was away. She was especially devoted to Sandor, since he had once saved her from an intruder who tried to shoot his way through her front door. To this day, Sandor had not told Florence that he was actually the man's target.

"How goes the acting gig?" he asked as he sorted through the pile of envelopes she handed him.

"I have a second call from one of the network soaps."

"That's great, which one?" he asked, not that he was

likely to recognize any of the names she might have given.

"Not sure, this is through an agency."

"Is that how it's done?"

"Sometimes, I guess. It's a blind audition."

Sandor looked up from his phone bill and gave her a skeptical look. "Just make sure it's a reputable outfit, right?"

"Yes, Daddy," she said with a smile.

Sandor gathered up the papers he had ripped through and stood up. "I'll take these and get out of your way." As he walked to the door he spotted a newspaper on the credenza. "Mind if I borrow this?"

"Keep it. I've been through it already."

As he trotted upstairs, he glanced at the front page of the *Times*. A small headline, on the lower left, stopped him in his tracks. It was a report of a United States incursion into North Korea. His mission.

He entered his apartment, dropped the box of mail on the living room table, and read the article. There were no names, a lot of "allegedly" this and "reportedly" that, but it was a highly inflammatory piece, especially since Bergenn and Raabe remained in harm's way.

Then he had an idea that might just help to retrieve his friends from North Korea.

Sandor finished packing his black leather bag, tossed the S&W automatic handgun on top, and slid his Walther into his waistband holster, then ran downstairs to the waiting car and slid into the passenger seat.

"Take me to the *Times*," he told the agent at the wheel.

————————

Sandor signed in at the security desk, where they called upstairs to tell Bill Sternlich he had a visitor. Sandor rode the elevator up to his friend's office, where Bill stood to greet him.

"Man, I'm glad to see you're back safe and sound."

"Thanks," Sandor said, then slapped the copy of the newspaper on Sternlich's desk. "So what the hell do you call this?"

"Excuse me?"

"Come on, Bill, what gives here?"

Sternlich shook his head. "Frank Donaldson," he said. "Eager beaver, wants to be Woodward and Bernstein and Murrow, all rolled into one."

"That so? And where did he get this information? How the hell is he tying the airplane crash in the Caribbean to North Korea? How did he even find out about North Korea?"

Sternlich walked past Sandor and shut the door to his small office, then stood facing his friend. "You asking me if I told him something?"

Sandor puffed out his cheeks and let out an angry lungful of air. "I don't have to ask that, do I?"

"No, you don't."

"Well, get H. L. Mencken in here and I'll ask him myself."

"Come on, Jordan, he's not going to tell you anything."

"No? Well, you get him in here and let's see. Or do you want me storming around this place to find him?"

"Okay, okay," Bill said as he went for the phone. "But calm yourself down, all right?"

Sandor did not reply as Sternlich called the reporter on the intercom and asked him to come in. A minute later they were joined by Frank Donaldson.

If Sandor disliked him before they met, he positively despised him at first sight. Khaki pants, oxford blue shirt open at the neck, with a red-stripe tie hanging down and Ivy League condescension written all over his face.

"Frank, this is Jordan Sandor," Sternlich said. "He wanted to meet you."

The reporter responded with a slight smirk. "Ah, your friend from Washington, we finally meet."

Sandor, who had remained standing in the center of the small room, responded with a malicious stare that brought the younger man up short. "Where did you get this information and who the hell gave you permission to print it?" he demanded, jabbing a finger in the direction of the article that still lay on Sternlich's desk.

Donaldson looked from Sandor to Sternlich. "What is this, Bill? I don't have to answer to him."

"If you don't," Sandor growled through clenched teeth, "I'll rip out your windpipe and shove it up your ass."

The young man blanched, then made a move to leave, but Sandor was ahead of him. He positioned himself between Donaldson and the door, then grabbed a handful of blue oxford shirt.

"You can't touch me," the reporter said.

"No? Listen, Joe College, I can kill you and toss you in a hole so deep they'll never find you." Then Sandor took him by the throat, shoving him hard against the wall, driving him off his feet onto his toes. "If anything happens to my men because of this, there's nothing they'll suffer that I won't triple for you, you understand me, you little weasel?"

"Jordan!" Sternlich shouted as Donaldson began to gag.

Sandor was still staring into the reporter's terrified eyes. "If you print anything that screws up the exchange of my men for Kim's minister, I promise you, you'll answer to me." Sandor let him down and the young man grabbed at his throat.

"I'm going to file charges against you, you Neanderthal."

Sandor laughed in his face. "And say what? That you're such a pussy you pissed all over yourself?"

Donaldson looked down at the wet stain on the front of his pants, then threw the door open and ran from the room.

"Are you out of your mind?" Sternlich demanded.

"Maybe," Sandor replied angrily. "But I've still got two MIA I need to get back and I don't want this little piece of shit causing an international incident that'll end up with my men evaporating into the North Korean ether. If we don't have deniability, we'll have no bargaining chip with Pyongyang. You understand what's at stake here, Bill?"

"I think I do, Jordan, but there are proper ways to handle things and this isn't one of them."

"It is in my world. I need to know where he got his information. There's a leak, and I'm going to have to plug it fast."

"I'm telling you, this isn't the way. All you're doing is making things worse."

"Really? Well trust me on this, if I see one line in your daily rag about me or my men or any connection we have to

North Korea, your staff is going to be short one obnoxious little reporter."

"You're out of control."

"No I'm not, I know exactly what I'm doing," Sandor told him. Then, without another word, he stormed out of the office, found his way to the elevators, and rode down to the lobby, a smile on his face all the way.

CHAPTER FORTY-SEVEN

TORTOLA, BRITISH VIRGIN ISLANDS

Aᴅɪɴᴀ ᴡᴀѕ ѕᴇᴀᴛᴇᴅ comfortably on the upper deck of the yacht *Misty II* as it rocked gently at anchor in Fat Hogs Bay on the eastern side of the island of Tortola. He was entertaining two honored guests.

Antonio Bastidas was a key player in the Chavez regime. He had traveled from Caracas to join the entourage gathered in this idyllic setting to plot the destruction of the American oil industry. He was a short man in his early fifties with coarse features, a pockmarked complexion, and a crude affect that was in stark contrast to Adina's elegant style.

Eric Silfen had been born and raised in Argentina, of German descent. Tall and thin and nearing sixty, he had thinning gray hair, a slightly stooped posture, and wire-rimmed spectacles that all worked together to promote the appearance of a world-weary college professor. In fact, he was a gifted scientist with an expertise in, and almost spiritual devotion to, nuclear and conventional explosive devices.

As soon as the steward finished serving their beverages and disappeared belowdecks, Bastidas got right to the point. "Are you concerned at all about the incident in North Korea?"

Adina responded with a slight tilt of his head, as if considering the idea. "It means nothing," he said. "We should monitor that situation, of course, but our preparations are right on schedule. Timing is critical."

"No need to move faster, just in case?"

"In case of what?"

"In case the Americans learned anything," he responded impatiently.

Adina treated them to his thin-lipped smile. "What could they have learned? They're still chasing their tails in St. Maarten and St. Barths. Who would possibly be looking at the Gulf Coast?"

Bastidas, one of Chavez's pit bulls, was not so easily assuaged. "After their disaster with the BP oil spill, they're always looking at the Gulf Coast."

"Their environmental zealots are looking, not their military."

"But we have no way of knowing if this team of American assassins got to anyone in Pyongyang with information that might compromise our plans. Can you be so certain they did not?"

"Certain? No. But what could our Asian friends have told them? We are the only ones with knowledge of the ultimate targets here."

"Are you sure?"

The indulgent smile reappeared. "It was I who traveled to meet with the North Koreans, and I imparted to them the limited outline of our intentions. Our ally is satisfied that we will act with appropriate ferocity, that is enough for them to know." He paused to take a sip of his drink. "I have also been informed that two of these assassins, as you call them, have been captured. We will know very soon if any breach has occurred."

That news seemed to placate Bastidas, at least for the moment. He sat back and had a gulp of his *mojito*.

Turning to Silfen, Adina said, "Shall we review the preliminary details?"

The Argentine-cum-German reached for the leather satchel beside his chair and removed several charts, laying them out on the large table before them. "As you know, we have determined that a nuclear strike is not practical. Although we may yet have access to one or more RA-115s, the likelihood of detection is too great."

"RA-115?" Bastidas repeated.

"Yes, the so-called suitcase nuclear bombs, some of which were developed in the Soviet Union. There are still more than a hundred on the black market, but the level of radiation leakage makes them easy to identify. It is too difficult to transport them without discovery. There is also the RA-115-01, which is the submersible version, but again we face the problem of transport. Not to mention that all of these are older weapons and many of them have leaked so badly as to become ineffective."

"Ineffective?"

"Duds, as the expression goes."

"Seriously?"

"Quite," Silfen replied to the Venezuelan, his tone making it clear that he was always serious when discussing weapons. "In order for these devices to remain potent they need to remain attached to a power source or risk the loss of their potency. Wherever they were stored, keeping them hot-wired for all these years would have made them dangerous, not to mention, again, easily detected."

"I assume you are proposing a viable alternative?"

"Of course. Back in 2004, the Ahmadinejad regime experimented with underground, implosion-type devices. The North Koreans provided some of the technology for those tests, which took place in the Iranian desert. The trials would have gone unnoticed, but Kim insisted that the last one include a nuclear component. The West became incensed, the International Atomic Energy Agency stepped in, all testing was halted."

"But the results were successful?"

"Extremely," Silfen assured him. "The most interesting result was the manner in which these explosions reacted underground." He pointed to the first chart and all three men leaned forward to review a drawing composed of various waves accompanied by numbers indicating the force of the expanding blast. "There is a mechanism known as a high-voltage detonator which can be joined to an EBW. That's exploding bridgewire," he explained without looking up. "When properly positioned the result is a series of shock waves that can approximate an earthquake or cause a tidal wave, or both, depending on the size of the charge and where it is deployed."

"So," Bastidas said, "if we can launch these underground, near the refineries in the Gulf of Mexico . . ."

"We can utterly destroy both facilities," Silfen finished the thought.

"And," Adina added, "it may even be possible to make it

look as if it is a natural disaster. This is certainly not crucial to the result, but it may help to add to the initial chaos."

Bastidas was confused again, and said so.

"You see, my friend, as I said to you earlier, it is all about timing." Adina was clearly pleased with this aspect of his plan. "We are within days of the first hurricane of the season in the Gulf of Mexico. As you have likely heard there is already a tropical gale forming off to our southeast. In the next week there are predictions of more intense storms and, hopefully, we will see the usual series of hurricanes veering into the Gulf. We don't need anything reaching the power of Hugo or even the recent assault of Ike on those coastal towns. A normal Category One hurricane should be quite sufficient to cover our tracks and, if it does not, there will be little remaining of our efforts to give the Americans any way to credibly fix the blame. They will have suspicions and accusations, of course, but the damage will have been done. That is the main thing."

Bastidas continued to study the first chart, as if there were something else he should understand. He finally sat back, lifted his cocktail, and said, "Surely these refineries have defenses in place for this sort of attack."

"Surely," Adina agreed pleasantly. "But we have three advantages in our little chess match. First, we are in the process of gathering inside information on those security mechanisms. Second, by taking out the communications center in Fort Oscar we have damaged the surveillance capabilities of the American military in the area. Not crippled them, I admit, but at least slowed them down. They still have naval reconnaissance and satellite capability, but we have helped our cause." He paused to take a sip of his cocktail.

"You said three," Bastidas reminded him.

"Ah yes. With Fort Oscar down, we can deliver these charges by submarine. It will be far more difficult for them to detect our movements until it is too late to prevent the attack."

"Submarine?"

Adina offered up another version of his thin-lipped smile. "A nice touch, don't you think?"

CHAPTER FORTY-EIGHT

MARAND, IRAN

AFTER THREE DAYS in custody Rasa Jaber was beyond hope. Her husband had fled to the United States without her. Her captors refused to believe she had no knowledge of his defection or the reasons behind it. Her life had become a jumble of fear, disappointment, isolation, and betrayal.

She sat on the cement floor of a windowless cell, her arms clutched tightly around her knees as she hunched in the corner, struggling to make sense of all this. After the initial interrogation, which had lasted more than twenty-four uninterrupted hours, she was tossed into this hole and left here. Alone. Stripped naked, she felt the rough concrete against the tender skin of her bottom every time she moved, a reminder of the utter degradation she was suffering. They had not tortured her. They had not beaten her. They had simply deprived her of her dignity and of any human contact. Her food, such as it was, came through a slot in the large, thick metal door once a day, or what she guessed to be once a day. She had no idea how long she had been there. She existed in total darkness, without sanitation or running water. It was warm and dank and she was sickened by the foul odor of the tiny room.

And so she endured her captivity, grappling with the loss of her faith and the desperation of her circumstances, wondering what miserable fate awaited her.

They could yet subject her to unimaginable agony but she would not tell them anything because she had nothing to tell. They could execute her at any time they chose—her husband had been with the IRGC from its inception and she knew that words did not exist to describe the ruthlessness of their techniques. Who would know how she died, or even that she had been murdered? She would simply disappear, like so many others before her.

But they were keeping her alive so far, she told herself again and again as the moments dragged on with cruel monotony, and there must be a reason for that.

As she engaged in what had become an interminable debate over her existence, there was a noise outside that made her start. It was too soon for them to be delivering another small plate of barely edible food, she was sure of that. She heard another sound, metal scraping against metal, and she thought the large bolt to the door was being pulled back. Suddenly the room was filled with light, blinding her as she raised her arms to her face.

"Stand," a voice ordered her.

She hesitated, huddling in the corner, her arms crossed in a vain attempt to cover her nudity as best she could. Then they tossed something at her, a single garment of coarse material, not worthy of being called a dressing gown, more like something one might be given in a hospital for indigents. She gathered it around her and rose, unsteadily, still trying to adjust her eyes in the glare, barely making out the three men who stood in the entrance.

"Come with us."

When she did not move one of the men stepped forward and grabbed her roughly by the arm. They led her down the hallway, then up a flight of stairs, where she stumbled twice. They dragged her along, finally shoving her into the room where she had first been questioned.

They sat her at the same table in the same straight-backed metal chair she had occupied for a day and a night while alternating teams of inquisitors had worked her over. Without a word, the three guards then turned and left her there, shutting and locking the door behind them. She remained alone for a few minutes, using the time to gather herself for what might come. Was this the end? If so, why bring her back here?

Then the door opened and two men walked in and sat opposite her. She had never seen these two before, at least she did not recall them. One appeared to be in his thirties, the other a decade or so older. They were handsomely dressed in suits and ties, their appearance stern, their eyes unfriendly.

"You have nothing to tell us," the older man said. "Is this true?"

Rasa blinked, then pushed some of her dirty, unkempt hair from her forehead. She did not speak.

"Come, come, woman. Answer the question."

"I am not sure what you are asking me," she replied nervously.

"Your husband," the younger man said impatiently, "has betrayed his country, gone to the sworn enemy of our people, left you behind. What do you know of all this?"

"I only know what you have told me. You have shown me photographs of Ahmad with the Americans."

"Yes, yes, and you knew nothing of his leaving the country to travel there, this is all you have to tell us?"

She nodded slowly, tears forming in her dark eyes. "I don't know anything, I really don't."

The younger man, raising his voice for the first time, shouted, "What you *do* know is that your husband abandoned you. Left you behind to face the consequences of his treachery."

Rasa remained silent as the older man placed a calming hand on his associate's forearm. Then he said, "You have a choice to make. You can die for your husband's betrayal of his country and his God, or you can atone for these sins."

Looking back and forth between these two men, Rasa Jaber hesitated, then finally said, "Tell me what you want me to do."

CHAPTER FORTY-NINE

ST. BARTHÉLEMY, F.W.I.

JORDAN SANDOR HAD been to St. Barths once before. It was on Company business, with a team that included Beth Sharrow from Financial Ops. That was a few years ago, when they thought they might have a future together, and so, once their assignment was concluded, they ended up spending a long, romantic weekend on the island. They stayed in a beachfront bungalow at Guanahani, and Sandor remembered the place fondly enough to book himself in there again, this time at government expense.

He had come to survey the damage at Fort Oscar, to make some sense of what the hell was going on in the Caribbean, and to visit a friend.

Arriving at the small airport, Sandor collected his bag, then proceeded to the booth that served as the customs and immigration checkpoint. Unlike that earlier visit, when a single attendant gave his passport a perfunctory stamp, today there were now three officers on duty, and an armed French soldier at the baggage claim area.

"You are here for business or pleasure?" one of the customs officers inquired in French.

Sandor grinned. "Does anyone come to St. Barths on business?"

The uniformed man looked up from the entry form and treated Sandor to a French scowl. He was obviously not amused. "*Monsieur,*" he said impatiently.

Sandor nodded. "*Plaisir,*" he replied.

"You have checked any luggage?"

"No, just this," Sandor said, holding up his black leather bag.

Sandor thought he might need to reach for his diplomatic papers, something he had hoped to avoid, but a soldier stepped up behind him and said to the immigration officer, "*Bonjour,* Jean-Pierre." Then he added something Sandor did not understand, his facility with the French language being rudimentary at best.

The customs officer responded by stamping the form and having another look at Sandor. "*Plaisir,*" he said derisively, then returned the passport and waved him on.

Sandor turned to face the uniformed soldier who had just saved him from any further bureaucratic entanglements. He had a handsome, intelligent face and dark, cautious eyes. His left arm was in a sling.

"Welcome to the new St. Barths, Mr. Sandor," the man said in heavily accented English.

"*Merci beaucoup.*"

Lieutenant Henri Vauchon responded with a warm smile. "I had a feeling I would be seeing you."

"Who else would they send, lieutenant? I have the advantage of knowing my way around here."

"And, of course, knowing me."

"*Mais oui.*"

Vauchon chuckled. "What say we do without your feeble attempts to speak my language, eh?"

Sandor also laughed. "Done," he conceded as the two friends shook hands. "We'll deal with your lousy English instead."

Vauchon pointed ahead and they began walking toward the parking area.

"I had no idea you were going to meet me at the airport, Henri. I'm truly honored."

"Time, as you Americans say, is of the essence."

"Yes, it is," Sandor agreed. "How's the shoulder?"

"Like a large toothache in my side. I'll live."

"So what are your orders?"

"I have been ordered to give you my full cooperation."

Sandor smiled. "Okay then, can you introduce me to a good-looking blonde in a bikini?"

"Perhaps later, yes? First we should drop your things at the hotel, then I'll take you to Fort Oscar."

"I'm going to need my own car at some point."

"We have arranged that. For now you will ride with me."

"Perfect," Sandor replied. "Let's go."

———

When they reached Vauchon's car the Frenchman removed his arm from the sling, assured Sandor that he was fine to drive, then set off for the pleasant ride up and down the hills of St. Jean, along the narrow roads of Lorient and the climb above the Grand Cul-de-Sac. They reminisced about the assignment that brought Sandor here the first time.

"I'm sorry about the circumstances of our reunion."

"Yes," Vauchon said somberly. Then, "I heard about Beth. How is she?"

"Recovering." He paused. "She's fine physically, but the attack left other scars."

"I understand. My shoulder, for instance, is the least of my concerns."

They pulled into the Guanahani resort and Vauchon waited in the car while his friend checked into a beachfront villa. Once inside, Sandor quickly changed into linen slacks and a Tommy Bahama shirt that draped over his drawstring waistband to secrete the Walther he had holstered at the small of his back. He had used the diplomatic papers Byrnes provided to pass his weapons through security in New York and St. Maarten, not wanting to embarrass Vauchon, whose superiors might balk at providing the American a gun on his arrival.

He returned to the car, and they headed back along the same road, past the airport and into Gustavia.

After some pleasantries about the sensational views from almost anywhere on the island and the changes St. Barths had experienced since becoming the "it" place for the rich and famous, Sandor got down to business. "Heard it was a rough fight."

"It was."

"They tell me you did well."

"Not well enough," Vauchon replied glumly. "Perhaps if we had been more alert there might have been less fighting and more survivors."

"Way I heard it, you were responsible for saving all the lives that could have been saved. Without you . . ." he said, then stopped to let the thought hang there a moment.

"I did what I could," Vauchon said simply. "I only wish I could have done more. Every time I think of those innocent people being held hostage on my watch I get sick to my stomach. I wonder if I did the right thing, the choices I made."

Sandor nodded, no stranger to second-guessing those split-second decisions that have to be made in combat. "Tell me what happened, from the beginning, everything you saw and heard and did."

The drive into town did not take long, so when they reached the main port Vauchon pulled the car to a stop along the quay. They sat there as the lieutenant took his time describing the assault on Fort Oscar, giving every detail he could recall about that night. He found Sandor's questions far more incisive and relevant than his debriefing in Guadeloupe, and he answered all of them. He also decided to share his final exchange with the man he believed had led the assault.

"At the end, after the explosion, there was chaos all around, as I am sure you can imagine. I did my best to help the people below, but once the explosions were ignited there was fire and heat and smoke everywhere." Sandor watched silently as the man grappled with the memory. "And then one man staggered to the opening by the stairway. He was bloodied and dazed, but I knew his voice from our exchanges. We had spoken over the radio, back and forth, when I tried to convince them to give up. He was on the floor and I dragged him to the stairs, but he knew he was dying. He told me his name was Renaldo. Then he said that he had been betrayed. He told me that his men had not set off the explosives, that it must have been done remotely."

Sandor waited, still not speaking.

"He said Adina had done this. I believe the name was Adina."

The recognition in Sandor's eyes was apparent, so Vauchon went on.

"Then he said something about a bay, or a town by a bay. I tried to get him to speak some more, but that was it. Another explosion rocked us from below. I was thrown to the floor. By the time I got back to him he was dead."

Sandor leaned back and gazed straight ahead. "Adina," he said with a nod. "That confirms our intel. And this bay, he didn't say where, or give a name of a bay, there was nothing else?"

Vauchon shook his head. "No, nothing else, that was all. I'm sorry this information was not made available sooner, but my commanding officer, to whom I gave this report, he is a bit, uh, shall I say, cautious."

Sandor turned to Vauchon. "Henri, you have absolutely nothing to be sorry about, believe me. I know all about commanding officers. What happened next?"

The Frenchman went on about the evacuation of the survivors and all that followed. When he was done, the sun was low in the sky, and he asked if Sandor would like something to eat or drink before they reached the fort.

"Later," Sandor said. "I want to see as much as I can in the daylight."

Vauchon started the car and pulled back onto the road, saying, "I am not sure how much there will be for you to see, with or without light."

As they drove around Gustavia harbor, the walls of Fort

Oscar were visible. What could not be seen, until they pulled up to the parking area just below the fortress and approached the main gate, was the extent of the damage done by the explosions. The guards on duty immediately recognized Vauchon and passed him and his guest through. Once inside the perimeter walls the detritus of the attack was everywhere.

Sandor approached the jagged opening that was once a doorway to the lower levels. "This is it?"

Vauchon nodded. "It may not be safe to use those metal steps. The engineers are still examining the situation."

"I'll be all right, you stay here. You've drawn me a pretty good map, I'll find my way."

The lieutenant had one of his men hand Sandor a flashlight, then stepped aside as the American made his way below.

The lingering smell of burned wiring and plastic and rubber, along with the stench of the charred bodies that had been removed, filled Sandor's nostrils as he maneuvered down the twisted staircase. One of the metal struts gave way as he neared the bottom, and he managed to grab the handrail and jump the distance of about six stairs to the floor below, just before the steps collapsed beneath him.

"You all right down there?" Vauchon called out when he heard the crash of metal and the thud of Sandor hitting the deck.

"Never better," came the reply.

Sandor moved forward with the flashlight, entering the remains of what had once been a high-tech computer center and was now just a cave lined with mangled steel and shattered electronic equipment. He had never seen the Fort

Oscar communications center when it was in operation, but even if he had, he realized that none of it would be recognizable now.

He walked around, searching for something, anything that might help him understand the why of this attack. All of the bodies had been removed, including the terrorists. All of the weapons were gone. Sandor shone the light on the metal floor and along the walls. It had obviously been an intensely hot chemical firebomb and, from what he had been told back in Langley and this afternoon by Vauchon, the worst of the carnage had been in the level below. He stepped to that opening and peered down. The remains of those stairs were worse than the ones above. He shoved the flashlight in his pocket, beam pointing up, splashing an eerie light across the ceiling as he climbed down, grasping whatever was left of the railings and supports and steel girders that now protruded from the damaged wall. At the end he made another short leap to the floor, then removed the light from his pocket and had a look around.

This room had certainly suffered the larger explosion. He took his time, sweeping the floors with the beam of the flashlight, checking the bent and twisted remnants of what had been desktops and workstations, not knowing what he was looking for or what he might find. And then, beneath what had apparently been a printer stand, wedged up against the corner where it could not be seen unless the light was shined directly on it, he spotted something. Bending down and reaching in, he found a cell phone. Apparently protected from the blast by the support panels of the metal rack, it was in fairly good shape. Whose phone was it? Sandor wondered.

Why would a worker on duty here have a cell phone out, unless they reached for it when the attack began? No, he decided, the terrorists would have quickly ensured that no one had access to the outside. No, it was far more likely to have belonged to one of the attackers.

He shoved the phone in his back pocket and continued his search, finally giving in to the odor and the futility and the sense of death all around him. When he was done, he climbed back up through the stairway shaft, hopeful he had at least discovered one thing that could help.

CHAPTER FIFTY

AN ESTATE OUTSIDE LANGLEY, VIRGINIA

AHMAD JABER HAD little to do to pass these end-less days other than to contemplate his uncertain fate. What had he expected when he put himself in the hands of these faithless Americans? He should have known better, he told himself.

The information Seyed Asghari had provided was suf-ficient to convince Jaber he had no option but to flee. Still, he should have realized that the intelligence Seyed imparted would not be enough to bargain with the CIA for a comfort-able future. He and Seyed had correctly guessed that the col-laborators were North Koreans and Venezuelans. But Jaber had no details of the planned strike because Seyed had never received those particulars.

With one exception.

The only thing Jaber had yet withheld from Byrnes was the general area of the intended attack. It remained the final currency he had to trade.

He knew it did not amount to much for at least two rea-sons. First, it was less than specific. Second, it might not even be true—it might have been disinformation passed to Seyed until he proved he could be trusted. And yet it was all Jaber had left to offer.

With his own prospects at risk, he now had the added concern of his wife. He struggled with the images of what they might have already done to her, what they might be doing to her at this very moment. The torture, the indignities—he fought to dismiss those pictures from his mind even as he wrestled with the possibility that she might already be dead. Here he was, seated in a comfortable armchair in the guest room of the CIA safe house that had become his new home. He knew that Rasa would be shown no such courtesy. She was the wife of a traitor and she had been caught in an attempt to escape from Iran. How could he have been so foolish to think his plan would work? His wife deserved better than the fate to which he had condemned her.

His anguished reverie was interrupted by a sharp knock at the door. He listened as the lock turned, remaining seated as Byrnes walked in.

"We have word from our agent in the Caribbean," the Deputy Director said without preamble.

"Sandor?"

Byrnes ignored the question. "Let me be as clear as possible here. If you're not able to assist us at this point then you've got nothing to sell."

The former IRGC officer did not reply.

The Deputy Director fixed him with a stern look. "You came here with the vaguest bunch of crap I've ever had a defector try to peddle. Since you've become a guest in our little bed-and-breakfast we've lost a commercial airliner and a major communications center. You gave us no warning, nothing to help prevent these attacks. Now it appears this may only be the beginning of a new wave of terrorism, and all you can tell me is that someone from the East has made a deal with someone from the West?"

"My wife . . . ," he began, but Byrnes cut him off with a wave of his hand.

"I don't give a damn about your wife. I want answers."

Jaber stood slowly and faced him. "If I tell you . . ."

The Deputy Director cut him off again. "There is no 'if' here, Jaber. You have no bargaining leverage, no trading power. If you have anything else to say you better say it now or I'll have you driven into D.C. and dropped off in front of the nearest mosque. You'll be dead in an hour and I won't blink."

Jaber actually managed a smile. "And so, Mr. Byrnes, you see that in the end we are all the same."

"Spare me the lecture."

The Iranian nodded. "The Gulf of Mexico," he said. "It's all I have."

Byrnes did not reveal that he had already received preliminary information from Sandor he would be trying to match up with anything Jaber told him. "That's it?"

"That's it. And I admit to you, before you ask, that I have no way of knowing whether Seyed was told the truth. But if he was, the attack is planned for somewhere along the American coast in the Gulf of Mexico. It's all I have left."

Byrnes stood there and thought about what Sandor had just related to him by secure satellite phone from Gustavia. "Well," he finally said, "it may be something we can work with."

Jaber hoped that the last piece of information he yet withheld would be enough to save him when the time came for his final plea.

CHAPTER FIFTY-ONE

ST. BARTHÉLEMY, F.W.I.

Sandor invited Vauchon to dinner at Maya's and the lieutenant readily accepted. As a modestly paid officer in the French army, a visit to Maya's was well beyond his pay grade. Not only is it regarded as the best restaurant on the island but it is also one of the priciest, even by the absurdly expensive standards of St. Barths. Still, it manages to be an unpretentious spot, set on a small jetty along the water in Gustavia, just across the main harbor from Fort Oscar. The tables are situated beneath a series of large cream-colored tents where the balmy night air is augmented by onshore breezes. The menu changes from night to night, depending on the available produce and seafood, not to mention the whims of the owner and her staff, who work in the kitchen that is set in a small building just off to the side of the entrance. The young waitresses are energetic, friendly, and a delight to watch in their minimalist island attire, leaving no shortage of scenery in any direction you look.

Sandor arrived late. He was greeted at the entrance by Randy, a tall, affable American who plays host, proprietor, sommelier, and translator for the daily bill of fare. He is also husband to the eponymous chef and his co-owner, Maya.

Randy led Sandor to a table on the deck just above the edge of the sandy shore, where Vauchon was already waiting.

"Glad to see you've opted for a relaxed look," Sandor said with a grin as he admired the Frenchman's flowered linen shirt and casual pants. "Uniforms tend to get on my nerves after a while."

"Mine too," Vauchon admitted with a smile.

Sandor had a quick look around the open space, then pointed to a table toward the rear. "Mind if we switch?"

Randy cordially obliged, showed them to their seats in the rear, then suggested cocktails. Vauchon politely declined.

"Come on, Henri," Jordan goaded him.

"How about a bottle of Domaines Ott," Randy suggested, and Vauchon agreed.

"But I need something to prime the pump," Sandor said. "Grey Goose, straight up with a twist of lemon, and a few slivers of floating ice to keep it nice and cold." He looked to Vauchon. "You aren't really going to let me drink alone?"

"Ah well," the Frenchman agreed with a nod.

Randy nodded approvingly, then went off to fetch their drinks.

"So," Vauchon said, "you always have to sit with your back to the wall, eh? Even when it isn't really a wall."

Sandor smiled. "Tradecraft," he said. "View of the room, no one behind me, a good look at the harbor." He gazed across the water, the imposing stone walls of Fort Oscar awash in the glow of the spotlights that shone up from the ground, just the same as they did every night. "Hard to believe anything happened there at all," he said.

Vauchon shared the view for a moment, then said wistfully, "For me more than for you, I can assure you."

Sandor nodded.

"I presume, after I left you at Guanahani, that you reported what I said to your superiors."

"Yes."

Sandor had phoned Byrnes and related everything he learned from Vauchon and his inspection of the fort. Sandor then contacted the technical support team that had traveled from Washington to St. Barths the previous day. He gave them the damaged cell phone, explaining the possibility that it may have belonged to one of the terrorists. Despite the heat damage they believed they might be able to trace the numbers recently called and received.

Just before Sandor headed to Gustavia for his dinner with Vauchon he heard back from the DD. Thus far, Hwang had been a tough nut to crack. They had gotten nothing more than the information Sandor elicited from him and Kyung back in North Korea—the confirmation of some covert alliance between Pyongyang and Venezuela. Piecing that together with the information they had from Vauchon and Jaber, they were focusing their attention on Baytown, Texas, home to one of the two largest oil refineries in the United States.

"Now," the Deputy Director said, "all we need to do is determine if this information is accurate or part of another elaborate ruse. If there's any truth to it at all you need to uncover what, precisely, is being planned."

"Is that all?" Sandor replied.

The DD said nothing; he just hung up.

The martinis were served and Vauchon made a traditional French toast to Jordan's health. Sandor returned the favor. The drink was cold enough, the air balmy, and the scenery spectacular. Then, taking a second swallow as he had a look around at the privileged group that crowded the other tables, Sandor spotted them walking in.

St. Barths is a truly international playground, where you are as likely to meet a tycoon from Abu Dhabi or Moscow as a celebrity from Los Angeles or New York. Sandor was not sure what drew his attention to the two Hispanic-looking men being seated at a table toward the front of the restaurant, but his instincts told him that something about them did not fit.

He continued to scan the place, as if looking for someone he knew, not allowing his gaze to settle on them. Then he turned to Vauchon and said with a broad smile, "I love this place, had a great time last visit here."

The Frenchman nodded as he finished a sip of vodka.

"Don't take your eyes from me, just keep smiling," Sandor told him in a casual tone, "then I want you to glance at the two men to your right, at that table up front. They're just sitting down. Give them a quick glimpse."

Vauchon did as he was told, then looked at a couple of other tables and returned his attention to Sandor.

"Well done, Henri. You see, it pays to have the proper seat."

"I suppose it does."

"So, you ever see either of them before?"

Vauchon shook his head.

"But they don't belong here at Maya's, you agree?"

"I think you are right," he said. Then he waited.

"Adina is the name used by Rafael Cabello," Sandor told him. "He's one of the most trusted men in Chavez's inner circle. We believe your information is correct, that Adina was behind the attack on Fort Oscar. And possibly the downed flight from St. Maarten. Assuming those things are true, consider why he might leave people behind. What would they be looking for?"

Vauchon nodded to himself, mulling it over. "Maybe to see what we do next?"

"Maybe," Sandor allowed, taking another swig of the frosty drink. "Or perhaps to see who might be doing it."

"Perhaps."

"Which means we need to find out who they are and what they expect to gain from that information."

"You mean bring them in for questioning?"

"Uh, I don't think so."

Vauchon gave him a curious look.

"You have no probable cause to interfere with their vacation here."

Vauchon smiled. "I am a French soldier investigating a terrorist attack, not a policeman."

"Understood. Then let's just say that bringing them in is not likely to net you any useful information. At least not anytime soon. Best you leave this to me."

Vauchon responded with a concerned look. He had seen Sandor in action before.

————

Sandor and Vauchon enjoyed a sumptuous dinner. The lieutenant ordered the *sashimi de thon* for his appetizer, then the *côte de veau Poêlée*. Jordan began with the *salade de concombre Créole* and, for his *plat principal*, the *crevettes au curry jaune*.

After finishing his martini Sandor was careful not to share too much of the wine, knowing how easily Domaines Ott can flow in this tropical climate. He was on full alert now and, while he and Vauchon continued to discuss the events at Fort Oscar, Sandor remained aware of the two men at the front table.

After finishing with a delicious lemon tart and espresso, Sandor paid the check and they prepared to leave. Sandor was not surprised to see that the two men called for their bill as soon as he asked for his. As they waited for the check, Sandor said, "I need you to do something for me." He explained, and Vauchon looked concerned.

"It'll be fine," Sandor told him.

Vauchon stood, then led the way to the front, where they bid each other good night.

"I'll check in with you in the morning," he said.

"Are you sure you don't need my help finding your way home?"

Sandor smiled. "I'll be fine. St. Barths is really just one long road, right? Anyway, if I get lost it's a beautiful night for a drive." Then without waiting for a reply he headed for his car, moving more quickly now as he got behind the wheel and started the small Suzuki 4x4.

The road to Maya's is a long, narrow lane. As Sandor drove up the hill above the port, the two men from the restaurant climbed into their car and started off. Vauchon had pulled out of his parking space and made a show of stalling his car for a moment as he kept them from moving around him.

Sandor had reached the crest of the road, a vantage point from which he watched approvingly as Vauchon delayed their pursuit. Then Sandor pulled off to the side, turned off the engine and lights, and waited.

If the two men intended to follow him they had already done a lousy job, thanks primarily to Vauchon's interference. When the lieutenant finally moved out of their way, they raced ahead in the direction Sandor had traveled. It's tough to lose someone on an island this small, but they rode up and back on the street along the harbor, not spotting Sandor as he sat in an area beside a stone wall along a short residential driveway. They finally stopped for a moment, apparently considering their next move, then turned in the direction leading from Gustavia toward St. Jean. As Sandor had noted, there is really only one main artery passing through the heart of the island. That meant it was difficult to determine what they had planned but easy to follow them. They might already know he was staying at Guanahani and be heading there, or they might be giving up their search for the night and returning to their own place. All he could do was keep his distance and watch.

Sandor stayed well behind them as they passed the airport and made their way to the other side of the island. They slowed at one point, and Sandor stopped and pulled into the parking lot adjacent to one of the nightclubs in Lorient. His main advantage was that most of the rental cars on the island looked alike. It would be tough for them to spot him as he resumed his pursuit, especially in the dark.

After a minute or so he pulled out. At the right fork that would have led to Guanahani, they turned left instead. Sandor slowed again and watched as they climbed the hill toward Pointe Milou. He knew the island well enough to take a side road that would lead him around to the same area. As he came from the right and over the rise that brought him back on course, he saw their car descending a steep driveway to a villa that was situated on a cliff overlooking the sea.

Sandor did not know that it was the villa Adina's men, Cardona and Hicham, had rented more than a week before. So far the French authorities had not identified Hicham from the plane crash, nor the place he stayed on the island.

Sandor pulled onto a narrow sandy shoulder, killed the lights and the engine, then stepped into the warm, breezy night. They had not gone to his hotel, meaning that they were satisfied to give him up for tonight, perhaps intending to make a move on him tomorrow.

But for them, tomorrow would be too late.

Sandor had his Walther, a spare magazine, and a silencer he had been given by the advance team sent by Byrnes. He climbed atop the rocks that sat above the complex of small buildings perched below him. He could not see much once the two men left their car and entered the compound. He had no way of knowing if there were more of them inside.

But it didn't matter.

He had come here for answers and he was determined to get them.

CHAPTER FIFTY-TWO

BAYTOWN, TEXAS

Peter Amendola was having a hard time sleeping. He rolled over for what seemed the hundredth time that night and squinted at the digital display on the bedroom clock.

Just after 3 A.M.

He quietly slid from beneath the sheets, pulled on his robe, and stepped into his slippers, then stole silently downstairs to the basement.

As he sat at the small metal desk in the corner of the room he wondered what the hell he had been thinking. He had never really bought the story about corporate espionage. After all, the refineries of the world were one huge conglomerate now, or at least the American companies were. Competition among oil companies? That ended forty years ago when two gas stations at the same intersection would cut their gas prices, give away coffee mugs, then wipe your windshield and check the oil. Now, he knew, prices were fixed in backroom deals. The giants of the industry remained giants and their pampered executives lived happy, pampered lives.

What the hell had he been thinking?

Amendola unlocked the desk drawer on the left, pulled

it all the way out, and set it on the floor. Then he reached into the back of the opening and removed a large metal box, setting it on the desk. He lifted the lid and stared at the contents. There were neat piles of hundred-dollar bills that already totaled well over $120,000. Sitting atop the money was a stack of papers he had collected over the past two days, papers that disclosed various aspects of the Baytown refinery defense system.

He knew, of course, that there were far more elaborate plans he would never have access to. He assumed his handlers would realize that as well. He only hoped that those other systems were sophisticated enough to do what they were intended to do, which was to protect the complex even after the information he was about to pass along came into the hands of the wrong people.

The wrong people. He almost laughed out loud as he silently repeated the phrase to himself.

He realized that he had somehow become one of the wrong people.

An attack on Baytown? It seemed unthinkable, but that had to be what these men were planning. Up to now he had been paid large amounts of cash for relatively innocuous data. But here he was, staring down at schematics for perimeter defenses and counteroffensive technology, much of which he didn't even understand. Who else would want this sort of information? Who would pay all this money for it unless they meant to use it? Who would threaten the life of his family to force him to get it?

"What are you doing down here, Peter?"

The shock of her voice, cutting through the silence of

night, stood him bolt upright from his chair, his left hand slamming the lid of the strongbox shut as he turned to face her.

"Uh, sorry, sweetheart, I tried not to wake you."

"You didn't," she said. "I turned over and you weren't there." Her eyes moved from him to the drawer that was sitting on the carpeted floor, then to the box on the desk. "What are you doing?" she asked him again.

He could not look her in the eyes, so he fidgeted with the sash on his terrycloth robe.

"I'll tell you what I'm doing, I'm working too damn hard, that's what I'm doing. Just came down here to think, is all. And what I think is that we need a vacation. That's what this family needs, a vacation together."

She stared at him for a moment, then slowly began nodding. "Maybe you're right. Maybe we do."

"Yeah, I worry about things at the refinery day and night, can't even sleep anymore. Been a while since we've gotten away. I have four weeks of vacation time coming. Be good for Thomas too, right?"

His wife pursed her lips as if giving it some thought. "Sure," she agreed. "That'd be nice."

"Good, good," he said.

"Well come on, let's go back to bed, we'll talk about it in the morning."

"You go ahead," he told her. "I'll be right up."

She hesitated. "You're sure you're all right?"

"Go on. I'll just be a minute."

After his wife left him alone again he sat down and gazed at the metal box without opening it. What choice did he have, other than to turn over these plans? If he went to the authorities he would have to admit what he had done. He would be ruined. He would probably go to jail. Not to mention that they would never be able to protect him and his family from the recriminations that might come. He couldn't just hide, he knew that these were the sort of people who would find him. Or his wife. Or children.

He had no choice, he knew that. These were serious people. The money, the attitude, the threat, it was all clear to him now. He had no choice. Tomorrow he would give them what they wanted. Then, as soon as he could arrange things at work without raising any suspicion, he would take two weeks of vacation and get away. Whatever was going to happen, he hoped that it would happen while he was gone.

CHAPTER FIFTY-THREE

ST. BARTHÉLEMY, F.W.I.

SANDOR FELT HE had waited long enough. It was after 2 A.M. and, as best as he could see from his aerie, all of the main lights in the compound had been out for more than an hour and there was no movement in the villa. It appeared that a young woman resided in the small structure nearest the driveway entrance. She was likely a housekeeper, and though he could not tell whether she lived alone, her lights had also been out for some time. He had neither seen nor heard a dog, which was a good thing under the circumstances, since the last thing he needed was a frisky animal waking everyone to announce his arrival. He thought he saw a cat—he hated cats, but at least cats are quiet.

The star-filled sky had enough clouds to provide him the cover of inky darkness as he made his approach.

With the cylindrical silencer already attached to the barrel of his PPK he began his climb down. There was no way he could determine if the driveway had motion or light sensors in place, so the outside route along the edge of the cliff made the most sense. In the event anyone was still awake it would also give him the best opportunity to arrive unseen.

The sheer drop to the Caribbean was off to his left. The

assortment of unfriendly rocks below was more than eighty feet down, the seascape illuminated with halogen lighting just above the waterline. Fortunately that lighting helped him navigate his descent as he continued along the craggy route he had chosen. He stayed well away from the edge, eventually finding his way to a flat area just above an artificial waterfall that splashed noisily into an infinity-style swimming pool that extended all the way to the precipice and seemed to disappear into the horizon. He said a silent thanks for the sound of the running water as it helped conceal his descent.

He was now only eight or so feet above the deck level, and he squatted behind a cluster of prickly shrubs to check the layout. A large patio ran from the edge of the pool and led to a spacious dining and living area open on two sides. The only light came from low-voltage fixtures around the base of the concrete decking. The kitchen, which was also an open-air design, was set off to the right and beyond that were separate structures he assumed to be the bedrooms.

Each of them was dark.

No one was in sight.

Sandor lowered himself onto the patio, then moved toward the first bedroom, off to the right of the pool. Keep it simple, he figured, pick door number one and go for it.

Unfortunately, the entrance to the room was a large, glass sliding door, making silent intrusion impractical. Behind the glass panels were floor-to-ceiling drapes that blocked any view of the interior. So he crouched down and crept past the kitchen entrance and into an outdoor corridor paved with tiles and lined with flowers he was certain offered a blinding assortment of color in the daylight, but for now just created an uneven wall of shadows as the walkway lighting cast its dim glow upward. Here, on the other side of the building, he found a normal, prehung hinged door leading into what appeared to be the rear of this first suite. If the sea air had rusted the metal, there would be a creaky announcement of his next move—but that was a chance he had to take. He took firm hold of the ceramic lever handle with his left hand and turned it down. Silence. He waited an instant, then slowly pushed, his PPK close to his side at chest height, just in case he met any surprises. The door cooperated, not making a sound as he swung it open just far enough to slide through. He took several quick looks ahead and over his shoulders, now aware of the rhythmic breathing coming from whoever was sleeping inside. He stepped into the room and eased the door shut behind him, using as much care as he had in opening it.

Sandor was in almost total darkness now and gave his eyes a moment to adjust. Then he acted swiftly, his rubber-soled shoes quiet on the terra-cotta floor as he traversed a short foyer and entered the bedroom. There he found the man lying on his side, sound asleep. Sandor leaned over and, in one quick move, pinched the man's nose with his left hand, causing him to open his mouth wide as he gasped for air, giving Sandor the opportunity to shove the barrel of the silencer down his throat.

The man reflexively grabbed for Sandor's wrist, but Sandor responded by pulling back the hammer on the PPK. The sound caused the man to stop moving.

"Now," Sandor whispered as he used his weight and the

strength in his right arm to pin the man down, "if you struggle, if you try to move before I tell you to move, if you do anything other than make me happy, this peashooter goes off whether I want it to or not, your brains are guacamole, and I'm on my way to room number two. You speak English, yes? Ah, ah, ah, don't try to talk yet, just hold up your left hand, one finger for yes, two for no."

The finger he held up was intended to convey more than "Yes."

"Now, now, no reason to be bitter." Sandor continued to speak in a soft voice, keeping their encounter as quiet as possible and forcing the man to concentrate on what he was saying. "All I need are a few simple answers, then you can go back to sleep. Please tell me you're going to cooperate or I won't waste another minute here, *comprende*?"

Even in the darkness he could see the man's angry eyes glaring at him.

"Now, tell me how many of you are here in this villa."

The man held up his left hand.

"Easy, big guy."

When he slowly spread out his five fingers, Sandor shook his head. "See, I know you're lying, and that really upsets me." He leaned on the Walther again and the man gagged as the metal drove into the back of his throat. "You want another chance?"

The man held up two fingers.

"Very good. Now I want you to tell me who you're working for. Do your best to speak now, but keep your voice low so I don't have to shove this barrel through the back of your neck."

The man responded with a guttural sound, so Sandor encouraged him to have another try. This time, it sounded something like "You're a dead man."

Sandor shook his head impatiently. "Uh huh. Well, just in case you haven't been keeping score, asshole, you're the one with the wrong end of the gun stuck in his mouth. So here we go," and he applied more pressure until blood became visible around the edges of the man's lips. "One more time, I want you to tell me who you work for. And remember, these are the easy questions, because I already know the answers. I'm just testing, see?"

The man winced, then managed something that sounded like "Adina."

"That's right, that's very good. You see, now you get to keep playing." Sandor thought he heard something moving outside. He gave a quick glance, then returned to his prisoner. "So, after your playmates blew up Fort Oscar and killed all those innocent people, why exactly would Adina still have you here?"

"I hope it's to kill you," the man hissed.

"Well, you're doing a helluva job, then. No kidding, I can see you're very good at this. And why would Adina want you to kill me?"

"I hope he orders me to kill all of you," the man said.

"So it's not personal, then, you just want to kill anyone having dinner at Maya's?" Sandor shook his head. "Look, I don't want you to feel insulted by this, but it seems like you're telling me you haven't been given that order yet, am I right? I mean, if you had instructions to take me out, you and your friend could have made a move earlier tonight, but you didn't. You didn't even go to my hotel after dinner. So I'm guessing there must be another reason you're here. Is Uncle Adina coming back to bring you and your pal to the festivities up north?"

The man did not respond.

"I want you to tell me about Baytown, and I want you to tell me right now."

The man's eyes betrayed no sense of recognition at the mention of Baytown.

"Your clock is running out and I promise, if you don't tell me what I want to know, your pal in the other bedroom will, and you're the one who won't be showing up for breakfast."

The room was quiet enough for Sandor to hear the sound. Someone was at the door he had just come through, although whoever it might be was not quite as adept as Sandor in disguising his entrance.

The man on the bed also heard it, making a sudden attempt to get free, but Sandor's finger was on the trigger and, as the man jerked his head to the side it caused the automatic to fire, the man's neck snapping back with a violent jerk.

"Just not your night," Sandor said.

The silenced report of the .380 was just loud enough to bring the second man charging toward the bedroom. He was almost at the end of the short corridor as Sandor managed to pull the lengthened barrel of his Walther free, but before either man could act a loud voice from the open doorway called out, "Stop where you are and drop your weapon."

The onrushing man came to an abrupt halt.

"I said drop your weapon," the familiar voice repeated. "I will not say it again."

The man slowly lowered his weapon as Henri Vauchon stepped from behind him, his pistol aimed in the center of the man's back, and relieved him of his submachine gun. The Frenchman then prodded his prisoner into the bedroom.

"So nice of you both to stop by," Sandor said.

"I had a feeling you might need help," Vauchon replied. "I knew there was no way you were going back to your hotel."

"How right you were."

Vauchon had a look over Sandor's shoulder. Even in the darkness, the grim fate of the man stretched out on the bed was apparent. "Was that absolutely necessary?"

"It wasn't my choice. He just couldn't learn to keep his mouth shut."

Vauchon led his prisoner to a chair. "Watch your eyes," he warned Sandor as he switched on a lamp. In the dim incandescent glow, Sandor now had a look at the burly man seated in the corner of the room.

"So, what is your name, *monsieur*?" When he offered no response, Vauchon asked him again.

"Jorge."

"Sorry about your friend, Jorge," Sandor said as he had a casual look at the dead man. "If you hadn't barged in here everything would have been fine. We were actually getting along quite nicely."

Jorge responded with a scowl.

Sandor stood up and wiped off the silencer with a corner of the bedsheet. "So, Jorge, are you going to tell us what we want to know or do you want to end up like him?"

Jorge stared down at his knees and gave no answer.

"We know you're part of Adina's team. We know

you're on the cleanup squad for the Fort Oscar attack. We know Adina has more excitement planned. Stop me if I'm boring you."

Jorge looked up, his sullen gaze meeting Sandor's determined stare. He still said nothing.

"Is Adina coming back here?"

As Jorge continued to sit there without speaking, Sandor leveled his gun at the man's right knee.

"We can do this with or without pain, that's up to you. I can tell you that a bullet in the kneecap is excruciatingly painful."

"*Mierda*," Jorge growled.

"Ah, a conversation at last."

Vauchon had been watching Sandor, realizing now that he meant what he said. "Let's place him in custody," he suggested.

Without taking his eyes off the Venezuelan, Sandor said, "He's already in custody. He's being interrogated."

"All right," the Frenchman agreed, "but you can't shoot an unarmed prisoner."

"No? How about all of the unarmed people they blew up in Fort Oscar the other night?"

"These men are terrorists."

"Hell, I'm a terrorist too, then." Sandor cocked the hammer on the Walther. "And I don't want to hear about how this makes me as evil as they are. I need answers and I need them now."

Vauchon took two steps away from Jorge and offered a theatrical shrug. "You're on your own," he said.

The three men were silent for a moment. Then the man

in the chair said, "I was sent here to see what you were doing about the fort. That is all I know."

"I doubt that, but it's a start." Sandor sat at the foot of the bed. "Why would Adina care what we do after the fact?"

Jorge provided them a convincing look of ignorance. "How would I know?"

"Then who are you reporting to, and when and how are you giving your reports?"

There was no way for the man to bluff here. If he was on a reconnaissance mission, he would certainly have to be conveying his observations to someone. He fell silent again.

Without warning Sandor fired a single shot, hitting the cushion of the chair just below the man's groin. Jorge instinctively rose, but Sandor waved him back into his seat. "Good thing for you I'm a crack shot," he said. "Now where were we? Oh yes, you were going to tell me a few things, like how you and your friend got to St. Barths, and where your cell phone is and when you're supposed to make your next contact with Adina."

CHAPTER FIFTY-FOUR

AN ESTATE OUTSIDE LANGLEY, VIRGINIA

Deputy Director Byrnes received the update on a secure phone from Baghdad. Rasa Jaber had crossed the border into Iraq and surrendered to an American unit on patrol in Halabjah, not far from the area her husband had chosen for his defection. She too announced that she was seeking political asylum.

Up to now Byrnes found Jaber's concern about the fate of his wife ironic on at least two levels. Obviously, there was the man's bloody history as the architect of the murder of so many innocent people. He hardly seemed a candidate for sentimentality. Second, and perhaps more relevant, was the fact that if he were indeed so attached to the woman, why had he left her behind in the first place? Jaber knew the tactics of the IRGC better than anyone, having helped to develop their cutthroat methods over the past two decades. Did he really believe his wife would go unharmed? Did he really believe they would let her drive cross-country to freedom?

Byrnes knew that the chess game he had been playing with the Iranian was at an end. If Jaber and his wife were part of an intricate deception intended to harm the interests of the United States, why would the IRGC release her now? They had to realize it would only heighten American suspicions regarding Jaber's claimed defection. On the other hand, if Jaber had been telling the truth from the outset—notwithstanding the Deputy Director's suspicions that the man was still holding out on them—then the IRGC might well be using Rasa Jaber to reach her husband.

Either way, Byrnes knew the woman's delivery into American custody must be treated with the utmost caution.

As he left his office in Langley to meet with the Iranian, the Deputy Director hoped Jaber's initial reaction might tell him enough to support his evaluation of this latest development. Seated in the comfortable den situated on the lower level of the safe house, Byrnes conveyed the news of Rasa Jaber's defection as dispassionately as he would deliver a weather report.

Jaber received the information in the same way. He paused before responding, then asked, "Where is she now?"

"On a military transport from Baghdad, on her way to Washington."

Jaber nodded. "They know I'm here in the United States. They've sent her to find me."

Byrnes pursed his thin lips, waiting a moment before saying, "To what end? They certainly don't think your wife is going to come here and assassinate you, do they?"

Jaber responded with a sad smile. "Who could blame her if she did? I cannot even contemplate what they might have done to her over these past days."

"You're obviously contemplating it now."

The Iranian nodded.

"Why release her?"

Jaber sighed. "They know I am in your country, but it is unlikely they know exactly where. Even if they do, I am beyond their reach. They may want to use her to draw me out."

"And you think she would cooperate in such a plan?"

He thought that over. "It is impossible for me to believe. It is more likely that she is unaware of their intentions. Or they may have convinced her she would be serving the state, that I am actually participating in some plot."

Byrnes responded with a look that said he might easily be convinced of the same thing. "You must know that bringing her to this house is an impossibility. They are undoubtedly tracking her. They almost certainly fit her with one or more homing devices. We have to assume they're determined to find you, and I would be compromising this facility and putting my men at risk if I let her visit you here."

"I understand."

"Frankly, I don't think you do." Byrnes pushed back his thinning salt-and-pepper hair with the palm of his hand, then leaned forward. "It is the policy of my government to extend every courtesy to political defectors. It's simply good business. The more attractive our hospitality, the more likely others will follow."

"Of course."

"In your case, there are various mitigating factors to consider. For starters, your past actions against my country and its allies have been, to say the least, heinous. There are many in my government who don't care what you've brought here to sell, they'd like to see you in solitary confinement for the rest of your days. Or worse."

Jaber stared at him, his coal-black eyes unblinking.

"Which brings us to the value of what you actually have provided us, which I judge to be woefully little."

Jaber remained quiet.

"You have one hour to make your decision as to whether you want to provide us your full cooperation. I will not insult you by suggesting the consequences."

Having said that, Byrnes stood up and left the room.

———

At Langley, later that day, Byrnes received his first back-channel communication from North Korea since Sandor's incursion in Pyongyang. In an unofficial communiqué that was padded with the typical spy-speak that enervated the Deputy Director to the point of distraction, the source had imbedded three critical pieces of information.

First, the DPRK knew that Hwang was in the United States and they wanted him back.

Second, Kim Jong-Il would regard any interrogation of Hwang as an act of terrorism.

Third, Raabe and Bergenn were in custody and still alive.

CHAPTER FIFTY-FIVE

ST. BARTHÉLEMY, F.W.I.

SANDOR FIGURED THAT Jorge knew very little about what happened in the attack on Fort Oscar and even less about Adina's upcoming plans. Someone as careful as Rafael Cabello would never entrust that sort of information to someone on a janitorial detail, and that is precisely what Jorge and his dead partner had been charged with, surveillance and cleanup. As Jorge's partner had admitted, they did not even have orders to take out Sandor or any of the others investigating the scene. However, just in case the man knew anything at all that might be useful, Sandor engaged in techniques he knew would be most effective when time was short and the stakes high.

For instance, the muzzle of a loaded automatic, when pressed hard into someone's eye, can be very influential.

Lieutenant Vauchon was becoming increasingly uncomfortable as Sandor ratcheted up the level of persuasion, but Jorge was sufficiently motivated to tell them what he could. He was supposed to phone Adina at eleven every morning and report on what he had seen. He had nothing to do with the attack on Fort Oscar or the downed airplane. He arrived in St. Barths after both of those catastrophes had already occurred. The only information he had about Adina's future intentions was that he was to await instructions here.

Although Sandor never said the word *Baytown,* he hinted around it, all of which received blank stares from the prisoner.

When Sandor was done, he gagged Jorge and tossed him on the bed beside his dead compatriot. Sandor figured it would do the man some good, stretched out there for a while beside the bloody corpse as he decided whether to cooperate when it came time for him to make his phone call to Adina.

That left Vauchon and Sandor to search the room. They found a cell phone, an Uzi SMG, and a Glock. They took the phone and weapons and went off to see what else they might find.

With guns in hand they checked the remaining bedrooms, all of which were empty. The master suite, where Jorge was staying, turned up several bricks of C-4 explosive, two remote detonators, an AK-47, a transponding device, a satellite telephone, a laptop computer, and another cell phone.

Sandor sat down on the bed, studying the transponder and two phones. "I can have these placed on a reverse trace, but whoever we find on the other end is probably on the move already."

Lieutenant Vauchon agreed. "I believe what he told us. The men who attacked the fort came here by boat. As I mentioned last night, that was our assumption."

"And they probably intended to leave by boat as well." Sandor sighed, figuring he was not going to like the answer to his next question. "Any way to track that?"

"There's really no effective immigration screening, boats

are in and out of here all the time. If the communications were up and running at Fort Oscar . . ."

"I got it. But there must be some other record of the major yachts that enter the harbor."

"Of course, but there are also vessels that anchor offshore. It's impossible to document every boat that comes and goes." Then Vauchon gave him a look that would have been an appropriate response to overripe Camembert.

"What?"

"This is a party island," the Frenchman apologized. "The government tends to look the other way when the rich and beautiful arrive with everything from cocaine to high-priced call girls."

"You mean models, don't you?"

Vauchon smiled. "They ignore these improprieties, which they regard as victimless crimes."

"My favorite kind."

"Armaments are a different matter entirely, but something we have never dealt with here before."

"I understand," Jordan said, "but it's worth a try. Maybe someone saw something on one of the big yachts. You never know unless you ask."

"Yes," Vauchon agreed, "we can try."

Sandor pulled out his own phone and called one of the techies Byrnes had sent as part of the forensics team. "Sorry to wake you, Leo, it's Sandor. I've got some communications links you need to have a look at."

Leo paused, obviously trying to shake the sleep away. "Is it morning?"

"It's morning for you."

"All right, all right, I'm listening."

"I've got two cells, a satellite link, and something that looks like a transponder. I need to find out who and where they've been used to contact, but I can't have anyone on the other end knowing we're running the trace. We can't take any chances; they're probably rigged somehow."

"Rigged?"

"Whatever you guys call it when the other party can detect a trace. Just get your ass over here, pronto." He told him where they were and rung off.

"You think one of these might lead us to Adina?" Vauchon asked.

"It might. It might also tell us who else is involved. How about you wake someone in port security and get us a rundown on the yachts in and out of the island over the past several days."

After Vauchon made a couple of calls Sandor told him they had one more precautionary stop to make, then he led him to the small building at the foot of the steep driveway where he had seen the housekeeper the night before. Dawn was approaching and they moved quietly, entering the tiny home through an unlocked door, moving past a small sitting room and into the bedroom, where they found the attractive young woman alone in bed. Stefanie was more than a little surprised to be awakened by two men carrying pistols.

Vauchon displayed his official ID, offering profuse apologies in an effort to calm the girl as she sat up clutching the bedsheet to her neck. The way the linen clung to her Sandor got a pretty good idea of what was underneath. He offered a polite smile of approval. He also gave the girl high marks for not screaming.

After a brief exchange they learned that she lived here alone, was employed by the owner of the villa as its caretaker—she made it clear she was no one's housekeeper—and she had almost nothing whatever to do with the recent guests, all of whom she found to be boorish and unpleasant. The two men left her alone to dress and, when Stefanie emerged just a few minutes later, Sandor marveled yet again at the mystery of how Frenchwomen can appear so sexy in the unlikeliest circumstances or attire. She had barely enough time to comb her hair and brush her teeth, but she had also managed to put on a touch of pink lipstick, did something to her eyes he could not quite figure out, and squeezed herself into a tight-fitting white tank top and a pair of extremely short denim cutoffs. The entire effect was unmistakably *soigné*, the best part being the cutoffs, which revealed that provocative crease that forms between the top of a woman's upper thigh and the bottom of her ass, which, when the thigh is slim and the ass is firm, was Sandor's favorite naturally occurring shape in all the world. It took a loud clearing of the throat by Vauchon to restore his companion's attention to business.

"Nice outfit," Jordan observed pleasantly. Vauchon began to say something, but Sandor added, "I forget which philosopher said, 'That which is offered for view should be admired,' or something like that."

Stefanie responded with an appreciative smile. "A philosopher said that?"

Sandor shook his head. "I actually just made it up. So, do we have any coffee around here?"

By the time the sun had climbed above the blue expanse of the Caribbean, the compound at Pointe Milou was populated with men from Byrnes's CIA team, an NSA advisor, two soldiers under Vauchon's command, and a French port security officer.

Stefanie was more than cooperative, making the coffee, squeezing fresh orange juice, and laying out croissants as well as baguettes with ham and brie. As she confessed to Vauchon, she was more than pleased to have "those people" gone.

Vauchon gave her no explanation of what had become of her guests and Sandor was careful not to allow her near the first bedroom, where the corpse and prisoner yet remained. He also asked Vauchon not to call in the coroner or local authorities, not yet anyway. He didn't want some officious French bureaucrat taking Jorge into custody and interfering with his singular style of interrogation—at least not before the eleven o'clock call to Adina. Vauchon had summoned two men he trusted, assigning one to stand guard over Jorge and the other to block the entrance to the villa.

"You are going to get me in trouble, Mr. Sandor."

Sandor clapped him on the shoulder. "No way, Henri. You're a local hero. For the time being I'm counting on the mileage that'll get us."

Sandor turned his attention back to the girl. "Tell me about the people who were here, why you didn't like them."

Stefanie told them that the men who arrived first did not allow her inside the main compound to fulfill her customary duties overseeing the cleaning and maintenance of the place. She explained that this villa, Villa du Vent, was one of the priciest on the island, and the owners were particular about its upkeep, not to mention the guests their broker allowed.

Sandor laughed. "I would say your broker needs to upgrade its vetting process."

Stefanie was not sure what he was saying, but smiled anyway.

"What else?"

The girl began in English, but quickly reverted to French, Vauchon providing the translation as Sandor gazed into her eyes, trying for the moment to decide if they would be called sea green or aqua.

"It seems there was something of a revolving door policy that made her uncomfortable," the lieutenant explained. "Other men showed up last week but did not stay. These men only arrived two days ago."

"Just after the attack on Fort Oscar."

"Yes," Vauchon said.

Sandor excused himself with a smile at Stefanie, then led Vauchon to the edge of the large deck. "Which means our friend Adina really did send a cleanup squad. But why? Why take the risk?"

Vauchon shook his head. "Perhaps this man Jorge is telling the truth."

"Yes, they want to know what we're doing here. Which means the fact we've taken Jorge and disposed of his friend is information we definitely don't want Adina to have."

Vauchon replied with a perplexed look. "I am not used to this sort of intrigue, my friend."

"Well, I am, and I know about Adina," Sandor said. "He has no conscience about sacrificing his own men."

Vauchon nodded solemnly. "Exactly what that man Renaldo was trying to tell me that night at the fort. He and his team had been betrayed."

"By the remote detonation of the explosives," Sandor said, finishing the thought. "That's typical of how Adina operates. So he sent these two on a recon mission. If they get him any valuable information that's a bonus. If we catch them it tells him something about how far along we've gotten in our investigation. Maybe even how close we are to reaching him." He looked over at the attractive young woman. "If we don't let him know they've been taken, he'll assume he's just that much farther ahead of us, *n'est-ce pas?*"

Vauchon winced at the butchered pronunciation. "Yes," the lieutenant agreed, "but it would be easier on my ears if you stayed with the English."

"All right," Sandor agreed with a shrug. "So when Jorge calls in today we'll let Adina think his boys are still on the loose."

"What if he refuses? Or tries to warn this Adina when they speak?"

Sandor shrugged, then began walking back to Stefanie. "Then I'll kill him," he said. Reaching the girl, he asked, "You busy for dinner tonight? Henri thinks I need to work on my French."

CHAPTER FIFTY-SIX

BAYTOWN, TEXAS

PETER AMENDOLA STAYED late at the refinery, waiting until it was dark before locking his office and heading off to the parking lot. Several of the men had gone for a quick beer at a local pub, but, as usual, Amendola was no part of that after-hours camaraderie. They had long ago given up on inviting him along.

He climbed into his Ford Explorer and headed past the gatehouse to the turnoff for West Main. Then he doubled back on Lee Drive and made a left onto Market Street, doing his best to see if anyone was following him. That's a laugh, he told himself, realizing there was little chance he would be able to spot a professional on his tail. Still, he followed a circular route until he reached North Civic Drive and approached N. C. Foote Park.

There was no indication that anyone at work suspected him as he had smuggled paperwork out of the plant. Yet in the past twenty-four hours he noticed an increased level of security at the refinery. It could have been his imagination or simple coincidence, but there certainly appeared to be additional guards on duty and a heightened sense of urgency at the various checkpoints.

The information he had previously passed on was fairly harmless, but this new data about defense systems was another matter entirely. It had been difficult for him to gain access to the schematics, and given the encryptions built into the computer systems and the vigilance of the security precautions, he had to believe they would detect the breach sooner or later. He only hoped they would not trace it back to him. Given the activity he observed today he was glad he had already removed the paperwork. The real question was, were they about to catch up with him? It had been over thirty-six hours since he managed to gain access to the information and that was enough time for them to trace his clearance numbers. His fingerprints were all over the use of the access codes, literally and in cyber-tracks. For a moment it occurred to him that it might actually be a relief if, instead of heading off to make the drop, he was greeted by the authorities and hauled away. But he made his way out and was now traveling the last stretch of North Civic without interruption.

His anxiety tonight was intensified not only by the sensitivity of the information he was carrying, but because of the instructions he received for this meeting. All of his previous drop-offs had been in Bicentennial Park. This evening they called for the exchange in Foote Park. This worried him. To use his wife's expression, it worried him mightily.

They had never insisted on a nighttime drop before. Up to now Amendola would take a morning run and leave his packages in a designated trash can or behind a specified tree, never venturing far from the jogging paths that crisscrossed through Bicentennial. He was more comfortable in broad daylight. At night he would have no chance to see who might be lurking in the dark, whether it was one of them or someone from security at the plant.

When Amendola told his handler that he was less than happy with this new arrangement, his contact made it clear these instructions were not negotiable. Amendola was left with no choice but to agree since, as he reminded himself, "They know where to find me."

He considered arriving early, while there was still light, searching for some position of advantage, but he knew better. He knew if he were spotted the consequences could be dire. He decided he had best start off by following their orders.

As he pulled the car to a stop at the curb near Civic Circle he repeated that last thought to himself.

Just do as they say.

He stared out the windshield, wondering how in hell he had dug himself in so deep. They had the names and photos of his entire family, proof of him making drops and picking up cash, and, most damning of all, they were holding the actual data he had already supplied them. He felt his chest tighten as he struggled to take a deep breath. Then he turned the engine off and sat there without moving.

There was nowhere to run, he knew that. What could he do to them? Who could he tell? How could he harm them? He was the one who had his neck in the noose. He didn't even know who the hell they were. There was only the possibility they would take these new plans and just let him go.

He had done his best to prepare. He had the papers in a brown envelope on the passenger seat beside him. Before he picked it up, he opened the center console and pulled out his Smith & Wesson .38 revolver.

He shook his head as he stared down at the gun. These bastards were professionals. He knew his life meant nothing to them. They had threatened the lives of his wife and children. They were prepared to murder innocents to get what they wanted. And here he was, with a .38 revolver, as if he were going to be able to stop them. His face tensed, a grim mask of realization. There was nothing heroic in Peter Amendola. He was not interested in stopping anyone. He was only interested in survival.

He lifted the S&W and shoved it into his jacket pocket, picked up the envelope and opened the car door, then began his walk into the park.

Amendola had no trouble finding the path they described. He plodded slowly along toward the train tracks that ran along the northern edge of the park. To his surprise there was plenty of illumination from the lampposts along the trail of packed dirt, at least in this area closest to the road. It was quiet, and he listened to the crunching sound of his boots on the ground, not breaking stride as he dropped the envelope in the second waste can he passed. Then he turned left as the path veered toward the interior of the park and he headed up a knoll, the darkness closing in on him now as he got farther from the lamplights and nearer the appointed rendezvous.

When he reached the crest of the hill he could see there were three men waiting. Amendola was surprised that his contact was one of them. For some inexplicable reason he never expected his handler to be there. His contact had always seemed so corporate. Amendola had imagined a tougher type for this sort of encounter and the other two men were more of that ilk—broader, less refined looking and, even in the dark, more sinister.

"Good evening, Peter," his contact said.

Amendola nodded.

"The papers?"

"We need to talk first."

The contact, who was leaning against a tree, took a step forward. "We're not here to have a conversation, Peter. We're here to exchange information for money." He reached into his sport coat pocket and took out an envelope.

Amendola managed a grim smile. "Three of you just to exchange cash for papers?"

"Where is the package, Peter?"

"I want you to leave my family alone. They have nothing to do with this."

The contact nodded. "Is that it?"

"What are you going to do with me?"

The contact sighed. "Isn't it a bit late for you to be worried about that?"

Amendola blinked. He was standing with his hands in the pockets of his zipper jacket, his right hand clutching the revolver. "I can't hurt you. I don't even know who the hell you are. If I ever breathed a word of this to anyone I'd spend the rest of my life in jail."

The contact appeared to be thinking this over. Then, with growing impatience, he said, "We know all of that, Peter."

"Why not just leave me alone. Keep your money. Just take what you want and let me be."

"Let me have the papers, Peter."

Amendola drew a deep breath. "I don't have them. Not with me."

The contact shook his head. "There are two things I must be wary of in my line of work. The first is conscience, the unfortunate possibility that someone's innate greed might be overtaken by a fit of remorse or an attack of latent morality. I was never worried about that with you. From the moment we chose you, we felt confident you were the sort of man who would, shall we say, stick to his principles." He paused, but no one else spoke. "The second problem is more complicated in its way. It can arise from a combination of fear or greed or stupidity which leads to a lack of truthfulness. It appears we have reached that crossroad in our relationship."

Out of the corner of his eye, Amendola saw a fourth man coming up the hill from the left. He was holding the envelope. "Here it is," the man said.

"Under the circumstances, Peter, did you really think we were going to allow you to enter this park unwatched? You might have brought the authorities. Or a meddling friend. You might even have armed yourself, as indeed you have. Please remove your hands from your jacket. Without the gun, of course."

Amendola did not move.

"Foolish of you, stashing the envelope that way. I thought we had a fair arrangement, you and I."

"You have what you came for," Amendola said, surprised to hear the timbre of his voice weaken.

His contact took the envelope from the other man. He opened it and, with a small penlight, had a quick glance at the papers. "Yes," he agreed, "it appears we have what we came for."

Without another word, the two men who were standing on either side of the contact raised their silenced automatics and opened fire. Amendola barely managed to get the gun out of his pocket, squeezing off two random shots as he fell to the ground.

"Damn," the contact said as he stepped forward and kicked Amendola's revolver out of his hand. "We didn't need the fireworks, gentlemen. Now let's get moving before we have company."

Amendola stared up at him. "You were going to kill me anyway," he gasped.

The contact nodded slowly. "If it's any consolation, yes, that is so."

Those were the last words Amendola heard. The last thing he saw were the two assassins silently approaching. One was leveling a pistol at his head. The other was carrying a large black plastic bag he would use to remove Amendola's body from the scene.

CHAPTER FIFTY-SEVEN

TORTOLA, B.V.I.

THE CREW OF the *Misty II* prepared to depart from the placid lagoon along the shore of Tortola. As Adina had predicted, tropical storms were gaining intensity in the southeastern Caribbean and he needed to advance his preparations.

His team had reported in from Texas, confirming they were now in possession of the information describing the perimeter defenses of the Baytown refinery. As expected, the design was similar in configuration to the fortifications used at other major facilities. Although the data obtained from Amendola provided less than the total specifications, they contained enough to enable their plan.

Adina also heard from the group that had begun their journey in Tehran, the men with whom Seyed Asghari had worked until he betrayed them to Ahmad Jaber. This cell was charged with obtaining low-yield nuclear materials similar in type to those employed in the tests jointly performed by North Korea and Iran a few years back. The materials had ultimately been obtained, not in Iran, but in Kazakhstan. They were secured with the aid of men from Kim's allegedly defunct nuclear program.

Over the years, officials from the Soviet Union—and then Russia—issued repeated denials that these "suitcase nukes" ever existed. When the highly placed GRU operative Stanislav Lunev defected to the West, he put an end to all efforts by Vladimir Putin and his subordinates to persuade the world that these bombs had never been built. Lunev gave irrefutable details about their composition, including the legendary RA-115s and, more importantly for Adina's purposes, the submersible RA-115-01s. Not only did these devices exist, Lunev explained, but the location of many could no longer be accounted for by the Russian government. The nightmare scenarios became almost endless, with the ultimate fear being the likelihood that they would fall into the hands of terrorists.

Some of the raw materials in these devices were used in the tests conducted in the Syrian desert by the DPRK, as it experimented with techniques it had developed at its Yongbyon nuclear reactor. The CIA confirmed both the tests and the sources of the enriched nuclear material and, in 2008, the United States negotiated and paid for the destruction of that facility with the nominal cooperation of Kim's regime. What could not be confirmed was a real end to Kim's efforts to utilize nuclear weapons if and when he chose to do so.

The men Adina had assigned to this part of his operation, Francisco and Luis, reported that they had now acquired sufficient firepower to implement the plan. They would deliver the first shipment to Cuba, then another directly into southeast Texas.

———

As the captain of the *Misty II* ordered his men to weigh anchor and set a course to the south, Adina was joined on deck by his chief technical consultant, Eric Silfen, and the liaison from Caracas, Antonio Bastidas. After bringing them up to date on the latest developments, he returned to the business at hand. Laying out a large map before them, the three men had a look at the geography of the greater Houston area.

"The issue, gentlemen, is the stretch of land that acts as a breaker outside Galveston Bay. As you can see, access to the interior Gulf waters, and ultimately to Baytown, is limited to a single cut between Port Bolivar to the north and Galveston to the south. Any vessel passing through, whether above or below the waterline, is subjected to the most rigorous surveillance."

"Why a submarine, then?" asked Bastidas. "Why all of this subtlety? Why not a ground-to-ground missile, or an unmanned air attack?"

Adina gave a patient nod. "These options have been considered, of course, but we must be realistic about the lack of sophistication of our systems when compared with American defenses. Missiles would be swatted from the sky like so many mosquitoes, and a drone attack would endure a similar fate. Even with the information we have gathered on their security mechanisms, stealth is absolutely required."

"But aren't you also telling us that a submarine has no chance of getting through?"

"No, I am not. I am telling you of the difficulty, not the impossibility. Given a hurricane for cover and the destruction of the communications center at Fort Oscar, it can be done."

Bastidas was not convinced. "The entire area is on high

alert, Rafael," he said, one of the few men who had the familiarity with Adina to use his given name. "They are investigating the plane crash near St. Maarten and the invasion of the
fortress in St. Barths. Why would you think such a plan will
not be detected?"

"I assume it will be detected, Antonio, I absolutely expect
it. But the discovery will come too late."

The man from Chavez's inner circle stared down at the
map again. "And what about the men on board? Won't they
be captured? Won't that compromise your intentions?"

Their host deferred to Dr. Silfen, who was only too
pleased to expound upon his plan to create the catastrophic
subterranean explosion that would annihilate the Baytown
refinery, including everything and everyone in the vicinity.
And he would do it, in effect, by remote control.

"So," Bastidas said when the proud scientist was done,
"you're telling me this submarine can operate without a
crew?"

"Precisely," Silfen replied. He described how American
ingenuity had created the Super Scorpio class of unmanned
submarines, also known as Autonomous Underwater Vehicles, or AUVs. The research and development had been
conducted at the naval base in San Diego and resulted in
what essentially became a submersible drone. In an ironic
twist of fate, Moscow had hastened the progress and use of
these vessels.

In August 2005, a Russian Akula class submarine became disabled, apparently having been caught in a maze of
high-tensile fishing nets off Russia's east coast. The lives of
the entire crew were in danger.

Knowing of the San Diego project, the Kremlin asked Washington for help and the U.S. Navy responded, sending two of its Super Scorpios from California via an Air Force C-5 transport, together with the ancillary equipment, crew, and technicians to undertake the rescue. The American AUVs led the successful recovery, resulting in increased cooperation between the two countries. The project was expanded and then moved to Norfolk, Virginia, where it became known as ISMERLO, for International Submarine Escape and Rescue Liaison Office.

"The Russians benefited from the new technology," Silfen continued, "as did others on the black market."

"The Russians sold the plans?"

"It's what they do," Adina observed with an indulgent smile. "The cooperation of our friends in North Korea has also been essential. You've heard of narco subs?"

Bastidas nodded.

"Those units are not nearly as sophisticated as the AUVs," Silfen said, then explained how drug runners from Colombia were using a simpler system for their SPSS boats, or Self-Propelled Semi-Submersibles, to transport cocaine. "They're not actually submarines in the truest sense, since they cannot dive. They merely glide unseen just below the surface. And, unlike the AUVs, they are operated by a two-man crew. If detected by the authorities, the pilots simply scuttle the craft. They are designed with side chambers that can be opened to let the seawater rush in. In a matter of moments they sink to the bottom like a stone, while the men on board are jettisoned from the cockpit to the surface. Under international law the crew must be rescued. They cannot be charged with any crime since the evidence by then has been dissolved in the seawater and washed away."

"But these narco subs would be easy to spot in a highly protected area, such as this," Bastidas said, pointing to the map.

"Of course," Silfen sniffed, annoyed at the suggestion he might employ such primitive technology, "but the North Koreans have taken the U.S. plans and created a hybrid between these crude models and the American Scorpios. Their unit moves faster than an SPSS, operates without a crew, and runs in relative silence."

Bastidas was impressed and said so. He also expressed surprise that he was not made aware that such a project was under way in Venezuela.

"Please take no offense, my friend," Adina said. "The secrecy has been fueled more by our concerns about the factions in Bogota than in Washington. At some later date we may be willing to sell the plans to the drug lords in Medellin, but for now we have a more important purpose in mind."

Bastidas let it go, but his dour look made it clear that being excluded from these discussions was a topic he would raise with Chavez when he returned home. "All right, I admit it seems very clever and perhaps it can work. But what about Baton Rouge?" Returning his attention to the map, he pointed at the long, winding route one would have to negotiate up the Mississippi River to reach that refinery. "You have already said that you cannot reach that refinery by submarine."

"Ah yes," Adina said with a smile. "We have plans for that too."

Before he could offer a further explanation, his steward came on deck.

"Are we about to get under way?" Adina asked.

"In just a few minutes, sir. But you have a call." He held out a satellite phone. "It's Jorge, from St. Barths."

CHAPTER FIFTY-EIGHT

ST. BARTHÉLEMY, F.W.I.

WHEN SANDOR AGREED that the body of the dead terrorist could finally be removed from the bedroom, Vauchon instructed the coroner to arrange for its transport directly to military headquarters on Guadeloupe. He also warned that if he heard of anyone on the island speaking of the man's death, the coroner would be made to answer for it himself.

With Stefanie and all other nongovernment personnel out of the way, the body was placed in a black bag, loaded into a police van, and carried away.

Jorge, still bound at his ankles and wrists, was seated in a chair. According to what he told Sandor it was time for him to check in with Adina. Sandor entered the number Jorge provided and held the cell phone to the man's face. Sandor was seated beside him on a table, listening to both ends of the conversation, which the tech staff was also taping. It began simply enough and, if Jorge was supposed to furnish a code of some sort, Sandor didn't hear one. They spoke in Spanish, which Sandor followed easily enough.

"So," Adina said after a polite exchange of greetings, "is there anything I should know?"

"An American arrived yesterday. He met with the French soldier who was at the fort that night. They visited the site, then had dinner."

"Any indication who this American might be?"

"Not yet," Jorge replied. Sandor was impressed with the man's even, almost casual, manner. "We have found out where he is staying and we intend to follow him there." Sandor thought the "we" was a nice touch.

"Why are you waiting?"

"I wanted your instructions. They seem to be moving slowly; we did not want to create any unnecessary problems."

Adina paused, as if thinking that over. "Was he NTSB, do you think?"

"No," Jorge said. "More like an undercover type."

"He might be NSA, or perhaps CIA. It could be helpful to find out. Go ahead, see what you can learn."

"Yes, sir."

"Anything else, any American military presence?"

"No, not that we've seen."

"Any technical services? Support teams?"

"Only the activity at the fort."

"Very well. Call me tomorrow, same time."

"Yes, sir," Jorge said, then the line went dead.

Sandor stood up, hit the end button, and shoved the phone in his jacket pocket. Jorge had basically kept to the script he prepared for him. "Nice work," he said, giving the man a hard slap across the face. The Venezuelan tried to spit at him, but Sandor had already moved away. "Send the guard back in," he told Vauchon and headed outside to the terrace.

———

When Adina ended the call on his end he appeared perturbed. He handed the phone to the steward and sent him away.

"What is it, Rafael?" Bastidas asked. "Is everything all right?"

"I don't think so," Adina replied. "He called me 'sir' twice." He nodded, as if confirming a thought. "Smart boy, that Jorge."

————————

When Vauchon joined him on the terrace, Sandor was giving instructions to Leo, the lead technician sent by Byrnes. Sandor handed him Jorge's phone and said, "I know they'll have this signal scrambled all over the map, but take a shot at locating the receiver's position on the call we just made, okay?"

Leo nodded. "I hope this works a little better than that fried version you gave me yesterday. Couldn't get a thing from that."

Vauchon looked confused and Sandor looked annoyed.

"Just see what you can make of this one, all right?"

Leo was about to say something like "Whoops," thought better of it, then made for the living room, where his team had already set up their electronics center.

When Sandor turned to Vauchon, the lieutenant was smiling. "Anything you want to share with me?"

Sandor described the cell phone he removed from Fort Oscar. "Probably nothing, just wanted to get a read on it as quickly as I could."

"Without interference from the French authorities."

"Something like that."

Vauchon offered a rueful smile. "As you know, I already have a pretty good idea of how you work."

"Meaning what?"

"As my mathematics teacher used to say, the shortest distance between two points is a straight line. With you, Jordan, even when you are shown a straight line you still seem to be looking for a shortcut."

"I try," Sandor admitted.

"Just remember," Vauchon chided him with more bemusement than rancor, "we're on the same side here."

"Point made," Sandor replied.

"Good. So tell me what you think about our friend Jorge."

Sandor rubbed his face as he thought it over. "It went too smoothly. Adina didn't ask enough questions, especially after Jorge told him that he made me as someone working undercover. I think Jorge said something that warned him off, but for the life of me I can't figure out what. Let's face it, Henri, this guy is a terrorist in the employ of Adina and Chavez. He isn't going to roll over that easily."

"Even if there were some code words in there, what signal could he possibly have given in such a brief conversation?"

"Maybe that we have him in custody."

"I see."

"They obviously know our governments are working together to investigate the airliner explosion and the attack here, but they don't know what we've discovered to date. They certainly have no way of knowing that one of their men spoke with you that night, and they can only guess at what we've learned in Washington." When Vauchon responded with another puzzled look, Sandor realized the Frenchman knew nothing of the Jaber defection. He said, "I'll explain that in a minute. The point is, from our perspective the less they think we know, the better off we are."

"Agreed. Perhaps we should listen to the tape of their conversation, hear it one more time, eh?"

"Good idea."

"And what have you learned in Washington?"

Sandor briefed him on what they knew from Jaber, without sharing the Iranian's name.

"So, this defector did not predict either of these disasters."

"No," Sandor conceded. "If he knew what was coming he never told us."

An officer arrived with a printout of the major yachts that had been in and out of St. Barths over the past ten days. Vauchon made the introductions and the three men sat at the dining table beside the pool and reviewed the data. It was difficult to re-create the information without the Fort Oscar computers available to help them, but the officer seemed to have an encyclopedic knowledge of all the large vessels and their owners.

"Impressive," Sandor said.

"If you are in St. Barths long enough you recognize them all," the man said in French, with Vauchon offering the translation.

The officer was particularly familiar with the yachts and other vessels that regularly visited the island, and it was a simple matter of eliminating those from the roster. There were a few that had docked in the harbor and various yachts that anchored offshore, which were the most difficult to identify. As Vauchon had predicted, those were simply impossible to monitor in the chaotic aftermath of the attack on Fort Oscar.

All the same, they had a dozen possibilities, so Sandor called over Leo's second in command and handed him the list of names with ports of origin.

"Find out everything you can about these. I know most of them will be owned by foreign corporations, but get behind that. I want the names of the principals who own the holding companies, the naval architects who designed them, the builders who built them, whether they're used on a strictly private basis or whether they're available for charter, and find out where they've been in the past twelve months."

The young man responded with a glassy-eyed look. "Wow," was all he could say.

"Wow? That's all you've got for me?"

"I just meant it's going to be tough."

Sandor fixed him with a look that froze the man. "Tough? Duty in Afghanistan is tough. You're about to find out what tough is if you don't get this for me pronto. You follow?"

Leo, who had just walked up to them, said, "If you're wondering, I can assure you he's serious. Get on it." When his assistant hurried away, Leo told them, "The trace on that call didn't give us much. All we could do was bounce the satellite signal back, and we're pretty sure it was a Caribbean hookup."

"That's not good enough, Leo."

"I know, but it's all we can get right now. They scrambled

their tracking link like an omelet; best I can get is that it's an offshore link."

"You mean like a boat?"

Leo frowned. "Yes, exactly like a boat."

Sandor's eyes turned dark and his mouth tightened.

Leo said, "Sorry. The more important information is that the boat, wherever it is, appears to be on the move."

CHAPTER FIFTY-NINE

Rasa Jaber was flown to Washington on a military troop transport. As an Arab woman on a flight otherwise filled with young men and women returning home from their tour of duty, she was something of a curiosity, especially since she was being escorted by two MPs.

Upon arrival at Andrews Air Force Base she was met by an interpreter. Still carrying the valise she had packed when she left her home in Tehran to visit her sister just a little more than a week ago, it seemed to Rasa like some sort of connection to another lifetime. When an aide tried to take the bag she protested, but they politely explained that this was standard procedure and that her belongings would be returned to her. She was then driven in a black Suburban to the Mayflower hotel in downtown Washington.

Unlike her husband, who had been secured under guard in the large estate outside the city as soon as he arrived in the States, she was ostensibly being given minimum-security treatment. All the while, Byrnes had men monitoring the actions of others who might be interested in her whereabouts. The Deputy Director had determined that the best and highest use of Jaber's wife was as bait. She had been in custody in Iran and her release was at best suspicious and almost certainly a purposeful ploy to help draw out her husband. Whether she was a willing participant or an innocent victim was immaterial. Byrnes intended to do his best to exploit the situation.

He had two men trailing her SUV in a sedan. One of them was already taking apart her suitcase, searching for homing devices. The IRGC did not disappoint, the agent locating two different types of transmitters, one in the lining of the bag, the other in her toiletries. The agent repacked the valise and, at a traffic light where the sedan could pull alongside yet another SUV, the transmitters were handed off.

When Rasa Jaber was shown to her room in the May-flower, she was given her bag and told to take some time to clean up and rest. The interpreter said they would be back in two hours for an interview.

Left alone, Rasa carefully unpacked her things, placed them in the closet, and arranged her cosmetics on the bath-room counter. Then she sat on the edge of the bed and, hold-ing her face in her hands, she quietly wept.

Meanwhile, the SUV with the two homing devices had veered off, taking a circuitous route around the Beltway. The two transmitters taken from Rasa's bags were being delivered by Byrnes's men to the FBI, where they would be placed on a desk in the Homeland Security liaison office.

An hour later the two Iranian operatives assigned to track Rasa Jaber's movements in Washington found themselves sitting in their car on Pennsylvania Avenue.

"FBI," the driver said. "Why would they interrogate her there?"

The second man shrugged.

"Why not the CIA?"

"Who knows, maybe it's one of those task force teams, or whatever they call them. Park around the corner and we'll wait."

And so they did, waiting in the heart of the capital until Byrnes's team decided where to send them next.

Rasa had cried herself into a fitful sleep. A loud knock roused her and she stood, straightened out her skirt and blouse, then opened the door. Deputy Director Mark Byrnes introduced himself and his assistant through an interpreter, then the three of them walked past her and sat around the small table in the corner of the room. Rasa locked the door and joined them.

"Forgive me if I seem abrupt, Mrs. Jaber, but my time is limited and I must get right to the point."

Rasa nodded, her dark gaze focused on the man across from her. She struggled to follow his English since she had a reasonable facility with the language, and she did not want to rely completely on the interpreter.

"We know you have come here to be with your husband."

Again she nodded.

"We also know that your escape from Iran was interrupted by the authorities, and that you were in custody for several days."

She did nothing to disguise her surprise. Even after all these years of marriage to Ahmad she did not understand the breadth and depth of international espionage. She simply could not fathom how her arrest in Marand could be known to these Americans. "Yes," she said in English.

"We must assume that your release is part of some scheme by the Iranian government, or the IRGC. You understand me?"

"Yes."

"What agreement did you make to secure your release?"

Rasa blinked several times. "Agreement?"

"Mrs. Jaber, we know that you are not directly involved in your husband's business, but there must have been some trade or concession that you made for them to allow you to leave their custody and travel into Iraq."

She appeared genuinely confused. "Only that I would see my husband."

Byrnes stared at her, waiting.

Rasa shifted uncomfortably in her seat, and then tears again began to well up in her ebony eyes. "Ahmad deserted me. I did not know he was coming to the United States. I have to see him again, to look at him and to ask him why. Do you understand?"

Byrnes said nothing.

"They imprisoned me. They might have killed me. They showed me photographs of Ahmad with Americans while I was abandoned to these, these, men. Men who subjected me to great indignities, who treated me as if I had betrayed them when I did nothing. Knew nothing." Her voice grew angry. "I want to understand. I want Ahmad to tell me how he could have left me to such a fate."

"And these men allowed you to simply get in your car and drive out of Iran, knowing you would defect?"

"Yes," she said, her tone making it clear that she felt this was as obvious as it could possibly be.

Byrnes shook his head impatiently. "I ask you again, why? What did you promise them?"

"Promise them? I promised them nothing."

"I'm sorry, Mrs. Jaber, I think you're a liar." Byrnes stood, followed by his aide and the interpreter.

Rasa remained seated. "I am not a liar. I came here to see my husband. I demand to see Ahmad."

"Demand? Well," Byrnes said, "whether you will or will not be allowed to meet with him remains the issue, but unless you agree to tell us the truth you will stay here, under guard, until we decide what is to be done with you."

Rasa stood now, a horrified look on her face. She stepped forward to confront Byrnes. "You are just as bad as they are. You are all the same."

Byrnes did not reply. He opened the door, and Rasa saw a uniformed officer standing in the hallway. Byrnes turned back to her and said, "Your fate is very much in your own hands, much as it was in Marand. Your husband's fate as well. When you are ready to speak truthfully with me you can let this gentleman know," he said, pointing to his man in the corridor. "Until then, you will be confined to this room."

Byrnes closed the door and headed down the hall to the elevator.

"You really don't believe her?" his agent asked.

Byrnes sighed. "I believe she knows very little, that much is true, but there's something she's not ready to tell us. That's what we need to get from her."

"Do you have any idea what it is?"

"Yes," Byrnes said, "I believe I do."

CHAPTER SIXTY

HOUSTON, TEXAS

THE TWIN-ENGINE KING Air is among the safest and most reliable of the classic-style prop jets. As the pilot banked his approach, he went through the LCD checklist posted above the familiar instrument panel.

"Easy as parking a car," he said as he lowered the landing gear.

His copilot nodded, then radioed their arrival to the ground crew at Coulter Airfield, a small airstrip just outside Bryan, Texas. After getting confirmation he looked over his shoulder to the two men in the small cabin. "Almost there," he told them.

It was a cloudy afternoon, with a slight crosswind, but the landing was smooth. The plane taxied to the end of the runway and turned left, where it came to a stop in the area designated for private aircraft. The copilot made his way into the cabin to open the hatch and drop the folding steps.

"Right this way."

The two passengers followed him onto the tarmac. They were attired in crisply pressed slacks, sport coats with open-neck shirts, expensive loafers, and dark sunglasses. They were tanned and well groomed, one sporting a full beard, the other a mustache. Each was a little too thick around the middle, having the overfed look of prosperous businessmen in their late forties. They carried their own overnight bags as they followed the copilot into the small terminal. They were met there by an attractive young woman who greeted them with a warm smile.

"Welcome to Bryan," she said. "Didn't have you on the manifest today."

"Hurricane coming," the pilot replied as he entered just behind them, then offered her his flight plan. "I'll be happy to get back up to Lawrence."

"Kansas," the girl said as she looked over the paperwork.

"Yeah, lucky to get in and out of here before this squall hits," the copilot said. What he did not tell the girl was that they actually took off from a small airfield northwest of Monterrey, Mexico, with a scheduled landing at the Love Field airport outside Dallas. Once they crossed the border, they circled north and set down at this tiny strip in Bryan.

"Weather's not so bad yet," the young woman replied cheerfully.

"Calm before the storm," the pilot replied.

The bearded man stepped forward. "Could we get some help? We have a few things on board and want to get on our way."

"Of course," the girl said, then picked up her two-way radio and summoned the baggage handlers. They were a couple of college students working part-time at Coulter Airfield, which was neighbor to Texas A&M just up the road. It was a quiet day, and the two stocky boys arrived, received their instructions, and set about removing the contents of the King Air and placing them on a motorized skid.

There were four large wooden boxes on the plane.

"Be careful there," the pilot said. "Electronic equipment."

In fact, the two larger crates held the disassembled components of programmable underwater conveyance devices. The smaller containers were packed with foam that protected, at the center of each, a lead-lined enclosure housing an RA-115-01—a submersible nuclear suitcase bomb.

"This is some heavy shit," one of the boys said as the pilot and passengers supervised the unloading.

"I'll say," his friend agreed.

The pilot said, "New systems for monitoring the weather. Weighs a ton and packed tight."

The first handler let out a laugh. "Weather? Are you kiddin'? Just look out the window if you want the weather. I heard someone say if you just tell 'em tomorrow is gonna be same as today, you're gonna be right two days outta three. What the hell? Guys on TV are wrong more'n half the time." He uttered a loud chortle. "You're better off to take your electronic shit here and play music on it."

His coworker obviously thought this was one funny routine. "I'll say," he finally blurted out through his laughter. "Play music on it."

The passenger with the mustache was standing off to the side. He forced a smile that rapidly turned to a grimace when the two burly young men mishandled one of the smaller packages. "Careful," he told them.

"Sure is heavier than it looks," the first kid repeated as he positioned the last box alongside the others. "That all of 'em?"

"Yes, that's everything. We'll handle our own luggage."

"You sure?" the kid asked. "Same price either way."

The man told him they were sure, bid the crew of their flight good-bye, then he and his bearded companion took a walk past the side of the building, watching as the young men guided the slow-moving tractor to the edge of the runway, where a sixteen-wheeler awaited them.

"Lotta truck for just these here boxes," the young man observed.

"You know, you're kind of a talkative type," the passenger said, but the bearded man interrupted.

"You just set those on the ground, our men will take it from here," he said. The boys removed the crates from the skid. Adina's man tipped them and sent them on their way.

Two men then climbed out of the truck and set about carefully lifting the boxes and placing them in the trailer. The boxes containing the underwater pods were loaded in the back. The other two, holding the nuclear weapons, were secured in a specially lined chamber they entered through the side.

Meanwhile, the two men who had arrived on the flight climbed through another side door into a forward compartment in the trailer that was fitted out with seats and other amenities. Once aboard, they closed the door behind them and began to remove their clothes, the facial hair they had glued on, and the padding they had wrapped around their stomachs. By the time they were done they looked twenty years younger.

They were two of the men who had murdered Seyed Asghari and destroyed Ahmad Jaber's home in Tehran.

"That stupid kid pissed me off with all his talking," said

the first man, called Francisco. "I wanted to put a bullet in his head."

Luis was slightly taller and thinner. "I would have taken them both out. And the girl too."

Francisco shook his head. "Adina is right, less chance of trouble without three locals disappearing."

Luis grudgingly agreed. "Let's just get the hell outta here. I feel like we've been babysitting these things for a month."

Over the past several days Francisco and Luis had shepherded their cargo from Kazakhstan through Turkey by ground, then on a series of private planes that took them to Indonesia, Caracas, Cuba, and then to Mexico. There they boarded the King Air, flying the circuitous route that took them well north of the border until they could circle southeast again toward this small airstrip in Texas. Their angle of approach had been intended to give the impression it had begun as a domestic flight. The pilot and copilot had already gotten back in their plane, preparing for the short flight to the Dallas airfield.

The Venezuelans in the truck were not staying around to see them off.

Francisco said, "All we've got to do is head south, get set up, then wait."

The door to their compartment opened and one of the drivers said, "We're all set."

Luis nodded as the door was shut and locked. A few moments later the truck's gears made a loud sound and they began to move. "Let's just hope we don't have to wait too long," he said.

CHAPTER SIXTY-ONE

ST. BARTHÉLEMY, F.W.I.

As always, Jordan Sandor began his day early. It was still pitch dark inside his beachfront villa at the Guanahani resort. He checked his watch, not yet five. He moved quietly as he sat up, not wanting to disturb Stefanie as she slumbered peacefully, facedown beside him.

The air was balmy and the ceiling fan provided the soothing feel of a gentle breeze, their sheets having been tossed to the floor sometime during the night. As his eyes adjusted in the darkness he enjoyed another look at her, examining the curves of her ass, the firm athletic legs, the smooth contours of her back and shoulders. He was tempted to lean over and kiss her neck, but he knew where that would lead. For now he needed to take care of business, so he slid off the edge of the low platform bed, grabbed his cell phone and Walther from the nightstand, then stepped noiselessly into the bathroom and silently closed the door behind him.

He hit the speed dial, waited, then said, "Sandor."

Byrnes picked up the call on the third ring, obviously rallying from a dead sleep, but still managing a sarcastic "Really?"

"Good morning to you too, sir."

The Deputy Director cleared his throat. "Don't you ever sleep, Sandor?"

"Tried it once, didn't like it all that much. Look, I think I've done all I can here. I'll be more useful back in the States."

"You're probably right. I was going to call you this morning at some civilized hour. What about this Jorge character? Didn't you say he has to check in with Adina again today?"

"So he claims, but our team is working with the French now; they can get it done. Lieutenant Vauchon is a good man, he can supervise the next contact. Anyway, I'm pretty sure Jorge gave some sort of warning signal in that call yesterday. I don't believe we're going to even get the call through today. As for Jorge, I just don't think he knows a goddamned thing."

"What if you can get the call through today and your friend Jorge takes a run at some other coded alert? Is Lieutenant Vauchon going to be as, uh, persuasive as you are about the likely consequences?"

Sandor smiled. "You're not suggesting I would threaten a prisoner, sir? Violate the Geneva Conventions? Take advantage of a situation just because I have an admitted terrorist in custody and innocent lives are at stake?"

"Do me a favor, Sandor, save the stand-up routine for someone with a sense of humor. What about it?"

"Lieutenant Vauchon lost some friends in Fort Oscar," Sandor replied. "He was also the man in charge of security that night. He'll be incredibly convincing if he needs to remind Jorge that his cooperation is a matter, as they say, of life and death."

"All right. Meet with your team and Vauchon, then clear out this morning."

"Thank you, sir." Sandor paused. "I'd like to get to Houston as soon as possible. Everything is pointing there."

"I agree. The intel is sketchy, but that seems to be the target."

"So, should I head directly there?"

"Not yet. We're already mobilizing on several levels, but first I want you back here."

"In D.C.?"

Byrnes told him about the arrival of Rasa Jaber in Washington. He also told him that the traces begun by Leo and his tech boys on the satellite phone links may have yielded information on Adina's movements.

"That's great," Sandor said, "but you don't need face time with me to handle those leads."

"Thank you for telling me my job, Sandor, and no, I don't need any more face time with you than I'm absolutely forced to deal with. The Director, however, feels it might be useful to get you in here to answer some questions about your assault of a reporter at the *Times*."

Sandor knew he would be in for it with Walsh on this one. "What a bunch of happy horseshit. We've got serious issues to handle and the Director wants to talk about a creep who might've put my men's lives at risk for a byline? Are you kidding me?"

"No, I'm not kidding you, so save your righteous indignation for someone it might impress because there's another reason I want you here."

"I'm listening."

"We had a back-channel communication about Bergenn and Raabe," he said, but before Sandor could ask a single question, he said he was not going to discuss it now, not even on a secure line. He ordered Sandor to saddle up and rang off.

Since his escape from North Korea, Sandor had kept his focus on the mission before him, but he also struggled with his responsibility to the men who were left behind in the DPRK. Sandor was their leader and when he was finished with this assignment he would return to Pyongyang if that's what it took to bring back Craig Raabe and Jim Bergenn. For now he knew that any communication Byrnes received was better than no word at all, since it likely meant the two Americans were still alive. The best part was that his ploy with that little weasel at the *Times* might be working.

He took a deep breath, then called Leo.

"This is the second day in a row you woke me up, you know that?"

"Gee," Sandor replied, "and I can't begin to tell you how bad I feel about it," then explained what was going on and arranged to meet him at Villa du Vent.

Next he called Vauchon, who, being in the military, was already up. He explained that the Frenchman was going to have to do without him for at least a couple of days. They also agreed to meet at the villa.

After next placing a call to Langley to organize his transportation home, he shaved, took a hot shower followed by a cold deluge, then dried and wrapped himself in a towel and let himself back into the bedroom.

By now, early rays of sunlight were filtering through the narrow openings of the cream-colored drapes, and he found Stefanie sitting up in bed. She was resting against a couple of pillows, long dark hair framing her lovely face, her eyes the color of the sea. She had replaced the sheets, which were now pulled demurely to her neck, and she was drinking a glass of the Champagne they had left unfinished in the silver bucket on her nightstand.

All in all one helluva picture, he thought.

"Well," Sandor said with an approving nod. "Did you know that Winston Churchill began every day with a glass of Champagne?"

She smiled, then went about pouring him what remained in the bottle.

Sandor sighed. "I'm not sure that's the best way for me to start my day," he said.

"*C'est parfait,*" she protested with an amused pout as she held out the crystal flute.

He stepped forward, took the offered drink, then had a sip.

"I am so glad you brought me to here," she said in her broken English. "I did not want to stay there. So many police. And that man they took away, who was dead," she added with a slight shudder. "*Horrible,*" she said in French.

Sandor grinned. "Is that the only reason you were happy to stay here?"

With a flick of her left wrist, she threw back the sheet on his side of the bed, then gave the mattress a pat.

Sandor had to meet Leo and Vauchon in less than an hour and then make his charter flight home. But what the hell, he told himself as he dropped the towel and climbed in beside her. There's time for everything if you plan carefully.

CHAPTER SIXTY-TWO

CIA HEADQUARTERS, LANGLEY, VIRGINIA

IF CIA DIRECTOR Michael Walsh ever drew up a list of My Favorite People, Sandor knew he was never going to make the roll, but he believed they at least shared a mutual respect. The problem with the Washington bureaucracy is that the chiefs are not elected, they are appointed, and the Indians they lead are neither elected nor appointed, but hired, with all of the attendant longevity and job security that makes the government so impossibly slow to move and so difficult to change.

When a man like Walsh is made head of Central Intelligence he has neither the right nor the ability to go out and replace his entire workforce. He inherits them, just as a new football coach is stuck with the team already in place. He can certainly appoint some assistants, make a few changes to the roster, and show favoritism to those most closely attuned to his own style and ethos. But in the end, he becomes the leader of a team he had no role in choosing.

This is true whether dealing with the Department of the Treasury or the Department of the Interior. It is particularly troublesome when tackling the leadership role in any of the branches handling intelligence, security, or law enforcement, since these organizations involve a unique array of problems, responsibilities, and, inevitably, personalities.

To Walsh's credit, he had held his position through the administrations of two presidents, which may speak more about his facility at playing politics than running the Agency. He was a "by the book" manager who despised any knee-jerk decisions and devoted his professional life to ensuring no one in his charge ever did anything to embarrass him.

Hence his less than enthusiastic view of Jordan Sandor.

Walsh knew Sandor's importance to the Company, having been informed of the important assignments Sandor had undertaken for his predecessor. He ultimately sanctioned Sandor's role in defeating the terrorist plot hatched by former CIA Station Chief Vincent Traiman, despite various misgivings. He reluctantly approved Sandor's mission in Bahrain. Even with plausible deniability for the recent North Korea invasion, Walsh acquiesced to the need for that operation as well.

On the other hand, he found Sandor to be insubordinate bordering on arrogant and a risk taker who at times was close to reckless. Also, like Deputy Director Byrnes, Walsh had no patience for Sandor's flippant style. The difference was that Byrnes realized he had no sense of humor of his own, whereas Walsh was unaware of his shortcoming.

Therefore, when the Deputy Director ushered Sandor into Walsh's office that night to discuss the pending complaint lodged by the *Times* in New York, neither of Sandor's superiors saw anything funny in his request that the reporter's slacks be made part of the official record.

"If the little rat is going to make a claim against me, I

think we should at least have some evidence, don't you? Exhibit A, the pants he pissed in. Where are they?"

"You find this amusing, Sandor?"

"Actually no," he told Walsh. "I find it pathetic. We have a Korean mole and one of our very talented agents lying dead outside Pyongyang. We have two of our best men, God knows where, inside that hellhole of a country. And this parasite is writing articles that inflame the diplomatic tension, making it more and more probable that Bergenn and Raabe are going to get two in the head and be dumped in a hole where they'll never be found. Freedom of the press is one thing, but didn't the Supreme Court say it doesn't give you the right to yell 'Fire' in a crowded theater?"

Neither man replied.

"You guys are in the game of politics, I'm in a business called stop-the-enemy. When we entered the DPRK the four of us knew the risks, we even understood that if we were captured it might be impossible for our government to get us back. We signed on as NOCs, and we took our chances. What we didn't sign on for was some punk reporter stirring up a shit storm that could make it all but impossible to deal with Kim and his gang of thugs."

Walsh was seated behind his desk, across from Sandor and Byrnes. He responded with a nod. "We are painfully aware of the delicate situation that exists. The North Koreans are claiming that we engaged in espionage, kidnapping, and murder, right under their noses, right there in their own country. At this point, they officially deny holding any of our citizens as prisoners—"

"That's perfect," Sandor interrupted. "I suppose they're

claiming that they're holding two Canadians, am I right?" He looked at Byrnes, but the Deputy Director said nothing.

"If it's not too much trouble," Walsh said, "I'd like to continue." He waited until Sandor sat back in his chair. "Fine. Right now they deny holding anyone, but claim to have proof that this Wild West shoot-out in and around the Arirang Festival was orchestrated and carried out by Americans. I take it, from your comments, that you comprehend the implications."

Sandor nodded. "Which is why these newspaper articles have only made matters worse for—"

DCI Walsh held up his hand, removed his reading glasses, and stood, coming all the way around so he could position his tall, lanky frame on the edge of his large mahogany desk and stare down at Sandor. "I want to get this straight. You believe the way to handle this situation is to go up to the man's office, point the barrel of your weapon at him, and threaten his life? I just want to be sure I understand you."

Sandor hesitated, then asked, "Who says I did that?"

"This fellow Donaldson made the allegation. Do you deny it?"

Sandor did not answer. "Any witnesses?"

Walsh and Byrnes exchanged a quick glance.

"There was a third man in the room," the Director said, "but he has not exactly confirmed Donaldson's account of your actions." Walsh reached back across the expanse of desk and grabbed his glasses and a sheet of paper, then read his notes. "He has suggested that his young colleague may have exaggerated some of the details of this encounter." He put down the paper and peered at Sandor over the frame of his spectacles. "We know all about your relationship with Bill Sternlich. His loyalty to you is touching, but at this point it's also creating quite a problem for him, as you might imagine. It may end up costing him his job, not to mention his career."

For the first time in their exchange Sandor averted the Director's gaze. He began rubbing his forehead with the fingers of his left hand.

"Do you want to say something, Sandor?"

Sandor looked up again. "Damnit," he said angrily.

"I must say, it's not up to your usual standard for witty repartee but it may be the most intelligent thing you've uttered this evening."

"What do you expect me to say?"

"Say to me? Nothing." Walsh took a stroll back around the desk and retook his seat, then leveled his steely gaze at Sandor. "What I expect is for you to apologize to this reporter, that's what I expect."

"Apologize? You must be joking."

"I never joke," he replied.

Sandor nodded, knowing how true that was. "And if I refuse?"

"If you refuse I will have to consider an immediate suspension and proceed with an investigation to determine if you should be brought up on disciplinary charges."

No one spoke for a few moments. Then Sandor grinned. He simply could not help himself. "I'm a field agent, sir, and, I believe I don't have to remind you, a reasonably good one. I'm never going to run for office or be appointed to a government post or win any popularity contests. What I am going to do, however, is protect my country, my men, and my integrity." He stood up. "The media gets to run roughshod over the safety, privacy, and reputations of our people. They get to tell lies and make slanderous statements, then shield themselves with a claim of good-faith reporting. If that's free speech, fine. But when it puts my men in harm's way, then I'm entitled to express *my* views, and that is exactly what I did, and I am not apologizing to anyone for it, suspension or no suspension."

There was silence again. Then Walsh looked at Byrnes. "Get him out of here," he said.

———————

Sandor and Byrnes hurried down the corridor without exchanging a word until Sandor said, "I thought that went well."

Byrnes frowned, appearing as if he had suddenly gotten a whiff of something putrid. "You're just asking him to fry your butt in oil."

"Come on, you can see he really likes me. He's just playing hard to get."

Byrnes shook his head.

"Trust me on this one, okay?" Sandor grinned. "I know what I'm doing."

As they rounded the corner and headed into the Deputy Director's office, Byrnes gave him a quizzical look.

"Trust me," Sandor repeated.

Since Sandor arrived back in D.C. earlier that afternoon Byrnes had been concerned about getting through the meeting with Walsh so they could return to more urgent matters. "Okay," he said, "I'll trust you on this, at least for now. Can we talk about something important?"

"Such as Jim and Craig?"

"Yes." They took seats in the room's small conference area. The DD had a file on the cocktail table between them. "Our source tells us that they're both alive, although Raabe is in bad shape and they haven't exactly been staying at the Ritz-Carlton."

"Or Walter Reed Medical Center."

"Precisely."

"But they're alive," Sandor said, "that's the point."

"The point is, Sandor, I'm told they want to make a trade."

"Hwang?"

Byrnes nodded. "They believe you took him alive and they want him back in one piece."

"A bit unusual for Kim, isn't it?"

"We thought so. He's certainly capable of letting his man rot over here."

"Unless the man knows too much to risk his interrogation."

"Perhaps."

"And unless, of course, the capture is made public and he's compelled to act to protect his own people and spare the embarrassment of abandoning a key official. I mean, how would that look?"

Byrnes stared at him. "So the follow-up article your actions provoked from this reporter Donaldson, the claim of an exchange of Americans for Kim's minister . . ."

"Hey, the press has to get information someplace."

The DD allowed himself a slight smile. "The day you grabbed this kid, you blurted out something he could print. About a possible exchange."

Sandor did not reply.

"Was your friend Sternlich in on this?"

"Not a clue." Sandor then nodded to himself. "I'm going to need to straighten that out for him somehow."

"Yes, you are."

"All right, what about Hwang? You still haven't gotten anything from him?"

"Not any more than he told you."

Sandor nodded without speaking.

"What is it? I know that look."

"It's the girl and her family."

"Hea?"

"Yes," Sandor said with a sigh, then puffed his cheeks and let out an angry lungful of air. "When we made our escape we visited her family home. Her brother Kwan used his truck to get us near the border. Hwang was unconscious for most of that, but he might be able to figure it out. They certainly know that she's missing by now, and I promised her that her family wouldn't be compromised."

"She knew the risks. We all know the risks in this lousy business."

"But that doesn't include our selling them out, does it?"

Byrnes looked down at the floor.

"What is it? There's more?"

Byrnes nodded slowly, then let the other shoe drop with a loud thud. "This is a two-for-two deal, Sandor. They're demanding Hea back as part of the trade."

CHAPTER SIXTY-THREE

WASHINGTON, D.C.

NIGHT HAD FALLEN and, after several hours of fruit-less surveillance, the two Iranians assigned to tail Rasa Jaber suspected they had been duped. They followed the signals sent from the transmitters that had been planted in Rasa Jaber's luggage. They moved twice, but had yet to catch a glimpse of the woman. They were now positioned outside a Holiday Inn, but there was no sign of government protection on the street or in the lobby.

"If they brought her here," one of them finally decided, "we would have seen her."

Just then the driver's cell phone rang.

Vahidi was the senior IRGC operative in Washington, a friend to Al Qaeda, but officially part of the Saudi Arabian diplomatic corps and thus protected by immunity—at least until there was proof he had engaged in some terrorist act.

He demanded an update and, when the driver admitted they had lost Jaber's wife, Vahidi told the man to put the call on speakerphone. Then he said, "You are both imbeciles. Why would they take her to the FBI Headquarters and keep her there all day? They have the same use for her that we do, to pressure her husband. What could she tell the FBI that could not be said in five minutes? The woman knows nothing and neither do the two of you. You are fools," Vahidi screamed. "Not a working brain between you."

When the tirade ended, the driver asked, "Where do you want us to go?"

"Go? Where do I want you to go?" He became quiet for a minute. "All right, all right. We received word the lead American agent they sent to St. Barths has returned to Washington. Perhaps it has something to do with Jaber. Find this agent and you should find the Jabers."

The two men in the car shared a look of utter incredulity. "How do you expect us to find this man?" the driver asked.

"It may be easier than you think," Vahidi told them. "The CIA maintains a safe house not far from Langley."

"And as well guarded as their Fort Knox."

"Of course," Vahidi said impatiently. "But if the Jabers are being held there, the agent may come and go to meet with them, am I right?"

His men did not reply.

"If we cannot get inside their fortress, perhaps we can reach their man outside, you understand?"

"Ah, yes."

"Good. Come to the southwestern corner of Massachusetts and Constitution in exactly ten minutes. I'll have someone meet you with a dossier and instructions."

———

President Forest's National Security Advisor said, "More bad news, sir," as he approached the desk in the Oval Office. Peter Forelli held an updated weather report. "That tropical storm is heading directly for St. Maarten, going to make a mess of the NTSB investigation."

President Forest responded with an irritated look. "As if a downed airplane and two hundred casualties isn't a mess already."

"They're going to call in all the boats conducting the search, probably no way to continue for the next couple of days." The NSA hesitated. "Worse than that, the remaining debris is going to be scattered all over the Caribbean."

"Not to mention the remaining bodies, is that what you're trying not to say?" The President leaned back and gazed up at the ceiling. "Sit down," he said. After a moment he looked across the desk again. "You didn't come in to give me another weather report, Peter. What's on your mind?"

"Well, sir, CIA set up their own team to investigate the attack on Fort Oscar. Sandor was there, now he's back in Washington, made his report, left men down there to continue working with the French." The NSA paused again. "Mr. President, you've said you're on a need-to-know basis only for all of this."

Forest peered at him from beneath his famously furrowed brow. "When I say need to know, Sam, I mean don't feed me a bunch of rumor with whipped bullshit on top, okay? You got something real, I want to hear it."

"Well, sir, Walsh thinks they may have a lead on some sort of alliance between Chavez and Kim."

The President began vigorously rubbing his eyes with the palms of both hands. "Well now, isn't that just dandy. And what about Ahmadinejad, wasn't he invited to the party?"

"Perhaps not. They have reason to believe the Iranians are being set up here."

President Forest shook his head. "If things weren't so awful I might have to laugh at that one. Ahmadinejad is being set up?"

"We're not sure, sir, but it's possible."

"Is this based on information from the Jaber defection?"

"Yes, sir, that as well as what Sandor developed in St. Barths."

"Do we know whether they're planning anything else?"

"Yes, Mr. President. That's what I came to tell you."

"Well spit it out."

The National Security Advisor removed his glasses. "Mr. President, Sandor thinks they're planning an attack on the oil refinery in Baytown, Texas."

————————

Rasa Jaber was staring out the window of her hotel room as dusk began to blur the Washington skyline. She realized, as if for the first time, that she had never been to the United States before. Odd, she thought, how that had not even occurred to her during this journey west. Her entire focus had been on reaching Ahmad.

There were so many things she wanted to say, so many things that she needed to tell him. But there was only one important question she had to ask.

How could you have done this to me?

In all of their years together she had been a faithful, even unquestioning, wife. She had never once revealed to him how difficult it was for her to reconcile the intimacy and tenderness of the man she knew and loved so completely with the evil deeds he had perpetrated on others. Oh yes, even as she tried to look away, and despite his efforts to shield her from the truth, she was forced to confront who he was and what he did. She came to know that he was the engineer of unspeakable horrors, all in the name of his country and his God.

Would Allah really approve such atrocities?

She knew that hate was a part of their culture. The despised Jews in Israel, the meddling infidels in America, the reviled barbarians in Iraq. But did such hate justify the murder of women and children and innocent men who were no part of these conflicts?

Even in an era where the education of women was discouraged, she had read of Hitler and the Holocaust, the genocide of Stalin, the contemporary horrors of ethnic cleansing throughout the world. Was this really Ahmad's goal, to rid the planet of every enemy, young and old, as if such a thing were possible? As if Allah would condone such carnage?

How could Ahmad pursue such an unthinkable destiny? How could anyone? Rasa did not imagine herself a political thinker, but she believed herself to be a person of intelligence and compassion. She knew, deep in her aching heart, that this was no answer to the problems men and women of the world faced. Death to all enemies was no solution. She knew from history, if history teaches us anything at all, that the destruction of your enemy only gives rise to another enemy. What better proof than Ahmad's defection to the United States?

But when he fled from Iran he left her behind, not explaining that they might never meet again in this lifetime, not providing for her safety. They had buried their sons, and now he was not giving the slightest consideration to what might happen to her. Or her sister. Or her sister's family.

What sort of man was this? Could this be the man to whom she had given her love and devotion for these many years?

Now, left to struggle with these harsh and painful questions, a bigger conflict loomed for her. Even in the face of his treachery, his abandonment, his faithlessness, was she capable of becoming his betrayer, and perhaps the instrument of his death?

The sky over Washington had darkened, but she took no notice. She stood there, unmoving, staring ahead without seeing, not knowing what she felt anymore, not knowing what she would do when the time came.

CHAPTER SIXTY-FOUR

WASHINGTON, D.C.

THE TWO MEN who were assigned to follow Rasa Jaber arrived at the corner of Massachusetts and Constitution Avenues at the appointed time. A man stepped quickly from the shadows of a nearby doorway and climbed into the backseat of their car.

They were surprised to see it was Ali Vahidi himself.

"Drive," he told them. As the car pulled out, Vahidi said, "Turn right, park in the first open space, then kill your lights." When they came to a stop, the head of the IRGC's Washington cell passed a folder to the two men in the front seat. It contained a map describing the general location of the safe house where Ahmad Jaber was being held.

The Agency's well-fortified retreat was an open secret in a netherworld where true secrets do not survive for long. Shortly after the first defector was taken there for interrogation several years ago the existence of this sanctuary was discovered. The inviolability of the facility was owed in part to an unspoken truce among foreign intelligence agencies—that such installations were both necessary and off-limits—but in an era of renegade adversaries its sanctity was even more reliant on security details, advanced weaponry, and sophisticated electronic systems. If its location could not be concealed, the Agency would leave no reasonable means for a hostile combatant to breach its defenses.

Ali Vahidi was well aware of these obstacles, but he was convinced that this was where Jaber was being sequestered. He needed to find a way to get to him, to determine how Jaber's defection was related to the recent terrorist actions in the Caribbean and how all of that might impact Iran.

No one under the IRGC's high command had participated in the preparation or execution of these attacks. Tehran made it plain to Vahidi that neither the aircraft explosion nor the destruction of Fort Oscar was an Iranian operation, but the timing of Jaber's flight gave them pause. Why had this loyal soldier suddenly left the country and surrendered to the Americans? Who had destroyed his home? And what happened to Jaber's subordinate, Seyed Asghari, who had seemingly vanished from sight shortly before these assaults?

The interrogation of Rasa Jaber in Marand convinced the IRGC that she was as much in the dark as they were, which meant her use as bait may or may not pay dividends. As matters stood they might never find that out, since Vahidi's men had lost her trail. Now, with no means of reaching Jaber directly, Vahidi decided his only play was to intercept the agent who was spearheading the investigation into these incidents.

"This dossier is on Jordan Sandor," Vahidi said as the two operatives looked through the papers. "Our other team was tracking the agents who met Rasa Jaber at the airport. They have been waiting near CIA Headquarters." Here he paused for effect. "In the hope of finding her again."

The two men shared a quick look of concern but said nothing.

"They have not seen the woman, but they spotted Sandor leaving Langley just before I called you. He is traveling in the back of a black Lincoln Town Car with his deputy director. His driver made several diversionary turns. I believe it is likely they are heading here." Vahidi leaned forward and pointed to the map. "They lost him, but from our location you have a head start; you have time to get there first." He paused. "I want this man alive."

Sandor was well known to the IRGC, and so the driver asked, "What if that is not possible?"

"You have already lost Jaber's wife today, I expect you to be able to take one man into custody."

"We understand."

"The map tells you where you are going. You should stay as far from the perimeter of this estate as possible. Intercept him before he gets there."

Without another word, Ali Vahidi got out of the car and walked away. The driver turned back onto Massachusetts Avenue and sped off toward McLean, Virginia.

———

Sandor and Byrnes were riding through the evening gloom, seated in the back of a Town Car being chauffeured by a junior agent, making the thirty-minute drive to the safe house.

"This really is a miserable business," Sandor said.

"Yes," the DD agreed, "it is."

"Hea is the reason I made it out of North Korea."

"I understand."

"It's only because of her I'm still alive," Sandor said, as if by repeating that simple truth it might help him solve the dilemma.

Byrnes remained silent, knowing there was nothing he could say to make any of this easier. There was no way to justify the exchange being contemplated. Once the girl was sent back she would be tortured and murdered. If the Agency refused to make the trade, Craig Raabe and Jim Bergenn would be left to suffer that same gruesome fate.

"We know they want Hwang. Maybe if we stonewall it they'll deal without involving her."

Byrnes shook his head. "We've obviously been making that offer. They want the girl."

"Tell them she was taken against her will."

"We tried that too, they're not buying it. They saw her on the train when you entered Khasan and she didn't look like any sort of hostage." He paused. "They also took long-range photos of her holding a weapon."

"Damn. Which means they have her picture to work with, and that already puts her family at risk."

According to KCIA sources from inside North Korea, the DPRK had yet to confirm Hea's identity. But that was only a matter of time, especially if they really had her photo. In Kim's totalitarian state the entire population was accounted for, and it would not be long before they matched her disappearance with the events at the Rungrado May Day Stadium. Her family would then be taken into custody and held in anticipation of her return. Once

Hwang was released, the end for Hea's family would be inevitable.

"We have no choice here, Sandor. We can't leave Raabe and Bergenn behind."

"Of course not, but there must be other options. Can't the State Department tell those bastards that if they don't release our men we'll treat it as an act of war?"

Byrnes shook his head again. "An act of war? Bergenn and Raabe were captured in North Korea engaging in espionage. Not to mention murder and kidnapping. Under any international law Kim could stand them in front of a firing squad today and there isn't a government in the world that would cry foul. The act of war was on our side of the table."

"In defense of our country, in case you forgot."

Byrnes let out a long sigh. "I'm sorry, Jordan, we've got to make the trade."

Sandor clenched his teeth. "Send me back. Talk to the DCI, give me a few days to try and get them out."

"Come on, we don't even know what city they're in, let alone what dungeon. I know you're frustrated, but you can't expect me to make a ridiculous request like that."

They were quiet for a few moments as the car turned onto Old Dominion Drive. "All right," Sandor finally said, "give me up in the trade, instead of her."

The agent at the wheel looked into the rearview mirror. Even in the darkness he could see the intensity in Sandor's eyes. They exchanged a quick glance.

"Forget it," Byrnes told him.

"I'm serious."

"I know you are but it's not happening. If you come up with something that makes sense I'll take it to Walsh. Otherwise you need to be realistic. Time is short and word is that Raabe is not going to make it much longer if we don't get him home."

————————

Vahidi's men had arrived in time to position their car amid some trees north of the intersection of Old Dominion Drive and Bellview Road. They only had to wait a few minutes before the black sedan passed in front of them.

The two Iranians were ready. The map showed that the main entrance to the estate was about four miles from the Old Dominion and Bellview intersection, which meant they had to act quickly. The compound consisted of several hundred acres, with multiple perimeter checkpoints. Their job was to reach the sedan before it got to that first entry gate.

The driver started his engine and pulled out, headlights off, rapidly gaining on the Town Car.

The road was totally dark, no streetlamps of any kind, no homes in view. There were rolling hills on either side of them, but all they could see were the red taillights of the Lincoln in the distance. The driver accelerated, narrowing the gap to just a few hundred yards. His partner pulled on night-vision glasses and helped guide them when the lights of the Town Car were intermittently lost as it made turns along the winding road.

————————

The agent driving Byrnes's car was the first to spot the approaching vehicle. "Sir, I think we've got a tail, no headlights, coming up fast."

Sandor spun around, peering into the darkness, straining to make out the onrushing shape behind them. He said, "Don't speed up, just make the first left you can." He drew out his Walther and snapped the slide back, chambering the round. "You should get low," he told Byrnes. Realizing a .380 pistol was not going to be much help against a speeding car, he asked the agent, "What have you got up there, Fitz?"

"Shotgun and a .45."

"Okay, as soon as you make the turn, flat-spin this thing off to the right and kill your headlights and the interior switch."

Fitzpatrick did as he was told. Before the car had come to a full stop Sandor threw open his door while barking at the young agent, "Cover your side," then he rolled out onto the asphalt and kept moving until he found the grassy shoulder of the road.

Within seconds the trailing car appeared, screeching to a halt as the driver realized they'd been made.

Fitz had opened his door and was crouching behind it, shotgun at the ready.

Sandor, who was on his stomach now, did not hesitate. He fired three shots, taking out both front tires of the attackers' car, then fired twice into the windshield, shattering the glass. He rolled over again, coming up on one knee behind a large tree. "You move and you die," he hollered.

The two IRGC operatives responded by opening fire, spraying the back of the Lincoln and the open driver's door with a rapid fusillade and scattering some rounds on the ground where Sandor had been.

Fitzpatrick got off three blasts from the shotgun, then ducked for cover again.

"Stay down!" Sandor yelled at the young agent, then fired off the rest of his magazine. Replacing it in one smooth motion, he took off at a run inside the tree line, coming even with the right side of the sedan. Sandor made out two men, each kneeling behind their open doors. He took aim from behind a large elm and hit the man on the passenger side, dropping him to the ground. When the driver spun in his direction Sandor shouted, "Put your hands up where I can see them." The man had no sight line on Sandor, so he dove back inside the car, threw the gearshift into reverse, and nailed the gas.

Sandor managed to take out the rear right tire as Fitzpatrick fired two more blasts from the shotgun, the second spray of buckshot finding its mark. The driver jerked backward and then slumped forward. The car slowed, rolling backward fifty or so yards until it ran off the blacktop where the rear fender hit a tree, bringing it to a stop with the engine still running and the wheels spinning in the dirt.

"Damnit," Sandor called as he and Fitzpatrick moved cautiously toward the vehicle. "We needed one of them alive."

"Sorry," the young agent said. "I thought he had a bead on you."

"Well then, I guess I'm glad you shot him." Sandor remained low as he approached. "Just be careful now. You never know what surprises they have in store."

Sandor had his pistol extended as he moved closer to the passenger side, Fitzpatrick coming from the front. Sandor kept low, first checking the man on the ground. "This one is dead," he called out.

"I think the guy in the car is a goner too," Fitz said.

Just as Sandor called out, "Don't be too sure," the driver yanked his head up and opened fire at Fitzpatrick. The agent managed to lunge for safety as Sandor fired two shots, the first knocking the man's weapon away, the second catching him in the shoulder. "Any more bullshit," Sandor barked, "and the next two are in your head. Now get out of the car."

"I can't move," the man groaned, his accent thick and his words slurred with pain.

"Tough shit, pal. You picked the fight, now get out. Ah, ah, ah, keep your hands where I can see them. You touch that gearshift again and you're dead."

The man paused for a moment, then turned slowly to his left and fell out onto the ground.

Fitzpatrick got to his feet and began moving forward again.

"Hold it," Sandor ordered. "He might still have a gun. Or a grenade." Sandor circled around the back of the car, making sure there was no one else inside. Then he came up from behind, still keeping several yards between them. "Who are you?"

"Drop dead," the man hissed.

"No need to be unpleasant."

The Iranian turned on his side and stared up. "You are Sandor?"

"I told you, keep your hands in sight. That's better. Now, I'll tell you who I am after you tell me who you are."

"Go to hell."

"Let me explain something," he said. "This can only go one of three ways. I can shoot you in the head. I can leave you here to die slowly. Or we can get you some medical attention if you're willing to cooperate. All I want to know is who you are and what you're after."

The man was obviously in pain, but he managed a grim smile. "You are wrong," he said.

"About what?"

"About everything," the man responded, his voice barely a whisper. Then he murmured, *"Allahu Akbar,"* and stopped moving.

Byrnes had gotten out of the Lincoln and was standing beside Fitzpatrick now. They watched as Sandor stepped forward and kicked the man, hard in the side. "Damn," Sandor said.

"Dead?" the Deputy Director asked.

"Completely." Sandor bent down and checked the man's pockets. There were no grenades, no self-immolation devices, only a wallet with some identification. Sandor held it up to the light from the dashboard in the car. "Probably phony," he said. "We'll check it out."

"What was this about?" Byrnes asked. "He knew your name."

"He certainly did." Sandor leaned into the car and found the brief dossier with his photo on the floor. He held it up for Byrnes to see. "Welcome to my world. How do you like field action, sir?"

"Not much," Byrnes said. He was not smiling. "Iranians?"

"Appears so."

"I thought the Iranians weren't involved."

Sandor shook his head. "Maybe they're not. Maybe they were just looking for a way to get to Jaber. Or to me."

"Let's go talk to Jaber."

"Splendid idea, sir." Sandor looked at Fitzpatrick. "You okay, Fitz?"

He nodded.

"Well, I think we're done here. Call this in and let's drive on."

CHAPTER SIXTY-FIVE

BAYTOWN REFINERY, BAYTOWN, TEXAS

THE HEAD OF security at the Baytown refinery, a former Army colonel name of Patrick Janssen, had his hands full. The feds were all over him with warnings of possible sabotage at the plant. The head of tech support was reporting a possible breach of the classified computer program that contained defense information. And now it seemed that one of their line supervisors, Peter Amendola, had gone missing without a trace.

Threats against the Baytown installation were nothing new, but 99 percent of them evaporated without involving a single tangible act. Disgruntled former employees, tree huggers from the left, eco-maniacs from any number of organizations with the word *green* in their titles, and the usual garden variety of crackpots—from time to time they all trumpeted the need to put an end to the refinement and transport of oil along the shore of the Gulf of Mexico. The BP oil disaster had only served to intensify the pressure.

The possibility of sabotage by foreign nationals was less common and more serious. In almost ten years as head of his department he had only dealt with three credible terrorist threats. One fizzled, the other amounted to a series of overseas communications that were intercepted at the source, and the third, the most frightening of the three, resulted in four arrests in Mexico. That last one was just a couple of years back. Janssen still shuddered at the memory of how close those men came to actually launching an attack.

Janssen was proud of his work. He was confident in the complex internal and perimeter defense schemes at the refinery, but he would never agree with the executives in the hierarchy of the company who regarded them as fail-safe. Janssen had spent too much time in the military to believe anything in life was foolproof. As long as people were involved, mistakes were possible.

There were automated systems such as the antimissile shield, high-powered sprinklers, and irrigation pipes that ran throughout the 2,400-acre plant in the event of fire; screens and sloughs in the event of a hurricane; mechanisms that segregated the numerous holding tanks to prevent the inflammation or explosion of one large reservoir from leading to a chain reaction igniting the others; and any number of structures and protocols to stop breaches of the property.

Nevertheless, this was the largest refinery in the United States, and as such it was a time bomb filled with crude oil and processed petroleum products. Safety was always the principal concern, every minute of every day.

"You're sure someone hacked into the program?" Janssen asked the head of the IT department.

"Not hacked, Pat. I think someone with a lower level of clearance hit it internally."

They were seated in Janssen's office, an austere room on the second floor of the administration building, with large windows overlooking what appeared to be an endless sea of circular tanks and enormous cylindrical conduits. "And you think that's possible."

"Anything is possible. Since you gave us the alert we've been checking every conceivable permutation."

"I don't get it," Janssen said. "If someone got into this data, wouldn't that come up in the normal course of your security checks?"

"Not necessarily. Whoever this was had the authority to enter the network without leaving a virtual fingerprint. I'm not sure how far they got beyond that. We're working on it."

"Well work on it quickly," Janssen told him, then sent the man on his way.

His next interview concerned Peter Amendola. The director of refinery operations had been present for the previous discussion. Now it was his own turn.

"I thought you said this Amendola is a solid citizen."

"He is. If he was going to take some time he would let us know. Amendola is not a spur-of-the-moment kind of guy."

"Uh huh."

"And then we got a call from his wife."

Janssen gave him an impatient look that said, "Get on with it."

"She called yesterday and asked if Amendola had to work the night shift or something. Seems he never got home."

"Maybe he has a girlfriend."

"Could be," the operations director admitted, "kind of

guy who keeps to himself, no telling what he might be up to. But she hasn't heard from him since and he doesn't answer his cell phone."

Janssen thought it over. "She been to the police?"

"Don't think so."

"Have we?"

"Not yet. Thought it best to start with you, Pat."

Janssen nodded. "All right. I want you to catch up with them at IT, see if it's possible this Amendola was our man on the computer."

"I can tell you for certain he had Level Four clearance."

"Which means it could have been him."

"Yes."

Janssen was sitting straight up in his chair, a posture learned during years in the military service that he was not apt to forget. He laced his fingers together and placed his hands on the desk. "We need to meet with his wife. Anyone see her yet or has this all been on the phone?"

"On the phone. Just me. Again, I figured this was your area."

"Uh huh. Well, leave me the info, I'll call her."

"That's what I hoped."

"His coworkers notice anything odd about this guy lately?" Janssen asked.

"Not that anyone has said. Bit of a loner, is all. Always has been."

The director of operations stood up to leave, then hesitated.

"Something else?" Janssen asked.

"Maybe it's nothing, but the way Amendola's wife sounded. I don't know the woman, met her once at a company outing, nothing to compare it to, no past behavior, if you know what I mean."

"Go on."

"When your husband doesn't come home that's cause for serious concern, but there was more to it than that. She sounded worried, but she also sounded guarded. It's hard to explain, but it was there in her tone."

"All right," Janssen said, "I'll get with her right away."

Adina trusted no one. None of his men were provided his full and final plans. Even Antonio Bastidas was being intentionally misled. The necessity of engaging the assistance of Dr. Eric Silfen was a potential problem that could easily be remedied in the endgame.

His two men in Texas, Francisco and Luis, were well under way with their assignment. The team in Houston, which had received the information from Amendola and then disposed of him, was also in place.

As the *Misty II* dropped anchor outside the Isla de la Juventud, off the southwest corner of Cuba, Adina readied himself for another briefing session. This time it would not involve Bastidas, who was already en route to Caracas to make his report. This time he would meet with the team of seamen who would program the submersible crafts that would be launched outside the Yucatan Channel and sent on their course up through the Gulf toward Galveston.

These were the North Korean hybrids that had been designed as something between the American Scorpio and a primitive SPSS narco sub. They were on board a freighter from Venezuela that was sitting at anchor nearby.

As the men gathered on deck, Adina studied the television monitor in the main salon. It was tuned to track Hurricane Charlene as it made its way northwest.

Everything, he told himself, was falling into place.

CHAPTER SIXTY-SIX

AN ESTATE OUTSIDE LANGLEY, VIRGINIA

At Byrnes's instruction, Agent Fitzpatrick had phoned the main security line at the safe house and, after providing a series of passcodes, reported the shooting incident about two miles southeast of the estate. The security systems had already monitored the incident and four vehicles were immediately dispatched to the scene.

Less than two minutes later the convoy came screeching to a halt in a circle around the bullet-riddled Town Car.

Sandor turned to Fitzpatrick. "The proverbial barn door," he said.

Byrnes stepped forward and identified himself to the agent in charge, who then hustled Fitzpatrick, Sandor, and the Deputy Director into the first Suburban and had them taken away. A second SUV rode shotgun in case there were any other hostiles still in play. Two panel vans stayed behind to mop up the situation.

––––––––

After arriving at the front gate they were passed through two checkpoints and escorted to the main building. Byrnes and Sandor did not take time to clean up, making their way directly to the lower floor.

Jaber had been brought to the comfortable study where Byrnes conducted most of their interviews. Jaber got to his feet as the two Americans entered and asked the Deputy Director, "You have news of my wife?" When he received no response he looked from Byrnes to Sandor. "What happened to you?"

Sandor's sport coat was torn at the shoulder and his pants and shirt were soiled from his roll on the ground. There were also bloodstains on his sleeve from his search of the two men they had left behind. "My dry cleaner is on vacation," he replied.

"We were followed here," Byrnes interrupted, "or at least intercepted on our way. We believe the men were Iranian."

"Of course," Jaber responded, as if that were to be expected.

"We assume they were trying to reach you. Or at least obtain information about you or your location."

"Yes," Jaber said impatiently. "And what did they say when you captured them?"

"They weren't in the mood to talk," Sandor said.

Byrnes gave him a disapproving look. "They were both killed at the scene," he explained.

"It would have been helpful if you could have spoken to them," Jaber said.

"I'm sure it would," Sandor agreed, "but since they were trying to blow our heads off, we decided it would be even more helpful if we put an end to that bullshit before we tried to have a chat."

Jaber uttered a long sigh. "What about my wife, please?"

"She's here, in Washington," Byrnes told him.

"I must see her."

"There are some things you need to know first. Sit down."

The three men took seats around the cocktail table and Byrnes patiently described the circumstances of Rasa Jaber's arrival. They were sure she was being followed. They had found two homing devices in her luggage. Any meeting between Jaber and his wife would put both of their lives at risk, and the American government would not be responsible for their safety.

"Bring her here."

"This isn't a hotel, pal."

Byrnes said, "Sandor is not wrong. This facility is designed for a specific use. Your wife is not a person of interest to us. It's also clear that any such attempt is likely to be tracked again, which would compromise my men as well as the two of you."

"What do you plan to do with us, then?"

"As we've discussed, the information you brought us has been, shall we say, a bit thin. To be perfectly candid, my government feels as if we're being played."

Jaber's eyes widened in disbelief. "You think I have placed myself in your custody as a ploy?"

"Not necessarily," Byrnes answered calmly. "We believe the fears you had for your safety were real, and that they caused you to defect. What we cannot understand is how a man as highly placed as you are in the IRGC can have so little information to give us in return for asylum."

Jaber sank back in his chair without speaking.

"Now your wife has arrived and we are convinced she was only released as part of an IRGC plan to bring you into the open. Until she is candid with us on her instructions, which she has not been up to now, we intend to do nothing. The risk of taking you to see her is too great."

"But it's my risk, and it's a risk I'm willing to take."

"Are you?"

"Yes, I am."

Byrnes stood up. "Is there anything else you have for us, anything you've withheld?"

Jaber said nothing, so Sandor also rose. "This is done," he said.

But Byrnes persisted. "If you have any information you have not yet shared, this is the moment. There is no time left to bargain."

"Promise me I will see my wife."

"This is not a negotiation, Jaber."

The Iranian looked up at him, his dark eyes as intense as Byrnes had ever seen them. "Promise me," he said in a hoarse whisper.

Byrnes stared at him, not saying a word.

Jaber stood and faced them. "I told you what little Seyed knew, that the strike will be along your coast in the Gulf of Mexico. He truly did not know where, nor do I. But he believed there was a secondary target. He was not sure if they would attempt both or only proceed with the alternative plan if the first was not viable."

"Where?"

"He did not know."

Sandor shook his head. "Are you making this up as you go along or did this Seyed really tell you this?"

"On my life," Jaber told him, looking directly at Sandor now. "And my wife's."

"Be assured," Sandor said, "those are precisely the stakes you're playing for."

———————

"What did you make of it?" Sandor asked after they left Jaber and hurried down the stairs to the basement level.

"Not sure, but I tend to believe him. I've come to know this man over the past couple of weeks. I can see how he would have tried to hold back one final piece of the puzzle."

"Maybe he's still holding out. It's not much of a lead."

"I think that's why I believe him," Byrnes said. "He could have invented some detailed story about an attack on Miami or Dallas or whatever, sent us running all over the map."

Sandor uttered a frustrated sigh. "If you're convinced he's not doubling on us we'll have to start looking for this second target."

In the basement they were vetted by the guards on duty, then a door was unlocked and they were passed into an area with several holding cells. A second door was opened and they entered Hwang's room.

The North Korean had been held here since his arrival in the States. Interrogation had yielded no more than the information Sandor had elicited in Pyongyang, the revelations Hwang had shared only because he never believed the Americans would escape. Hwang regarded this misjudgment as a weakness and a complete disgrace to his country, refusing any further cooperation. He was a true believer, or so he insisted, and would rather go to his final reward than disappoint the Great Leader.

It was also quite possible that what he had told Sandor was the extent of his true knowledge. Whatever deal had been made between the Venezuelans and the North Koreans, it was becoming increasingly apparent that the former were in charge of the operation, while the latter were not involved in the execution of the plans.

"How's the shoulder?" Sandor asked with feigned cheerfulness. "No gangrene, I hope."

Hwang treated Sandor to his best scowl, then directed himself to Byrnes. "Why have you brought him here? Do you expect to frighten me with his barbaric tactics?"

"Hey," Sandor said, "your English is getting better. Rosetta Stone?"

Byrnes said, "We are in discussions with your country regarding your release."

"Ah. I will have the opportunity to face my Great Leader and make reparation for my failings."

"You would be exchanged for the two men who are being detained by your country."

"Two spies, you mean. I would rather die than see them released."

Sandor felt the blood rush to his face, but he said nothing.

"And what of the girl?" Hwang asked. "The Great Leader does not suffer traitors. I am sure she will be expected to accompany me on my journey home."

Now Sandor stepped forward and, before Byrnes could utter a "Stand down," he had kneed Hwang hard in the groin, grabbed a handful of the man's hair, and, twisting his head to the side, slammed him against the wall and pressed his left forearm against his larynx. "You miserable sonuvabitch," Sandor hissed into the Korean's face. "I'll kill you first."

Byrnes called in the two guards. They pried Hwang loose from Sandor's grip, helping the breathless man to take a seat on his cot.

"Kill me," Hwang gasped, as he rubbed his neck, "and you will never see your men again, Mr. Sandor. Oh yes," he added as he saw the look of surprise. "I know who you are, and our acquaintance will not end when I am returned to my homeland."

The guards were standing beside Sandor now, looking somewhat equivocal over whether to intervene if Sandor decided to have another go at breaking the Korean's spine.

"Threats are not helpful," Byrnes warned. "Our arrangements have not been finalized. I would be careful if I were you."

"So," Hwang said, still panting, "you *have* brought Mr. Sandor here to intimidate me."

"No," Sandor said, "I'm here to tell you that there's no deal involving the girl. You want to go home, you're going to have to tell your pals you're coming alone." With that, he spun around and left the room.

––––––––

Upstairs on the main level he used one of the bathrooms to clean up. Best he could manage was to wash his face and run a comb through his dark, wavy hair. His clothes really were a mess, which he hadn't even noticed until Jaber mentioned it, but there was nothing to be done about that now. He needed to speak with Hea.

She was staying in one of the guest rooms on the second floor, where she was free to roam the house, except for the high-security areas on the lower levels, and to stroll a large fenced-in area of the beautiful grounds that sprawled over several hundred acres. He knocked on her door and she let him in. She was looking much better than the last time he saw her.

She had gotten a little sun, and they were feeding her well, or so it appeared, because she was shapelier than he recalled. Maybe, he thought, he just hadn't noticed before.

It was not in her culture to greet him with a hug. As Hea stood there with an uncertain look she prepared to make a demure bow, but he stepped forward and wrapped her in his arms. It took her an instant before she warmed to the moment, then drew him closer, and they held each other without speaking. Then he backed away and said, "You look great."

"Thank you. You look as if you have been fighting again," she said with a smile. "Is this what you do all the time?"

"Not all the time," he replied with a grin. "Just most of the time."

"You are all right, though?" she asked as she pointed to the dried blood on his sleeve.

"Not my blood, so I'm fine. But we need to talk. Want to go for a walk?"

They headed outside into the darkness, the cool night air bracing him for what he had to say. After the attack by the two Iranians and his assault on Hwang, it felt good to wander the grounds and collect himself.

"You are very troubled by something, Sandor. It would be best if you told me sooner, if that is the proper English. You know I try hard to speak well."

Sandor nodded. "You do just fine," he said, and then he told her. He explained the capture of Bergenn and Raabe, the possibility of an exchange, the rumors of Raabe's failing health and, of course, the fact that they were insisting Hea be part of the trade.

She neither spoke nor broke stride when he told her; they just continued on, side by side into the night.

"I have another concern," he said.

"My family," she answered. "Yes, as you know, that has been my worrying from the beginning. Worrying?"

"Worry."

"Yes, my worry."

"Mine too. Once Hwang is back, with or without you, he'll be able to identify your brother."

"He may, this is true. But first he must find him."

Now Sandor stopped, gently took her by the arm, and turned her toward him. "What are you saying?"

Hea showed him a diffident smile. "We have plans for such things, you see? Your arrival in my country was not a surprise, Sandor. You know that?"

He nodded.

"You Americans are funny people, I think. You act as if nothing exists until you arrive. You understand this? There are many cultures for thousands of years before yours, yet you believe you are the inventors of everything, that nothing happens until you do it. Am I saying this right?"

Sandor laughed for what seemed the first time in quite a while. "I get the point, if that's what you're asking."

"It is not an evil thing. I believe you mean well by it. It is, um, charming, I think is the word."

"So are you," he said, then thought he saw her blush in the moonlight.

"We worked with Kyung, he knew you were coming, we arranged the, um, contact at the festival, yes?"

"Was your brother always part of the plan too?"

"Yes," she replied simply.

"From the beginning?"

"He was ready if he was needed."

"And the rest of your family?"

"Arrangements are made for such things. It is not easy, and I can see from your face you do not believe me, but we do things even when you Americans are not there to help," she said, the smile returning. "My people are all prisoners, and some of us work for our freedom. Do you understand?"

Now Jordan gave her his best smile. "Do *I* understand? Yes, yes I do. So your family is safe, but where? In the South?"

"It does not matter. It was time for them to go."

"But what about you? What happens to you if they send you back?"

Her look of amusement vanished as she said, "This is the risk we take. Perhaps it would be better if I was never leaving the country with you. We had no way to knowing your men would be captured."

"So what is that supposed to mean, that you'll agree to go back? Hea, they'll murder you. And worse. And then your family will be at risk again. They'll force you to tell them where they've gone."

A look of serenity replaced the fear that had flickered for a moment in her young eyes. "I cannot tell them things I do not know."

"That's true," Sandor said with a nod of comprehension. For the first time he felt some real hope. "If your family is safe, even with Hwang's return, then all I've got to do is figure out how to protect you."

She shook her head and began to say something, but he stopped her.

"Look, you had a plan even before I got there, right? Well, I have a plan too. Just trust me."

She gazed up at him for a long time without speaking. Then she whispered, "I do. I do trust you, Sandor."

There was nothing more to say. Together they had survived the onslaught in Pyongyang and the flight into Russia. He was certainly not about to surrender her to the grizzly fate Hwang and his compatriots would arrange.

Sandor stared into her unblinking eyes, a shared moment where kissing seemed almost superfluous.

Then he took her in his arms and kissed her anyway.

CHAPTER SIXTY-SEVEN

BAYTOWN, TEXAS

THE NEXT MORNING, as he prepared to travel south, Sandor told Byrnes he would not leave Washington without a firm commitment that no trade involving Hea would be concluded until he returned. Sandor realized time was running out, but he also knew these diplomatic negotiations never moved quickly. He also banked on the fact that the North Korean government would keep Raabe and Bergenn alive long enough to make the exchange.

Then, just to be sure there was no misunderstanding his position, Sandor took Hea with him to Texas.

It was not easy, doubling back on his way to the airport, gaining access to the safe house under the pretense of needing to speak with the girl again, then taking Hea with him for an imaginary meeting at Langley. It was tougher still at the airstrip, explaining how an unauthorized person was joining their flight south on one of the Agency's G4s. But Sandor had the respect and confidence of enough of his fellow agents that he was able to talk his way through. Soon he and the girl were in the air on their way to Houston.

"Are you out of your mind?" Byrnes demanded when he learned what happened and was patched through to

Sandor on a sat-phone. "This kind of stunt is over the top, even for you."

By this time the flight was over West Virginia. "I could have her parachute out, sir, you can pick her up in the Smoky Mountains."

"Stow the sarcasm, Sandor. When you land, you leave that girl on the plane and they'll bring her back here straightaway. That's an order."

"I can use her help down there."

"You can use her help?" Byrnes's voice had become an apoplectic garble.

"You okay? Sounds like you're drowning."

"Listen to me, Jordan, the girl is a foreign national and we cannot be responsible for her safety. On top of that she's an informant, not a field agent. And she barely speaks English. Even if I could somehow put all of that aside, we need her so we can get Bergenn and Raabe home. This is not open to discussion. You will send her back by return mail, you read me?"

"Yes, sir."

Hea had been able to hear the Deputy Director yelling on the other end and, when the call ended as abruptly as it had begun, she said, "You are in great trouble for bringing me."

"Not at all."

She gave a look that said she knew he was lying. "What did Mr. Byrnes say?"

Sandor slouched in his seat. "He wished us good luck," he told her, then closed his eyes and tried to get some rest.

———————

As they got farther south the flight became bumpy, early effects of the coming hurricane. By the time they touched down at Ellington Airport, Byrnes had already gotten word to the flight crew as well as his agents on the ground that Hea was to remain aboard. When the plane taxied to a stop the pilot came back and explained. "I have my orders, Mr. Sandor," he said.

"Me too," Jordan said. He took Hea by the hand and disembarked, wind whipping around them as they walked down the steps. Two operatives were waiting to greet them. One was a complete stranger to Sandor but the other was an old friend. "What the hell are you doing in Texas?"

"Temporary change of scenery," Brendan Banahan replied with a grin, then the two men shook hands.

Sandor nodded to the other agent. "So, were you guys sent here to help me or stop me?"

"We're here to help you," Banahan said. "But we need to put this young woman on the flight back to D.C."

"And if I don't agree? Are you ready to shoot me or what?"

His old friend smiled. "Just one or two in the leg, slow you down a bit."

"You know what's going on here?"

"I do. And I know that we need this lady to get Jimmy and Craig home, or at least that's what Byrnes told me."

Sandor nodded. "He's telling you the truth. Problem is, Hea is the reason Craig and Jim are still alive. Not to mention the only reason I'm here. If we send her back to North Korea you can just imagine the warm reception Kim's going to give her."

The two agents had a look at the girl, who stood there impassively as they haggled over her fate.

"I'm sorry, ma'am," Banahan said.

"I need twenty-four hours," Sandor told him. "I've got my reasons, and you know me well enough to know I'd never hang my own men out to dry."

"Come on, Jordan, you can see what we're up against. We have orders."

"Look at this weather," Sandor said, pointing up at the cloudy sky. "Probably shouldn't be flying out of here anyway, right? Take her, hold her, tie her to a post, I don't care, just give me twenty-four hours before you send her back."

Banahan shook his head as if someone had just told him something incredibly sad. Then the second agent spoke up, surprising Sandor when he said, "Let me call the Deputy Director. Weather here really is pretty dicey."

Sandor responded with a curious smile. "Have we met before?"

The man held out his hand and Sandor took it. "I'm Ronny Young. We've never met, but I know who you are."

———

Young pulled out his cell phone and reached Byrnes, who, after offering some loud and uncomplimentary opinions about Sandor's insubordination and downright disobedience, agreed to the twenty-four-hour moratorium on Hea. "But no excuses after that. If the weather gets worse, you get her back if you have to drive her up here yourself," the Deputy Director barked at his agent.

Young agreed.

Then Sandor interrupted. "Ask Byrnes if he's seen the *Times* this morning."

Young responded with a curious look.

"Here," Sandor said, reaching into his back pocket and

pulling out an article from the morning paper. The head-line read:

NORTH KOREAN DIPLOMAT RETURNING HOME IN EXCHANGE FOR AMERICAN TOURISTS

Young read the headline to Byrnes, then the lead para-graph:

> Government sources have confirmed the planned exchange of a North Korean diplo-mat, who has been detained in Washington on suspicion of improper activities, for two Americans being held in Pyongyang in con-nection with violation of their visitor visas.

Sandor could hear Byrnes snorting into the phone on the other line.

"Tell him he doesn't have to thank me," Sandor said. He told Hea to stay with Agent Young and hurried off with Ba-nahan, then climbed into a GMC Yukon and sped away.

———————

Less than half an hour later their SUV was approaching Baytown. When they reached the refinery they passed through the clearance centers and were escorted to Patrick Janssen's office.

The former Army colonel introduced himself, had his secretary bring them coffee, then took his seat behind his large, metal industrial desk. "You boys mind if I talk plain?"

"I like plain talk," Sandor told him.

"That's good, 'cause for the life of me I can't figure why Washington would send two spooks to investigate a rumor like this. Forget that phony State Department horseshit you showed me," he said, referring to their standard credentials. "Look, fellas, I get visits from the FBI, Homeland Security, hell, Department of the Interior is up my ass every other week. But two agents from the Company, well, I don't get that at all."

Sandor grinned, not even bothering to deny anything the man had said. He had already checked out the various commendations and photos on the walls. Janssen was ex-military and, as Sandor was advised back in D.C., he had already been given a Level 2 clearance for these discussions. Plain talk, as Janssen suggested, was in order. "Whatever these rumors may or may not turn out to be, sir," Sandor began, allowing the man his rank, "we have reason to believe they're connected with the downed airliner and the attack on the communications facility in the Caribbean."

"Communications facility?"

"State of the art. Fort Oscar, which has been portrayed in the media as an essentially defunct old fortress, actually housed a multinational communications linkup."

Janssen nodded without speaking.

"We have no particulars on the when or the how of another attack, if one is really planned, we only know the where. And that's here."

Janssen called in the director of IT, who explained their concern about a possible breach of the computers controlling the automated security procedures. As of yet they had not been able to determine the extent of the information obtained or to identify the intruder. They were confident none of the systems had been damaged, but information had definitely been extracted.

Then Janssen told them about the recent disappearance of Peter Amendola.

"How many days?" Sandor asked.

"Going on forty-eight hours. Actually his wife alerted us. He never made it home after his shift night before last. He scheduled some time off or we wouldn't even know he'd gone missing, at least not yet."

"Anyone meet with her?"

"Spoke with her on the phone. We were going to see her today, then I heard you guys were coming."

Sandor nodded.

"For all we know," Janssen said, "he's got a girlfriend or he's off on a bender."

"You know this guy? I mean, anyone think it's likely that he'd run off that way?"

"Actually, that's a negative on both counts. I met him, but don't actually remember him all that well. We spoke with his coworkers. They say there's no way he took a flier. Doesn't even stop for a beer with the boys. Keeps to himself mostly, very buttoned-down."

Sandor glanced at Banahan. The perfect type for a flip. "All right, have someone call, tell his wife we're coming over right now. Meanwhile, let's just do a quick review of your current defense resources, see what we might do to help."

—————

The Amendola home was a modest ranch house on a suburban street west of Hedwig Village. There was nothing unusual about the place, nothing to set it apart from the other homes on the block.

As Sandor and Banahan headed up the walkway Jordan whispered, "I feel like a cop."

"I know what you mean," Brendan said.

"Let's keep this simple."

Kate Amendola was waiting for them at the front door. She was wearing a plain housedress, had her hair pulled back, and wore no makeup to conceal the tired lines around her eyes. Under other circumstances Sandor figured she might be reasonably attractive, but today she appeared older than her years.

He flashed some federal credentials and she showed them into the living room.

"Can I get you something? Coffee? Water?"

"No thank you," Sandor said. "We'll only take a few minutes of your time."

She responded with an odd look, and for a moment Jordan thought she was going to laugh. "My time? Take all the time you want. I have nothing to do but hang around here and worry."

Sandor gave a short nod. "Well, I'll get right to the point, then. I take it this behavior is out of the ordinary for your husband?"

Mrs. Amendola stared at him as if he were speaking a

foreign language. "Out of the ordinary? Yes, you can certainly say that. In all the years we've been married Peter's never disappeared before."

The three of them were standing in the middle of the room, and it was apparent no one was in the mood to sit.

"Have you noticed anything unusual lately? Has he been under a strain of any kind? Trouble at work? Difficulty at home?"

"You mean, have Peter and I been having marital problems, is that what you're asking?" Her voice grew louder now. "Are you asking if I think he just up and ran off on me?"

Sandor decided it was easier to interrogate a terrorist than to question an angry housewife. "Actually, no ma'am," he responded quietly. "I'm asking if you've seen anything in your husband's general behavior that you regard as unusual. Has he mentioned problems at the refinery? Has he been short-tempered? Anything at all like that."

His calm demeanor helped to defuse her mounting anger. She stared at him, as if suddenly comprehending that she was speaking to a federal agent, not a marriage counselor. "Is Peter in some kind of trouble?"

"To be honest, we're not sure," he admitted, "but if he is, and if we're going to be able to help him, we need a starting place."

"We have two children," she told them. "Our son has special needs." When Sandor gave an inquiring look, she said, "He's mildly autistic and he has serious respiratory issues. Peter is a devoted father. He comes home from work and spends as much time with him as he can."

Banahan, who had been silent up to now, said, "Then

it's fair to say you have no explanation why your husband wouldn't have at least called you these past two days."

"None," she replied dully, her anger receding into the sad realization of that fact.

"We understand you've tried his cell phone a number of times."

"Of course. Many times. And I've tried texts. And e-mails." Then, as if remembering something, she hesitated, then said, "Peter hasn't been sleeping very well lately." Her reluctance in making the statement was obvious, as if she was somehow betraying a secret she and her husband shared.

"How do you mean?" Sandor asked. "Like tossing and turning?"

"He would get out of bed and go downstairs. Sometimes he didn't know I was awake, but it's been happening a lot, especially this past week."

Banahan asked whether she and her husband had discussed what was bothering him, but she shook her head.

Must be a close couple, Sandor noted, then asked, "Where downstairs?"

"I'm sorry?"

"You said he would go downstairs. Where would he go? Was there someplace specific or would he just walk around the house?"

She winced, telling Sandor that he was treading on their private life again. It was exactly where he wanted to be. He abandoned his pose as an understanding officer and fixed her with the intense look of a man who knew how to get answers when he needed them.

"Where did he go, Mrs. Amendola?"

She paused for a moment, then said, "Peter has a little office area, in the basement. He would go there."

"Show us," Sandor said, more by way of an order than a request.

She led them down a narrow flight of stairs to the finished basement and pointed to the corner.

Sandor made a cursory examination of the desk and the area around it. There was a small filing cabinet to the left and he had Banahan begin a search. Then Sandor started opening the desk drawers and riffling through the papers.

"I'm not so sure you should be . . . ," Kate Amendola began to say, but Sandor shot her a look that told her she had best shut the hell up for the moment.

The drawer on the upper left was locked. "You have a key for this?" he asked.

She shook her head.

Sandor found a letter opener and pried it open.

There did not seem to be anything of interest in there, so Sandor got down and began looking into the knee well and underneath the desk. Then he rose and began yanking the drawers all the way out and stacking them on the floor, one atop the other.

"Bingo," he said. Banahan turned around to see Sandor pulling a metal strongbox from the back of the top drawer cavity.

Sandor stood and placed it on the desktop. "You ever see this before?" he asked the woman.

"No," she said, but the look on her face told them she was lying.

He flipped the top open and the three of them stared at

several stacks of hundred-dollar bills, a manila folder, and a small white envelope with the word "Kate" written on the front.

Sandor studied the woman's look of complete astonishment. "You've seen the box before, haven't you?"

She nodded slowly.

"But you never knew what was in it, did you?"

She looked up at him. "I swear, I never did. I didn't even know where he kept it."

Sandor fixed her with a hard stare, then opened the envelope and read the letter.

Amendola told her everything, making it clear he finally realized that he had put himself and his family in serious danger. Assuming her husband was still alive, Kate Amendola might yet be used as a target or even as a hostage, and so Sandor figured taking her into protective custody would be a hedge against further distractions. He pulled out his phone and called Ronny Young to arrange for the Amendola children to be taken out of school and also brought to the plant for safekeeping. "Here," he said, handing her the cell, "tell this man where he can pick up your children. Then get dressed, you're coming with us."

CHAPTER SIXTY-EIGHT

WASHINGTON, D.C.

Byrnes called a meeting of the counterterrorism task force in Washington that had been assembled to deal with the Baytown threat. They met at the Pentagon, convening in a steel-encased room on the second floor where signals could neither be transmitted nor received except on secure lines. Eavesdropping from inside or outside the building was impossible.

The gathering was attended by representatives from the FBI, CIA, NSA, Homeland Security, Department of Defense, and the White House. They ringed the large conference table, studying the reports that had been compiled to date. The team had pieced together the information Jordan Sandor had gathered from Hwang, the investigation in St. Barths, the sketchy intelligence provided to Deputy Director Byrnes from Ahmad Jaber, and now the papers left behind by Peter Amendola.

They believed they were finally in possession of a general concept of what they were about to confront.

The North Koreans had apparently made a deal with Venezuela to provide weapons technology in exchange for a guaranteed supply of oil at a below-market price. The lack of fuel was choking Kim's economy, making the arrangement irresistible for the DPRK. The regime in Caracas would more than cover its losses on the cut-rate sales to North Korea from the benefits it would derive in destroying America's largest refinery—not only causing political and economic panic in the West, but also creating an immediate inflation in the price of processed crude.

The attack on Baytown was being spearheaded by Rafael Cabello, known in the intelligence community as Adina. He also appeared to be responsible for the assault on Fort Oscar and, in all likelihood, the downing of the passenger flight outside St. Maarten. The logical conclusion was that the destruction of the communications center in Gustavia was intended to weaken the ability of Washington to monitor Adina's intended movements in the Caribbean. This in turn suggested that the assault would be coming by water, rather than land or air. Perhaps the explosion of the jetliner was geared to draw more attention to the skies than the sea, and in the double-think world of espionage there were those who subscribed to every imaginable variation on those themes. In the meantime, Hurricane Charlene had increased in speed and intensity and was only twenty-four hours away from striking the Gulf Coast with its full force, complicating their defensive strategies.

Having agreed on this analysis, the brain trust in Washington was convinced that they would be able to prevent the attack and were already congratulating each other on averting yet another terrorist threat to the United States. Despite interagency rivalries, there were even some outside the CIA who had to admit Sandor had done one hell of a job.

Sandor, however, was not so sure.

———

Sandor and Banahan had returned to the Baytown refinery with Peter Amendola's strongbox, his wife in tow.

"You got the kids?" Sandor asked.

"They're on the way," Ronny Young told him when they met in Janssen's office.

"Good. Make sure they're not scared to death by this whole thing, okay? My guess is they're going to have enough to deal with over the next few days."

Young nodded.

"And how's my friend Hea doing?"

"At the moment," Young said, "my constant companion." He gave a nod to the right. "She's in an office down the hall. She's fine."

They sorted through the contents of Amendola's manila folder, which provided a fair summary of the information for which he had traded his soul. In his note to his wife he did not specifically admit his treachery, but he asked her forgiveness and understanding.

And yet, Sandor thought, and yet.

He asked Janssen to vet the information Amendola had sold, and to confirm just how much damage the release of the data might cause. Then he headed for the privacy of a small, empty office where he called Byrnes. The DD left the task force meeting to take the call.

"You got the fax of the Amendola file?"

"We did. Good work on that."

"What preparations is CTC making to secure the refinery?"

Byrnes described in general terms the measures being taken by the joint counterterrorism team, and Sandor listened without interruption. "You're uncharacteristically quiet," Byrnes observed when he was finished.

"I'm not sure I buy it."

"What does that mean?"

"I mean it's been too easy. Like we've been following the breadcrumbs they've dropped along the path. I'm not sure I buy it," he repeated. "Take Amendola, for instance. The guy disappears, the wife hasn't heard a word, no one has seen him, so we've got to believe they removed him, right?"

"I'm listening."

"Why kill him now? They've obviously been paying him, he apparently gave them the information they wanted. Why not just let him go home?"

"I would answer with the obvious," Byrnes replied. "He might have a change of heart, maybe he was ready to blow the whistle on them."

"True, but factor into the equation that he hasn't done that up to now. Why would he suddenly expose himself to a long prison term? An attack of conscience? Not likely. The note to his wife shows he came to realize that these people mean business. They know where he lives, where his family lives. It sounds to me like a man who was afraid, not a guy who was going to turn on them."

"So what're you saying?"

"I'm not sure, but let's think it through. By making him disappear it became a certainty that within a day or two people would be looking for him. Questions would be asked. The cash might even turn up. Or he might have left something behind, one of those 'Open in the event someone blows my brains out' notes."

"Which he did."

"Not exactly, but pretty close. It was enough to make it clear he was no Boy Scout, and that someone was obviously paying him a lot of green for information on the refinery's security systems."

"And you think the fact that it all came to light was intentional."

"I think, as Sun Tzu taught us, you must never underestimate your enemy. These terrorists are animals, but they're savagely clever animals. They wouldn't take Amendola down without purpose. Or without considering the consequences."

Byrnes mulled it over. "So, if they left Amendola alive . . ."

"They would have actually bought more time," Sandor finished the thought. "They could have even held him, let him call his wife to say he had to go out of town for two days. She would have been angry, but she wouldn't have started calling around to report him missing."

"I suppose not."

"Add this to what that dying terrorist told Lieutenant Vauchon that night at Fort Oscar. Not to mention the airliner they took out in St. Maarten. And what about the story our friend Jaber is spinning, letting the line out a little at a time?"

"Jaber," Byrnes repeated.

"It's all too pat for my taste."

"Which leaves us where?"

"We've got to continue making preparations for Baytown." Sandor drew a deep breath. "But it also leaves us looking for their secondary target."

Byrnes was quiet for a moment. "I see your point. That would be a typical Adina ploy."

"Exactly. Misdirection."

"And what about Jaber?"

"I think it may be time to grant his wish and cut him loose. He wants to see the missus so badly, let him go."

"He's a political detainee, Sandor."

"He's a murderer, and he's counting on Uncle Sam's generous nature to protect him. Don't be fooled by his polished act. He's a terrorist, sir, remember that."

Byrnes was in no mood to debate ethics with Sandor, who was colorblind when it came to discerning shades of gray. "Tell me what the hell you're doing with the girl."

"What girl?"

"You can't jeopardize the lives of our men."

"As if I ever would," Sandor bristled. "Look sir, Hwang may be up to his neck in something that could cost the lives of thousands of people, so you know damn well that we're not dealing him away until we clean this up. You also know I'm totally loyal to my men, but for now no one is going anywhere."

For once Byrnes backed off. "All right," he said, "but you better be ready with an explanation . . ."

"I am, believe me."

"You mean that article in the paper?"

"That's part of it. The more public this becomes, the more likely Kim will deal for Hwang alone. He couldn't lose face by admitting he wanted this girl as part of the trade."

"So that's why you threatened the reporter?"

Sandor did not answer. "Baytown is on high alert. Tell

them in D.C. they need to start thinking about a secondary target, sir. That's what I'll be doing down here."

————————

When Byrnes returned to the meeting he wasted no time advancing Sandor's concerns, giving his agent's analysis and some of his own thinking.

"The information we received from Ahmad Jaber has been disappointing, to say the least. But he has told us that his man, Seyed Asghari, believed there were two targets. In fact, the attack on Baytown may be more a ploy than a real threat, if you carry this thinking to its logical conclusion."

"You're not suggesting we pull back from the Baytown operation," the man from Homeland Security said.

"Quite the contrary," Byrnes said. "The more we learn the more we need to make it appear we're buying their primary target. We need to make it obvious we are shoring up the defenses at Baytown."

"What about the surveillance you've requested?" asked the colonel from the DOD. "With Fort Oscar out and the hurricane coming, it's going to be difficult to monitor movement in and out of the Gulf."

"Difficult but not impossible. Everything points to some sort of attack by sea, or at least the transport of weapons by sea. We need to keep the fleet on call."

An admiral from the Joint Chiefs nodded, then reminded them, "We're in the middle of a hurricane."

"Yes," the Deputy Director of the CIA agreed, "but it's going to be a hurricane for them too."

CHAPTER SIXTY-NINE

BAYTOWN, TEXAS

SANDOR RETURNED TO Janssen's office in time to catch the end of a phone discussion between Brendan Banahan and an FBI agent in Houston who was coordinating the efforts of the local staff there. Banahan completed the call, then looked up and said, "We need to talk."

They excused themselves and huddled up in the hallway where Banahan said, "We may have something."

"Go."

"They've got the Coast Guard and Navy on alert and they're stepping up harbor inspections. We also had them do a rundown on local airports. We may have a lead at a small strip up in Bryan, at Coulter Airfield, near Texas A&M."

"I'm all ears."

"Private plane came in yesterday morning, dropped off a couple of businessmen, dumped some cargo that was loaded on a truck, then the plane took off and the truck left."

"What makes it a lead?"

"We've been calling every private airstrip in the area, having them double- and triple-check recent activity. Turns out the flight plan for this arrival didn't match the itinerary the pilot filed."

Sandor responded with a slow nod.

"They came in unannounced, claimed they were flying in from a field up in Lawrence, Kansas. We checked, there was no record of that plane in Lawrence."

"And where's the airplane now?"

"Seems it went on to the private strip outside Dallas, then took off again for Lawrence . . ."

"And don't tell me."

"Never arrived."

"Okay," Sandor said. "I'm on my way."

With Janssen's cooperation Sandor commandeered one of the Sikorsky helicopters at the refinery and told the pilot to head north to Coulter. He had Banahan stay behind to oversee efforts at the plant and to organize a forensics team to follow him to Bryan, just in case.

It was a short ride on the high-powered chopper and Sandor was set down beside the private terminal at the end of the small airfield. The young woman and two baggage handlers who were on duty the day before had already been contacted and were told to await his arrival.

Sandor did not flash any identification as he entered the small building; he simply walked up to the fair-haired girl behind the counter and introduced himself. "I understand you were here yesterday morning when you had an unscheduled arrival?"

"Yes, sir," she said uneasily.

Sandor had a look at her name tag. "Take it easy, Karen, I'm not here because you did anything wrong, I'm just doing a routine investigation."

"Routine?" The girl gave him a nervous smile. "Mister, I

gave some information to a man in Houston over the phone less than an hour ago. Twenty minutes later I get a call telling me to round up Brad and Freddie and then stay put. And now you blow in here on a helicopter and you want me to believe this is routine? I don't know what this is about, but whatever it is, it isn't routine."

"You're right," Sandor agreed. "This is not routine, but I promise you're not in any trouble. Just tell me what happened."

Karen did her best to recall every detail. When she finished with a description of the two passengers, Sandor knew he was in the right place. "Where are the boys?"

"Waiting outside," she said, then led him out the door and around the side of the building, where she introduced Sandor to the two young men sitting on a couple of boxes.

"Thanks for coming over here, guys."

The taller boy, named Brad, said, "No problem. Made it sound kinda important."

"Might be," Sandor said. "You guys go to A&M?"

"Aggies through and through," the other boy, Freddie, told him.

"Excellent. Well, I've just got a few questions. Maybe Freddie can go back inside with Karen. I want to hear from each of you separately, okay?"

The three young people already had the sense they were not in the position to argue with anything this man had to say, so Freddie followed Karen, making themselves scarce as Sandor got to work interviewing Brad. When he was done he repeated the process, then sat all three of them down in the terminal. "You've been great giving me the facts. Now I want some opinions."

"Like what?" Karen asked.

"Anything peculiar you noticed about these people, what they did, how they acted?"

Brad spoke up immediately. "Shit yeah," he said. "We told you about the truck, right? Thing was freakin' huge. I mean, they had these boxes, could've fit in the back of a pickup, but they had this gigunda sixteen-wheeler. What was all that about?"

"Yeah," Freddie agreed.

"And the boxes, they weren't all that big, but man they were heavy."

"I'll say," Freddie chimed in.

"We're only here part-time and this ain't exactly Dallas–Fort Worth, but we've lifted our share o' crates, and these babies were heavy for their size."

Sandor nodded. "No one here checks contents, no scanners or anything?"

"Not for incoming domestic flights," Karen said.

"And not much outgoing," Brad admitted with a nervous laugh. "Hell, these private flights, you could toss anything aboard, who the hell is gonna know?"

Sandor shook his head. Even in the face of a worldwide epidemic of terror, the naïveté of the American people survives. As does its basic trust in others. "You said they were bringing in some sort of meteorological equipment. They were going to track Hurricane Charlene?"

"Something like that. You say you want opinions, I can tell you they didn't look like no weathermen to me," Brad said.

"Me neither," Freddie agreed.

Sandor turned back to the girl. "And their itinerary listed this as a domestic flight."

"That's right," Karen agreed. "From Lawrence, like I said."

"But you have no tracking facilities," Sandor said, thinking aloud, "and you don't check with the port of embarkation when an unscheduled flight arrives."

"No, sir."

"So, regardless of who would have been working here yesterday, there was no way to know that plane was coming in or where it was coming from. It could have flown in from anywhere."

Karen nodded.

Then Brad said, "But those guys in the truck, whoever they were, they sure as hell knew they were comin'."

"I'll say," Freddie agreed.

Sandor asked them to give him one more description of the tractor-trailer, to consider any detail they might have left out.

"I'm pretty sure it said something about 'refrigeration' on the back," Brad remembered.

"Company name?"

"Not that I can recall. But they had the guys on the truck load the crates themselves, and they didn't open the back hatch, like you might expect, they opened some kinda side compartment. And then the two guys from the plane, they got inside through a different door on the side. Weird, you know?"

"Weird how?"

"Well, I mean trucks don't usually have all these extra

compartments, if you catch my drift. Trailers usually have flat panel sides and a rear hatch. I dunno, thought it might help."

Sandor said that it did. "Karen, you never got close to the cargo, that right?"

The girl nodded.

"Okay." Sandor stood. "There's a team of specialists coming here in just a few minutes." He glanced at his stainless steel Rolex, then told them, "They actually should have been here already." Looking back at the two young men, he said, "I want you to stick around, go through some tests."

"Tests?"

"Just a precaution."

Brad and Freddie shared an uneasy look.

"Probably nothing," Sandor assured them, then headed outside. He pulled out his cell, phoned Banahan, and said, "I've spoken with the three kids who were here, I'll fill you in later. When your gang from Houston shows up, be sure they sweep the area and check out the two boys."

"For what?" Banahan asked, feeling as if he'd just entered the middle of a conversation.

"They say the crates they unloaded were small but extremely heavy, and I'm guessing whatever was inside could have been lined with lead. The trailer also had a couple of different compartments, wouldn't be surprised if those were lined too. I want the boys and their luggage tractor tested for exposure to radioactive materials."

CHAPTER SEVENTY

ISLA DE LA JUVENTUD, CUBA

Adina's yacht rocked gently on the quiet sea, moored just off this small island situated to the southwest of Cuba. A large freighter flying a Liberian flag under the name *Morning Star* was now anchored some fifteen hundred yards away.

Its only cargo was two North Korean–built mini-submarines.

The shipyard outside Maracaibo Bay in Venezuela had retro-fitted this old double-bottomed freighter, working in the lowest cargo hold, number four, isolating it from all other belowdeck areas. A moon pool and cranes were inserted so the submersibles could be loaded aboard, ready to slide out into the sea along newly installed launching rails. A single hatch was cut into the outer skin of the hull, rigged to open outward on hydraulic levers. The mechanisms and hinges were set inside the vessel while the outside joints were fixed with watertight seals, making them virtually indistinguishable from the rest of the weathered steel. The large metal access flap could be operated while the freighter was moving at speeds up to four knots, allowing the vessel to stay on course so as not to arouse any unnecessary suspicion by slowing to a stop on the open water.

Once the hatch was lifted the subs could be released along their steel rails. They would immediately throttle up to ensure that they would break free of the quick water running beneath the freighter's large hull. The hatch would then be closed, the amount of water taken in being negligible for an empty freighter, since the small hold had been sealed off from the other areas and pumps installed to flush the seawater out once the two craft were deployed.

The subs would then follow their northerly course into the Gulf of Mexico to Galveston Bay and toward the waters due south of Baytown near Barbours Cut.

As to the payload the submersibles would carry, Francisco and Luis had already made their delivery to an abandoned airstrip just south of Guane on the Cuban mainland. They had stopped there before proceeding on to the Coulter Airfield in Bryan, Texas, carrying the deadly cargo they had brought from Kazakhstan.

In Cuba, the two packages were off-loaded while the plane was being refueled. Then they promptly took off again. The parcels were whisked by truck to the south shore, where a speedboat brought them out to the freighter, all with the sort of military precision and timing Adina favored. That efficiency, coupled with the bribery of a local Cuban official, ensured that the transfer was neither intercepted by nor reported to the local shore patrol.

Now that all these pieces were in place, Adina knew he must not linger. The Cuban authorities would eventually become curious about a freighter sitting idly off the coast. Or an unreported flight into and out of Guane. The less attention they drew the better, even from a regime that might look favorably upon their plans. He picked up his radio, for the third time in an hour, to request a progress report.

"We are almost done," he was told again.

"Almost," he muttered in response and clicked off.

The plan was simple. Once the two submersibles were properly fitted, the freighter would begin moving slowly to the south, then circle back around the western tip of Cuba on a northwesterly course heading through the Yucatan Channel and into the Gulf. As Hurricane Charlene tracked a parallel path, the freighter would turn back, sixty miles or so short of its apparent destination, as if deterred by the weather. As it made its turn the two Autonomous Underwater Vehicles would be released below the waterline and sent on their way.

Once the two AUVs were launched, the ship would be as conspicuous as possible in making its movement back south, hopefully drawing attention away from any surface traces of the two small guided vessels that would then be motoring their way along their programmed routes. The AUVs would eventually pass through the cut between Galveston and Port Bolivar, into Galveston Bay, and ultimately be detonated just as they reached the Baytown refinery.

This, Adina believed, was the genius of his plan, or so he had described it to his associates. There were defenses in place all around and above the Baytown plant, protecting it from attacks that might come from the air, by land, or across the water. What had not been calculated was the damage that could be wrought by a subterranean explosion of the magnitude nuclear charges would cause. This would have the effect of an artificial tsunami that would not only devastate the refinery, but once the chain reaction began it would destroy all of the surrounding area. The destruction, following the Gulf oil spill, would be overwhelming, and the bonus would be the residue of radioactive fallout.

He sat back and had a look across the calm sea at the *Morning Star*, hoping the hurricane would move in soon, wondering who might suspect that this rusty, nondescript tanker could be the instrument of the deadliest attack in the history of the United States.

Then he smiled, reminding himself how well he had done in leaving nothing to chance.

CHAPTER SEVENTY-ONE

SOUTHEASTERN TEXAS

THE NIGHT BEFORE, the large tractor-trailer that had met Francisco and Luis in Bryan, Texas, pulled into a truck stop outside Beaumont, along Interstate 10. All four men stayed on board. They had food, water, a portable toilet facility, and strict orders that none of them was to leave the vehicle until they received further instructions. They spent the night there as many long-distance drivers do and, as other rigs came and went, they remained unnoticed in the rear of this large parking lot.

The two men up front slept in the living area behind the main cabin. When morning broke they passed through the opening to the trailer, joining Luis and Francisco in their compartment. The four of them had met back in Caracas, and they immediately began comparing their impressions of this mission. The one thing upon which they all agreed was that they wanted it over sooner rather than later.

These men were not religious zealots, they were mercenaries. They worked for pay, as they freely acknowledged. They had trained as soldiers, served in the military, and were now using their skills to escape the poverty of their homeland, risking their lives for the promised windfall that would set them up for life.

The driver said, "This hurricane cannot come fast enough, eh?"

The others could not agree more. They had been told they would not be given the command to move until the storm intensified. None of them knew exactly why, and they spent some time guessing at the reasons.

In the end, they all acknowledged that Adina was a master strategist, and whatever reasons he had must be good ones.

CHAPTER SEVENTY-TWO

"Be CAREFUL WHAT you wish for," Mark Byrnes told Ahmad Jaber when he informed him that his request was going to be granted, that he was going to be reunited with his wife.

Jaber responded with a solemn nod. "I understand the risks."

The Deputy Director was not sure that he did. The issue had been debated at Langley until Byrnes could not bear any more discussion on the subject. There were still a host of unanswered questions about Jaber but, in the end, Director Walsh made the call and, as usual, determined that the most obvious explanation was usually the correct one.

"Occam's razor," Walsh said, invoking one of his favorite expressions. "Jaber defects, but has given us very little. His wife is captured by the IRGC, then released. She is either working for them to get to Jaber or she and her husband are working together on some elaborate disinformation scheme we have yet to decipher. Either way, we will never get any further than we already have until we put them together. The simplest solution is the best, am

I right?" He did not await a reply, looking to his deputy. "And you have said yourself that time is running out if Jaber is going to have any more value to us as we try to intercept whatever Adina and his cohorts have in store."

"If we put him on the street, I believe he will be killed."

Walsh fixed his steely gaze on Byrnes. "As your man Sandor would say, 'So what?' Jaber is a murderer of innocent people. He has sought refuge here because his gang of IRGC cutthroats wants him dead. He offers us only snippets of information, in return for which he expects a lifetime of support and protection. What rubbish. The man has demanded to see his wife, so let him see her. It's your job to monitor who does what here, am I right?"

"Yes, sir."

"You give him the best protection possible, that's all we owe him."

And so, as Byrnes delivered the news to Jaber, he felt a mix of guilt and relief. On some level, he knew he was exposing the Iranian, and likely his wife, to an attempt on their lives. On the other hand, he, like Walsh, needed to know. If there was something else to learn from or through Jaber, time was indeed short.

The Deputy Director stood there, staring at the Iranian. "I hope you understand the risks, Ahmad," Byrnes said, using the man's given name for the first time. "I truly hope you do. My government is not able to guarantee your safety. Or your wife's."

The Iranian nodded again. "You have done your duty," he said. "Let's go."

As they left the grounds of the safe house and drove

into D.C., Jaber wondered if he would ever see this place again.

Then, he decided, it didn't matter.

During these long days, spent almost entirely alone, he had time to contemplate his life in ways he had never before done. He was always a man of action, not reflection, a man defined by his beliefs, unquestioning in his pursuit of justice for his people. He even saw the deaths of his only two children as justified in the context of those values. While he mourned the loss of his sons, he knew their sacrifice was worthy of a greater cause.

Over the years he had never wavered in his convictions, at least not until now.

It was too late for him to regret his decisions or to feel remorse for the countless lives he had stolen from the young and innocent. It would have been utter hypocrisy. Yet he wondered at the overriding futility of all he had done, and the faithless end that had become his destiny.

For these past two weeks he had entrusted himself to the protection of the very infidels he was sworn to destroy. Now he faced the possibility of execution by those he had devoted his life to serving. And this man, this Mark Byrnes, actually appeared sorry to subject him to that risk.

Where was the sense in all of that? The order? Where was the guiding hand of Allah?

He spoke the truth when he told Byrnes that he understood the risks. He actually welcomed them, because there was no other way for him to resolve these conflicts, no other way for him to reconcile his life.

———

When Rasa Jaber was told she would be allowed to see her husband she felt a sudden flash of joy that was quickly replaced by fear.

I am not prepared for this, she told herself. I am not prepared.

She longed to see him, of course, but her excitement was tempered by anger. Sitting alone in the hotel room she imagined how he would behave, how she would react, hoping there was some explanation he could offer for what he had done that would allow her to forgive him.

And then she thought of the phone number she had been given by the IRGC.

They told her the Americans could not be trusted. Her husband could not be trusted. Only her countrymen could protect her. As soon as contact was to be made with Ahmad she was to let them know. They would take care of everything, they would bring her and Ahmad home. They would sort it all out there, in Tehran. Just call the phone number they had her commit to memory. Call us and you will be safe.

Rasa sat in the chair at the small writing table, staring straight ahead and wondering, *What should I do?*

CHAPTER SEVENTY-THREE

BAYTOWN REFINERY

SANDOR HAD THE pilot fly the helicopter back to the plant, then told him to stand ready to leave again shortly.

"Skies are getting pretty bad."

Sandor nodded. "I won't be long."

Inside, Sandor found that Banahan had been joined by several local agents from Homeland Security, the FBI, and a technical support team. Janssen was continuing to give his full cooperation. Sandor asked for some privacy, and everyone except Banahan and Janssen cleared out of the office.

"What have we got?" Banahan asked.

"I'm not sure," Sandor admitted, "but let's try to piece a few things together." He described his interviews with the three young people at Coulter Airfield.

"So," Janssen summarized, "someone flew into town under the radar, dropped off God knows what, then flew out leaving behind two men and the goods to be loaded on a specially fitted tractor-trailer that had separate doors on the side."

"Right. And the crates were not large but very heavy, as in possibly lead lined."

"Which means nuclear, is where you're going," the former colonel observed with a grim look.

"That's where I'm going."

"Damnit," Janssen roared, slamming a flat palm hard onto his desktop. "It just can't be that friggin' easy to bring a nuke into this country."

"I'm afraid it can, sir. That's why I wanted to speak to you two alone before we create a panic here." They were standing around Janssen's desk, and now Sandor began pacing back and forth across the small room. "There's something else nagging at me here. As I told them in Washington, everything has pointed to Baytown, right from the beginning. It was almost too easy to follow the trail here."

"What are you saying, son?"

"I'm saying maybe that truck is not heading here. I'm saying maybe that truck is heading somewhere else."

There was a knock on the door and all three men turned. Banahan let one of his agents in, who promptly announced that the team had arrived at Coulter Airfield. "The preliminary reports are positive," he told them.

"For radiation?" Banahan asked.

"That's affirmative. Traces were found, particularly in the area they identified as the loading point."

"What about the kids?" Sandor asked.

"Clean so far, but they're taking all three to the hospital."

"Good. You keep this to yourself for now, and that's an order."

The agent nodded, then shut the door behind him.

Sandor turned to the others. "Any questions?"

All branches of the military had been warned. The Coast Guard had patrol boats running back and forth along the Gulf Coast. The Navy had several destroyers in the area from the Ingleside Naval Station. The Air Force and Air National Guard were on standby.

But the Gulf of Mexico is an enormous area to cover, the ninth-largest body of water in the world. The United States coastline alone runs more than 1,600 miles. And the weather was getting worse.

As Hurricane Charlene continued its destructive path northwest through the Bahamas and into the Gulf, the more difficult it would become to stay in the air and monitor movements at sea.

The Coast Guard was the main watchdog for the Gulf, or GOMEX as it is referred to by the military. Using their computerized Automatic Identification System they were able to monitor all ships in the navigable area. As a requirement of the International Maritime Organization, every ship entering the Gulf had to radio in its identification numbers, indicating country of registry, and would have to report its course, speed, type of vessel, as well as ports of departure and destination. Foreign ships were also required to give advance notification before being allowed to enter a port of call.

Hurricane conditions would complicate matters, especially if they were going to be dealing with a rogue craft. The Coast Guard had various classes of vessels, many of which were agile and fast and all of which were armed with Automatic Identification Systems and radar. At the moment, as the skies darkened and the first rains arrived on the front edge of the fast-moving storm, Sandor's concerns about the weather were complicated by another fear that simply would not go away.

At his request, Janssen had tied together a conference call with the Police Commissioner in Houston, the Chief of Police in Baytown, and the Captain of the State Highway Patrol.

They all knew Janssen and, given the nature of his responsibilities, he was treated with appropriate respect. They also knew he was not someone who was going to flash this sort of SOS unless there was a damn good reason.

Janssen offered a preamble, describing what they might be up against, then introduced Sandor.

"Let me get right to it," Sandor said into the speakerphone on Janssen's desk. "In my business we're often asked to look for the proverbial needle in a haystack, and that's what I'm asking each of you to help me do today. The Navy and Coast Guard are doing their best to cover the coastline, but my concern is the truck Colonel Janssen has described to you. It picked up its cargo more than thirty hours ago at Coulter Airfield and could be almost anywhere by now. It could be hidden in a warehouse right down the street, it could be on the road, it could even have its markings changed. It could have off-loaded the goods or it could be in Tennessee, we just have no way of knowing. But I can tell you this, gentlemen, I have reason to believe it's carrying a deadly cargo, and if we don't intercept it there's going to be hell to pay."

The Houston Police Commissioner identified himself,

then asked, "You have any idea at all where they might be truckin' this stuff?"

Sandor looked at Banahan and Janssen. "I wish I did, but I don't. All I have is a guess."

"Better than nothing," one of the other voices suggested.

Sandor nodded his agreement, then said, "From the beginning of this intelligence operation, we've been led to believe a terrorist attack is being aimed at the Baytown refinery. That, of course, is the first possibility for the destination of these explosives. But if you want my guess, I think there might be another target in play." Sandor paused, but none of them spoke. "You're all in law enforcement, and you all know that sometimes the best clues are the least reliable. You also understand that bad information is more damaging than no information at all. My concern is that we may have been led to Baytown for a reason. These terrorists are evil, but they're not stupid and they're not careless. Landing that cargo in Bryan may even be part of the scheme. Drop the goods off at an airstrip near enough to Baytown to have us believe they're part of this assault. But what if they're headed someplace else entirely? What if we're concentrating our attention and resources here while they're targeting a different location?"

"You said you had a guess," Janssen urged him.

"I do, but I don't want to distract your men from a broader sweep."

"Mr. Sandor, I'm Captain of Highway Patrol in this area. If you've got an idea, I think we should all hear it."

Sandor hesitated. "If their plan is to cripple our economy

by destroying the largest refinery in the country, what would their next target be?"

"The second largest," the captain answered.

"That's my guess, gentlemen."

"Baton Rouge," Janssen said.

"Baton Rouge," Sandor agreed.

CHAPTER SEVENTY-FOUR

WASHINGTON, D.C.

THEY BROUGHT JABER to the Mayflower hotel. Agent Fitzpatrick drove while Byrnes sat in the backseat of the Lincoln sedan with the former IRGC operative. It was just the three of them, a quiet ride, no one speaking, although the DD retrieved several cell phone messages, one of which he would return as soon as he was done with the Iranian.

"This is it," Byrnes said as Fitzpatrick pulled their car to a stop at the entrance. Then he gave Jaber the room number.

The Iranian was genuinely surprised. "That's it? I'm free to go upstairs, on my own?"

"We'll be waiting for you right here when you're done," Byrnes replied. He did not mention the SUV that had tailed them from the safe house, in case there was another attempt to intercept Byrnes's vehicle, nor the men stationed inside the hotel.

Jaber, however, knew the score. "Of course, there is always the all-seeing eye of your Agency."

Byrnes nodded. "You don't have to do this," he said.

"Do what? Act as your human bait?" Jaber smiled his thin, mirthless smile. "I understand what your superiors want. I have not given you enough information, so now I am being used to draw out my own countrymen, to give you a chance to capture one or more of them and perhaps learn something more about this business with the Venezuelans and North Koreans." He shook his head. "I have played this game too long not to grasp the situation, Director Byrnes, but in the end you are giving me what I have requested, are you not? I am going to see my wife." He leaned forward and grabbed the door handle, then stopped and turned back. "Whatever comes of this, I will not forget that you have treated me with respect. And a modicum of hatred, anger, and condemnation, all which were to be expected," he added with another brief smile. "But always with dignity."

"You sound surprised."

"I am," he replied, then he yanked on the lever, swung the door open, and stepped outside. He took a deep breath, then bent over and looked inside the car. "I really will see you later?"

"You can count on it," Byrnes told him.

Fitzpatrick got out and accompanied Jaber into the lobby. Byrnes remained in the backseat, where he pulled out his cell and dialed Sandor.

When Jaber and Fitzpatrick reached the bank of elevators, the young agent made a show of stepping back.

"Good-bye, then," Jaber said.

"You know the room number," Fitzpatrick replied, then turned and returned to the lobby door.

Byrnes had made a show of removing the security detail stationed right outside Rasa Jaber's room, but he still had men on hand. One agent was behind the front desk dressed as a hotel trainee and one was working as a bellhop, for which he would be endlessly ribbed back at Langley. He was the rover, moving around the building as needed. A third agent remained in the stairwell on Rasa Jaber's floor.

Once Jaber entered the building, the black Suburban pulled up behind Byrnes's sedan and three other agents stepped out. One stayed with the DD while the other two joined Fitzpatrick in the lobby.

The man assigned to Byrnes leaned down and opened the door. "No hostiles in sight," he said.

Byrnes nodded, said, "You guys know the drill," then got on his phone.

———————

Jaber rode the elevator alone, got off on the fifth floor, and found his way to his wife's room. It was the middle of the afternoon and the hallway was quiet. He knocked and waited, listening as she had a look through the peephole. She opened the door and they stood there facing each other.

"Rasa," he said, then they fell into an awkward silence. He wanted to take her in his arms, to tell her how sorry he was, but something felt wrong about that. He looked past her into the room, then asked, "Are you alone?"

"I am alone," she told him. Then, as if her statement needed confirmation, she swung the door wider. "You should come in," she said, and he followed her inside.

———————

The agent positioned in the stairwell reported that Jaber was inside. Fitzpatrick was standing at the hotel entrance when he got the message. He relayed the high sign to the Deputy Director.

The two men who had followed Byrnes in the SUV now made their way up the stairs.

_____

What none of the agents knew was that word of Rasa Jaber's location had already been discovered and passed to Vahidi. One of his men was already inside the hotel and ready to act on word of Ahmad Jaber's arrival.

The word had been given as soon as Jaber entered the lobby.

_____

Rasa was standing in the room with her back to the window, framed by the Washington skyline. Jaber closed the door behind him and sat in the club chair where his wife had spent so many hours anguishing over what would become of her. Of them.

"You look well," he said.

"You sound surprised. Is that because you expected that your former friends in the Revolutionary Guard would torture me? Humiliate me? Leave me to freeze and starve while you came here without me to live in comfort?"

"Rasa, I can explain."

"Of course you can, Ahmad, you can always explain. But can you give an honest answer? I have come to realize that these are two different things. The one is nothing more than an excuse, the other is about the truth. Can you look at me and tell me the truth?"

"I can, but you are angry," he replied calmly.

"Angry? Why should I be angry? Because you left me to

die? Because you put the lives of my sister and her family at risk? Because you have betrayed the memory and honor of our sons?"

"I know you have good cause for your upset but please, sit down and collect yourself. There is much we have to discuss and there may not be much time."

She drew an uneven breath, his equanimity only further infuriating her. Grabbing the straight-backed chair from the writing table she turned it toward him and sat down. "Go ahead," she said, maintaining an erect posture as she glowered at him. "I will listen."

"These men from the IRGC. What did they tell you?"

"What did they tell me, you ask? What do you think they told me? That my husband had defected to America like a traitor and left me behind to suffer for his betrayal. They told me that you were living in luxury while I was stripped of my clothes and possessions and sent to rot in a cell as if I were some sort of criminal."

Jaber felt himself wince, but he struggled to remain composed. "Did they tell you why I came here?"

The question seemed to take her by surprise. She hesitated, then admitted, "I believe that's why they let me go. I don't think even they know. They want me to find out why. For myself as well as for them."

Jaber nodded. "Then ask yourself, my wife of all these years, why would I have come here without you unless I had a very good reason?"

"I have been tormented by that very question for the past two weeks."

He stood up and stepped toward her. "I was betrayed and marked for death. I was left no choice but to flee."

Rasa jumped from her seat so abruptly that he almost fell backward. Then she shrieked at him, in a voice he had never heard from her. "And what about me, Ahmad? What about me? What did you leave me to face? What choice was I given?"

Outside, the agent stationed at the far end of the landing remained in the stairwell, out of sight but connected by radio to the rest of his team. Even through the thick walls and substantial door of the Mayflower, he could hear Rasa Jaber scream.

"Ah, married life," he whispered into his mike.

The man at the lobby desk, hearing him through the ear-piece, said, "Are they having a happy reunion?"

"Love in bloom."

One of the two men in the stairwell announced that they were on their way up.

Just then, the agent on Rasa Jaber's floor heard the sound of the elevator door opening. From his vantage point to the left, he could see a young man wheeling a tray into the corridor.

"Control, we have company here. Anyone on this floor order room service?"

The man downstairs at the front desk had his eye on a computer monitor. "That appears to be a negative, but we'll double-check with the kitchen right now." The agent dressed as a bellhop was on it immediately.

"Should I move or wait?" the agent asked. But before he received an answer the waiter abandoned his cart and began racing toward Jaber's room. A pistol was suddenly visible in one hand and an electronic keycard in the other.

"Hostile on the floor," the agent barked into his mike as he burst through the door, "move, move, move!" he hollered to his teammates, but it was too late. He managed to get off three shots, but the man had already used the keycard to enter the room and slammed the door shut behind him.

———

Rasa was wide-eyed with fear at the sight of the slightly built Arab man aiming his pistol at her. The assailant, who could not have been more than twenty years old, glared at her, then turned to Jaber. "You are a disgrace to our great country and to Allah," the young man announced in a loud, nervous voice.

Rasa was astonished at how impassive her husband remained. She realized, in that instant, that she had never before seen him in action.

"And who," Jaber inquired, "has filled your head with such lies?"

"Those whom I trust with my life," he declared.

Before any of the three of them could speak again, they heard a noise at the door. Someone else was coming in, and their assassin had clearly been instructed not to delay.

In that final instant, Rasa looked at Ahmad. "I never called them," she said, tears filling her sad, beautiful eyes. "They told me to call them, but I swear to you I never did."

When her husband turned away from their murderer to share a final look with her, she expected to see hatred or anger or at least doubt in his eyes, but there was nothing but kindness there. "I understand," he said. "And I am so sorry."

The next few moments passed quickly in a blaze of noise and smoke and blood, and yet for Rasa Jaber it felt like the eternity it would become for her. The young man fired first at Ahmad, three rapid shots, and she watched helplessly as her husband fell onto the bed. She remained frozen as the assassin then aimed his weapon at her and, just as he squeezed the trigger, a large man burst through the door, his gun riddling the young Iranian with shots she did not live long enough to see.

CHAPTER SEVENTY-FIVE

SOUTHEASTERN TEXAS

Hurricane Charlene was moving with a vengeance now, the rain and winds that augured the arrival of the storm just a hint of what was to come. Breakwaters along the Gulf Coast were already rising, waves crashed above retaining walls and battered the shore, and clouds darkened the skies.

Adina's men, who had been huddled together in the trailer of their large rig, received instructions earlier that morning to move from the truck stop outside Beaumont to a similar area just south of Opelousas in Louisiana. They proceeded through the torrential rainstorm, barely reaching their new destination when another encrypted message came through.

"It's time," Luis told them.

The four men readied themselves, checking their weapons and preparing for the final phase of their mission. They left the truck stop and took a back road that had almost no traffic in the midst of these blinding weather conditions. They turned into a wooded area, donned plastic ponchos, and stepped out into the storm, where they quickly removed the thin, off-white adhesive vinyl sheeting that had been attached to the sides of the trailer, proclaiming the truck McSHANE REFRIGERATION. Underneath was a darker, metallic gray color with a logo and stenciled lettering that read FOSTER TRANSPORT, another fictitious company. The two drivers also climbed atop the trailer, tearing away the paper that bore one identification number on the top, now displaying another. Then they came down and reentered the truck, removed their rain gear and dried off, then headed for the highway to carry out their orders.

They were to travel east along Airline Highway, across the bridge to Scenic Highway, where they would turn north and head straight until it became Samuels Road and turn off just past Port Hudson. There they would proceed to a specified site on the eastern bank of the Mississippi River, north of Baton Rouge, a couple of miles above the large refinery that sat along the shore.

In two crates were the nuclear devices brought from Kazakhstan. They had been secured in the small, lined compartment at the center of the trailer. The other crates held two motorized fiberglass craft into which these suitcase bombs would be strapped, the timers and guiding systems set, then the two packages placed in the river and sent downstream. The sites of the eventual explosions would not have to be precise; it would be enough if one or both of the RA-115s detonated anywhere near the refinery.

Before they armed the two devices, they would detach the trailer and make ready to leave as fast as they could travel once the bombs were activated and their pods launched. Their planned route was east across Louisiana Highway 10 until they hit Interstate 55. They would get as far north as they could before the explosions rocked Baton Rouge. They knew that even with the weather, there would still be more than enough time to get clear, but they were not going to take any chances.

————

The freighter *Morning Star*, rigged with the two drone submarines, was running on a northwesterly course through the Yucatan Channel into the Gulf of Mexico on a heading that paralleled the angry tack of the hurricane. The ship moved slowly, staying clear of the few other vessels to be found in these choppy waters, but its entrance was noted almost as soon as it turned around the western tip of Cuba and approached GOMEX.

"This is the United States Coast Guard," a disembodied voice proclaimed over the USCG frequency. "Identify yourself."

The skeleton crew of the *Morning Star* was under strict orders to maintain radio silence. Their task was to get as close as they could to the Texas shore, launch the two AUVs without being detected, then turn for home. They did not expect to be intercepted by the Americans this quickly, even with the weather reducing the usual traffic in the commercial lanes of the Gulf.

The two men in the pilothouse shared a concerned look when the voice from the USCG crackled across their radio speakers a second time.

"This is the United States Coast Guard. We order you to immediately provide us proper identification."

"*Mierda*," one of the men said.

The other worked a pair of high-powered binoculars, trying to see something through the soupy skies. *"¡Imposible!"* he exclaimed, barely able to see the bow of their own ship.

They exchanged another look, and the decision was made. The second mate put down the binoculars and headed out into the pouring rain. He hurried down the metal stairs to the deck below, where he found his men waiting for their orders. He told them to prepare the hydraulic pumps.

The mate returned to the wheelhouse as the pilot brought the *Morning Star* around to the port side, slowing almost to a stop as they turned, giving them time to raise the hatch. The position of the freighter made the maneuver invisible to the north and, in this weather, to anyone who was not within a hundred yards of the ship.

The crew belowdecks released the chains that secured the two subs, and they slid along their descending rails, disappearing below the surface of the sea as the hatch was lowered back into place.

When the compartment was shut and they finished their sweeping about-face, they increased speed and headed south for Venezuela.

CHAPTER SEVENTY-SIX

ABOARD THE U.S.S. *BURGWYN* IN THE GULF OF MEXICO

Lᴉᴇᴜᴛᴇɴᴀɴᴛ Lᴏᴜɪs Sᴘᴀɴᴏ on the U.S.S. *Burgwyn* was the first to spot the two AUVs on his radar screen as they made their way through the water on their route north. Standing in the communications room using SOSUS, the United States Navy sound surveillance system, he noticed two new blips on the LCD monitor. He immediately radioed the captain.

"Sir, we have subsurface movement on a north-northwest heading, running at twenty-two knots. It appears to be two different vessels."

The *Burgwyn* was an *Arleigh Burke*–class guided missile destroyer, over 500 feet long with a beam of some 65 feet, carrying more than 300 servicemen. It was equipped with state-of-the-art sensors and processing systems, including the standard AIS, AN/SPY-1D radar, AN/SPS-67(V)2 surface search radar, and AN/SQS-53C sonar array, together with a modern arsenal of tactical and defense armaments.

The communications center on the *Burgwyn* had already heard the report from the Coast Guard, that an unidentified freighter had entered the Gulf and that when calls for identification went unanswered the ship had turned and made its way south.

The *Burgwyn*, using sonar buoys that are passive hydrophones while also "dipping" their sonar, could determine whether the submersibles were manned or drones, their size, engine capability, and, of course, speed.

While the crew worked on gathering that data in response to Spano's observation, the skipper contacted the emergency command center that had been established at the naval air base in Corpus Christi. The *Burgwyn* was fitted with an SH-60 Seahawk helicopter, but in this weather it would be a high-risk sortie to attempt to track the renegade freighter as it headed south. There were enough USCG fast boats in the Gulf to chase it down. The important issue for now was tracking the two subsurface vessels.

———

Byrnes was standing on Connecticut Avenue, speaking with Sandor on his encrypted cell phone about the possibility of a secondary target, when the agent in the lobby of the Mayflower came running out to tell the DD about the shootings.

"The Jabers are both dead," he reported.

"What about Agent Karipides?"

"He's fine, he was able to take the assassin alive. Badly shot up, but alive."

Byrnes responded with a grave look, then remembered that Sandor was still on the line. "You heard all that?"

"I did," Sandor told him. "I'm surprised the shooter wasn't wired for a religious send-off." Sandor knew that was a favorite Al Qaeda ploy. After you thought you had disarmed the man you discover he's wired with explosives to take you and everyone around him on that final journey to Jannah. "Make sure he isn't rigged up with anything."

Byrnes relayed Sandor's concern to his agent, who told him that was a negative. "First thing Karipides checked."

"All right," Byrnes said dully, "let's get the shooter to the infirmary."

"And set him up for interrogation," Sandor hollered into the phone. "Let's find out what we can from the sonuvabitch."

Before Byrnes could respond, Banahan came to the door of the side office.

"I've got to go," Sandor told the DD. "We've got action in the Gulf. I'll report back."

———————

Sandor and Banahan hurried into Janssen's office, where they found themselves in the midst of another huge conference call, this time with participants from the United States military. The captain of the U.S.S. *Burgwyn* reported subsurface movement that appeared on the sonar array as two small vessels. They had no response to attempted radio contact and believed the subs to be unmanned.

The Coast Guard weighed in, describing the actions of the renegade freighter that ignored their demands for identification, instead circling south and heading back through the Yucatan Channel.

Everyone wanted instructions on how to proceed.

The commanding officer from the U.S. Navy air base at Corpus Christi was also on the call. Michael Krause was an Annapolis graduate with two tours of duty in the Middle East, a chest full of ribbons, and a charge-ahead attitude that earned him the nickname Moose among friends and enemies alike. "This is Captain Krause," he announced over the speaker. "The hell with that freighter for now. We'll catch up with them later. I'm ordering an immediate intercept of both submersibles. We can't go airborne in this weather. You'll have to take them out from the *Burgwyn*."

"This is Jordan Sandor. I'm coordinating the antiterrorist task force out of Washington, captain, and I think we should take a moment to consider our approach."

"There's a hurricane brewing, and if you're in Washington—" Krause began, but Sandor cut him off.

"I'm right here in Baytown, sir, and I fully understand the weather issues. In case you have not been fully briefed, my problem is not the means of interception, it's the potential payload of these two underwater vessels."

"Let's get the chain of command straight, son. This is Captain Krause, officer in charge of the Corpus Christi base. Who the hell passed you the baton?"

Sandor gave the name of the President's National Security Advisor, Peter Forelli, and a scrambled number. "Have your aide decode that and check it out for yourself, captain, but we're on a short fuse."

There was only the slightest hesitation, followed by, "All right, Sandor, what have we got here?"

Sandor was concerned that the line was not secure, but time was short and he had no choice. "We have reason to believe these AUVs may be hot. Probably low yield, but hot all the same."

"I hear you," Krause said. "Now please tell me this is some sort of doomsday fantasy they're dreaming up in D.C."

"I'm afraid not, sir."

No one spoke until Krause said, "All the more reason to get hold of these submersibles on the double."

"Agreed," Sandor replied, "but we can't risk detonating them."

"Understood. You got an idea?"

"Disabling their navigation system. Simply stopping them in their tracks, then attempting to disarm them."

"How do you figure they're wired?"

"They could be rigged for impact explosion, but that's unlikely. If they hit something before they reach their target they would go off, which would defeat their purpose. My guess is a digital timer or a remote device."

"And you're betting on a timer."

"Yes, sir. A remote would be fairly undependable at long range in this weather. If we're right, and we can stop them, at least we'd have a chance at defusing them. Better than setting them off ourselves."

Whoever this Krause was, he impressed Sandor when he took absolutely no time making up his mind. "Damn right," he said. "Let's get the SEALs on this pronto. *Burgwyn*, you still on this call?"

The skipper of the *Burgwyn* acknowledged he was there. "We have four SEALs on board, sir."

"You get us coordinates and we'll get a second team there."

"Yes, sir."

"Let's get moving, then," Krause ordered. "How much time you figure we have?"

"We assume they're heading this way," Sandor told him, "to Baytown."

The Captain of the *Burgwyn* said, "On their present course, if they maintain speed, that would give us less than two hours to be on the safe side."

"Roger that," Krause replied. "Position yourself so you're running alongside, just in case we have to blow them out of the water at some point."

"Aye aye, sir," the captain responded, then rung off.

Sandor asked, "I want to go with the SEALs, sir."

"It's a mess out there, son, and I've got a team can be in the air in the next few minutes."

"I'm willing to take the risk," Sandor told him. "Just give me a few minutes. I'll be on a chopper and at your door."

"Well get your ass in the air, then," Krause barked. "We'll have a Seahawk going up in ten minutes with or without you." Then he signed off.

CHAPTER SEVENTY-SEVEN

BAYTOWN, TEXAS

Before Sandor left, he turned to a map they had tacked to the wall. "After Baytown and Baton Rouge, what are the biggest refineries in the area?"

Janssen stood with him and pointed them out. "Texas City just to the southwest of here. Lake Charles and Belle Chasse in Louisiana. Plants all along the coasts of Texas and Mississippi."

"We need to warn every one of them."

"You're sure a secondary hit is going to be a refinery?"

"I'm not sure of anything," Sandor admitted, "but that's my guess." He picked up his jacket and turned to Banahan. "Alert their security forces. Especially around Baton Rouge."

"Will do," Banahan said.

"You may be wrong about the second strike," Janssen said, although he did not sound at all convinced.

Sandor shook his head. "If Baytown is really the play and they're coming at us by water, then where the hell is that truck?"

"Could be a lousy coincidence is all, may have nothing to do with what we're up against?"

"Sorry, I don't believe in radioactive coincidences."

Janssen frowned. "Neither do I."

Sandor nodded, as if confirming a thought. "Then you guys stay on this. I'm going to do what I can to help them find these nukes in the Gulf," he said, then bolted out the door.

———

When Adina received word of the early launch of the two AUVs he did nothing to conceal his fury. "Too soon!" he hollered at the men gathered around him in the main cabin of the *Misty II*. "Too soon! Those miserable cowards will pay for their weakness. The Americans will have too much time now, far too much time." He slammed his hand on the table. "Contact Luis by text, find out their position."

Two of his aides scurried off to the communications room as Adina paced angrily around the main salon. "What could they have been thinking?" he wondered aloud. His yacht was nearing Puerto la Cruz, where he would monitor the events from a land-based site. "Let's hope this weather worsens quickly," he told the others, who remained to attend his orders. "Let's at least hope for that."

———

Outside the administration building at the Baytown refinery, the pilot of the Sikorsky chopper expressed more than a little reluctance to go up into a sky that was black with rain and clouds and a vicious wind.

"You only need to get me to the landing pad at the LBJ Space Center," Sandor told him. "They've got a military transport waiting for me there."

Now the pilot looked at him as if he were insane. "That's flying dead into the storm."

"'Dead' is a bad choice of words," Sandor said as he ran up the steps to the helipad. "Now crank this thing up," he ordered, then climbed aboard the helicopter.

As they rose into the dark sky, Sandor grabbed the radio headset and had another quick discussion with Captain Krause, then was patched back on the line with the men assigned by the various state and local authorities to coordinate the search for the missing tractor-trailer. Given the time elapsed since the truck left Coulter Airfield, the absence of any information on its direction and the scope of its possible destinations, there was little cause for optimism among them.

"They could have even changed the markings on the trailer by now," the officer with the State Highway Patrol said, "or switched the cargo to another vehicle."

"Possible," Sandor said, "but not likely. The trailer we're looking for appears to be specially fitted out. And no matter what they do to the logo on the back, they can't disguise all the doors that are cut into the side. No, my guess is that they simply don't believe we'll be able to find them in time." He paused. "They may be right."

"We're hard at it," the man from the Houston Police Commissioner's office assured him, then hung up.

The helicopter ride was a brutal roller coaster, with strong headwinds and shears that rocked the small chopper to and fro. The pilot had that white-knuckle look Sandor had seen so many times when inexperienced men came under fire.

"Never flown in combat, eh?"

The pilot shook his head, continuing to stare into the darkness ahead. "Never."

"Well, take a deep breath, then," Sandor said, "and pretend you're on a ride in Disney World."

They reached the Space Center without further conversation, where the pilot gratefully set down on one of the designated platforms, obviously hoping to remain on the ground until the hurricane blew past. Sandor, meanwhile, ran straight for the Seahawk that Captain Krause had ordered up. It was waiting across the tarmac, the rotors already whirring overhead.

The SH-60F is a multipurpose helicopter with numerous upgrades over the earlier model that enhance its offensive and defensive systems, as well as its range and survivability. The current weather conditions would certainly test those last two features.

It was armed with the Hellfire Missile System, Hydra 70 Rocket System, and an M230 30 mm chain gun. This chopper had also been loaded with variable-depth sonar and sonobuoys to detect and track enemy submarines, an air-to-water torpedo system, various aquatic devices, and a remote Geiger system. Sandor clambered aboard, already drenched from his short run through the driving rain.

"Jordan Sandor," he said as he wiped away some of the water that was dripping from his dark hair. Then he held up his credentials.

The pilot, a Marine by the name of Tom Martindale, introduced himself. "Call me Marty," he said. "This is Jake," he said, pointing to the copilot.

In the rear, four SEALs were suited up and ready to go for a swim. Sandor shook hands with each of them.

"I know you men have all been briefed, and you all know what's at stake." He turned back to the pilot. "Let's get this baby in the air."

CHAPTER SEVENTY-EIGHT

GULF OF MEXICO, SOUTH OF GALVESTON BAY

THE SEAHAWK IS a highly sophisticated asset that can search and destroy under the most difficult circumstances, day or night. However, as the sleek helicopter cut through the sky on a heading toward the destroyer U.S.S. *Burgwyn*, the winds had increased to gusts of over sixty miles an hour and the ride was as dangerous as enemy fire. Sandor was seated in the rear with the stoic complement of Navy SEALs who were already adjusting their scuba gear, the helmets fitted with wireless radios and mikes, and their oxygen tanks.

Sandor, needing to holler above the roar of the rotors and the hurricane, asked, "You guys sure you can stop these subs?"

"Yes, sir," snapped the lieutenant in charge.

"The *Burgwyn* has the tracking vehicles ready to go?"

"That's affirmative, sir."

Sandor nodded, the lieutenant's formal demeanor reminding him that he was with four of America's most well-trained and disciplined fighting men. It also reminded him that he did not miss his days in the military, not one bit.

The lieutenant held out a helmet. "You'll be able to communicate better with this on, sir."

Sandor pulled it on and adjusted the microphone.

The Seahawk F Model is nearly sixty feet long, flown by a two-man crew, and can reach a speed of 180 miles an hour. Along with its advanced weaponry and attack capabilities, it carries a digital target-acquisition system that can locate, classify, and prioritize any one of more than 120 different types of potential threats, then launch a strike against the target, all within less than thirty seconds. For now Sandor was more interested in disabling the two submersibles than blowing them out of the water, but it was good to know they had options.

Even running into gale-force winds they were soon nearing the *Burgwyn*. Sandor reached out for one of the extra neoprene suits that were stacked against the armored wall of the chopper.

"Sir," the lieutenant interrupted, "what are you doing?"

"I'm getting ready to take the jump with you boys."

"I'm sorry sir, that's not possible."

Sandor paused, staring into the lieutenant's determined eyes. "Washington has put me in charge of this operation. If the four of you are going to risk your lives jumping into this oversized bathtub, I'm going with you."

"I'm afraid that's a negative, sir," the young man said firmly. "Do I have your permission to speak freely, sir?"

"Free as a bird."

"We're professionals, specially trained for this work. Whatever it is that you do, sir, I am sure you are equally capable at your job. But this situation calls for a very specific set of skills and your involvement will only prove a hindrance."

Sandor smiled. "So you're telling me I might screw this up for you, is that it, lieutenant?"

The young man allowed himself the faintest grin. "That would be affirmative, sir. You will almost certainly screw this up for us."

Sandor sat back on the hard bench. "Well, I guess you told me," he said.

"The last thing we need is to have to worry about you down there, sir."

Sandor nodded.

"Sir, as I understand it, our first task is to determine if there is radioactivity on these AUVs."

"That's correct."

"If we find that they are hot, we will need to disable the vehicles and disarm the weapons. If they are not, we'll need to clear out so we can destroy both submersibles. Either way, time will be precious. I meant no offense."

"None taken. I'll stay aboard and monitor your actions."

"That would be excellent," the young man said, breathing a visible sigh of relief.

"There's another four-man team meeting you below."

"Roger that, we've been fully briefed."

The copilot turned to the five men in the rear compartment. "There it is," Jake told them, pointing off the starboard side at the destroyer.

The Seahawk banked slightly, coming astern of the Burgwyn. They listened on the radio hookup as the skipper barked out instructions. The destroyer was now running alongside the two AUVs, which were just below the water level. Sandor stared out through the torrential rain and dark sky, peering down into the even darker sea. He could not see a thing.

The captain on the Burgwyn reported that the four

SEALs on board were in the process of dropping two high-speed launches into the Gulf. Unfortunately, the sea was already rolling with twenty-foot swells and chops at least half that size. The four men aboard the Seahawk with Sandor would be lowered into the Gulf on ropes operated by automatic winches, two men to be picked up on one launch and two by the other. Each team would then be assigned to one of the AUVs.

The captain of the *Burgwyn* said, "The launches are fully equipped, including remote radioactive sensors."

"Excellent," Sandor replied into his microphone, then turned to the lieutenant, who was working with his men to strap on their oxygen tanks and hook onto the winch lines. "You guys ready?"

Just as the lieutenant gave him the thumbs-up, a powerful wind shear caused the helicopter to lurch hard to the side, causing all five men to stumble across the small compartment.

When they righted themselves, Sandor got up and placed his hand on the lieutenant's shoulder. "You all return here in one piece," he said, "I'll dry you off myself."

The lieutenant nodded, then told Sandor to operate the winch mechanism on high speed. "Our best chance is to get in the water as quickly as we can."

"Done."

The copilot looked back at them again. "Ready?"

"Take her down," the lieutenant said.

The most dangerous part of their trip was about to come. With the Seahawk rocking unsteadily the pilot needed to bring them as close to sea level as possible, not wanting the four men swinging violently back and forth in the air and suffering injuries before they even hit the water. Martindale maneuvered as best he could, barely able to see the two small launches below them as the copilot suddenly yelled, "Go, go, go."

Without a moment's hesitation, the four young men stepped up to the open hatch and jumped into what appeared to be a bottomless sky. Sandor sent them down as quickly as the system would allow, watching as one after another unsnapped his harness and fell into the angry sea.

CHAPTER SEVENTY-NINE

WASHINGTON, D.C.

THE DEPUTY DIRECTOR'S team had a man in custody, which was at least something to take from the Mayflower hotel debacle. His agent had shot the assassin in the legs and arm, then prevented him from taking his own life. With time at a premium two agents had already begun interrogating the shooter as they rode together in the back of the ambulance that was carrying them to the Agency's clinic.

In great pain and having suffered a considerable loss of blood, he was now being pumped with morphine. There was little chance the man was going to be able to withhold much.

The problem was that he did not seem to know anything.

He told them his name was Ashraf and that he took his orders from a handler in Washington who in turn reported to Ali Vahidi. Vahidi was known to work with the IRGC and Al Qaeda. Unfortunately, his affiliation with the Saudi Arabian diplomatic corps gave him immunity, a political invention that drove Jordan Sandor to distraction.

It would be helpful if this Iranian killer would implicate Vahidi in a terrorist plot—that would remove Vahidi from his diplomatic protection—but Byrnes knew the coerced confession of a murderer was not going to be much help on that score. If all else failed they could bring Vahidi in for questioning, but the only thing that would net them was another battle with the weak sisters on Capitol Hill who were afraid of antagonizing their Saudi ally.

With an ally like that . . . , Byrnes said to himself, then dismissed the thought.

Ashraf gave the location where he and his comrades met, but Byrnes realized news of this shooting would already have been passed along. The address would be as worthless as the mention of Vahidi, who would have already ordered his crew to clean up their cell and move on.

Nevertheless, Byrnes dispatched a team to check it out, amusing himself with the notion that if they found Vahidi there he might hold him until Sandor returned.

Otherwise, it appeared that the man they had in custody was a low-level zealot who had been ordered to eliminate Jaber, his wife along with him, and then to join his fellow martyrs on the road to Paradise.

As Byrnes contemplated all of this on the ride back to his office, it occurred to him that Jaber had apparently died for nothing, and it surprised Byrnes that he felt a pang of sympathy for the man. After all, Jaber had engineered the deaths of countless people, pursued an evil war in the name of a distorted vision of his God, then sought sanctuary for fear of his life. But in the end, he was willing to face inevitable death to make amends with his wife.

Given the opportunity, even the worst of people can surprise you and as Byrnes had experienced before, when one comes to know an enemy it invariably alters your view of that person forever. It introduces a human element that cannot be ignored.

Back in his office he reached Sandor through a satellite link and received an update on what was going on in the Gulf.

"Unfortunately, we still have no lead on the truck," Sandor told him.

"Then get out of there and head back to Houston."

"I've got eight Navy SEALs in the drink right now," Sandor protested.

"Fine. And when they complete their mission they'll be picked up by the Navy, not some helicopter being bounced around in the middle of a hurricane."

"True," Sandor reluctantly agreed. He then switched back to the radio, tying into communication with the captain of the *Burgwyn*. "How are they doing?" he asked.

CHAPTER EIGHTY

GULF OF MEXICO, SOUTH OF GALVESTON BAY

A‍LL EIGHT SEALs had successfully found their way to the two Navy launches. Four men boarded each boat and they were now running just above the two AUVs as they pursued their deadly course toward Galveston Bay.

The sea was a combination of swells, chops, and waves that constantly pushed the two small pursuit crafts off course. The winds were intensifying and, for the first time, the helicopter pilot advised Sandor that they would have to seek landfall before conditions worsened.

Sandor did not divulge the order from Byrnes that he was to return to Baytown. "Hang on just a minute," he told Martindale. Then, speaking into his microphone to the captain, he asked, "Have they set up the remote detectors yet?"

"Almost done," the captain reported.

The SEALs were using two systems to determine whether there was radioactive material aboard the AUVs. The first was a remote laser-guided Geiger counter, not the most reliable approach in these climatic conditions. The second was a new device that used gallium arsenide to detect neutron emissions. That device, referred to as a GA, is small, uses very little power, and is fairly stable. The problem is that it requires actual contact to work, meaning that they would have to be attached to the hulls of the submarines.

The two teams, designated Red and Blue, were each outfitted with sets of both types of detection equipment. The voice of the Red Team leader came crackling through the headphones, saying, "So far we are negative on both vessels based on these laser readings. Repeat, negative on both."

"How close have you come?" the captain inquired.

"Hard to say, sir, the sonar reading is jumping all over the place. We're getting hell knocked out of us down here."

Just then a huge swell crashed across his bow, almost capsizing the small craft.

"Can you get close enough to attach the GA device?" the captain asked.

"Affirmative," the team leader reported with a confidence not justified by the difficulties they faced.

In order to fasten the GA devices to the hulls they would have to race their speedboats ahead of the subs, then each would send a two-man team into the open sea, all four secured to their pursuit crafts by a long, braided nylon rope attached to the stern. With the launches staying in motion at a slower speed, they would allow the subs to catch up with them and, as they passed, the men in the sea would attach these small instruments to the outside skin of the AUVs with a water-resistant adhesive already affixed to the back of the device. The good news was that the reading on the GA would be almost instantaneous and reliable, but the bad news was twofold. First, a miss would cost them valuable time, since they would have to bring the men back aboard the launches and then repeat the process. Second, after the men in the water were done, the draft of the rear-powered submarines might draw them toward the propellers, tearing them to shreds.

"Do it," the captain ordered.

Both launches took off at once, riding over the large surges that slapped at them, often tossing their small pursuit vessels into the air, the engines spinning uselessly in space as they were slowed and thrown off course. But in a few minutes their sonar indicated that they had managed to outrun the AUVs. The *Burgwyn* kept apace.

Without delay, two SEALs from each launch flipped over the side, tethered to their boats, disappearing from view into the murky darkness of the roiling sea.

Their headpieces were fitted with halogen lights, but the beams were useless in these conditions except perhaps for the ability to spot each other. When they hit the water they did not swim, they merely stayed submerged, allowing the nylon ropes that had become their lifelines to reach full length and begin to drag them forward as their boats slowed.

In less than a minute they could make out the oncoming subs. The Red Team was too far astern, so those two men began paddling furiously to put themselves in the path of the AUV. The other two were soon staring directly at the nose of a small craft as it churned toward them. Only one of them had to succeed, and each knew his role, one to the port side, one to the starboard.

The AUVs were about thirty feet long and moved with

remarkable stealth, running almost silently as they relentlessly followed their programmed paths through the sea.

As the subs drew nearer, one of the men spoke into his microphone. "Blue Team here, we need more speed," he said, "three more knots, and pronto."

In a moment, all four men felt a slight tug on their lines as their movement increased, nearly at the same rate as the subs'.

The men on the Red Team, who had been too far away, had pulled closer, and one of them was near enough that he managed to slap the GA device toward the rear of the AUV, then flipped backward, barely clearing the propeller. "Red Team done!" he shouted into his microphone. "Red Team done!"

The SEALs on the Blue Team each had a good position, and both men were able to paste a GA sensor onto the hull. Then, just as one of them reported, "Blue Team done, Blue Team done," his rope was caught in the propeller. Before he could be dragged into the lethal path of the swiftly turning screw, the cord was severed, and he was set adrift.

On the launches, as soon as they heard that the GAs were in place, they began reading the monitors. Then the SOS came.

"Blue Team, one man cut loose, repeat, Blue Team, man cut loose."

The other three men were being pulled back to the launches, their teammates aboard the launches drawing in their cords hand over hand. The *Burgwyn*, which had kept a safe distance, was shining all of its spotlights on the two pursuit crafts during the mission. As soon as the distress call was sent they began sweeping the area with high-powered beams, searching for the lost man.

Tossed about in the inky water, the abandoned SEAL had immediately surfaced and ignited his flare. Even with his electronic chem-lite shining into the darkness and his homing beacon working, the movements of the sea and the darkness of the sky made it impossible for the crew of the *Burgwyn* to spot him. Added to the problem of identifying his position was the time it would take for a destroyer the size of the *Burgwyn* to come about. The distance between the SEAL and his mates had vastly increased in just these few moments and the danger that he would be lost was rapidly increasing.

Meanwhile, the captain aboard the *Burgwyn* called for the monitor readings.

The Red Team leader called in. "All readings are negative. That's negative for any radioactivity."

"Blue Team, report in," the captain ordered.

"We confirm, sir. Two devices report no radioactivity."

"Please reconfirm those readings," the captain ordered.

"Reconfirming, sir, there is no reading of radioactivity on either craft."

Meanwhile, the small pursuit boats were turning course as the SEALs struggled to get a visual on their missing teammate. Much smaller and more agile than the large destroyer, they were taking a two-flank approach in estimating the winds and currents and, with the readings on his homing beacon, they hoped to narrow the search area.

Sandor heard everything. "Captain, this is Sandor. I'm

heading back. After you pick up your men, do whatever you need to destroy those subs."

"That's affirmative."

"Remember, they may not be carrying anything nuclear, but we have no idea on the total payload."

"We know what we've got to do," the captain said, his voice betraying the obvious concern—he needed to pull his men out of the water before he could take out the AUVs, but time was indeed growing short. "We'll stand back, then launch our torpedoes."

"Sir, this is Red Team leader," came a voice from below. "We copy that, sir. You do whatever has to be done, but we're all staying down here until we find him, sir."

"That's affirmative from Blue Team," another voice promptly added.

"You listen up," the captain snapped, "you've got exactly ninety seconds to locate him and then you all return to the *Burgwyn*, and that is an order, son."

No one spoke as the seconds ticked by, the two launches frantically negotiating the stormy sea, the large spotlights from the destroyer sweeping the water like huge klieg lights. Sandor had Martindale throw the forward searchlights on, but from this high, through the stormy sky, they were little help.

Sandor told Martindale not to leave the scene while the man remained missing. Everyone fought against time and the weather, the two launches circling in a deliberate pattern that canvassed the area in the hope of picking up a signal.

And then, suddenly, a glimmer could be seen about a

hundred yards from the Red Team boat, the beacon bobbing up and down on the chops and swells like a drunken buoy.

"We see him," Red Team reported. "We've got him."

Sandor blew out a full lungful of air, then tapped the pilot on the shoulder. "Marty, it's time to go find out where they really sent those nukes."

CHAPTER EIGHTY-ONE

OVER THE GULF OF MEXICO

A<small>S</small> T<small>OM</small> M<small>ARTINDALE</small> piloted the Seahawk back to the mainland he was becoming increasingly concerned about the accelerating winds that buffeted his craft, sending it back and forth like some airborne rocking horse.

"I'm not one to leave a party early," he said into his microphone, "but we're getting our asses kicked up here."

The copilot said, "Roger that."

Sandor had moved to the jump seat right behind them. "How are we on fuel?"

"Depends how far you want to go," Martindale replied with a chuckle, just before another gust sent the chopper reeling. "Shit, that felt like a hundred-mile-an-hour crosswind."

"Can this thing take a hundred-mile crosswind?"

Martindale laughed again. "Hell no."

Sandor steadied himself, then said, "I'd like to reach one of these refineries, and it'll be a whole lot better if we don't have to stop. Can we make it?"

"Depends which one. The only good news is that we're running northerly with this hurricane, not fighting the headwinds anymore."

Sandor said, "Good," then tapped the copilot on the

shoulder. "Jake, hook us up with security in Baytown, then I've got to speak with D.C."

As he was about to make the connection, the voice of the captain from the *Burgwyn* came through. "Gentlemen, don't know if you'll be able to see this off your rear port in this soup, but we're twenty seconds from contact."

"What the hell," Martindale said, banking the chopper to the left as they peered through the dense rain at the sea behind them.

Just a few seconds later they heard the crew aboard the *Burgwyn* whooping it up over the radio as they were barely able to make out the distant flash of the fiery destruction of one submarine, then the second, MK-32 torpedoes taking out both vessels.

"You boys see that?" the captain asked.

"We saw enough," Sandor told him, "but we heard your men and that was even better."

"We'll do a full recon, make sure we didn't leave any moving parts behind."

Sandor thanked him, then told Jake he had better contact Washington before he called Baytown.

Deputy Director Byrnes had already been informed that the two subs were not "hot," news that was immediately passed to the joint task force. That good news was tempered by Sandor's concerns about the missing truck and the possibility of a second target.

"It's worse than that," Sandor told the DD after he confirmed that both subs had been taken out. "I think these subs were an elaborate version of an old-fashioned bait and switch."

"You don't believe Baytown was ever their real objective?"

"It was just too easy for us to connect the dots. The attack plan was too impractical. I think Adina told the men who invaded Fort Oscar that it was all about a strike on Baytown; that way if they were caught that's what they would tell us. Same with the two idiots he left behind in St. Barths. Why put them there unless you actually wanted them to be captured? I believe even Hwang was dealing disinformation and didn't know it. Adina's too good a chess player for all these mistakes."

"And the two AUVs they just took out?"

"How in hell were they going to make it through the cut into Galveston Bay, then all the way to Baytown without being stopped? Anyway, they were carrying conventional explosives; how much damage would they have done?"

"I understand."

"And the entire game they played with this guy Amendola selling them security information, then making him disappear just before the attack. All too pat."

"So you figure it's all about this tractor-trailer."

"I do. Adina is using this hurricane as cover. It's perfect for him. He's got us chasing a couple of drone subs armed with TNT and everyone else in the area is fighting Hurricane Charlene. We need to find the damn truck, then take it out in some way that minimizes the damage."

Byrnes said he would report all of this to the joint task force and rang off. Sandor's next call was to Brendan Banahan and Patrick Janssen to find out what they had heard about the tractor-trailer.

"Nothing," the Baytown security director admitted. "Not a single lead."

"Well, the only good news I've got is that we took out the two subs and, unless I miss my guess, your refinery is in the clear." Sandor gave a quick description of what had taken place in the Gulf.

"Hell," Janssen said, "that's something anyway. Meanwhile, your boys in Washington spoke with the governors of Texas, Mississippi, and Louisiana; they've got the National Guard mobilizing and every state trooper that isn't tied up with Hurricane Charlene is out there on the roads."

Sandor was not encouraged. "We're missing something, guys, something obvious." He thought it over for a moment. "This truck isn't going to be on the move. It's got to be in a warehouse someplace. The packages arrived thirty-six hours ago; they're not riding around risking the chance of being caught. Let's assign a couple of agents to cross-check every possible warehouse that might have taken in a large rig since yesterday." He paused again. "And truck stops, what about truck stops? That's the oldest ploy in the world, hide in plain sight."

"We're already working on the truck stops, but we'll double up on that, and we'll do a computer run on all the independent garages that might take in a tractor-trailer like this."

"All right," Sandor said, his voice betraying his concern. "Be sure to let everyone know we're running out of time, if we haven't already. You hear from Krause?"

"No, want me to patch him in?"

"Why not?"

They connected to Corpus Christi and brought the commanding officer up to date. "Damn," he said, "that's great work those boys did on the AUVs, wish we had something more on your truck, Sandor."

"Me too."

"You heading back here?" Banahan asked.

"What do you think, captain?"

"They've got things under control in Baytown and you're running low on fuel. I say you play your hunch and check out Baton Rouge."

CHAPTER EIGHTY-TWO

OUTSIDE BATON ROUGE, LOUISIANA

JORDAN SANDOR HAD been right about two things. First, his guess that the refinery in Baton Rouge had become the real target. Second, that it was too late to stop the truck from reaching its destination.

By the time the all-points bulletins had circulated through the three states and the law enforcement personnel and National Guardsmen could be mobilized, Adina's men were already driving along Scenic Highway, circling the refinery on their way north.

As Hurricane Charlene hammered the Gulf Coast, there were just too many logistical issues and not enough manpower to blanket the entire southeastern United States with the level of surveillance Sandor wanted. Every available trooper, soldier, and police officer was already on duty trying to prevent another Katrina-like calamity. The plant at Baton Rouge had temporarily shut down operations—it had sustained so much damage in the hurricane season two years before, it had had to be closed and refitted over several months, and they had no interest in sustaining another similar loss.

Adding to the difficulty was the sheer impracticality of disclosing to the world at large that a truck with nuclear weapons was barreling through the storm somewhere in an area with a radius of up to a thousand miles. The panic that would result and the devastation the public reaction would cause might be worse than the explosion itself.

Given that risk, most of the law enforcement officers and soldiers involved were told nothing about a possible plutonium bomb; they were only warned of a potential terrorist strike.

Patrick Janssen's counterpart at the Baton Rouge refinery was on high alert. Between the storm and the newly released warning of a terrorist threat, military units were moving into place at all the refineries in the region as quickly as the weather allowed.

Sandor worked the radio lines while Marty and Jake guided the Seahawk through lethal crosscurrents until they reached landfall over Louisiana. All manner of information was being fed from law enforcement personnel and military on the ground, filtering it through Captain Krause's office at the naval air base in Corpus Christi and the temporary communications center in Baytown. Although nothing had turned up yet, every man in the field was being encouraged to relay even the most insignificant data they came across. Nothing should be considered inconsequential, they were told—the stakes were too high to overlook a single detail.

Their first break came on a call that was routed through Baytown.

"I know this isn't much," Janssen told Sandor over the satellite hookup, "but the police have been rousting every truck stop from Little Rock to Miami. You talk about terrorists to these truck drivers and that's a hot button, as you can imagine."

"I got it," Sandor replied. "So what's the news?"

"Found a guy in Opelousas who had a strange observation."

"I'm all ears."

"There's a big diner and rest area right off Interstate Ten. This driver noticed a tractor-trailer show up, didn't stay but a few minutes, then took off again. Says he only noticed it because they pulled up right beside him and nobody ever got out."

"When you say it isn't much, you're not kidding," Sandor replied.

"Hang on, there's more. When the truck left, it didn't get back on the interstate. He said it made a turnoff to the side road. This trucker calls it one of those roads to nowhere." As Sandor thought it over, Janssen continued. "In this storm, why come to a rest area, immediately leave, but not get back on the highway?"

"When?"

"This morning. A couple of hours ago."

"Did he describe the truck?"

"Freightliner cab, sixteen-wheel rig, trailer plain white, didn't catch any logos, but get this—when we gave a description of what we're looking for, he said he noticed the trailer had some unusual-looking doors on the side."

"And how far is Opelousas from Baton Rouge?"

"How about, down the road a piece?"

"You hear that, Marty?"

The Marine nodded. "Copy that."

"Okay," Sandor said, "it's a long shot but you never know. Let's get word to everyone in that area, scope out every road that could lead from Opelousas to Baton Rouge. In fact, every road from Opelousas to anywhere."

"Already done."

"Good. Order them to identify but not to engage. If there's any chance we can take them down before they ignite those nukes, it's worth a try."

Banahan was on the line. "Got it, Jordan."

"Good. I'm getting on the horn with Washington; we'll get the Air Force and the Air National Guard on this right now."

Sandor cut them off, made the connection through Langley, and gave his latest report to Byrnes. Meanwhile, Martindale was approaching Baton Rouge from the southwest. The helicopter was still being tossed about and fuel was becoming an issue, but now they had no choice except to stay in the air and try to find the truck.

As Sandor finished with the Deputy Director, he was peering out the windows, but there was still nothing to see but rain and dark clouds. "Marty, if you were coming at this refinery in a truck, would you try to make a direct hit?"

"Hell no, couldn't get close enough, not with a low-yield nuke. And they've gotta assume we're on watch for them by now."

"Agreed. So the questions are, how would you go at it and what's in that truck besides the weapons?"

Jake said, "Sir, the Baton Rouge refinery is right along the bank of the Mississippi River."

Sandor nodded. "And water seems to be their preferred medium of attack."

"Any kind of airborne assault is too likely to get shot down."

"I'm with you on that too," Sandor said. "And the Mississippi, last time I looked, runs south, that right?"

They both agreed.

"Which means, if we're going to find this damned needle in a rainstorm, we've got to get north of the refinery."

"Aye aye," Martindale said, then increased his speed.

"But we've got to run low enough to see the damn thing."

The Seahawk took the turn smoothly, even in the gale winds, and Martindale banked the craft in an arc that led them west so he could circle back around from north to south along the sweeping curves of America's largest river.

Sandor radioed back to Janssen and Banahan.

"It's only an educated guess," he told them after he explained the approach they were taking along the Mississippi, "but we're on our way now. Call and have some of the men positioned for an attack from that direction."

Banahan assured him he would take care of it.

"How's my Korean girlfriend?"

"Safe and sound."

"No flights north today."

"That's right. Ronny Young is babysitting her as we speak."

Sandor nodded to himself, wondering, if these nukes went off, whether he would have done Hea a favor after all, putting her in harm's way. "Keep pushing for information," Sandor said, then signed off and contacted Captain Krause.

The two drivers who were ferrying Luis and Francisco and their deadly cargo to their destination had already made the turnoff from Samuels Road and were heading west to the area above the eastern bank of the Mississippi.

They had been spotted by a state trooper when they passed Port Hudson, but the officer had not yet received the APB, so he didn't think much of it—other than the fact that it was an odd place to take a large rig in this storm. Now that he had the alert, he called it in.

Sandor was making another vain attempt to see something on the ground when Banahan relayed the report, immediately patching in the trooper to provide details.

"There are a whole lotta places a trucker can pull off the road in a hurricane like this," the officer told them, "but headin' down to the river, you've gotta have shit for brains to be anywhere near the water today."

Sandor asked him for the precise location of the turnoff, then told him to stay where he was. "Do not approach or engage them," he said. "We'll be back to you in a few minutes."

Martindale, who was listening in, swung the Seahawk around while Sandor got back in touch with Captain Krause.

"It's sketchy at best," Sandor admitted, "but it's all we've got right now, and I'm not far from there. Two problems, though. First, we're about to run out of fuel. Second, if we get too low they might spot us before we see them, which is going to be a real problem if they actually turn out to be the guys we're after. You've got Coast Guard and Navy running up and down the river?"

"That's affirmative, we've asked them to get moving, although we're about to get slammed by the brunt of Charlene so I don't know how much good they can do."

"And I don't know how much longer we can stay in the air," Sandor admitted.

Just then the copilot, who was working with binoculars, saw a sixteen-wheeler parked near what appeared to be a municipal boat launch. "Off the port side!" Jake called out.

Through the rain he could make out the tractor-trailer sitting just beside a concrete ramp used to roll small craft on their trailer hitches into the river. In these conditions, there was no one with a boat anywhere near the area. In fact there was no one in sight but the large rig.

"Marty, take us back hard to starboard!" Sandor hollered, then he told Krause what they'd seen.

"Roger that," the CO replied. "I'll have two CG vessels there pronto."

"We need to approach with caution," Sandor reminded him. "We don't know how or where these devices are supposed to be detonated. We go barging in and we may be the problem instead of the solution."

"All right," Krause agreed, "give me the coordinates and we'll make an oblique approach. But remember, I'd rather have these things go off three miles upriver than right beside the refinery."

"Understood," Sandor agreed. Then he turned to Martindale and his copilot. "You boys know what this is about, so here's the deal. You're going to set me down somewhere in the woods on this side of the river and I'm going after them. You're short on fuel and you've risked your lives for the past two hours, so you get the hell out of here, nothing to be gained by hovering around in the middle of a hurricane, especially given the payload they're carrying."

"And what are you supposed to do when you get down there?" Martindale asked. "If that's really the truck those kids at Coulter told you about, there are at least four men aboard. Maybe more by now."

"I'll try to get close enough to take a couple of them down, delay them until the cavalry shows up. Then we'll figure out how to disarm the bombs."

"Easy as that?"

"As long as our friends get there in time."

"Well, sir," Martindale said as he unbuckled his harness and climbed out of the pilot's seat, "at least you'll have me for company in the meanwhile."

Sandor smiled. "I guess this is not a debate."

"No, sir," the Marine replied with a grin. "Jake can land this thing on a dime, and two of us on the ground will be a whole lot better than one, don't you think?"

CHAPTER EIGHTY-THREE

ALONG THE MISSISSIPPI RIVER, NORTH OF BATON ROUGE

Jake took them toward the river, north of where they had spotted the truck. Sandor and Martindale lowered themselves from the Seahawk with the same ropes and winches the Navy SEAL team had used to enter the Gulf of Mexico. As soon as they hit the ground they disengaged their harnesses, unhooked the bundle of weapons they had packed, then hurried into a wooded area that was about half a mile inland.

Given the strong winds and relentless rain, they hoped their landing went unnoticed by the men near the truck. Whether it did or not, they were ready to move as soon as they unclipped themselves. When they signaled to Jake that they were clear he hit the recoil switch that drew in their lines, then banked the chopper hard to the northeast and disappeared into the storm, away from the sight line of the targeted area.

Martindale was in full assault garb, Sandor in black slacks and sweater, although he was still wearing the helmet from the helicopter with the two-way radio connecting him to both Marty and their COMCENT in Corpus Christi.

Each man was armed with an S&W .45 1911 automatic, an M-4 carbine with extra clips, grenades, and flares. In the knapsack they had one pair of binoculars, a satellite phone, a portable Geiger counter, and an array of other monitoring devices. They went through the package, setting themselves up with their weapons as Martindale shouldered the backpack with the remainder of the electronic hardware, then they pushed off at a trot, heading south and toward the edge of the river.

It was possible, of course, that this truck was not the one they were searching for, but logic told Sandor otherwise. Not only had they run short of leads, but there was something about a large tractor-trailer stopping at the shore of the Mississippi River three miles north of the Baton Rouge oil refinery in the face of an oncoming hurricane that defied any reasonable explanation other than enemy action.

Occam's razor, DCI Walsh would say.

They moved swiftly through the sparsely wooded area until they were less than a hundred yards from the boat launch.

Unfortunately, the maneuvering of the Seahawk had not gone undetected. Luis and Francisco spotted the helicopter when it banked east across the river and, although they did not see Sandor and Martindale disembark, Francisco told the other two men to be on alert.

"We may have company soon," he told them. "Could just be some sort of aerial patrol related to the hurricane, but be ready."

Meanwhile, the four of them were unloading the large

crates from the trailer. Their jobs were relatively simple. They were to assemble the two ovoid-shaped vessels that were custom crafted of gray fiberglass, virtually undetectable once they were in the water, especially in the midst of this storm. Each craft had a preprogrammed navigation system and gyroscopic balancing mechanism. When they finished putting these devices together they would open the smaller crates containing the nuclear weapons, each of which was equipped with a digital timer. The plutonium orbs were packed separately. After the detonation systems were lowered into the pods and secured in place, the timers would be set and the navigation programs initiated. Only then was the plutonium to be inserted.

Then the hatches on each pod would be snapped shut and the fiberglass shells slid down the ramp into the Mississippi, where their small engines would run them downriver with the current. Assuming the timing was reasonably accurate, two nuclear blasts would occur just along the banks of the Baton Rouge oil refinery, the results of which would be an obliteration of the facility; a fire that would rage for months because of the impossibility of getting near the epicenter of a nuclear blast to deal with the conflagration; radioactive fallout that would impact the surrounding area; and, if the stars aligned for Adina's plan, damage along the Mississippi that would cause inestimable harm to the neighboring areas to the north and the south.

The key, as far as the four Venezuelans were concerned, was to put these bombs into play, get into the truck, and drive as fast as they could to escape the impending cataclysm.

———

It did not take long before Sandor and Martindale came within range. "Looks to be four of them," Sandor whispered into the microphone imbedded in his helmet as he watched them working in the pouring rain. The truck had been backed up to the river, the doors to the trailer now wide open.

Martindale, who was thirty feet to his left, gave him a thumbs-up. "I also see four."

"What the hell are they doing?" came Captain Krause's voice over the radio.

"Stay tuned," Sandor said, "we need a closer look."

They were nearly at the edge of the tree line and could not move nearer without risking exposure as the men around the truck busied themselves at the top of the concrete ramp that was used to lower boats into the river. Sandor held up two fingers and pointed to his eyes. Martindale nodded, then pulled out the binoculars.

"Appears to be some boxes on the ground. Hard to tell what they're working on."

"Are they armed?" Krause demanded.

"Also hard to make it out from here through rain," Martindale told him.

"They must be armed," Sandor said.

"Take them out!" the CO barked into their earphones.

"Sir," Martindale responded, "we have no confirmation they're hostiles."

"That's affirmative," Sandor said, "and even if they are, we have no way of knowing whether the weapons have been set. We might want one of them alive."

"Damnit," Krause snapped back at him, "we're not gaining anything by waiting, are we?"

Sandor could not suppress a smile. It was not that he found anything amusing about their situation, he simply liked the captain's style. "Sir, I think the circumstances are suspicious enough to warrant action. What's our position on the river?"

"Closest to you are a pair of CG Defenders heading north, be there in a few minutes."

"A few minutes may be too late," Sandor said, looking across at Martindale. "Let's move."

Before Krause could respond or Martindale could react, Sandor took off at a dead run. In the rain he was not immediately visible to the four men, but then one of them looked up and suddenly all four turned in his direction. In that instant, there was no longer any question about whether they were armed or hostile.

Two of the men did not hesitate, grabbing automatic rifles that had been on the ground, opening up a fusillade that sent Sandor diving for cover.

As Sandor hit the dirt and returned fire, the barrage of shots from Adina's men flew past him, several hitting Martindale, who had followed him out from the cover of the trees.

Martindale's combat gear included body armor, but he was knocked backward from the impact. As he lay still for a moment sprawled on the ground, the other two terrorists had time to get their assault rifles and join in the onslaught.

Sandor steadied himself behind some rocks off to the right. Before the Venezuelans could take cover, he hit two of them with a series of shots that put them down. By now Martindale had recovered, although he realized that he had been struck in the left side with one shot that managed to find its way through the seam of his protective vest. "I'm hit," he spat into his mike.

Sandor had a quick look across the field at Martindale, who had crawled behind a tree, pulled off his backpack, and checked his injury.

"I'm all right!" the Marine shouted into his mouthpiece, then scrambled to a kneeling position and squeezed off a series of shots. "Let's go."

Sandor was not sure how badly he had hurt the two men who had fallen, but he knew there were at least two others who had taken cover behind the truck. "I'm going directly for the parcels," he told Martindale. "You okay to circle around the front of the rig?"

"Affirmative," Martindale replied.

"Let's go," Sandor said and raced forward.

Martindale rose to a crouch and also took off, moving in a crossing pattern with Sandor toward the front of the tractor-trailer as Sandor went left.

As he came to the top of the boat launch, Sandor was able to see what appeared to be two gray pods sliding down the concrete ramp, entering the river below. The shooters who were positioned behind the truck had managed to shove the two ovoid shells into the river. Now they resumed firing and Sandor was forced to lunge for cover again, this time behind a concrete stanchion at the top of the bulkhead. He steadied himself, returning a series of shots from his carbine, catching one of his attackers in the side and spinning him to the dirt. One of the men Sandor had previously hit suddenly rose from the ground, his weapon extended, but Sandor reacted in time to strafe him with a barrage that sent him tumbling backward, dead before he hit the ground.

When Sandor heard the sound of gunfire coming from the far side of the trailer, he knew Martindale was in position.

"We've got two packages already in the drink," Sandor advised.

"Roger that," Martindale replied. "You seem to have things under control up here. I'm going after them." Before Sandor could respond, he added, "Need to ditch my helmet in the water, so I'll be out of radio contact." Without another word, Martindale yanked off his headpiece and made a dash to the right, where, about twenty yards from the loading platform, he dove headlong into the Mississippi.

In the storm, and under fire, Martindale misjudged the height of the bank, hanging in the air long enough to be exposed to another series of gunfire from the remaining terrorist, who was positioned behind the truck, but the shots narrowly missed. Martindale broke the surface of the water and plunged into the darkness, the impact driving most of the air from his lungs, his side already aching from the gunshot wound. He remained submerged as he began swimming with the current of the mighty river, stroking furiously to catch up with the two amphibious packages.

The diversion gave Sandor the opportunity to circle back and come around the rear of the trailer, where he took out the last of Adina's men with a head shot. He moved forward with caution, first confirming that this last shooter was dead. Then he stepped slowly toward the other man behind the truck cab, the one he had hit from the other side. He was on the ground writhing in pain, and Sandor swiftly disarmed him, then slammed his foot onto the man's shoulder and jammed the short barrel of the M-4 into his chest.

"How many are you?" When the man did not give an immediate response, Sandor moved the barrel to his throat and repeated the question.

"Four," the man barely managed to croak as Sandor leaned on the stock of the carbine.

"What do you know about the bombs you carried on board?"

Pain and fear were evident in the man's face. "Nothing, man," he said, "nothing. We were just the drivers, man, just the drivers."

"Just the drivers, man," Sandor repeated through clenched teeth, then spun the man onto his face and expertly bound his wrists and ankles with plastic restraints.

After that, still moving watchfully with his weapon in front of him, he made a quick review of the area and headed for the back of the truck. As he drew near the two men he had shot on the other side of the tractor-trailer he could see one was clearly dead, Sandor having successfully dispatched him in the second attack. The other was crawling on his hands and knees toward the edge of the woods.

Sandor came up from behind him. "Stop right there and let me see your hands. Do it now!"

The man stopped moving and raised his arms. "I've been shot."

"Really? Well, turn around now, nice and slow, or I'll shoot you again." The man turned slowly, until he was sitting on the ground. "That's good," Sandor said. "Now, how many are you?"

"Four."

"How many bombs?"

A flicker of fear was apparent in his eyes.

"How many?"

"Two."

"And now they're both in the water."

He responded with a slow nod of his head.

"You going to tell me how to disarm them or you want me to take you downriver so you can be there when they go off?"

The man said nothing.

"You don't look to me like one of those Islama-psychos, wants to get all blown up in the name of some holy war. Am I wrong about you or what?"

Luis hesitated, then said, "You're going to kill me anyway."

"Not necessarily, not if you tell me what I need to know."

Luis was in pain, but he figured his injuries were not fatal. Maybe, he thought, survival was an option. "Where are the others?"

"You're the last man standing," Sandor lied to him, "which means you only have yourself to save here. So what's it gonna be?"

"You gotta promise . . ."

Sandor stepped forward and kicked him hard in the chest, sending him sprawling onto his back. "No deals, no negotiations, just tell me what I need to know."

"Timers," he said, "they're on timers."

"How long?"

"A little more than half an hour now."

"Nuclear?"

"I think so, yeah."

"Those gray pods, how are they programmed?"

When Luis hesitated, Sandor aimed his M-4 between Luis's eyes.

"Hey, take it easy, I'm talkin' to you, right? They've got low-speed propellers, gyroscopes, each set to reach the refinery as the timer runs out."

"Any booby traps in the setup?"

"No, I didn't see none."

"You telling me the truth?"

Luis nodded. "The truth. Now get me the hell outta here."

"Oh sure," Sandor said, "I'll have you on your way to the local Ritz-Carlton in no time." Then he rolled the man on his face and trussed his wrists and ankles with plastic ties, all the while making his report over the microphone to the communications center at Corpus Christi.

Once Sandor had the man secured, he continued to describe the scene while he ran for Martindale's backpack and pulled out the digital Geiger counter. As soon as he placed it on the ground beside the trailer and turned it on, it confirmed that the area was hot.

"We're affirmative on the weapons," he reported. "We're dealing with weapons-grade plutonium. These are nukes and they're set to go."

Captain Krause spit out a string of expletives.

"We need to get a team that can disarm these," Sandor said, "and we need them in place right now."

"Roger that," Krause responded. "Any chance we can just blow them out of the water?"

"That's a negative. We need to catch up with them first and have a look. I'm not so sure there isn't some triggering device if we interfere with their program."

"All right," the CO said, "but we don't have much time if this asshole is telling you the truth."

"Get the bomb squad on those Coast Guard speedboats as soon as you can," Sandor said. He was standing on the bulkhead now, looking downriver for Martindale. "The pods are running with the current," he told Krause, then ran to each door of the trailer, finding the compartments empty. The remnants of the crating were scattered about on the soaking wet turf. "Looks like whatever they meant to do is already done," he reported.

"What the hell does that mean?" Krause demanded.

"It means I'm going to follow Martindale."

"Hang on, Sandor, we've got Coast Guard on the way. If you go in the water, we'll have no radio contact."

"Damn," Sandor said, knowing he was right. "I'm not just going to stand around here, I can tell you that." He moved quickly, dragging the two bound terrorists, one at a time, to the side of the trailer. He lifted them, shoving each one into a different compartment, slammed the doors shut, jumped into the cab, and started the engine. "I'm heading for the refinery," he said into the microphone. "It's only three miles, and I'll get there in the truck. Maybe the two I have with me will have more to tell us once they're staring at those pods coming downriver."

At that moment the Coast Guard speedboats arrived from the south. They were Defender-class vessels with dual outboards and, as they came around the bend of the river, the crews spotted the two floating bombs. They also saw a man just behind the two gray crafts and proceeded to open fire.

"What the hell are they doing?" Sandor yelled into the microphone as he was maneuvering the gears on the large truck. "Order a cease-fire, they're shooting at Martindale."

Martindale also saw the USCG boats as they raced into view, then heard the first rounds go whizzing by his head, the bullets slowing as they entered the water all around him.

He had no choice but to dive, using the two large fiberglass pods for cover.

Krause, who was surrounded by a team of officers in the communications center at Corpus Christi, quickly had the situation under control. "This is Captain Krause, commanding officer at COMCENT," he bellowed into the speakerphone. "Get those nitwits to cease firing. They're not only about to kill one of our own, but we don't know enough about those pods or how they might be wired to set them off."

Sandor was listening as he steered the rig onto Samuels Road and accelerated toward the refinery entrance, just a couple of miles south. "Tell security I'm coming," he said to Krause, then got the large rig moving south.

CHAPTER EIGHTY-FOUR

BATON ROUGE REFINERY, LOUISIANA

Hurricane Charlene had reached Category 3 and was at full force now, battering the entire region with winds that gusted over a hundred miles an hour and rain that was falling so hard that roads began to resemble rivers and fields had become swamps. The Mississippi was a torrent of roiling water.

After barreling down the deserted highway, Sandor reached the refinery entrance in just a few minutes. He pulled the tractor-trailer to a stop at the first security checkpoint, which today was being manned by fully armed members of the United States military. When Sandor threw the door of the truck open, four soldiers leveled rifles at his head.

"I'm Sandor," he told them, but they stood at alert. He still had his helmet on, with radio access to Corpus Christi. "Hey, I'm glad you guys are on top of this, but Captain Krause is coordinating this defense, he'll vouch for me."

At the mention of Krause's name, the senior man on duty stepped forward. "They've got a team that just arrived down at the dock, Mr. Sandor. Come with me."

"Two hostiles in the trailer," Sandor warned the others. "Keep them bound and alive and get them down there with us, they may be useful." When one of the younger soldiers gave him a curious look, Sandor added, "After we clean up this mess, as far as I'm concerned you can do anything you want with them."

Sandor climbed into the Jeep being driven by the captain in charge and they raced through the next two security stations, not stopping until they came to a long wharf overlooking the Mississippi. Sandor checked his watch. Nearly ten minutes had elapsed since Adina's man told him they only had a little over half an hour.

The team waiting onshore in the driving rain consisted of various skilled personnel. The only people Sandor wanted to speak with, however, were the members of the bomb squad. The lead man was a Major Formanek, his second in command a young woman wearing captain's bars by the name of Franz.

"We've likely got two low-yield nuclear weapons set on timers that may go off in fifteen minutes," Sandor told them. "We have no idea if there are booby traps in the pods carrying them downriver, and we don't have a lot of time to figure it out." He fixed the two officers and their subordinates with his dark gaze. "Are you guys the right people to intercept and disarm them?"

"We are," Captain Franz replied, her eyes locked on Sandor's.

He stared at her for a moment, then nodded. "All right, let's move out."

The Coast Guard Defenders had already picked Martindale out of the water and the two speedboats were now moving slowly on either side of the two pods as they made their way downriver. By now, Washington had tied into the call with representatives from the entire task force huddled together in the White House Situation Room to monitor the situation in real time.

Sandor was still wearing the SEAL helmet, his headphones now constantly ringing with the various voices that were on the call, a headache in the making when he needed a clear mind. He stepped ahead of the others as they made their way to the end of the pier.

"Gentlemen," he broke in, his voice loud and firm over the microphone, "with all due respect I would appreciate it if you would all shut the hell up right now except for Captain Krause. We're in the middle of trying to resolve this crisis and you'll just have to stay tuned for results. Sir?"

"Go ahead," the CO said.

"I've got Major Formanek and Captain Franz heading the team to disable these nukes. I need a straight answer, sir. Am I dealing with the best available technicians?"

There was silence on the line for a moment. Then Krause said, "Let me get this straight. You're in the middle of a hurricane with fifteen minutes to go before your ass winds up in the center of a nuclear explosion, and you want to know if there's a more qualified group to handle this situation?"

"That's exactly what I'm asking."

"You've got balls, son, I'll give you that, so let me set you straight. If the sun was shining and I had two days to put a group together, I'd still want Carol Franz leading the charge. You copy that?"

For the second time that day, Krause made him smile. "Copy that, and thank you, captain."

Sandor turned back to the river, where two Coast Guard boats awaited. He looked to Formanek, Franz, and the other six members of their squad. "So, we need to jump in these speedboats, corral the pods while they're still running downstream, then disarm them both. That's the plan?"

"That's the plan," the major agreed.

"All right, anyone not absolutely necessary to the mission should get the hell out of here now. We have no idea what's really in these floating coffins, but let's put as few people directly in harm's way as we need to."

"We're all necessary," Captain Franz told him.

"We have two of the terrorists, both have been shot, any chance they might be helpful to have along?"

"Highly doubtful," Franz said. "There's still the chance they're willing to die for this cause, whatever it is, and so they may lie to us or slow us down. I'd rather we rely on our own team," she said.

"All right, then," Sandor agreed, "let's move out," and they jumped into two waiting speedboats and took off upriver.

It took less than two minutes for them to reach the Coast Guard cruisers that were heading south as escorts alongside the two bombs. The pods had been set to track slowly, actually fighting the current so the detonation of the nuclear devices would occur as close to the refinery as possible while giving the terrorists time to get away in their truck.

Sandor was on the boat with Captain Franz, Major Formanek in charge of the other.

"If they're on timers we can't waste another moment,"

Franz told her squad. "From what we know, it's unlikely that any sort of triggering mechanism is tied to the hatches. The men involved had neither the time nor the expertise to rig that, would you agree, Agent Sandor?"

He nodded, for an instant trying to recall the last time someone had referred to him as "Agent Sandor."

"You agree, major?" she asked into her headset.

Formanek gave the thumbs-up from across the way.

"If we're wrong," she went on, "it could be a disaster, but I think it would be worse to lose the opportunity to disarm these weapons because we allowed the clock to run out on us while we tried to figure a safer way to get inside the pods."

"It's your show now," Sandor told her.

Each of their boats was fitted with a large netting device that could be employed for various purposes. Today they would be used to haul in the fiberglass encasements, allowing the technicians to work on them as they continued to run alongside the USCG vessels. This way they did not have to interfere with the programmed navigation systems in case they were somehow part of a triggering device. With long, expandable aluminum rods, the nets were extended to corral the pods and secure them while still moving downstream.

The maneuver was fairly simple and within less than two minutes each pod was drawn next to the railing of the boats. The two teams immediately went to work, Franz leading the way to open one, Formanek the other.

The captain had been correct: unbolting the hatches did not ignite any sort of defensive device. Once they got inside, however, the real danger began.

"You were right," Captain Franz reported to Sandor.

"There's a digital display and it shows there's not more than ten minutes still remaining here."

"And mine," the major reported from the other boat.

"The problem is that the timer appears to have been set with an acceleration device." She looked across at Formanek, speaking into her headset. "Is that what you get, sir?"

"Affirmative," Formanek replied.

"Which means," Sandor said as he peered over her shoulder at the interior of the gray fiberglass shell, "any attempt to disarm the mechanism . . ."

"Is designed to bypass the timer and set it off." She finished the thought.

"How do you work around that?"

Franz and two of her men already had their heads and hands inside the pod now. "The nuclear device is fairly antiquated," she explained, "appears to be an old Soviet RA-115. But the timer is modern, digital, and hardwired on a circuit board. No red or green wire to clip here." She turned around and looked up at Sandor. "So, if you can't take a chance playing with the trigger, it's time to unload the gun."

Sandor's earphones suddenly filled with a battery of questions, one voice atop another from Washington, until he again reminded all of them to pipe down and wait until he had an update. Captain Franz and Major Formanek, meanwhile, agreed that there was no room inside the pod for anyone to enter and work on the nuclear weapons that way, and there was no way to get them on land with enough time to tackle the problem from there. Without wasting another moment, Franz pulled off her helmet, took a couple of hand tools from her kit, and had two of the men grab her by the ankles and lower her, head down, into the pod. Formanek did the same with his team.

All the while the rain pelted them, the winds rocked the small craft, and they continued their inexorable path downriver. Sandor tried to stay out of the way, but he could not resist inching forward to see what progress, if any, she was making.

After a couple of tense minutes hanging over the edge of the boat into the fiberglass shell, Franz said, "Weapons-grade plutonium."

One of the young members of her team glanced at Sandor. "The radioactivity exists," he explained, "but until it's detonated it poses no real danger."

"I understand weapons-grade plutonium," Sandor replied. "If we all don't get blown to smithereens, at least we don't have to worry about glowing in the dark afterward."

No one laughed.

Captain Franz asked for a ratchet wrench, 24 mm. They handed it down to her and, after another few minutes, she said, "I think I've got it. Tell the major to try twenty-four millimeters on the interior plate."

The information was promptly conveyed to the other boat.

Then, a few moments later, she said, "I've got it open. Now pull me up. And slowly."

They did so and, as she emerged, she was holding a sphere in her hands, smaller than a soccer ball and appearing as harmless as that. They helped her to her feet as she continued to cradle the destructive orb in her hands. "Open the box," she ordered, and carefully placed the plutonium into a lead-lined case on the deck, then grabbed a headphone from one of the men. "How far has the major gotten?"

When one of the team on the other boat told her he was still working on his, she took a quick check of the time. Sandor did as well, and saw there was less than three minutes left.

"Ask the major if he wants my help."

"That's a negative," she was told. "He's almost there."

Franz turned to Sandor and the others, saying, "This device is still live, although it's no longer nuclear. There are explosive components designed to detonate the nuclear blast. We need to release this pod and let it run downstream. We can detonate the charge ourselves at that point by firing at it, or let it blow itself up. Either way we need to get it away from this boat."

Sandor was impressed at her calm demeanor and the way she delivered the information, especially since they were only a couple of minutes from being incinerated. As Franz's team went to work to unhook the pod from their cruiser, Sandor had a look across the water. He could see that Formanek was still facedown in the fiberglass shell.

"Is he going to make it?"

Franz glanced at the other boat. "He'll make it," she said.

Another anxious minute passed. Captain Franz's team had cut their pod loose and it was already proceeding down current as their boat made a turn back upriver. They stood at the railing, watching anxiously until they finally saw Formanek being raised out of the fiberglass shell holding the plutonium.

Only at that moment did Sandor sense the slightest panic in Franz's demeanor.

She was clutching at her headset and, as soon as she saw the major get to his feet, she was barking orders over the line.

"The device is still live, repeat, the device is still live. Secure the nuclear fuel and cut the pod loose. Repeat, cut the pod loose and reverse course. Sir, do you read me?"

"Roger that," came the reply but at the same moment the passengers on Sandor's vessel witnessed the first pod, the one they had sent floating free downriver, ignite.

It was not a large explosion, nor, in the midst of this hurricane, was it particularly loud. Their boat had already motored upriver far enough to create a safe distance but, before Formanek's team had the chance to fully release their pod and get clear of it, the device in their pod erupted.

As the second pod detonated, it spewed flames into the air and showered burning fragments across Formanek's small craft. In an instant the boat's fuel line caught fire, and the sky was suddenly filled with fire and debris and, even amid hurricane winds, the screams of pain and horror could be heard.

The two USCG Defenders that had first encountered the pods, one of which now carried Tom Martindale, were holding their position north of where Sandor stood beside Captain Franz as they helplessly watched the fire rage upward into the pouring rain. They now gave full throttle to both outboards and took off toward the burning speedboat. Captain Franz also gave the order to move into position to assist.

All three boats swiftly came to the aid of their stricken mates, but it was too late. Major Formanek and the two sailors who had held on to him as he prevented a nuclear catastrophe paid the highest price of heroism. They were closest to the pod and now all three were dead. The others aboard were injured in the explosion and ensuing fire.

Captain Franz wept openly, as did the men on her team.

In the haze of smoke and noise and tears and drenching rain, Sandor could not bear the cacophony of voices that filled his headset. He pulled off his helmet, tossed it into the river, then stared across the water at Tom Martindale, sharing that moment of ineffable sorrow that always comes after intense combat and the inevitability of death. They had ridden to the precipice of massive catastrophe and successfully faced it down, but now they were left to confront the personal tragedies that follow in the wake of the grotesque actions visited on this world by those who traffic in evil. No one who has not experienced the horror of battle can ever understand that moment, no one who has not engaged the enemy can feel that pain.

All they could do was nod to each other. Then Sandor turned away, sat on a bench off to the side, held his face in his hands, and wondered again what needed to be done to put an end to all of this.

CHAPTER EIGHTY-FIVE

BATON ROUGE, LOUISIANA

THE SURVIVING MEN and women were evacuated from the horrific scene on the Mississippi and whisked off to Baton Rouge General. An excellent hospital, it was fortunately close enough so that ambulances and military vehicles could transport all of the wounded there quickly and without the need to risk helicopter flight. As Hurricane Charlene continued to intensify, the latter was not a viable option.

Baton Rouge General features a burn center that is one of the finest such facilities in the South. Its state-of-the-art capabilities would be tested as the twelve-bed unit suddenly found itself crowded beyond capacity.

The others were left at the refinery to sort out what had just occurred—and what had almost occurred. Back on land Sandor assisted Captain Franz as she organized a cleanup operation. They were in possession of two containers holding weapons-grade plutonium, the remnants of the two fiberglass pods, and the two wounded prisoners. Military personnel appeared in force now to take control and, once matters were put in a semblance of order, Franz stepped away for a moment and found Sandor standing off to the side, soaking wet and staring out at the rainstorm.

Her eyes were still rimmed with red, bearing that vacant look that Sandor had seen too many times. "If you hadn't found that truck in time . . ." She hesitated. "What would have happened is unimaginable."

"Unfortunately, in my line of work the unimaginable is very much the reality, captain."

She nodded slowly. "You saved so many lives here today." She wanted to express her gratitude, to say something else, but her voice trailed off.

"I know," Jordan said in a soothing voice. "But we couldn't save everyone."

Her eyes welled up again.

"You did a great job today. And so did Major Formanek."

She drew an uneven breath. "Yes, I guess we all did."

———————————

Sandor was shown to an office in the refinery administration building. He called CENTCOM and was promptly tied into Captain Krause as well as the team in the SitRoom at the White House. He made his report, and the group in Washington was obviously elated at the news.

"We lost some good men and women today," Krause broke in.

"Of course," the man from NSA replied, "but those men and women helped avert a major catastrophe."

"Pieces on a chessboard," Krause muttered. Sandor heard him and responded with a grim smile. The others did not make out what he said, or pretended not to.

"Gentlemen, I still have two prisoners down here," Sandor reminded them, "and I think they may have a thing or two to tell us."

"Sandor, Walsh here," the Director of Central Intelligence said. "You need to get those men up here straightaway."

Sandor stared out the window again and shook his head. The gale was blowing the rain sideways and he suddenly realized he was drenched from head to toe. "Well, sir, I could start driving north and probably make it back in a couple of days. Maybe I can stop over in Busch Gardens and show them the sights."

Sandor could picture the grimace on the DCI's face as he replied. "We understand you're in the midst of a hurricane."

"That would be affirmative, sir. I think it would make sense if we secure the hostiles on premises until this blows by, then perhaps Captain Krause could arrange transportation for us out of Corpus Christi."

"I'll send a chopper for you as soon as we can get one safely in the air," Krause told him.

"All right," Walsh agreed. "You keep them under lock and key for now. You have military on premises."

"That's correct."

"Well use them." He paused. "With Captain Krause's cooperation, of course."

"At your disposal," the Navy man told the bureaucrat, his voice dripping with sarcasm.

"And Sandor," Walsh added, "don't engage in any of your unique interrogation methods in the meantime."

Sandor almost laughed, knowing the DCI was in a room full of Washington toadies. "Oh come on, sir, just a little torture?"

Before Walsh could ream him out, Sandor heard chairs

and people moving, followed by the familiar voice of President Forest as it came booming over the line.

"Just got back down here, my NSA briefed me. Good job, Sandor."

"Thank you, sir."

"When you get back here I'll want to hear all the details. And I'll want them directly from you, you got that?"

"Of course, sir."

"And Sandor."

"Yes, Mr. President?"

"I heard that last comment you made."

"I apologize, sir."

"No apology required, son. You're in charge down there, and you have my full confidence, all right?"

"Roger that, sir."

CHAPTER EIGHTY-SIX

PANMUNJOM, DEMILITARIZED ZONE BETWEEN
NORTH KOREA AND SOUTH KOREA

KIM'S GOVERNMENT WOULD not agree to an exchange of prisoners inside the United States. They resented any implication of wrongdoing on their part or that of their minister, Hwang Hyun-Su. They claimed his kidnapping was an unprovoked violation of international law and they would not sanitize the barbaric actions of the United States by having him released to them in Washington, D.C. There should not even be an exchange, they insisted, since he was entitled to diplomatic immunity and should be returned to his country as a matter of course. They also categorically denied any involvement in an attempt to sabotage the refineries in Baytown and Baton Rouge, which attacks were not officially reported or confirmed by Washington.

James Bergenn and Craig Raabe were quite another matter, according to the emissary from Pyongyang. They were Americans who had posed as Canadian citizens, entered North Korea under false pretenses, wreaked havoc on the peaceful people of the Great Leader's nation, and committed any number of capital crimes. They were spies and subject to the death penalty.

The White House saw things a bit differently.

There was no hard evidence of North Korean involvement in the failed attacks on the American refineries. However, as President Forest put it so succinctly in response to the North Korean denials, "I may not be able to tell the difference between *foie gras* and chicken liver, but I sure as hell know chickenshit when I smell it." He made this observation in a debriefing just thirty-six hours after a nuclear cataclysm was averted through the efforts of Jordan Sandor and Captain Krause's team. That meeting included the President's National Security Advisor, DCI Walsh, and DD Byrnes. Sandor was also in attendance. He had just been flown back to Washington together with the two Venezuelan terrorists and Hea, who had spent the past two days under the safekeeping of Ronny Young.

Unfortunately, as the President conceded to the assembled group, without proof of Kim's collusion in the assaults, the best he could do was trade for the safety of their men. Hwang was of no use to them now and, as Sandor observed, they were not doing him much of a favor by sending him back home, where he would be made to explain how the Americans had managed to frustrate their scheme to blow up two oil refineries.

Up to now the media had been kept away from the story, the explosion on the Mississippi being described as a Coast Guard accident amid the violent storm. There was no telling how long they could keep the terrorist assault under wraps, but for now the matter was referred to the State Department.

Later that afternoon Byrnes and Walsh met with a representative of the State Department to discuss the extraction of Raabe and Bergenn. When the Brooks Brothers–clad, thin-nosed, briefcase-carrying bureaucrat arrived, Sandor requested that he be allowed to attend the meeting. Walsh agreed, his generosity due in no small part to the gratitude the White House continued to express for the remarkable services Sandor had provided his country.

Sandor remained uncharacteristically civil throughout the meeting as the functionary from State gave a presentation of the "back-channel" list of Kim's complaints about the actions of Sandor and his colleagues.

"You have got to be kidding," Sandor finally said.

The man from State suggested that a more measured response was required.

"Does 'Kiss my ass' get it done?"

Deputy Director Byrnes quickly interceded, sharing some of the information they were permitted to divulge— that they had reason to believe agents of the Kim and Chavez regimes had engineered an attack on the United States that had only recently been frustrated by the efforts of Jordan Sandor and others, including the men being held by the DPRK.

This was obviously news to the diplomat.

When Byrnes was done, he added, "There will be no apology or any Asian face-saving nonsense here. You can tell them it will be an even swap, Hwang for Bergenn and Raabe."

And then, to Sandor's amazement, Director Walsh added, "And you can tell them from me, if they don't like the deal, we'll keep Hwang and I'll send Sandor over there to pick up his friends personally."

_____

The transfer occurred two days later, with the State Department voicing its strenuous objection to Sandor attending the exchange. Sandor made it clear to anyone within earshot that he didn't give a damn what the State Department had to say, he was going to be there.

And since President Forest liked the idea, no one was in a position to refuse.

So it was that, along with a relatively unhappy representative from State, Jordan Sandor and Deputy Director Mark Byrnes accompanied Hwang on his trip to Panmunjom.

_____

The so-called Demilitarized Zone between North and South Korea is anything but. The joint security area looks like a temporary barracks designed by a group of Bauhaus architects on a bad day. Both sides of the border are seen by the North and South as an opportunity to prove their military preparedness for each other, and anyone else in the world who happens by. Soldiers march back and forth, weaponry is constantly on display in the distance, and at times it is rumored that the collective troops from both nations populating the few miles on either side of the supposed DMZ exceeds a million in all.

Sandor was not impressed.

The American delegation sat in the neutral building where meetings and exchanges between the two countries usually take place. It is a long, single-story structure, as cozy as a tomb, and they were left there to cool their heels for more than three hours before someone from the North arrived.

When the DPRK diplomat finally pranced in, Sandor

judged him a smug little embassy type, just the sort to get along with their own boy from Foggy Bottom. The North Korean immediately began speaking and the interpreter went to work, creating a version of discordant stereophonic sound that went bouncing off the blank walls until Sandor held up his hand.

"Let's knock off the pretense. You undoubtedly speak English as well as Laurence Olivier, so why don't we cut the interpreter crap. Where are Bergenn and Raabe?"

When the two diplomats started stammering about protocol and propriety, Sandor broke in again.

"We're not here to make friends or influence people. We've got Mr. Hwang sitting in a car out there, under guard, and he's waited a long time to get home to all of his other little Kim groupies. I've got two friends I want to see right now so I can be sure their brains haven't been fried or their balls cut off. Now either we move this along or I'm going to stop sugarcoating this and tell you what I really think."

The little Korean turned on his heels and stormed out of the room. Then, just as Mr. State Department was going to read Sandor yet another chapter from the Diplomat's Riot Act Handbook, several men began filing into the room from the North Korean side. The first two were bulky and nasty looking and, although weapons were clearly forbidden here, Sandor figured they were trained to rip him apart with their bare hands in any one of several different martial arts. After what he had been through in the past week, Sandor was actually inclined to have them take their best shot.

Then Bergenn and Raabe were ushered in.

Jim Bergenn looked all right, a little worse for wear, of

course, given the torture and beatings he had certainly endured, but he managed a wry grin at the sight of Sandor sitting between Byrnes and the guy from State.

Craig Raabe was another matter. He barely made it into the room under his own steam and, at first look, it didn't appear he would survive the plane ride home.

Sandor began to rise from his seat, but the little Korean diplomat stepped into the room. "I suggest you sit down, Mr. Sandor. Yes, we know exactly who you are and, if it were up to me, neither you nor your two friends would ever leave this room alive." He paused, as if to allow that idea to sink in. "But the Great Leader has a fondness for Mr. Hwang, and he also has many questions he would like to ask him. So you and your friends will survive this day, but only if you henceforth conduct yourself in an appropriate manner."

Sandor looked to Bergenn, who gave him a safe sign, letting him know that both he and Raabe were all right. Sandor turned back to the Korean. "Henceforth? Appropriate? I guess I sold you short when I compared you to Olivier."

"I am one of those many people who do not find your American sarcasm funny, Mr. Sandor. Likewise, I am not amused by the games you have played in the media. Oh yes, do not appear surprised, we are fully aware of how you have engineered the release of information regarding Mr. Hwang and these men."

"You guys read the papers?"

"Again, if it was my choice, you would have been forced to produce the traitorous young woman who paved the path of your escape, or you would never see these two again."

The man from the State Department finally began a protest, actually rising from his chair. "Threatening American citizens . . . ," he began, but the Korean cut him off with a look.

The man from State resumed his seat. After all, this was really not his problem.

"You know," Sandor said, "I'm really sorry you and I have gotten off to such a lousy start. Maybe someday we'll have a chance to chat again. Privately. Like in a dark alley somewhere in Harlem."

The diplomat ignored him and turned back to the man from State. "Have your people bring in Mr. Hwang."

CHAPTER EIGHTY-SEVEN

NEW YORK CITY

"YOU'RE A REAL pain in my ass," Bill Sternlich said, "you know that? You have any idea of the trouble you caused me?"

Sandor picked up his Jack Daniel's and took a sip. He did not answer and he did not smile.

"You used me, Jordan."

"That's such a cold way to put it, Billy. Let's just say you helped me without realizing it."

Sternlich frowned. "Are you going to tell me what it was all about?"

"What do you want to know?"

"That scene in my office, that was staged, wasn't it? You wanted to provoke Donaldson."

"Who's Donaldson?" Sandor replaced his glass on the small table between them. They were seated in the comfortable old armchairs in the lobby bar of the Algonquin Hotel, their favorite spot for cocktails together. Sandor had returned from Panmunjom a few days earlier, spent the rest of the week in Washington, where he went through debriefings, visited Craig Raabe and Jim Bergenn in the hospital, then returned home.

"Come on, Jordan. Donaldson. The reporter you roughed up in my office."

"You mean that punk who pissed all over himself, you mean that guy?"

Sternlich had been leaning forward. Now he collapsed back into the soft cushions. "I give up, I really do."

"Yes," Sandor finally admitted. "I got what I wanted from the little prick."

"The exchange for your two men."

"Correct."

"I'm listening."

"There was a girl," Sandor said.

Sternlich laughed.

"What's so funny?"

"Preston Sturges said, 'There's always a girl,' remember that line?"

"*Sullivan's Travels.*"

"Top grades. Go on."

"She was the reason I got out of North Korea. They wanted her back with Hwang in the trade. We couldn't let Jimmy and Craig rot over there, and I knew State would give her up if they had to. So I needed to make it impossible for Kim and company to demand her as part of the deal. Once I told your little Jimmy Olsen I was angry about his articles and I let it slip about our two men there and Hwang here, I knew he would print it. He's just that sort of scumbag. What he didn't understand was how much he helped me. At that point Kim was screwed. What was the Great Leader going to say once the story was in the media? Was he going to admit that he wanted to get some young woman back so she could be raped, tortured, and murdered?"

"Very smooth."

"And he wasn't going to risk being exposed as part of the plot down south, not after the exchange was made public."

"Risky play."

Sandor took another gulp of whiskey. "It was just a shot, there was no guarantee it would work."

"And if it hadn't?"

Sandor stared ahead for a moment. "I've never left a man behind, and I wasn't going to start now." He shrugged. "I would have thought of something."

"And the girl?"

Sandor grinned. "We're having dinner tonight." The smile quickly faded. "Sort of a farewell. We're going to give her a new identity, a new place to live. You know the routine." He picked up his glass and took another swallow of the Jack Daniel's. "Someday I hope we can put her back together with her family." He put the glass down. "Quite an extraordinary young woman."

"I guess I should be sorry I never got to meet her."

Sandor nodded but said nothing.

"How did the exchange go?"

"It went all right." Sandor laughed. "I had Hwang dressed up in one of those ridiculous suits Kim Jong-Il wears. Looked just like him, actually. When we had him brought in I thought the jerk from North Korea was going to faint."

Sternlich shook his head. "So how are your guys?"

"Jim's okay, he'll be back chasing the skirts in no time.

Craig's on the DL for a while. But Kurt is dead, I haven't forgotten that."

They sat quietly for a minute, then Sternlich asked, "What really happened down there, in Louisiana?"

Sandor turned to his friend and fixed him with that serious look that had frightened many adversaries who had crossed his path. "Is this between you and me or is this for publication?"

"Come on, you know our ground rules. Strictly you and me."

Sandor didn't say anything.

"Was it a nuclear threat?"

"Why do you say that?"

"I know how you operate. You weren't chasing down a couple of sticks of dynamite. And everyone in the government seemed too relieved, even though you lost those men outside Baton Rouge."

Sandor nodded. "Yeah, we were chasing down a hot one."

"Who was behind it? Was Al Qaeda in league with Kim?"

"Not this time. It was Chavez. You remember his Richelieu, name of Rafael Cabello?"

"Calls himself Adina?"

"And high marks to you, sir."

"He was behind it?"

"Appears so. Which means he and I have some unfinished business."

Sternlich let that sit for a moment, then asked, "What about the Jaber defection? Wasn't the IRGC involved?"

"Apparently not. We're still trying to piece that together, but it looks like it was Adina's show and Jaber just got in the way. A lot of good people went down, and that Venezuelan sonuvabitch never even showed his face. Someday he will, though, and when he does, I'll be there to—"

Sternlich held up his hand. "I get the idea," he said, shaking his head slowly. "So now it's Chavez. And the North Koreans. When does all this end?"

Sandor put down his glass and looked at his friend. "You know, Billy, I was asking myself the same question just the other day as I stood there and watched those people die on the Mississippi."

"You come up with an answer?"

Sandor stared ahead without speaking. "No," he finally said, "but I wish I could, I truly wish I could." Then he lifted his glass and took a sip. "Until I do, though, I promise you— I'll be on duty."

ACKNOWLEDGMENTS

As I created this novel, I did my best to ensure authenticity with regard to locales, weaponry, and technology, as well as the inner workings of the military and the government departments described. With that goal in mind, I imposed upon many friends and associates for their advice and expertise, a list of generous people far too numerous to name. I trust that each of them knows the importance of their help.

I must nevertheless single out a few individuals for their contributions:

Rick Kutka is an armaments expert, as tough as his subject matter, who does not allow a shot to be fired, a helicopter to be boarded, or an explosive device to be detonated in any of my stories without first verifying the accuracy of the event and the equipment.

Michael S. Krause, USNA Class of 1963, CDR USNR, is not only a great friend but he is also the real deal when it comes to American service and heroism. His assistance was invaluable in describing naval operations, vessels, and procedures. He also allowed me to use his name in the story, and it will not be the last time Jordan Sandor and I are going to call on him for help.

Captain Nicholas J. Lewis has been as close to me as any brother could have been for my entire life. He furnished information on ships, boats, and marine practices that have been essential in taking the reader on this journey.

Thanks to my son Trevor for the creative ideas he contributed to the path of this novel.

And finally, my gratitude to a patriot who lives in the shadows, protecting this great country and our way of life without public appreciation or fanfare, without the world at large knowing, who asks for nothing more than the certainty that his work makes the sort of difference that it does.

Special thanks to my editor Kevin Smith for his fine work and support; my agent Robert Diforio for his never-say-die determination; the group at Simon & Schuster led by Louise Burke and Anthony Ziccardi for their faith; my son Graham for his encouragement; and my wife, Nancy, for her insight, honesty, and almost mystical patience in reading draft after draft of my work.

God bless you all, and God bless America.

Can't get enough
JORDAN SANDOR?

"A RIPPING, GOOD YARN OF INTRIGUE..."
VINCE FLYNN, New York Times BESTSELLING AUTHOR OF
EXTREME MEASURES

TARGETS
OF DECEPTION

WELCOME TO PORTOFINO!

JEFFREY STEPHENS

Check out *Targets of Deception*, the first explosive
Jordan Sandor thriller by Jeffrey Stephens.

AVAILABLE NOW IN HARDCOVER AND eBOOK FROM VARIANCE PUBLISHING

WANT A THRILL?

Pick up a bestselling thriller from Pocket Books!

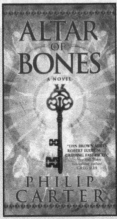

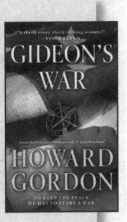

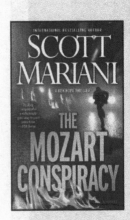

Available wherever books are sold or at
WWW.SIMONANDSCHUSTER.COM

28553

GET SOME ACTION

Blockbuster thrillers from Pocket Books!

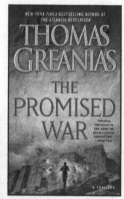

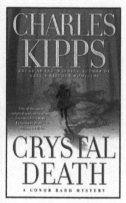

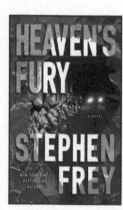

Available wherever books are sold or at
WWW.SIMONANDSCHUSTER.COM

27584